MW00576329

Erich Anderson

FRIDIUM
PRESS

This is a work of fiction. Names, characters, places, and incidents either are the product of the author's imagination or are used fictitiously. Any resemblance to actual events, locales, organizations, or persons, living or dead, is entirely coincidental and beyond the intent of either the author or the publisher.

FRIDIUM PRESS
http://www.fridiumpress.com

Cover design by Katie Pyne
More information at http://www.erich-anderson.com
ISBN: 978-0-9882511-6-8
LCCN: 2022908760

Publisher's Cataloging-in-Publication (Provided by Cassidy Cataloguing Services, Inc.)
Names: Anderson, Erich, author.
Title: Rabbit : a golf fable / Erich Anderson.
Other titles: Rabbit: a golf memoir fable
Description: [Los Angeles, California] : Fridium Press, [2022] | Title page reads "Rabbit: a golf memoir fable" with the word "memoir" crossed out.
Identifiers: ISBN: 978-0-9882511-6-8 | LCCN: 2022908760
Subjects: LCSH: Golfers--United States--Fiction. | Ex-convicts--United States--Fiction. | Life change events--Fiction. | Adjustment (Psychology)--Fiction. | Loss (Psychology) --Fiction.
Classification: LCC: PS3601.N54331 R33 2022 | DDC: 813/.6--dc23

To Saxon

There was only a tiny fraction of my early life where I was considered normal. Just before my third birthday, professionals were brought in to confirm it to the world.

There had been murmurs of confusion and disappointment coming from the two people who called themselves my parents for a time, but I was not aware in the moment. By the time cognition arrived, I was labeled and my future had been charted.

They use the term "on the spectrum" now and I think that's apt. I don't see this designation in gradations that start at mild and span to severe, but like the way a prism bends light and presents a band of colors.

Luckily for me, the colors of my Asperger's turned out to be somewhat sharp and in focus. I experienced symptoms that would be considered classic, but I was not one of those souls whose colors are so blurred that they'll never be able to access the gifts this condition offers.

There was a lot of work to be done to get me to what the rest of the world would refer to as "the mainstream," a stupid metric that was designed by what? Society? Psychologists?

I was taught how to do everything. There was no option for discovery, for trial and error, or the familiar stumbles of youth that lead one to eventually try to adopt a confident stride.

Every advance I made was acknowledged in the most annoying way possible—hand claps of joy, cheers of victory, requests for high-fives.

Every setback was met with subtle headshakes, imperceptible sighs, and whimpers of phrases like, "Okay, Charles, that's okay; let's try that again."

When frustration overwhelmed me, I lashed out or shut down like a toy with a dying battery. If the dials of my behavior went from zero to ten, I never seemed to spend much time at level five in those early years.

Golf changed all of that. It gave me back all that the protocols instituted after my diagnosis had muted.

But there was certainly a disconnect when it came to processing the mental into the physical and I still deal with elements of that to this day.

Golf was my salvation, then and forever.

Let me add the presence of Jim to that creed.

There is a trait of my kind that is considered symptomatically classic—the inability to be empathetic. I use this as an example of how there is no perfect diagnosis. The academic laziness displayed by many studying my condition is galling. I wish that they would just toss the textbook and take a long look at an individual's soul.

The world makes up their mind without your input. They tint you with colors that they know, usually just black and white. Here are two ordinal instances that have been used to assess me:

Example #1: I once overheard a medical professional tell the woman who'd adopted me that I would never express or accept love for/from another human being. As he imparted this wisdom, as the tears of resignation caused her eyes to glisten, I proved the guy wrong by walking over and kicking him square in the testicles for making my mother cry. I was four, and to this day I'm convinced that I did that out of love for her.

When that anecdote emerged at my trial as a cheap prosecutorial tactic, promoting the theory that I continued to display a pattern of violent behavior, I laughed so hard that my court-appointed idiot shrugged in solidarity to the state, the jury, and the judge. The bailiff had to remove me from the proceedings.

Example #2: As a fourteen-year-old playing in the U.S. Junior Amateur, I won my quarterfinal match seven and six. My opponent had cried for most of the match after missing a putt to halve a hole midway through the front side.

When I holed my chip from just off the green to end the match, he threw his hat to the ground, kicked his dad-caddie in the shin and stomped away. I stood in the middle of the green, doffed my visor, shook hands with myself, and said some pithy things like, "Great match, Chunk!" and "You are just too good, my man!"

The Golf Network had cameras out there that day; they played that footage easily fifty times over the next twenty-four hours.

The blowback was gale force. I was called "impertinent," "spoiled," and "arrogant." If they hadn't been so stuffy, I'm sure one of the hosts would have called me a "little asshole."

That night, my guardian, Jim, and I were summoned to a hastily arranged meeting of officials from the United States Golf Association. They held the option to disqualify me in abeyance as long as I made an apology to the field, the organization, and the world.

Like a boy tasked with putting the square block through the square hole, I did what was asked. Which kept me in the tournament, but given that I have this tendency to speak in a monotone, no one believed I was sincere.

It was only after Jim told them that I wasn't being disrespectful—that was just the tone of my voice, the way I spoke—that they let me stick around to be smoked by Gary Houston in the semifinals.

Jim knew that I wasn't this person who everyone had decided was a dick. He knew me to be Charles "Chunk" Dawson, just an odd, extremely awkward boy in his mid-teens with extraordinary talent to play a very difficult game.

He'd told me not long after we'd met that I would have to have thicker skin than most. Honestly, I must've had that, or at least I had no idea what he was talking about. I'd been bullied fairly badly as a "short bus" elementary school student and was not the worse for wear at the time.

I can't explain why nearly all of the ridicule never pierced me. I do know that along with all of my issues, from the moment

I was introduced to golf, I had this innate feeling: that of a rising sun always on the horizon.

Having to go prison for a time nearly snuffed that light out, but I'm convinced that it was that ethos that got me through.

Jim talked a lot about Ben Hogan, and he saw some similarities in me that he could not shake. He'd told my adoptive father, not long after our first lesson, that he had witnessed elements of my natural ability in only one other player in his lifetime. He never mentioned who that was, but I took it to be "The Hawk" himself.

Jim had worked as a range boy at Shady Oaks during the era when Hogan rehabilitated his car-wrecked, broken body, and fully cemented his conversion from being a hooker to a fader.

He couldn't break eighty from the ladies' tees, but he knew more about the game than anyone I was sure to ever meet.

He said one of the greatest myths about Mr. Hogan was that he had convinced the world that he knew the secret to being excellent at this game. This ruse had every one of his opponents fixated on him, distracted from their own experiences, wondering what he knew that was so special.

I have my own secrets, some not dissimilar to that hardscrabble, chain-smoking man from central Texas.

There is the Asperger's whopper I've alluded to here, that I was forced to divulge only because of circumstances.

That might also have been something that we commonly shared. Perhaps, if Ben had been born in a later era, he might also have had someone poke, prod, and test him. He might have been placed in a category that would have designated him different and altered every part of people's perceptions from that day forward.

The other secrets are mine alone. I've mentioned to Jim through the years what's going on in my head—the arcs and angles I see; the exact amount of spin I try to impart upon the ball with each unique strike; the instincts associated with the internal and external rotations of the club and the body; factors involving the environment, and even the supernatural.

None of it made sense to him. He used to just shake his head and tell me what Ben would say—that I needed to practice about ten times longer than I did. But he knew that I was seeing some of what Hogan must have envisioned in his mind. He knew that we had access to information and the ability to execute on that knowledge like few in the world ever had.

I once knew how to play this game as well as nearly anyone on the planet in this space in time. At least I thought so. I'd been in the midst of a steady climb to the upper echelons when fate intervened.

The state of Missouri did not wish for me to continue this pursuit for a specified amount of time. It felt like they'd cloaked the sun for nearly half the decade. But somewhere between the smallest of openings, I searched for a bit of the glare and endeavored to have a ray or two warm my skin.

I am a professional golfer but will readily admit that I am an amateur human being.

To my delight, I can make a ball come to a screeching stop from fifty yards out with V-shaped grooves.

It turns out there are a whole host of things I cannot stop. Turns out, if it's not spherical, logoed, and dimpled, I may have zero control over it in the end.

2

On most nights, flat atop the mattress in my cell, I would stare up at the water-stained ceiling and conjure past experiences of glory or how I could improve on my technique in the future.

For the latter, I paid particular attention to my putting stroke.

There were other times that all I could produce in those moments were examples of failure and disappointment.

This one recurred a couple of times a year: Round of sixty-four at my first ever U.S. Amateur. I'd just turned sixteen and was the youngest to make it to the match play portion of the tournament.

My opponent was a man in his late twenties, a gentleman amateur by the name of Billy Mars, a scion of the owner of Mars Bank and Trust.

I was pretty freaked out that I'd made it that far and had convinced myself that the only way I had a chance to beat him was to go for everything. I cut the corners on every dogleg, tried to stuff it in the hole on every approach, and hole every putt regardless of prudence.

I found myself six holes down at the turn.

Finally, Jim said, "Are you done messing around?"

"He's too good," I said.

"No, that's not it. He only made two birdies on that side and you only halved three holes."

"I'm going to have to really turn it up."

"No, that's not it either. Why don't you just try to make a par here?" Jim asked.

"I'm six down," I whined.

Jim nodded and walked over to the side of the tee. He functioned as my caddie, but his arthritic body made it impossible for him to tote my sticks at that point in his life. I thought about it for a second, put my driver back in the bag, grabbed a three iron and laid up to the widest part of the fairway.

I birdied that hole and two of the next four to cut Billy's lead to three up with four to play.

Billy bogeyed fifteen and sixteen to my pars. I was one down with two to play.

The seventeenth hole at Cherry Highlands was a healthy par three that played 242 yards.

It took me awhile to account for the elevation and the wind, but I grabbed a four iron and knocked it hole high, about three feet to the left of the flag. One of the purest golf shots I'd ever hit in competition.

I smiled at Jim. I was going to head to eighteen all square

after being six down at the turn. He did not acknowledge me. He just took his towel and wiped the residual turf and sand from the sole of my club.

Billy Mars hit a slight cut. The ball landed on the very front edge of the green, crept up the ledge that fronted the pin position, hit the center of the flagstick dead square and plopped down into the hole for a one.

That ace ended the match.

About halfway to the clubhouse, Jim offered what will always be the truth. He'd said it many times before and it was a universal axiom.

"That's golf," he said.

Three years into my stretch, I happened upon a fellow in the yard; he used to caddie for marginal players on the various minor league circuits that I played.

Everyone called him Buzz, which I thought was a paean to the empty real estate on the top of his head. I never caught his real name.

Turns out he had gotten that name because he was the guy who sold marijuana to the other caddies and a larger number of players than one might think.

Missouri is not one of those states that is looking to legalize weed, let alone decriminalize it. He was caught with just over thirty-five grams, which made his possession a felony with intent to distribute. That distribution just happened to include a player, who when caught, readily gave him up as his supplier.

That player was a guy I actually knew, Marty "Party" Leebo

and he was just about to end his dream of making it as a touring professional.

He had stepped out of his Springfield Regal 9 motel room on a rainy Friday to take a couple of hits off a joint and try to forget that he'd just missed another cut at the United States Development Tour event being contested down the street.

A clap of thunder distracted him just long enough that he failed to take note that the Greene County Sheriff's SWAT team had rolled into the motel parking lot. They were looking to serve a fugitive warrant on a burglary suspect who just happened to be holed up in the room next to Marty's.

There was a moment when the deputies incorrectly connected the stunned and newly-stoned Marty to the object of their warranted search: a two-time loser named Salvatore (Sally) Dio, the cross-dressing bank robbery bandit who had set a record that summer for knocking over more banks in Missouri than the James gang.

The brothers James' record had stood for nearly a sesquicentennial, but Sally had ambition and plans and he/she was only halfway to his/her goal when the probe of the sheriff's Bearcat busted through his/her flimsy motel room door to find him/her in bra and panties stacking the nearly sixteen grand the teller at the Joplin branch of NASB had handed him/her just over two hours before.

Whether it was an abundance of adrenalin or just straight-up confusion by the arresting officers, Marty was cuffed and transported along with Sally.

They shared a ride to the Sheriff's substation, and were booked simultaneously. Marty was released on his own recognizance within a couple of hours, while Sally was held without bail.

"You know, I heard Marty had to answer more than one question about the nature of his relationship with that he/she," Buzz said as he spat some tobacco juice on the caked mud of the yard.

"Did he?" I asked.

"That was probably my fault, though. I really tried to push that angle to see if I could get myself some leverage over his testimony," Buzz said.

"Did it work?"

"Nah. They had his caddie, Freddie, and he told them all kinds of shit about me," Buzz said.

He spat again and stared up at a cloudless sky.

"I'll be all right. I'll keep my nose clean and get back to my life after this bullshit. I'm a hustler. I always get by. This ain't my first time in the joint."

I nodded in fake prison solidarity.

"I heard a little about how you ended up here," Buzz muttered.

"Yeah?"

As was my custom, I wasn't going to elaborate. I had no interest in being seen as anything that smacked of legend.

"Just that you killed some guy."

"I guess that would be the technical explanation," I said.

There was a silence as Buzz clammed up. He'd gotten the confirmation he was seeking, and I had nothing else to offer.

I finally asked the question that had lingered for the bulk of the conversation.

"What did they do to Marty?"

"I heard he got a six-month suspension from the tour for being a weed head. That screwed him pretty good. No tour school. No status for next year. He's probably done, and looking to sell insurance about now."

No one had officially suspended me throughout my entire ordeal, and I was concerned that there was another shoe to drop on my release. That was another one of those things that kept me up at night.

Like few at the facility, I was actually incarcerated at the Western Missouri Diagnostic and Correction Center. Buzz was just passing through.

It had been my home for three years and four months by the time Buzz transferred out to the penitentiary where he would serve his three to five year stretch.

I was housed in a special unit of the W.M.D.C.C., intended to serve those who had a special need or were not considered suitable for the general prison population.

As I've mentioned, for most of my life, certainly for the years that I have qualified as an adult, I never told anyone that I had been diagnosed with Asperger's Syndrome. It was hard to hide in my elementary school years, but by the time I entered high school, my classmates didn't seem to notice.

I still suffered the indignation of having to start my years of secondary education in remedial classes, but my fellow laggards—mostly the stoners and the guys and the gals who liked to stare out the window, or draw dresses or motorcycles on their workbooks—didn't exhibit enough awareness to determine that I was that much different from them.

My success in my golf life had preceded me, so instead of any focus being placed on my developmental issues, I was labeled a jock and given all the considerations and shrugs that go with trying to keep an athlete eligible.

Later on, during my years as a playing professional, I worried that someone might bring it up. I certainly didn't want the truth to ever come out. I wanted them to fear, not pity me. I also wanted to retain the power of a secret, like the philanderer, or boozer, or embezzler who draws strength from the excitement of the initial impunity.

Even during my trial, I tried to keep any discussions directed at the evidence and the witnesses. I was convinced that I would be acquitted on merit.

I had briefed my cretinous advocates on my desire to leave my condition out of it. They'd argued that they could use the information to evoke some sympathy from the jury—something they were sure that they didn't yet possess.

But when the guilty verdict was announced, it was a punch to the gut like few I'd ever received. Though, that Billy Mars hole-in-one had been a pretty good one.

In the moments that followed, I gathered every scrap of information about my disability and had it turned over to the court prior to my sentencing.

I was terrified of incarceration for so many reasons, the bulk of them thanks to the TV shows and movies that depicted prison as a hellscape where the odds were highly in favor that I would be raped, tortured, disfigured, rendered lame, blinded, or all five in the first week.

The judge, who turned out to be a single digit handicap with a correctable loop in his swing, sensed my terror and used my suddenly plaintive excuse to have me placed in the W.M.D.C.C. for the entire term of my sentence—in that special section for the "hard to house" category of convicts.

He could have given me the maximum of the fifteen years that a class B felony carried, but imposed a soft cap on my term at the minimum, which ended up being a term of five to seven years.

There had been an early offer on the table to have me plead to a Class D felony, but that was with a deal that included a five-year term with no possibility of early release. On advice of my worthless counsel, I went to trial on a Class B. As it turned out, thanks to the generous jurist, I had a shot at bettering those five years when it came to my possible parole date.

When I ran into Buzz that day, I was a year away from my first opportunity to petition for release.

3

The story of my origins is not that unique in this day and age.

Taylor and Cissy Dawson had only two years of marriage under their belt when the decision was made to seek out an addition to their family. She was nearly twenty years younger than Taylor. He had already endured three marriages and the subsequent dissolutions. None of his previous unions had produced any offspring.

Taylor and Cissy's pre-nuptial agreement failed to include a provision for children. Taylor never thought to instruct his lawyer to include it because he had secretly gotten a vasectomy during the last year of marriage number two.

He never told Cissy, and when a few too many months passed without fertilization, he explained the lack of sperm motility on a baseball incident from his youth.

I'm not certain why Cissy felt that she needed a child to make her life complete. Perhaps, her intention was to alter the pre-nup that she had signed in haste. Motherhood couldn't have been nestled too deeply in her hope chest.

I was delivered in a hospital in Mobile, Alabama, to a young girl who was paid $25,000 to be relieved of the inconvenience of having to raise me.

The birth father never knew his status had been changed to parent; the mother never saw him again after their single night of passion in the back seat of his Charger, in the parking lot of the aptly named Vigor High School.

With the notable alumni confined to a whole host of guys who made it to the NFL, I've always chosen to imagine him as the solid back-up quarterback for the Wolves' Varsity.

I spent fewer than twenty-four hours in the great state of Alabama before I was shuttled to our house in Spring Valley, California, a suburb located in south-central San Diego County.

I have come to believe that my presence in Taylor and Cissy's life started the countdown clock to the end of their relationship.

There were other mitigating factors like the burst of the housing bubble that essentially shut down Taylor's thriving mortgage brokerage firm and the honing of Cissy's palate to discriminate between ever-finer vintages of red wine.

I cannot say that they didn't try with me.

It couldn't have been easy for them, especially when the ruts that only I could produce caused them to veer off whatever smooth road they had wanted to travel in their lives.

When it comes to my parents, there is a nagging guilt that resides deep in my psyche. It is about my inability to be seen by the world as normal. It's a bit twisted—given their gnarled histories—that I could have had much influence on their eventual trajectories, but still, I feel that my presence in their life was just too intrusive to be sustainable.

Early on, when they had the means, they procured the best that the therapy industry had to offer. At one time, they had a concierge who shepherded me through all the various state-of-the-art treatments.

I am convinced that the thousands of hours of occupational and behavioral therapy I endured got my brain and personality to a place that eventually allowed me to walk through life without the suggestion of pathology.

Cissy tried for a time. She even brought in shamans and believers in the powers of crystals and rare earth elements in an effort to explore every corner of the perplexity I presented for her.

For a spell, I was made to drink something called clustered water, which professed to be an autism cure.

I will flat out state: I am eternally grateful for all of the effort that was displayed in those early years. I think it had a positive effect for the length of time it was in full flight.

My progress was frustratingly slow. When the money started to wane, my treatments were one of the first items to be jettisoned.

I was eventually handed off to a babysitter by the name of Leah who was frequently high and had a steady stream of boyfriends always hanging about. Taylor spent most of his days at his office or on the road; Cissy went to "lunch."

One afternoon, when I was six, there was a guy, a US Navy

E-4 named Mark, who needed for me to not be a distraction so he could get busy with the always-willing Leah.

On the way over, he popped into the Walmart and purchased a set of no-name brand plastic golf clubs. They came with a little cloth bag and an array of five colored Wiffle balls—yellow, green, red, orange, and blue. A spectrum.

I was dazzled by the colors. I'd never been allowed to play with anything that could remotely be used as a weapon, and the big orange plastic-headed driver (it even had grooves) could have definitely qualified as a bludgeoning tool. I needed to know how these things worked together, and I needed to know it immediately.

Mark took me over to a part of the back yard that was away from the house while Leah made sure the gate of the pool fence was locked.

She seemed brittle, suspended in a purgatory between horniness and responsibility. She had ceded her power to the skinny Petty Officer (third class) for the moment, and it made her anxious as hell.

"This looks like a good spot," Mark said to no one.

Mark opened the garage door, and rummaged around for a bit. He eventually returned with a good sized piece of cardboard from an empty TV box, and a fat roll of painter's tape. He closed the door, affixed the cardboard to an area in the center of it. He dropped the golf bag and scooped some dirt from the base of the old ash tree nearby.

Leah fidgeted and harrumphed, letting everyone know that she considered this whole thing a really bad idea.

"What are you doing?" she finally asked in exasperation.

Mark didn't answer her, but he whispered to me.

"I'm building you a driving range, Chucky," he said.

He took the dirt and made what looked like a two-inch high teepee, then ripped the plastic packaging away from the balls and placed the yellow one on top of the mound.

"Stand back, son," he commanded.

I wasn't having any of that.

"No," I said, "I want to do it!"

"You don't even know what you're doing, you little retard," he said.

"Mark, goddammit! I've told you before . . ." Leah screamed.

"Yeah, yeah," Mark said, "I'm just going to do it once for you, Chuck. After that, it's all yours, okay?"

My willfulness was legendary, and no one—with the exception of a talented therapist—wanted to experience the consequences of denying me something, but for some reason I relented. Just seeing that equipment and trying to figure out how they worked was mesmerizing.

"You are going to swing this club at these balls. One at a time, okay? If you hit it, it should fly into the cardboard. After you've hit these five, you need to pick them up, and do it again. Got it?"

He held the short club in his hand in a baseball grip, and squatted so he could reach down far enough to make contact. Leah laughed.

He swung, and flat-out whiffed it. Maybe a grain of sand was whisked off the mound by an air current.

"Me!" I screamed, adamant that he'd had his turn.

I ran straight at him, and in a blink clamped both of my hands on the shaft of the club.

"Hang on, kid, I'm trying to show you."

"Me, now!" I screamed again.

He let go, and I used the club to push him away.

"Hey, ya little brat."

"Mark, stop it." Leah snapped.

I set my hands in a similar baseball grip with a good couple of inches of gap between the right and the left. I don't know how I knew to stand perpendicular to the target; I guess I was just copying Mark. I took the club back, swung through, and smacked that ball right into the cardboard protective.

"You lucky little shit," Mark said with a laugh.

"Mark, please, if he uses that word later, they are going to blame me," Leah pleaded.

"Do it again," Mark asked.

I placed the blue ball on the mound, gripped the club in the same exact fashion, and lashed at it. The result was another center of the face strike followed by a concussive smack into the garage door.

I did not turn around to see them stroll back into the house. And I did not hear her scream with pleasure and him grunt with satisfaction for the next half hour. I just kept smoking those balls into the cardboard until they wandered back outside.

Mark had copped a beer from the fridge, and he was hearing it from Leah as he came over to check on my progress.

"How many have you missed?" he asked me.

I'm sure I didn't answer him.

"C'mon Mark, you have to put everything back the way you found it and get that thing away from him, and either hide it or take it with you. I don't know how I'm going to explain the missing beer."

"Aw right," Mark said. "We got to shut this down now, Chucky."

Of course I refused, but he devised a pretty good plan, then roamed the grounds until he had collected four of the balls. One remained on the tee and he stood there waiting for me to put it into play.

He had a wry grin of impending success plastered on his face. I was about to lose the moment; I needed a way to keep going.

I drew down on him by moving ninety degrees to my left, setting up to drive the green ball straight into his torso. I think he thought I might catch it a little low on the face, because he squeaked like a suddenly exposed mouse. He covered his junk and ran down the driveway toward the front yard.

He did not let go of the other four balls in his free hand, though.

In a flash, Leah was there, standing in front of me with her hands extended. She could be as hard as cured concrete at times.

I was way beyond having access to rational thought at that point. To be sure, that wasn't yet a part of any pre-frontal cortex response. All I had at that age was the visceral—invariably tantrum-based shrieks and screams.

She continued to stare, as if cataloging in her mind the penalties she planned to enforce.

I reached down, snatched up the forest-green ball and bolted into the house with the driver held tight to my chest. No one chased me. Leah and Mark destroyed all evidence of my driving range. Mark departed with all of the other equipment he had brought.

Since I wasn't pursued, I had plenty of time to stash my treasures in a place that would never be discovered: in the laundry room, behind the stackable appliances, tucked into area where the studs were exposed.

I never liberated them again for fear that they be taken away, but from that day forward, every stick-like item from a broom handle to a barbeque brush became something I would grip and use to swing at an imaginary ball.

Everything changed and the acknowledgement of that was never clocked by those around me. I didn't know it at the time, either, but my normal cycle of progress followed by regression was terminated by the experience of getting to whack those Wiffle balls into the garage door. The regression component disappeared completely after that day.

Taylor and Cissy were completely oblivious. I was putting out the signals, but it took others to notice.

You had to be pretty dense to not see my reaction to anything that had to do with golf. Eventually, some did. That part became the basis for behavioral modification rather quickly and the babysitters who followed Leah figured it out. I would roll over and play dead if they let me watch an infomercial about some stupid practice gadget.

I suppose this repetitive behavior was lumped together with

other actions that could have been deemed as symptomatic of my condition. Perhaps that is why it was overlooked by so many, for so long.

It was a teacher at my school who mentioned to Cissy that something like a golf class, or lessons, or even a camp, might be beneficial. It was during a parent/teacher conference that Taylor had not showed up for—I remember an excuse about a calendar mix-up, but he might have already started up with the woman he thought might wear his fifth wedding ring.

Cissy, likely numb from self-sedation, did not recall most of the conversation with Mr. Fleck, but she did pull the word "golf" out of the air later when she briefed a tousled-haired, slightly musky Taylor.

He still didn't get it; it would take an extraordinary set of events to make my desires known.

On a side note, one of the clubs that disappeared from the driveway—and later probably tossed in the dumpster outside of Mark's enlisted man's quarters—was the plastic putter. It was one of the great regrets of my life that I wasn't able to secure that starter implement at the time. That's how most kids are first exposed to the game, through the use of a putter at a mini-golf course. I kind of did it ass-backwards.

Bantam Ben Hogan had issues with the putter for most, if not all of his career, and it is another trait we have in common. It was and still is something that I struggle with constantly. I haven't gotten to the knees pinched in, shaft straight down, wrist-flicking, yippy, choking, stance and stroke like he did yet, but I've tried it. I've tried everything at some point or the other.

As to the Dawsons and their experiment as a family, well, oops. They would stick it out for just eight years after my arrival before she ran off with the drummer of a band that backed a burgeoning country music singer. Taylor hung around for a bit as a single parent, but eventually ceded full custody of me to Jim when I had just turned twelve. His engagements to two women were spoiled by my presence, so he moved to Australia to pursue a wealthy widow who would become his fifth and last wife. I assumed at the time that I would never see either of them again.

4

The Western Missouri Diagnostic and Correction Center sat smack in the middle of St. Joseph, Missouri, a town of less than 100,000 about an hour's drive from Kansas City.

St. Joseph's history can be summed up pretty briefly—the starting point for the Pony Express, and the spot where the coward Robert Ford put a bullet into the back of Jesse James' head.

It had fallen on hard times more than once and the central part of the once thriving town had a bit of a Fukushima/ Chernobyl vibe. The W.M.D.C.C. slotted into that environment perfectly.

The vast majority of my fellow inmates were those who had physical disabilities or suffered from substandard intellects.

Because she was still in the process of transitioning, and had yet to undergo gender reassignment surgery, Sally Dio ended up in our special wing. She had wallowed in a county lockup for over six months as she went through the trial process, which is why Buzz preceded her matriculation.

Like me, she was made aware that she would never be tossed into the savanna where the wild animals roamed as long as she followed the rules. I was a golfer, and so that would never be an issue. Playing by the rules was a given in my case.

Sally was quite different in the way she conducted her life, so I found myself constantly trying to keep her focused on the task of adhering to the prison's proscriptions. Though she would never admit it, she came to rely on me to remind her to walk the straight and narrow within days of her incarceration.

She had reasons to worry. There were powerful political figures who fought to have her status changed, and there were concerted efforts to place obstacles in her path that might lead her out of the protected enclave we occupied.

She had set the bank robbery record that one summer, and to get that far and become that famous, she had embarrassed the entire universe of Missouri law enforcement for an extended period of time. They were never, ever going to forget it.

Add to that the tabloid nature of her legal proceedings where nightly media discussions often centered on the type of dress and shoes she had donned on any particular day. Suffice it to say, the collective temperature of the men in that conservative state registered just under the standard metric required for blood to boil.

Sally had delayed her sentencing by having her lawyer petition for her to be imprisoned with the gender she identified with: women. By the time of her arrival at our unit, her case had wended its way through state and federal court before eventually being struck down by the Eighth Circuit.

For now, until the next step, she would be housed as a man. In the cell next to mine.

Sally revealed the core of her character on the first day she landed on our block. I was down in the common area on the ground floor playing cards with an inmate named Steven "Shorty" Williams, a former college basketball star who was with us because he was suffering from advanced stage prostate cancer.

Like Sally who was trying to fund her surgery, Shorty felt he had to resort to crime to pay for his medical needs.

His insurance had lapsed well before his diagnosis, so he went to work for a neighbor who had a business in East St. Louis distributing Mexican tar heroin. The income he generated provided him with the money for his initial cancer treatment, as well as easy access to pain medication that didn't require a prescription.

High during his waking hours, he continually forgot to visit the doctor. The cancer metastasized into his bladder and eventually his liver and pancreas.

He was arrested by chance in Ferguson during a rollup of civil rights protestors on a hot summer night. Shorty wasn't there to vent his rage about some ongoing injustice; he was there to make a delivery to one of the local news mimbos—strictly a weekend user—who was covering a civic flare-up after another young man of color was beaten senseless during a routine traffic stop.

As was the case for a lot of his life, it was just bad timing. Like the time he blew out his knee while working out for the Milwaukee Bucks in anticipation of the NBA draft just after his sophomore year at St. Louis University, or the time he signed a contract with a Croatian team only to find the arena and the hotel that was to accommodate him recently leveled by a terrorist attack that signaled the start of a civil war, or the time his car blew a tire on a rain-slicked state road and skidded into a bridge abutment killing his girlfriend and their child.

Through it all, Shorty maintained his grace and wit—all six-foot-eleven of it.

He taught me many things in our time together.

On the day that the guards escorted Sally Dio to her cell, Shorty and I were sitting downstairs playing Rummy Five Hundred.

He was bitching that I was doing some sort of "Rain Man" card counting voodoo on him, but then, that was Shorty—whining only about his bad luck at cards, never about the avalanche of astonishing curses that had still failed to completely bury him.

"C'mon, Chunk, you got to put that electric mind to sleep, you know? Click that shit off. You are playing a dyin' man, who is on serious pain meds. It ain't fair that you know what cards I'm holding in my hand," he said.

He pulled out one card, tried to find a new place for it, slid it in between two others, then removed it, clucked a couple of times, and put it back in its original position.

"You know, Shorty, I'm not doing anything devious. It's not

hard to tell what you have. I can easily subtract what I have as well as what I've seen you discard. You should be doing the same thing."

"Oh, I should, huh? Okay, smartass, what am I holding?"

I knew, but wasn't going to say. I liked wasting time with him playing this game, and if he knew he had no shot at winning—and he had no shot—it would likely come to an end.

"Let's just play," I said.

I loved hanging out with Shorty. He was certainly a game rival. There wasn't a thing we did in our daily interaction that didn't evolve into some type of competition.

A discarded piece of paper could entertain us for hours—origami football, or a tearing game we developed where any separation of that paper resulted in a loss.

When we first met, he was still fairly spry and sharp. Even when the pain increased and the morphine dosages elevated, Shorty could give me everything I could handle.

But, by the time Sally showed up, I was beating him pretty regularly. I began to devise ways for him to win without him knowing that I was making that possible.

My plan for that particular game of cards involved me roaring out to a huge lead only to stall as Shorty mounted a comeback that would result in him cresting the 500–point barrier needed for victory. It was not surprising to me that it was at the maximum point of his ass getting whupped that he had begun to whine.

But on that day, our cone of concentration was shattered by an otherworldly shriek with a timbre that startled the both of us. Shorty's first thought was to swivel his head toward the loudspeaker, because we had only ever heard a sound even close to that coming from there.

There was a second scream followed by these words:

"There is no way on God's great Earth I am wearing that!" the voice yelled.

"Shut the hell up, freak!" screamed one of the guards from above us.

I scrambled from my seat and bounded up the stairs.

"Stay away, Dawson," the older guard, Cappy, said pointing his hard rubber sap in my direction.

I didn't advance, but I didn't retreat. All of us in the system had a tacit pact to be witnesses to anything that smacked of abuse.

"Gray?" the person asked in plaintive voice.

"Put it on now," Cappy demanded.

"This facility dresses people in gray?"

"Shut up and get out of that dress and put on your clothes."

It took Shorty awhile to make it up to where I was, but he eventually came to my side.

"Hey, Cappy, why don't you give that person some privacy? You and I both know all of the contraband checks and cavity searches were done well before they got here," Shorty said.

This would have been true, and the two guards finally relented. They stepped aside and allowed the person a moment to change into their jail clothes—gray T-shirt, gray ill-fitting chinos, and because they rarely heated the place, a gray coat made of heavy denim.

The person reemerged, gathering a waterfall of dirty-blond hair, holding it together in their slender fingers.

Cappy held out a pen, an implication that a form needed to be filled out and a box checked to make sure the task had been completed.

"You should make sure that you can account for everything that has been requisitioned before you sign off," I offered.

"Dawson, goddammit, get the hell back downstairs and leave us be," Cappy said.

"Just trying to make your job easier, Cappy," I said.

But I wasn't doing anything of the sort. I'd already seen them pull some shit on many an incoming soul, including myself. If you didn't count everything they had issued—two pairs of pants, three pairs of underwear, two T-shirts, one jacket, one pair of shoes, three pairs of socks, one sheet, one pillowcase, one blanket, one pillow, one towel, one washcloth, and one laundry bag—they would charge you for what might turn up missing.

I knew the items and their quantities so intimately because I probably registered their presence at least twenty times a day. Of course, that was just a natural response for me. I can be obsessive about things like that.

There is a rule in golf, 4b, that confines one to a fourteen-club limit and there is a minimum of a two-stroke penalty for breaching that rule. That's all I needed to know when I was told about it. Paranoid about being assessed that penalty, I routinely counted the clubs in my bag at least six times during a round.

Later, like the inventory check in my cell, I began to see that vigilance as meditative; a way to ground myself and put an accent on the importance of staying in the present.

The job finished, the guards made for their exit.

"You kinda sweet on the new one, Dawson?" the younger guard, someone who was just brought in for that duty, asked.

I didn't respond. When they had made it back down the stairway, I told the person to join us at the card table downstairs after they were settled.

"Thank you, darling, but this ain't the first time in the hoosegow for me. I'm going to be just fine. I'm Sally."

"I'm Chuck and this is Shorty."

Some hellos were exchanged between them before Shorty tugged at my shirt.

"Let's finish our game, Chunk."

"Yeah, all right."

And we did. My plan worked perfectly. Those moments post Sally's arrival saw me go on an extended losing streak. Shorty emerged from the depths to conquer me. He never saw it coming because I was an experienced hustler when it came to things like this.

I got such a kick out of watching his eyes blaze with excitement as he crept closer to me in points with each successive hand.

For a fleeting instant, Shorty reverted to something that I hadn't seen recently: a dominant opponent. He was merciless with the banter espousing his governance over the weaker. It was glorious.

As the crescendo neared, and my defeat loomed, Sally reversed course and came downstairs to hang out with us. She stayed silent as we played, and when Shorty celebrated his victory, she offered a round of dainty applause.

But when Shorty headed to his cell to pee and wait for the arrival of his medications, Sally turned to me and in a breathy whisper asked, "What is wrong with him?"

"He has cancer," I said.

"Shit."

"So that's why you let him win?"

"What?"

"Oh, come on, darling, I'm not blind. That was the worst dive I've ever seen anyone take."

I almost fell off the bench.

"You could see that?" I asked.

"Please."

There was a fairly long moment of silence before I brought up the subject I'd been wanting to ask about.

"I've heard of you before," I said.

"Yeah, I guess I'm pretty famous now. Not sure what that gets me."

"No, the guy who was busted at the same time you were, the golfer, I knew him a little."

"Oh, god, you know Marty?" Sally asked with a guilty laugh.

"Kind of. But we were never friends."

"Oh, my lord, his face. I will never forget that look in the back of the black-and-white when they first hauled us in. I watched someone's whole world completely disappear in the space of about twenty minutes. Here I was, getting ready to spend the rest of my life in the can, and all I could do was try to keep him from crying."

"I'm willing to bet he's over it now," I said.

"How do you know that?"

"He plays golf. You move on. The next hole, the next round, the next tournament. What's past is past."

"What's with the calluses on the pads of your hand?" she asked.

I smiled, impressed by the attention to detail.

"Well, I'm a golfer, too."

I held up my left hand to show her that, even though they were softening, there were still gristly humps along the pads below my first three fingers and a healthy patch of leathered skin on the inside of my forefinger.

"That's eighteen plus years of holding a golf club for nearly every waking hour."

"How long have you been in here?"

"Three years, one hundred and ninety-four days today," I answered.

"Wow, and you still have the hint of them."

"I've been known to place my grip on any stray broom handle, or even on the bars of my cell. It's my hope that there will be some remnant when I walk out of this place."

"And when is that supposed to happen?"

"My window opens in about two months," I said, trying not to let the excitement invade me quite yet.

Sally nodded, then stared into the distance. She sighed, her face darkened, and her hands moved to prop up her chin. It suddenly seemed that she needed the extra support or her head might plunge onto the table.

"I fucking hate gray," she said.

5

The early therapeutic techniques were pretty simple. I was taught to sit still. I was trained to look another person in the face when I attempted communication. I was instructed about body awareness and how I took up space in the world.

There were iterations designed to give me a sense of time, the rules of human interaction and discovery associated with the nature of curiosity. These were all things that were not being naturally processed by my brain as I developed.

One sees, questions, and is hopefully led on a journey to answer the origins of something new. I was told what it was before it was even presented to me for inspection.

The need to perform became my norm. With that as the only acceptable result, something was stolen from my sense of wonder.

Me being was never an option. Education through failure

was out. Scrutiny was constant. Any tic, or jumbled thought, led to a possible new diagnosis.

I was, and would always be, sick.

Sweetwater Municipal Golf Course was constructed on an area of flat horse country that sprawled just east of the city of Chula Vista, California.

It was one of those courses that had started out as a middle-class private club. Within a year after its debut, the course fell into disrepair from neglect and stupid agronomic choices made during its construction. The owners went belly up and all those with equity stakes begged the county for relief. Somewhere along the line, a deal was struck, and the town of Sweetwater City took over control of the property.

Their gamble turned out to be wise one. The city used its large banquet facilities to host the Elks and the Rotary. The Junior League ran their cotillion out of there, and all of the various professional social organizations took advantage of the attractive rates for outings and local tournaments.

It took some time, but the golf course began to come around. They started a men's and ladies' club, and a junior program. They made an investment in an innovative greenskeeper who brought natural protocols to the course's care.

Eventually, like all golf courses in the proximity of the coast, *Poa annua* invaded the once bent grass greens and the surfaces finally became uniform and ultimately readable.

And then they hired Jim Wellington to be the head pro.

Born in Texas, on the day Hitler had invaded Poland in

1939, Jim was delivered in the back bedroom of his parents' house in suburban southwest Fort Worth.

When Jim turned ten, he got a job after school at Shady Oaks Country Club cleaning the clubs of the members. At twelve, he'd been promoted to driving range custodian, and was afforded the first opportunity to witness the cranky mien of Ben Hogan.

Mr. Hogan had survived a horrific car crash that had nearly ended his golf career. One look at the photos of the remnants of his Cadillac, demolished head-on by a Greyhound bus in a pea soup fog, and it is truly a wonder that he would ever walk again, let alone resume his golf career.

He won the 1950 U.S. Open at Merion just fourteen months after he was released from his fifty-nine day stay in the hospital.

There are other parts of the Hogan lore—that he witnessed his father's suicide, how he was forced into becoming a caddy to supplement the family's lack of income after the patriarch's demise, and trouble with temper and demeanor, but the man was nails, and Jim often said that none of his celebrated success would have been possible without all that he had experienced in his life.

He said the same thing to me.

My adoptive dad, Taylor, was a little dense, and definitely distracted by Cissy's departure and/or whatever gal he was romancing at the moment. I'd been leaving clues to let him know I was interested in exploring this whole golf thing, and everyone, except for him, had noticed.

My frustration grew until one day I snapped.

To get to the city of Chula Vista, the main center for commerce in the area, we had to drive past Sweetwater Municipal Golf Course.

Every time we had passed by the track, somewhere between the seventeenth green and the tee for the finishing hole, I would roll down my window and try to breathe in the intoxicating amalgam of freshly mown grass, stagnant pond scum, and ammonium sulfate fertilizer.

But one day, while stopped at the light that abutted the eighteenth green, I became transfixed by a group of youngsters who were walking along the fairway, their junior bags slung across their bony shoulders.

In a flash, I unlocked the passenger door, unsnapped my seatbelt, and bolted for the dry wash that ran parallel to the medium-length par five. I heard Taylor yell something peppered with a curse word, but I did not turn around.

I charged through the scrub bush, forded the tiny stream in the arroyo, and bounded up to the kid who was nearest the road. He was in the rough on the left side, not two paces from the red hazard line.

"Hey," I yelled. "My name is Charles. What are you guys doing out here?"

The kid freaked out, dropped his bag to the ground, and went running toward the one adult in the group.

The terrified kid pointed me out.

I froze. I realized I wasn't supposed to be there and heard

the voices of all of my occupational therapy trainers screaming, "No!"

I spun around to look for Taylor's Fusion, but the light had changed and it was no longer where it should have been.

The semblance of panic began to orbit me, as I had no idea what I should do next. A booming, "Hey, you!" rang out from the man standing on the edge of the right side of the fairway.

I looked to him and his posse of kids, who had now huddled around him in case the crazy kid who crashed their round turned out to be vicious.

He waved me over.

Something caused my feet to move, and I started the march toward his beckoning. I only covered a couple of steps, when the grass under my feet changed from the two-inch ragged shag of the rough to the .45 of an inch tightly mown fairway. That first crunch under my feet was a brand on my brain.

It felt weird and I soon found that I couldn't walk normally over the expanse. It was like a recently swabbed deck, or something so pristine, that I ended up on my tiptoes, trying not to spoil its virginal nature.

The gaggle of young golfers surrounding the man began to laugh.

"Go back to your balls," the man said, firmly.

They did. I suppose that since I was close to him, they felt secure enough to safely disperse.

"My name is Jim," he said.

He was a man of average height, with a stern gaze, dressed in slacks and golf shirt and sporting a tan woolen flat cap. The man held out his hand as I arrived.

It wasn't really a hand in the anatomical sense. At that point, it was almost like a claw—the joints stuck in an arthritic half clasp that I would later recognize as a precursor to the perfect golf grip.

I knew my training. I reached out to accept his invitation, and said, "I'm Charles Dawson."

"Okay, Charles, let's watch these boys play their third shots, what do you think?"

I couldn't see the joy on my face, or the gleam in my eyes, but I felt them welling. He exhorted the kid closest to us to go ahead.

"Okay, Cameron, what's your yardage?"

The kid looked at the red marker on the side of the fairway, triangulated the distance to his ball and then to the flag, which sat in the dead center of the green, just in front of a pretty sharp upward slope.

"I've got it at about a hundred yards, Mr. Wellington."

"And how much of a factor is the wind at this point?" Jim asked.

The boy plucked a couple of tufts of grass and threw them in the air. The emerald blades fell directly to the ground.

"Not that much, Mr. Wellington," he said.

"So, what are you going to hit?"

"Seven iron," he said.

"But you don't want to be long, right? You don't want to have that putt from the top of the hill."

"I'll hit a hard eight," the kid said.

He pulled the cut-down junior club from his bag, took his stance, waggled a time or two, and took a rip at it. The ball just barely got up in the air, but it did travel in a straight line, and just crawled onto the front of the green.

I made some kind of sound with my lips closed, and followed that by saying, "I could do better than that."

"Quiet son, that's not the point of what's going on here. He knows what he did wrong. Your correct response should be something like, 'That'll work,' or 'You've got a putt at it,'" Jim said.

The other boys each took their turns, but no one hit a shot like the players did on TV.

After the four had completed their efforts they picked up their bags and trudged forward toward the setting sun.

"Let's go, Mr. Dawson," Jim said to me and so I walked with him.

A figure appeared on the mound at the back of the green. Lit from behind, it was dark to us and larger than reality. It was Taylor, and I could intuit from his crossed arms and staggered stance that he was angry.

When we got within the distance his voice could travel without yelling, he said, "C'mon, Chuck, leave these people alone."

The boys who made it on the green were marking and cleaning their golf balls. One of the kid's shots had landed in an area between the two bunkers left of the hole, and he was preparing to play his next shot by taking a couple of practice swings.

Jim just held up his two fingers at Taylor, kind of like an admonition that it was not his time to infringe on the proceedings. Why Taylor didn't react to Jim and let the moments cascade toward their conclusion, I'll never know. He was usually impatient and certainly always felt a need to scratch out his territory amongst other men—be it a neighbor, store clerk, or any of those he had to share the road with in his car.

But Taylor waited, arms still crossed, possibly a little tighter than before.

The boy who was off the green hit a pretty decent chip. I felt a hand on my shoulder.

"Pull the flag, please, Mr. Dawson," Jim said.

I'd seen players and caddies do this on TV, so I purposefully walked toward the hole. If the fairway was a beautiful luxurious carpet, the green was like exquisite Carrera marble, but I didn't hesitate. I kept putting one foot in front of the other.

"Try not to step in their line, Mr. Dawson," Jim warned.

I had no idea what he was talking about. I continued straight to the hole, only to hear the kid who was farthest from the cup say, "Stop, dude."

I did as he said. He walked over to me and pointed out where the other players' balls lay, and told me to steer clear of stepping on their line to the cup. He lightly grabbed my arm and led me on a circuitous path to a place of entry that would be inoffensive.

"Guys don't like it when you step in their line. It's cool—everyone learns this at some point. No time like now," he said with what appeared to be knowledge from direct experience.

It was the first of many of my lessons in golf etiquette, but the most indelible because it was learned amidst the daggers of six sets of eyes being thrown by these boys, Jim Wellington, and the frowning Taylor, still posing with his straitjacketed arms on the hillock above the green.

In true Arthurian fashion, I withdrew the flagstick like the sword from the stone. I retraced my steps to the edge and watched as the boys finished the hole. Replacing the flag, I looked over to Jim, who nodded his approval.

"All right, Chuck, can we go now?" Taylor asked.

"Yes, sir," I said.

But I really didn't want to wake from the dream just yet, and Jim somehow knew this. He walked over to Taylor and stuck out his rheumatoid stricken hand. As they shook, Jim smilingly said:

"Hi, there, my name is Jim Wellington, and I'm the head pro here at Sweetwater."

"Taylor Dawson," Taylor said as he tried to fit his hand into the claw that Jim had proudly offered.

"Your boy seems to have a bit of interest here. Perhaps you'd like to come down here sometime and we can gauge the level of that," Jim drawled in florid Texan.

"My boy has some issues, Mr. Wellington. I'm not sure he or you are quite ready to take on something like this."

I stayed silent. I really didn't want to upset Taylor any further.

"Well, your choice, Mr. Dawson. Interest is a powerful thing. When I see it, I'm kind of a sucker in trying to find out if it can be expanded," Jim said.

The accent gave his statement a sort of magnetic gravity, and

Taylor actually paused to consider it. Anything optimistic about my future was usually dismissed because I'd never really given him a reason to think my struggle would ever ease.

"I would really like to try this," I said.

It was kind of a complete sentence—certainly a rarity when speaking to Taylor.

"Okay, maybe we'll check it out," Taylor said.

"You know where to find me," Jim said with a grin.

Having impressed Taylor for the first time in my recollection, I suddenly felt a need to keep the ball rolling.

"Thank you, Mr. Wellington," I said and held out my hand.

"Thank you for tending the flagstick, Charles," he said as he encircled it.

"All right, let's go now," Taylor butted in.

But that was said without the normal brusqueness; a usual command that frequently involved physical steerage toward his geographical goal.

"Just call the club here and ask for me," Jim said.

He wandered off to rejoin his students as Taylor and I silently returned to his vehicle in the parking lot.

Nothing was said between us during the rest of the ride. I was in a daze for most of that time.

When we returned to the house, I did everything I was supposed to do without my normal level of protest. I put on my pajamas and brushed my teeth, all without being asked, and crawled into bed at my pre-determined time.

I only imagined what Tayler did next. He got out a bottle of bourbon and sat in the dark for a good long while. He thought about where he was headed in life with his wife gone, his kid afflicted, and a business that had yet to show signs of recovery.

He'd come to this fork more than once to this point, and he'd always chosen the route that put it all in the rearview mirror. As much as he wanted to do that again, he had a solitary complication this time: me.

The next day, he called Jim Wellington and scheduled my first lesson for that coming Saturday.

6

I made my application for parole on the very first day that I could. I'd served three years, eight months and two weeks of my sentence. I didn't know a whole heck of a lot about what was supposed to happen next.

I relied on Sally since she had gone through the parole process multiple times during her first stretch in prison.

She related the most amazing story about how she was suddenly set free from serving her first term.

Like me, she'd been convicted of a Class B felony. In her case, it was for a pattern of jewelry store heists that did not involve strong-arm robbery. She would saunter into the store in full drag, and ask to look at a variety of items. A couple of those baubles just happened to never make it back into the display case.

"I'd been told that no one gets parole the first time, but I'm an optimist by nature," she told us.

At the time, she had spent most of her existence as a man.

She'd even been employed for a long period operating a skip loader for an environmental remediation firm. She had a flattop and droopy mustache during that period of her life—desirous of fitting in with the crew who worked alongside her.

We laughed when we heard that because it was all so incongruous by the time she showed up in our world. No one would have checked the "desire to fit in" box on any subjective assessment of her.

In Missouri, the parole board is made up of seven folks who are selected by the governor. Though a part-time endeavor, each member makes nearly $86,000 a year to serve; these are patronage jobs in their purest sense.

At Sally's hearings (both resulted in denials), she was asked to present her version of the events, what she planned to do should she get out, and the rest of the stuff on the boilerplate hearing protocol.

She admitted to being reckless and stupid. She promised them that she would never be in their presence again during the rest of her lifetime, and that she had been a model inmate and committed no crimes since being incarcerated.

"Did you ever use drugs, Mr. Dio?" a parole member asked her the first time around.

"No, sir."

"Never tried Lucy in the sky with diamonds?"

Sally remembered doing some kind of quick double take at the time. She polled the faces of the other members of the board, but they were stoically implacable.

"I'm sorry, did you say Lucy in the sky with diamonds?"

"Yes, Lucy in the sky with diamonds," the guy repeated.

"Uh, no. I'm not sure I know what that is, sir," Sally replied.

The guy nodded, looked down, and wrote something that Sally said looked like hash marks on his notepad. She also saw him try to suppress a bit of a crooked smile.

There were a couple more queries about whether he—Salvatore at the time—could reform his dastardly ways. Someone brought up the concept of sin, and someone else asked if all of the merchandise that had been lifted had been recovered (it had not).

Sally could tell this was going nowhere. There were some victims' statements read, including a particularly funny one from a Norwegian jewelry storeowner who had little facility with the English language.

Her lawyer brought up all the usual qualifiers: first-time offender, the struggles of class inequality, and some other stock bullshit.

Finally, as it was all wrapping up, the man who had asked the strange question in the beginning asked this, "Mr. Dio, did you ever find yourself at a bazaar trying to sell your ill-gotten goods?"

"I'm not sure I understand. A bazaar? A bazaar for what?" Sally asked.

"You know, a criminal enterprise where stolen merchandise is exchanged. An evildoer's bazaar."

"No sir," she replied, curtly.

He did that nodding thing again and put down another group of slashes on his yellow legal pad.

She found out the next day that she had been denied. There was no mention of the strange questions from the board member, and she subsequently reapplied on the next possible date.

The second hearing was almost a shot for shot remake of the first one, including the man asking this question, "Have you ever walked in Central Park, singing after dark, and people think you're crazy?"

Sally just looked at her lawyer, and asked if she needed to answer that one. He shook his head in the negative.

Later, while answering another question about what skills she could use to seek employment if granted parole, Sally said, "I've done heavy construction and am licensed and certified to operate a variety of work site machinery."

The bald guy butted in, "Did any of these machines have a nickname like Babe Ruth?"

Again, Sally looked to her lawyer, who proceeded to change topics and bring the hearing to a close.

Once again, she found out the next day that she had been denied parole. Though thoroughly dejected, she decided to not give up and renewed her application on the first day she could.

Before that third hearing could be scheduled, she was suddenly released from prison on a Mandamus writ. A higher court had ordered nearly all of those who had appeared before that parole board to be granted release because, as it turned out, the man who had asked the odd questions, two other members of the board, and a full-time clerk were cited and dismissed for abusing their responsibilities.

Seems that the guy and his cohorts were running a game

where they would use pre-selected phrases, song lyrics, and/or words during the proceedings. They got a point for getting it out there, but if the inmate repeated it, they got three more. Each point was worth a double sawbuck, and at the end of the year, the four had a dinner at a Kansas City steakhouse, drunkenly paying off their wins and losses.

It was a stupendous stroke of luck that got her released. She told us she was processed out within an afternoon, and was so stunned, so sure that fate had dictated her fortune, that she robbed a liquor store on her first night of freedom.

She was back in prison serving two sentences concurrently within a fortnight and didn't come up again for parole until she had served nearly fifteen more years in the pen.

On the day before my hearing, the guard we called Cappy shoved a Manila envelope through the bars of my cell. It was most of the material from my trial, including my statement to police on the day of the incident.

I was going to meet a new public defender, Deidre Agugliero.

Sally, being half-Italian, had to coach me on the pronunciation of her name.

The Missouri Voluntary Manslaughter Law separates the distinction from murder by classifying this crime as purposefully causing the death of someone, but qualifying that the act happened in the moment and was the result of passion or emotional excitement.

I might have added things like rotten luck, or poor

representation at trial, but the state's description was an adequate summation of the category.

From the first seconds of this ordeal, I knew that all I ever had was my truth, and there would be no embellishments or entreaties that weren't grounded in objectivity or facts of that day.

I ran my story for Sally and Shorty; both said that my matter-of-fact recollection, though totally riveting, lacked any sense of empathy or compassion.

"So, I'm a little confused," Shorty began. "Not about the story or the details—that shit you present very clearly. It's just . . ."

"You don't seem to care about what happened," Sally offered.

"Yeah, that's it in a nutshell," Shorty said.

"Well, if the truth be told, I don't," I replied.

"Is this what you've told me about your condition, Chunk? That sometimes when you talk, you don't have any emotion or stuff?" Shorty asked.

"I suppose it could be a little of that, but what happened, happened, and given a similar situation, I believe the outcome likely would've been the same."

"Well, please don't say that, darling," Sally said, "Whatever you do, don't go there."

"This isn't even in a live setting anymore, is it?" Shorty asked.

"No. All video conference now," I said.

"And your attorney isn't here either?"

"No. She's probably in a room somewhere in St. Louis."

"Just tell her to tell the board about your condition. Tell her to tell them that though you come off as insincere and uncaring, it's only because that is your nature genetically, your handicap, as it is." Sally said.

"Well, I'm not doing that."

"And you know, the whole fact that it's being done on a screen, where your voice is coming out of a speaker, and you look puffy because the camera adds some weight—well, that will just make it that much more worse." Sally said.

"I'm sorry. It's all I've got," I said.

The next morning, I shaved away the wisps that had accumulated on my face, put on my cleanest denim, and waited on my bed for the escort to take me to the video conferencing room.

Cappy came and got me. He fit a manacle belt around my waist, cinched it tight, and ratcheted the cuffs on my wrists.

"Why do I need this?" I asked.

"They do this stuff in an office in the administrative building. It's all still kind of new, and they haven't worked out all the details. I have to take you out of the prison. I ain't doing that without this shit," Cappy explained.

"Okay."

I twisted a little in place. I suppose the restraints might have some value as a golf training aid—keeping the torso connected to the arms and all that.

"Knock that shit off, Dawson."

"Yes, sir."

He picked up the Manila folder, led me out of my cell, and

down the stairs into the common room. Sally was thumbing through a tattered fashion magazine and Shorty was nodding off at the table we used to play cards on.

Shorty was set to shuffle off of the planet soon. Both Sally and I made sure he was never alone for very long.

"Oh my god, Shorty, wake up and get a load of this," Sally squealed.

Shorty raised his head and offered a forced smile through the fog of pain.

"You know, they do that because he might be around a girl," Shorty slurred, referring to my restraints.

"Well, now I'm a bit insulted," Sally said.

There were a couple of others in the room, but the three of us were the only ones who usually had any form of interaction. Cappy tugged on the belt and pushed me to the door.

"Knock 'em dead, kid. Not literally, of course. You don't want them tacking anything on," Sally chirped.

"Shut up, Dio." Cappy said.

"Yes, sir."

The door buzzed on our arrival and we exited into a holding area where Cappy gave me a quick pat down. There were two court officers waiting on the other side of what could only be described as an airlock.

I started feeling a little hinky—the hair on the nape of my neck began to stiffen. Where they were taking me was unfamiliar. Some old behavior reared its head and memories of panic—long quelled—crept back.

I flashed back on many instances from my youth: new doctors, or food, or relatives I'd never met, or a store I'd never visited, and the crippling terror that would often overtake me in those circumstances.

Cappy handed me off to the two officers.

"You got him," he said, before handing over the envelope.

He disappeared back through the door.

"Hi, my name is Charles," I said.

"Don't talk, dickhead," the younger of the two said.

They pushed me through the door, then another, and finally out into a long hall. It was obvious that this was not part of any secure facility. I tried to focus on all of the details being presented around me and not on the quickening of my breath, or the pearls of sweat oozing out from just below my hairline.

A group of non-incarcerates was moving around with paperwork in their hands. I saw an inordinate number of reusable coffee cups occupying the balance position in the off-hands.

I caught a couple of the notices tacked upon the wall. A big softball game was nigh, and the coming Tuesday was the warden's secretary's birthday.

And then we were outside, in the parking lot where there was no fence or wall preventing me from looking at anything more than the sky.

I stopped and tried to will the blood to cycle through my body. It had been over three years since I had been in the proximity of freedom.

The air was different from the stuff we got to breathe on the yard, and it puzzled me to no end because that space couldn't have been more than a couple of hundred yards from where I was standing. Something smelled familiar.

"C'mon, Dawson, let's go," one of the officers urged, as he tugged on my manacle belt.

"You smell that?" I asked.

I didn't expect a response because I wasn't asking anyone else but myself.

I knew what it was. My eyes darted toward an opening in an ivy-covered fence across the street. Behind the greenery lay a golf course. The aroma was the variation on the theme of all the ones I had spent the bulk of my life roaming.

A tractor flashed past my sliver of a view, pulling a fairly new aerator. I got a glimpse of the belt-driven tines puncturing the desiccated earth and egesting two-inch plugs in its wake.

Of course, it was spring. The smell was fertilizer. Its application was intended to burn up the water-distressed rye and resurrect the Bermuda from dormancy.

One of the officers nearly tugged me off of my feet, and the other aided him by giving me a solid push. I craned my head to see if I could see anything else, but one of the two grabbed my neck and directed it forward. I savored the last bit of the odor as its pungency waned on my retreat.

We entered another door and another hallway. After a sudden stop, I was pushed into a windowless office with a wooden chair in the middle of the floor. I sat and looked up to a large monitor that seemed to float on the wall.

A woman, surely younger than I, sat at a desk examining the nail on her right index finger.

"Hi," I said, assuming that the audio was working.

It was not. She kept gazing at the fingernail with a look that could have been anything from wonder to contempt.

I tried waving at the camera that was perched above the monitor. She had a bit of a start, composed herself, and signaled to someone across the room she was sitting in.

Through the little speaker, I heard, "I'm Deidre Agugliero; I'll be representing you for this hearing. Are you okay with that?"

"Yeah, of course."

She seemed sturdy. Her voice sounded confident and oddly soothing. I wiped the slickness off my brow and listened as she prepared to give me a rundown of what was about to take place.

7

On the eve of my first golf lesson, I crawled into bed well before my assigned time and tried with all my might to sleep. Back then, I believed that the hours flew by faster at night. I did not sleep, though, and the morning drive to the course seemed to take forever.

It was spring; there were only a couple of weeks of school left. When we pulled into the parking lot and I saw the tide of players toting their golf bags toward the starter's shack, the flood of anticipation overwhelmed me. I could feel my heartbeat in my fingers.

Taylor bitched about how far he had to park away from the entrance, but I didn't do my normal cowering at his curses because I'd accomplished what seemed previously impossible. I was actually about to get a golf lesson at Sweetwater Municipal Golf Course.

I marveled at the stucco-cladded clubhouse and banquet/meeting facilities at the end of the parking lot.

At the far end of the buildings, you could see some of the golf course, laid out underneath the shadows of looming foothills where mid-twentieth century ranch houses snaked along the switchbacks.

The first tee and the ninth green were the first to come into view, the latter flanked by a wall of oil-soaked phone poles—a forest of masts for the netting that enclosed the driving range.

"What a waste of good real estate," Taylor stated.

I was the first to see Jim. He was at the far eastern end of the range, sitting on a high canvas chair, umbrella attached to one of the arms, leaning forward and studying the address position of what Taylor would later say was a very fine-looking lady.

I sprinted to Jim's position, using the thrusting burst from Taylor of "Goddamnit, Chuck" like an afterburner.

"Mr. Wellington!" I screamed.

Many of those practicing turned to see my charge. Jim noticed me out of the corner of his eye, and without altering his focus on his student, put his gnarled hand up as a stop sign. I obeyed.

Taylor arrived and grabbed me firmly around my meager bicep.

"This is not a playground, Chuck!" he seethed.

He let go and targeted his gaze on the white cotton shorts that just barely concealed the rear end of Jim's student.

Jim rose from his perch and squared his student's shoulders so her upper body was parallel to her feet.

"I want you to understand," Jim said, "that when you aim

too far to the right, you are going to have to come over the ball to get it back to the target."

He used the club in her hands to lightly trace the swing path, so she could feel the awkwardness she had manifested with her setup.

He stepped away. She made the adjustment, threw in a waggle or two and a little squat (Taylor eyes probably widened in their sockets at that moment), drew the club back, and clicked the ball off of her five iron out into the sea of grass and golf balls. The ball stayed pretty straight and landed within the area of her intention.

The warmth she exuded with her smile could have thawed the Alps.

"All right, take it out there and play with it. You've got this, Martha. I'll see you next week," Jim said.

She never dropped that smile as she gathered her things, walked over to Jim, and put her SPF-15 frosted lips on his left cheek. It might have been the only time I ever saw him blush.

Taylor followed her departure.

I stood, heart still pounding, waiting to be released from Jim's request to remain motionless.

He rooted around in a large Hogan tour bag that was parked next to his chair and pulled out what was a smaller version of a mid-iron.

From a large bin of balls nearby, he grabbed a warm-up bucket and dipped it in.

"Welcome, Mr. Dawson," Jim said to me.

"Hi."

"Can I call you, Chuck?"

I nodded.

Why don't you step over here?"

There was a kelly-green artificial turf mat close to the fence. Jim laid the bucket down and placed a ball on a low rubber tee.

"You want to show me what you got?" he asked.

He handed me the club. I gripped it similarly to the plastic one that I had swung in the back yard many years before—slightly split baseball grip. I stepped onto the mat, and aligned my feet and shoulders in the same exact fashion Martha had done after being corrected. I took the club back, swung, and flat out whiffed it.

I heard Taylor smirk.

Jim didn't bat an eye.

"Try it again. Eye on the ball. Slow it down."

I did and ripped that second one on a low line drive straight out into the range.

"All right, do it again," he said as he placed another beaten, striped range ball on the tee.

I did with the same result. He didn't say another word; he just kept putting a ball on the tee, and waiting for me to rip it out into the air.

I don't recall whether I even looked to follow the result most of the time; I just kept going through my routine and taking a swing. My eyes were always on the ball at contact, because that's what Jim had told me to do.

After about twenty-five whacks, Jim reached to grab the

club away from me. Like before, my instinct was to never give it up—I had lived years with the regret from having to disappear the "Walmart Walloper." But this time, after just a brief moment, I relented.

Jim turned to Taylor.

"Your kid, young Chuck here, has got some very special tools, Mr. Dawson."

Taylor squinted with the obvious scrutiny of how much all this was going to cost him. He knew how these deals worked: a lot of bullshit praise with the sole purpose of making yourself crucial to your child's survival. He had used this technique in his business, as well.

"And what would those be, Mr. Wellington?"

"Good concentration, repeatable coordination, able to accept and understand instruction. Other intangibles. Something that I would qualify as innate talent."

"Ha. Not sure you nailed that last one," Taylor said with an eye roll.

"I can tell a lot by just what I've seen your son do. I wouldn't say it if it wasn't true."

Taylor was in a particularly sensitive place at the time. The divorce was final and he had just finished paying Cissy her half of the value of the house. The custody thing had never been formalized. He seemed to remember some kind of joint thing being discussed, but she had been out on the road with her drummer for a good, long time, and he never got her to respond to any of his queries about her responsibility.

And now, this municipal golf pro guy was trying to tell

him that his afflicted, adopted son was talented after watching him for less than fifteen minutes? Talented? He had never heard anything even remotely like this being directed to the boy in all of the years he had been part of his life.

I had never heard anything like that before either. I searched Jim's sun-bronzed face to try to determine whether this was fact or fiction. I had spent most of my life being given a whole shit ton of praise for doing the simplest of actions. The amount of times that I would see a therapist, or babysitter, or teacher paste on a fake smile, open their eye orbits in wonder, and hold up their hand to make me slap it in congratulations was into the gazillions by that point.

I went through the motions because all of those folks seemed to enjoy it, but Jim was not standing there screaming at me to give him five. He was looking at me differently than I had ever been looked at.

I can only say that for the first time in my life, I didn't feel like a specimen. So many of the people I had contact with dealt with me from a relative distance. I was a thing to be manipulated to produce the result that they had been hired to achieve.

After that first lesson, a new normal was established. It was me who wanted to achieve, and that was different.

"I don't know," Taylor said.

I wanted to scream. *How could that be his response?* I wanted to throw myself to the ground and beat my fists on the sparse turf, but I uncharacteristically held myself back.

"I'm going to give you a book, Chuck," Jim said.

"He can't read, Mr. Wellington," Taylor sighed.

Jim kept his gaze leveled at me.

"There are a lot of pictures in it, Chuck. You can also get someone to read you parts of it, or better yet help you to read it yourself."

Taylor never entertained the thought that someone might be him. That would have been a bridge too far, but he clearly thought that my minders might be able to use all of this as a type of reward when the need arose.

"Okay, so what's this book?" Taylor asked.

Jim reached into a pocket that hung off the side of his chair and withdrew a well-worn hardback copy of *Ben Hogan's Five Lessons: The Modern Fundamentals of Golf*.

He opened it to page nineteen. There were two drawings of Mr. Hogan. The one on the right was a penciled reproduction of the master striking the golf ball. There were active lines around the shaft of the club to give the observer the sense of speed and motion.

The drawing on the left side of the page is the one that immediately drew my attention, though. It was the exact replica of the other with the outlines of Hogan's body at the time of the strike, but there were no facial features, bulging biceps, or the unmistakable flat cap on the head. Instead, encased within the frame of the body was some type of electrical circuit.

There was a big motor in the area of the heart with wires connecting through the arms, and resistors lodged in the area of the hips and the hands. Bolts of electricity flew out of the hands and oscillated in a direct target for the ground.

There was a second, smaller motor where the head should

have been. I studied the difference in size and determined, in that moment, that the bigger force—the bigger motor—was not in the head, but the heart.

For one who had struggled so mightily with all things intellectual, this was a monumental revelation. It also set me on the course that led me to calling myself a "feel" player.

The irony there is that Jim didn't open up the book to that page to show me that. He opened it to show me what was on the previous page—eighteen, which showed a dark black numeral one followed by text that I later learned said, "*The Grip*."

He handed me back the club.

"Take both of these with you, Chuck. If you think you might be interested in exploring this further, cover Chapter One and we'll meet again."

I looked up at Taylor, who half-nodded. I added the club to my right hand and cradled the book with my left.

"So next week, same time?" Taylor asked.

"That would be ideal," Jim said.

Taylor fished a twenty and a ten out of his wallet and handed it over to Jim's claw.

"Thanks, Mr. Dawson," Jim said.

"Yeah, sure," Taylor said. "Let's hit the road, Chuck."

I spent all week, every waking hour, thinking about, creating, and executing Hogan's suggestion of the perfect grip. I could hardly wait to show Jim the following Saturday.

8

I couldn't stop staring at her. Deidre Agugliero wore a navy-blue blazer over a cardinal-red cashmere sweater. A string of white pearls hung like a quarter moon just below the crew neck. The whole getup was kind of like an abstract representation of the U.S. flag, but that was not what grabbed my attention.

Something was off with her eyes. I thought the right one might be fake. The iris was a light gray, startlingly contrasting with the hazel hue of her left. She must have noticed my interest because she halted her explanation of the events to come.

"Are you all right?" she asked.

"Yeah."

"Is that how you normally listen to someone?"

"I'm not sure what you mean," I said.

"I don't mean to be rude, and of course it is perfectly fine, but you appear to be fixated on something."

"What?" I asked.

She looked down at some papers in her hand.

"I guess I'm just curious about your right eye," I said. "It's a totally different color from your left one."

She blushed initially, before getting a little pissed off.

"Is that important to you? Are you going to become so distracted by that mystery that you'll be unable to focus on the future proceedings?"

Now it was probably my turn to blush, but I don't actually do that. I'm not sure I process embarrassment like others might. I did react to being admonished, though.

"No," I stammered.

"Okay, good. So, as I was saying, you are going to be required to give your version of the events of the situation that put you in this prison. You could just tell the board that you would like the record to stand, but my experience has shown me that the board wants to hear your story. They want to hear you. They want to see if you are remorseful, or if there's been some significant growth in your understanding of the events, or even if you've gotten religious."

"I'm not religious," I stated.

"Okay. That's fine," she said, and then in an aside that was nearly under her breath, she offered an axiom: "That kind of thing goes pretty far in this state."

She looked at me as if to see if I had a reaction to that last bit; I didn't. She rifled through another couple of pages.

"I'm looking at this sentencing report and, uh, I was wondering how you feel about divulging anything pertinent as to your, uh, condition?"

"You mean my Asperger's? My spectrumy stuff?"

"Yes."

"Do you think that might help? I no longer see it as a hindrance to anything. I've overcome aspects of the difficult parts of it. I've actually accomplished getting a college degree in just the first two years of my sentence."

"Yeah, I see that. A B.A. in English. Congratulations. I'm just saying that it might help to mention that you have a disability."

"I don't see it as a handicap. I see it purely as a gift. Without it, I would have no shot at achieving my goals."

"How so?" she asked.

"I'm not sure we have time to get into it, Ms. Agugliero. But, look, if you think it might help, I suppose you could bring it up. I need to get out of here and I'll use whatever works to make that happen. The only thing I can't pull off is a lie. So, between you and me, I have no remorse. I haven't grown while being incarcerated. In fact, I've likely regressed. I just count the days, try to be distracted by this or that, and when one is finished, I move onto the next. And I believe in myself, not myths.

"Yeah, you said that already."

"Okay, sorry."

"You do represent a first for me, Mr. Dawson. I've been at this gig for nearly three years now, and you are the first incarcerate seeking parole who does not have a single statement from a victim."

"Well, the victim is dead, ma'am."

"I'm referring to the victims who are still living. The ones affected by the loss of life. There is not one of these statements, not a complaint from a friend or family member, in the file I was given. By all accounts, there was not a single one offered at your trial."

"Yeah, that doesn't surprise me."

"Why?"

"The guy was—excuse my language, please, but there is no other real descriptive term that fits—a complete dick. When asked, I've remarked that the planet is better off rid of him. I'm pretty sure any of those people you described, if they existed, probably felt the same way."

"You're not going to say that, are you?"

"I don't know, Ms. Agugliero."

"Try not to volunteer it, please."

"Yes, ma'am."

She stuffed the paperwork back into the folder and turned to someone I couldn't see.

"We're ready," she said.

She turned back to me.

"Birth defect."

"Excuse me?"

"My eye. I was born with little or no pigment in my right eye. Kind of like those cats."

"Oh."

"Sometimes, I wear a contact lens that would match the color of the other eye, but today, I just didn't feel like it. I see it as a gift too sometimes," she said with a smile.

The screen went blank, but I still saw that smile in the blackness of the characterless pixels.

A new image appeared. Before me was a large boardroom,

its walls covered with framed photos of white men in blue suits with captions offering their titles and tenures. A long oaken table created a gulf between the camera angle and a gaggle of semi-interested individuals occupying the chairs on the other side.

The pinned-on nametags were a little hard to make out in the harsh light. There was a fair mixture of genders along with a smattering of diversity.

"Are you Charles Dawson, Missouri state inmate number 5-678097?" asked an older woman with a high hairdo.

"It's actually 5-6780991," I said.

The woman lowered her glasses on the bridge of her nose and looked at the form again.

"Yes, of course; thank you for correcting me."

"We all good?" a guy in a short sleeve white shirt and dark tie asked.

There was a nod from the woman.

"Okay, Mr. Dawson. We've looked over and briefly discussed your application for parole, and we would like you to please explain again how you ended up in the facility you are currently being housed in," the man said.

"I was convicted of manslaughter. A class B felony," I said.

"Yeah, we know that. Can you give us your version of the events that resulted in that conviction?"

"You want me to go over the trial proceedings?"

"No, sir. We would like you to take us back to the day of the crime. Tell us what happened."

"Oh, okay."

The head guy took a deep breath and exhaled loudly.

"I guess it's been nearly five years almost to the date, sir. I was in Cape Girardeau for the tour event there. I had four-spotted on the Monday, shot a 63 at Pocahontas Country Club, and played in the morning wave of the pro-am for the tournament on Wednesday morning back at the host venue."

Quickly, nearly everyone began to fidget.

"Let's back up, Mr. Dawson," the man said. "You're a professional golfer, correct? That is how you make your living?"

"When I make the cut, sir," I said with a hint of a smile.

"Yes, yes. Could you just use a little detail for those of us who don't exist in that world?"

"Sure thing, sir. Okay, I had been fully-exempt on the big tour for the first time in my career. But, my mentor, my guardian, the guy who really was my father, got very ill, and I stayed at home to take care of him. Well, the tour started without me, and by the time I was able to get back out there, I had pretty much lost my exempt status. Priority was based on earnings and I had earned zero to that point. So, I did what rabbits do."

"I'm sorry, can we stop? How did we change the subject to rabbits?" someone asked.

"They used to call guys who chased the tour and tried to qualify for each event individually rabbits. It's an old term from the sixties, I think, but that's what my guardian, Jim, used to call those who did that back in the day."

I plowed forward.

"Anyway, I shot 63 on that Monday to qualify, and that put me in the field for the tournament that week. It also obligated me to play in the pro-am on that Wednesday. I was paired with a group of salesmen from a suburban St. Louis insurance company. One of those was a guy named Ed Custis."

"The victim," the man explained to the board.

"Yes, sir. We played the round and I tried to make it a good experience for them by being jovial and positive, but they were truly intent on winning, and they were willing to do anything they could to make that happen. They started cheating. They conspired to write inaccurate scores down, pick up putts that would never be conceded, remove their balls from trouble, that sort of thing. When this had happened in the past, I would just tell my playing partners that they couldn't do that, and having been unmasked, that usually put the matter to rest. But these guys didn't care what I thought, and kept it up throughout the round. They weren't smart enough to understand that I carried the official scorecard. When we finished, I told the tournament chairman what they had tried to do. He thanked me and tossed the scorecard in the trashcan. I didn't wait around to hear their response when the calligrapher put a big DQ, as in disqualified, next to their team name up on the leaderboard."

I could see—and certainly thought—that the entirety of the parole board was with me at this point. I'm pretty sure that my story was the only one they'd heard that day that didn't involve a drug buy or weapons violation.

"So, the tournament began on Thursday, and I had a pretty good start. I'd been away for nearly eight months, but I felt good and birdied three of the first five holes. Since I was one of the early starting times, all of the electronic leaderboards had the name Dawson at the very top. Somewhere between the fifth green and the sixth tee, I heard a voice that sounded familiar say something vulgar to me. I turned to find it was Ed Custis, and he was already pretty lit even though it was likely somewhere between eight or nine in the morning."

Out of the corner of my eye, I saw a younger man with a buzz cut whisper to the parole board member sitting on his left. That person nodded and then craned his neck to look behind at another member, whispering something to her. The man who seemed to be running things saw the communication, held up his hand to halt my story, and turned to the assembled.

"Why don't we just let him finish, and then we can ask questions later," he said.

"I'd like to know what the victim said to the applicant," a youngish Latina said to the man.

The man looked at me.

"Mr. Dawson, would you care to recount what the deceased said to you?"

I hesitated. I had used the term "vulgar" to describe his statement, but that certainly didn't do it justice.

"Could I confer with my attorney at this point?" I asked.

"Just tell us what he said to you, Mr. Dawson."

"He said, 'Hey Dawson, you fuckhead, you're going to fucking choke, you motherfucking pussy. You're going to choke you retarded piece of shit. I'm going to make sure of it, cocksucker.'"

There was a moment where I thought I might have crossed the line. Deidre was right. These folks were likely pretty religious—the governor who had appointed them was certainly a Bible thumper. I wondered whether I had blown it, and if the hearing were already over.

"Thank you, Mr. Dawson, we can return to using the words like vulgar or profane to describe further interactions now that we've set the benchmark for the flavor of what was said."

"I'm sorry, sir."

"Okay, noted. Please continue."

"I hit a solid shot on the sixth hole and made like a twenty-footer for a birdie. I immediately thought, you know, *take that, Mr. Custis.* That I even thought that was the first big error that I made. That I let this guy distract me was unforgivable. Forget the score, or that I was leading the tournament, or even that I might actually see some money for the first time in a really long time—all things that I never allowed to be part of my thought process when I played. I had let this guy in somehow and that realization broke me in that moment. I proceeded to triple bogey the next hole. Then I drove it into a cypress tree on the eighth and had to take an unplayable. That's a penalty. While I was initially searching for the ball, I heard his voice rise above the crowd again. He was confirming what I already knew; that he had gotten to me and it had showed up in my performance."

"So, we can assume your subsequent actions were a reaction to this behavior?" the man asked.

"No. My caddy immediately called a marshal over and had him removed from the course. The incident that led to my incarceration didn't occur until two days later."

"Wait a minute, I'm confused," someone in the back said.

"Yeah, me too; none of this is in my report," someone else said.

"I'm sorry, I'm just trying to provide context," I said.

"Can we skip to the day where the crime occurred, Mr. Dawson?" the man asked.

"Of course, sorry, sir. So, all of that was on a Thursday. I played my second round on Friday and failed to make the cut by a wad. Easily the two worst rounds I have ever played as a professional. I paid my caddy for the week, took my clubs out to my courtesy car, and who was there waiting for me in the parking lot? Ed Custis. He apologized for being a drunken idiot the day before and he wanted to know if I was interested in a proposition. He proposed a match at his home club up I-55 in Festus. It was in the exact opposite direction of the next tour stop, but I really needed the money, so I asked him what he had in mind. He wanted a shot on every hole but the par threes, ties carry over, and you could press when you got two holes down. Wager was $200 per hole, per bet."

"Could you explain some of the terminology?" one of clerks asked.

"I got this," said the young Latina. "He's saying that for him to win on most of the holes, he had to beat the other guy—this Ed Custis person—by two shots. That if he beat him by only one, they would just tie. If they tied, the next hole would be played for 200 more. If either got down $400, you could press which means you could start a new bet, right?"

"Yes, ma'am."

“So, you were gambling?” a woman asked with a bit of disappointment.

“Yes, ma’am. This kind of thing happens all the time. Quite often, people approach us with the intention of testing their games against a professional. Usually, it’s a CEO or a different type of sports star, or even a politician. I believe that Mr. Custis desired to not only show off for his friends and cohorts, but he could get me to fold as he seemed to have done during the first round of the tournament.”

“But gambling like that is illegal. Are you confessing to further crimes, Mr Dawson?” she asked.

“Margaret, please . . .” the man said.

“Yes, sir. Sorry, sir,” she said.

“Go on, Mr. Dawson.”

“So, I said ‘yes’ to his proposition. He gave me directions and told me to be there the next day at 10:00 a.m. I drove up as the sun was setting, waited until it was pretty dark, hopped a fence, and did a little reconnaissance of the course before finding a quiet street so I could sleep in my car. The next morning, I got up at first light, found a nearby municipal course with a driving range and practiced for nearly three hours before heading over to the Festus Country Club. The parking lot was pretty full, but I didn’t see a lot of players on the course. Ed had spent the previous evening at the bar in the clubhouse telling everyone to come out and watch the spectacle that was sure to unfold. There were close to a hundred people milling about when I arrived, and you could just see that the side money that was being wagered would dwarf the figures that Ed and I were playing for.

I paused for moment. Everyone seemed to be listening.

"Now Ed was not a bad player. He hit it pretty straight with his miss being a bit of a hook at times. On a good day, he could break eighty with ease, but his short game was a little wonky, and he definitely got uncomfortable over any putt that was longer than two feet. I beat him by one on the first and second hole to tie, but on the third I failed to get it up and down out of a really nasty pot bunker, and suddenly he was six hundred bucks up. Now, mind you, I did not have more than about forty bucks in my golf bag total, but I was not anxious. I was hoping he might get off to good start. That way I could increase the wager. So, I pressed on the fourth tee."

I pointed over to the woman who had explained the elements of the wagering earlier.

"Like she said, I started a new bet that would only run the remaining fifteen holes. Now we had two bets going: one where I was down six hundred bucks and one that stood at zero. We tied the next three holes even though I birdied them all, but I eagled the par five eighth to his par, and suddenly I was up fourteen hundred dollars."

One of the clerks raised his hand. The smart gal who knew the game straightened him out.

"He's up 400 on the original bet and a thousand on the second," she said with a smile.

I nodded.

"So, did he press back?" she asked.

"Yeah, of course. There were all these people who would have forever ridiculed him had he not. He didn't hesitate because

I think he was holding onto the memory of what had happened a couple of days before where he believed that he had heckled me into playing poorly. He'd been saving that for the right time, and as we approached the ninth tee, you could see that he was getting ready to fire those bullets. We now had three bets going."

I had them. Interestingly, their focus was on the result of the match, not on the incident that took away my freedom.

"So, Ed started in on me again. He began playing slower to mess up the rhythm of our round. On nine, ten, eleven, and twelve, I had to wait for him on every single shot, as he chatted with his buddies, tested the wind, walked miles around putts to survey the break, that kind of thing. We tied every hole because, though I beat him by a shot on every one, as you now know, it was still not a win for me. Thirteen was a really good downhill par three, with a stiff breeze blowing across the depression from the left side. I hit one of the types of shots I had worked on in the morning practice session, a low liner that took most of the effect of the wind out of play. I started it at this huge, yawning bunker on the left and just bored it out there. The wind took it in toward the middle of the green, and I ended up with a fifteen-footer, just under hole high on the right. 'That's bullshit,' Ed said to the crowd. 'He almost flat whiffed it. Tell me, you didn't nearly whiff that, Dawson. That was a total mishit. You hardly got it off the ground.' I put my club back in the bag and started thinking about the putt that was to come. Ed's ball got up in the wind and ended up on the front fringe, probably forty feet or so from the hole. He putted up to about three feet and marked his ball. Now at this point, because it was a par three, all I had to do to win the previous five holes was make the putt I was staring down."

I sought out the woman who understood the wager.

"Now, I make it, and it's worth how much?" I asked her.

She had been keeping track, making notes on the yellow legal pad she had in front of her. Her answer came quick and sure.

"You make that putt, and you are fourteen hundred up on the original bet, two thousand up on the first press, and a thousand up on the second press?"

"Exactly. I make the putt and I'm up forty-four hundred with five holes left to play. I'm feeling pretty good. I'm going to be able to get a motel room for the following week, and not fret about anything but trying to qualify for the next event on the coming Monday. But, you see, there I go again. I'm not thinking about the putt. I'm letting my mind drift to things that have no bearing on the moment. So, I miss the putt on the low side and my ball comes to rest near his mark. I can't quite finish out, so I mark my ball, then move it out of his line."

I saw that someone at the table—previously silent but obviously a golfer—predicted what was coming. He produced a big eye roll, followed by an obvious shake of the head.

"Ed made his knee knocker—he really grinded over those short putts. I then put my ball down on the green and quickly one-handed in my putt to tie."

"You didn't replace your mark. You didn't move it back to its original position," the guy who had been reacting blurted out.

"Exactly right," I said.

"You lost?" the mathematician asked.

"Yeah. One shot penalty for playing from the wrong place. Rule 20–3, in fact. So instead of being up over four grand, I was now . . . ?" I asked the woman.

She quickly moved some figures around on her piece of paper.

"Six hundred down on the first bet, even on the first press, and a thousand down on the second," she said without a hint of uncertainty.

"Yeah, that's right. I was just looking at a putt that would have made me a winner for the day, and now, because I'm an absolute idiot, I'm down sixteen hundred dollars that I don't have."

I could see the wheels turning in the heads of the people who were sitting at the table. Now that the bubble of my sure success had burst, they were beginning to parse all the various motives or scenarios that might eventually lead them to the circumstances surrounding the death of Ed Custis.

The guy who seemed to be the leader was losing interest. I felt he was starting to wonder whether he was going to be home in time for dinner.

"Can we cut to the chase, Mr. Dawson?" he asked.

"Just let him finish, please," someone said.

"Okay, but give us the *Reader's Digest* version," the man said.

I had no idea what he meant by that, but I did try to trim off an extraneous detail or two as I pushed on.

"Okay, so now I'm sixteen hundred down, five holes left. Ed's gotten a little high with this sudden turn of events. He starts really yakking about how I'm a loser and possibly mentally deficient. He's strutting and crowing for all the spectators. It felt like at least half of them were hoping that I would have really smoked him and put him in his place. As it looked more like that wasn't going to happen, the gallery began to thin. I pressed back and won the next two holes outright, two birdies to his two bogeys.

That straight ball of his was starting to go to the left and he had to play out of the trees on both of those holes. He pressed back and we tied the sixteenth and I eagled seventeen to his par to win those two holes. So now we've got a total of five bets on the table with just the eighteenth hole to play."

I pointed to the scorekeeper.

"Okay. You're up 200, up 800, down 200, up 800, and up 400. You're up 2,000 total?"

"Right," I said. "I can't lose at this point. Even if he presses, and he wins the last hole, I still walk away with 800."

"So, does he press?" someone asked.

"Not initially."

"Ha! He's had enough?"

"Not exactly. I think he was confused and still thought he could beat me. Finally, he cursed out loud and announced that he was pressing. I nodded and said something about it being my honor and he cursed again. The eighteenth hole was an absolute beast. A 460–yard par four designed by some real genius back in the forties. There was trouble lurking in every direction. Plattin Creek meandered up the right side of the rough until about the 260–yard mark where it jutted into the fairway and cutoff the landing area. Unless you could carry the ball at least three-ten or so you were forced to lay up in front of it. I hit it pretty far, but not that far and a quartering wind had begun hurting us from the northeast. On the left was a steady line of water oaks that really framed the hole. If you hit it into them, you were dead. I decided to blast the ball over the water oaks and see how far up the tenth fairway—the hole that ran alongside it—I could get it. An unconventional route, but one I had thought might be the only way to make birdie. I figured Ed for a bogey, so I stepped up, aimed directly at the tree line, and tried to hit a slinger of a hook. I was hoping that wind would help move it too. As the ball left the club, I heard the crowd collectively hoot, certain that I had knocked it right into the trees. Then the ball began to turn. It landed right in the middle of the tenth fairway just about twenty yards from the tenth tee. The sharp breaths of shock changed to murmurs of curiosity as everyone seemed to be figuring out that this had been my plan all along. I picked up my tee and changed places with Ed, who said in a near whisper, 'I'm going to gut you, you piece of expletive.' The moment might have been too big for him. He flinched at impact and snap hooked his ball right into a particularly nasty group of those water oaks. I won't say what he said; I think I've already used up my entire quota of bad words to this point."

The board leader cracked a hint of a smile, the first time that his face resembled anything other than alabaster.

"So, the gallery set off toward Ed's ball, which, sure enough, had come to rest right behind the trunk of one of those oaks. I thought his only shot was to try to give it a swipe with a left-handed swing, and see if he could get it back out into the fairway. He would still have nearly 300 yards to the green, but he would be free to take a full swing at that point. He was pretty mad about his predicament and as he cursed god, country, and his three ex-wives, he straddled that tree as if he were a grizzly bear and took a swing. Miraculously, he got some club on the ball. It ricocheted off the next tree that was closest to the fairway and found its way into the left rough, but out in the open with a clear shot to the green.

The ruckus also dislodged a nest of bluebird chicks. It clattered to the ground near Ed's feet. Frustrated that he would be hitting his third shot before I hit my second, he whipped his club at that nest and killed two of those baby birds right in front of their hovering mother."

I could see the heartstrings being yanked on those who were listening to the story. This was in no way meant to throw anything like sympathy in my direction or to justify my actions later, but I knew where they were coming from because, in that moment, I had been sickened by his actions and was completely rattled that he had done that.

"He scuttled his third shot to within about eighty yards of the flag and the entire group scattered over to where my ball lay. 'You planned to do this?' someone asked. I gave him a wink to confirm. I had about one-sixty to the middle of the green, but the pin was in the front third, on a bit of knoll above a steep incline. This is the kind of pin placement that nearly any pro I've ever played with would have called unfair, because if you got the ball above the hole at any time, you better make the putt or the ball would roll all the way down the hill and off the front of the green. So, the top portion, the flatter portion of the green, was off limits if I wanted to make a three or even a four. I turned to one of the members of the gallery and announced, 'This hole is awesome, y'all must be proud to have this as your finisher.' They collectively nodded with pride and someone in the crowd said, 'C'mon, man, you can do this.' I pulled an eight iron, put the ball back in my stance a tad, tried to hit a draw that would stay lower than my normal flight, but get up over the barrier of trees. I hit it a little too high, and the wind ballooned it. It landed exactly the right distance, but a little right of my target on the lower edge of steeper part of the green. It spun pretty well, stopped for less than a second and then started to trickle away from the hole and toward the front. As it picked up speed, I could see that it was never going to stay on the green. It rolled through the fringe, and back down into the fairway. I could hear a groan or two from the people around me, but I was ecstatic. I had maybe a beach towel's worth of area to play with, and I landed it right in the middle of that space. That pin position was just plain ridiculous. But, with Ed still preparing to hit his fourth shot, I was pretty sure that I could win the hole by getting the ball up and down for my par. Ed had to hit the shot of his life. He nearly pulled it off, but his sand wedge landed about eight inches too far. It took a hop past the hole and sat down on the flat part of the green three feet above the cup. The spectators parked their carts and took positions around the green. Many more from the clubhouse had joined on the last hole and I would have to guess there were somewhere between two to three hundred folks awaiting the outcome of the match by that point. I walked up to the green to pick the spot where I wanted to land my chip. I was going to hit something with hardly any spin and a let it run up the hill. I stood over the ball and just as I got ready to hit, I heard Ed say, 'Did you see that? The ball just moved! It . . . uh, I'll substitute the actual word, uh, effing . . . moved!' I stepped away. The ball was sitting in the exact same place that it had been when I addressed it. The logo and my personal mark were in exactly the same orientation that it had been when the ball came to rest. Ed turned to the gallery who were standing behind me. 'You saw that, right?' And then he repeated, 'The ball effing moved! That's a shot, and you need to replace it.' I looked around to those who were standing near me. They were kind of in stun mode; quizzical looks of disbelief. I didn't want to ask them to confirm that the ball hadn't moved because I felt that would give some sort of validity to Ed's declaration. Ed found some toadie that he knew standing about ten feet away from me. It was actually one of the clubhouse boys, a zit-faced, beanpole named Tommy, a person who would have to deal with Ed for far longer than I ever would. 'Hey Tommy, you saw it move, right?' he asked. Tommy shrugged, but kind of half-nodded at the same time, and Ed treated that as affirmation. 'Ya effing cheater. That's a shot. Return the ball to its original position. You lie three, uh I'll substitute again, uh, a-hole.'

I stopped to make sure I didn't have to get into a whole thing about the rules of golf and the violation I was being accused of committing.

"I didn't argue after that. I was outnumbered and even if a

single person there believed Ed in that moment, I would not be able to convince them otherwise. I abhor controversy. I marked my ball, picked it up, put it back down in the same exact position it had been in, stepped up, and holed my chip for a par. The crowd erupted in this wild spontaneous celebration. There were hoots, hollers, claps on the back. Even Tommy seemed elated. I had given them a story they could tell at the bar, at their next business meeting, or even on their deathbeds. I plucked my ball out of the hole, took the pin out, and moved to the side of the green. Ed had his three-foot downhiller for bogey to tie me on the hole. If he makes it, I win two thousand bucks because we tie the hole. If he misses, I'll win twelve hundred more.

"He missed it?" someone asked.

"Didn't even come close. The ball missed on the high side by more than a ball's width, paused near the hole, then started rolling all the way down the length of the green, through the fringe, and back onto the fairway. It stopped in almost the exact place that I had hit my chip from. Well, he started screaming that I was a cheater, and he sure as hell was not going to make good on a wager with a cheater. The gallery looked pretty upset. They were definitely on my side by that point, and a couple of them had the stones to actually confront Ed. Ed told them to F-off, got in his cart, drove out into the parking lot and threw his clubs into his Lincoln. A battalion of carts with spectators followed him out there and you could hear some of the people who had witnessed the match trying to get him to come back and make it right. Ed started his car, peeled out of his parking place, nearly hitting a few of those folks and headed for the exit to the lot. He drove past the back of the eighteenth green where I stood. He had his middle finger out of the window as he passed, screaming a steady stream of profanities at everyone. I still don't know why I did it, but after he passed, I reared back and threw my golf ball at his car. The ball hit the windshield. He swerved and smashed right into a parked Mercedes. A lot of people rushed to the car, but he was dead. The autopsy said heart attack. I was arrested that evening for causing his death. And so, that's why I am here with you today."

There was a long silence. The guy who knew a little about golf, the clerk the leader had called Margaret, and the young Latina all gave the impression that they were sympathetic. The board leader, ever the stoic, gave zero indication of a lean, one-way or the other.

"All right, I think we've used up enough time here. I would prefer that we let Mr. Dawson return to his sentence for now, and we can speak to his attorney. Unless someone has a burning question that would sway your decision, could we just move on, please?" he asked.

Even if they wanted to, no one voiced an objection at that point.

"Thank you, Mr. Dawson. We'll have a decision for you in no longer than forty-eight hours,' he said with finality.

Deidre's face came on the screen in a box that opened in the bottom right. She nodded her head at me. I took that as a good sign.

"Thank you, parole board," I said.

I rose and walked to the door, where my handlers whisked me back to my unit.

Sally met me on my entrance.

"How did it go?" she asked.

"I think it went well," I said.

She nodded and gave my cheek a pinch.

"That's good."

I looked around for Shorty, so I could tell him too. Sally grabbed my arm. Her eyes were moist, and she struggled to speak.

"They took him to the infirmary. He was really having a hard time getting a breath."

"Damn," I said.

"I not sure, he's coming back, darling."

I'm sure I didn't react with any emotion in that moment. It wasn't related to the lack of empathy thing that people have accused me of in the past. I had prepared for Shorty to pass for nearly two years. The man was really sick, and though he had to spend the closing chapters of his life in that place, he did not spend them alone. To this day, other than Jim, he might have been my truest friend.

Sally gave my arm another squeeze, before trundling off into her cell. I sat at the table in the common room for a good long time. Maybe, just maybe, I thought, he could hang on for a couple of weeks (he had already lasted nearly a year over what the prognosis had been), I would get out, and then I could make sure that he was treated in death with the respect he deserved.

Of course, he and I had never discussed any of his wishes post-life, but if there were to be anything resembling a service or memorial, I wanted to be there.

9

Taylor brought me back for the second week's lesson with Jim. If he hadn't, there might have been a headline in the *Spring Valley Star-News* about an autistic kid violently dispensing with his adoptive father. There would be a serious incongruity there, because we are known as gentle souls by nature, except we might knowingly or unknowingly inflict some mayhem on ourselves. But, if I had been thwarted, I am quite certain my wires would have been crossed or frayed or both.

My lesson with Jim was another inflection point—akin to the lack of regression that presented after I hit those plastic balls into the garage door.

Like I had been reprogrammed, or had an alien walk into my body, I had spent the week parsing my every movement and action to coordinate with what I reckoned Taylor would have wanted. Cause for reprimand or blame in any form needed to be tabled, so I could get back to Jim and the driving range the next Saturday.

Every other waking hour that Taylor was not around was taken up with my babysitter–du jour helping me through chapter one of the *Five Lessons* book.

Hogan's ghostwriter had a lively style and tried to channel the irascible gentleman in his prose. He portrayed the Hawk fawning over certain players, who had impressed him with their grips.

The irony, of course, is that the man himself started playing the game cross-handed. When he was instructed on how to properly grip the club, it took him a bit of time to embrace the new over the comfortable. Initially, he did not see results that were better than his instinctual leanings. Even his early attempts at orthodoxy, though acceptable, changed over the years. It took nearly the whole of his early professional career to settle on the grip that he demanded of all golfers.

My split baseball grip—the one I copied from the horny sailor—was what felt right to me. When one of my care persons started walking me through the numbers on the Hogan grip, there was some initial reluctance, but I relented when the babysitter said, "You don't want to disappoint your teacher on Saturday, do you?"

That did it, and from that point, I did my best to produce an exact copy of what Hogan would have called "a handsome grip." Taylor had no reason not to bring me back, as my watchers reported that I had been more docile and adaptable than they had ever seen during that week.

And so, Jim and I started on our journey. Each week, I was assigned another chapter in the book, and each Saturday we would adjust the learned knowledge to fit in with something that was amorphous—that odd innate ability in me that Jim had identified from the outset.

Unlike so many of my experiences to that point, Jim chose to not treat me with all of the types of deference that every other single person had.

Our sessions were focused, and he really plugged into how my brain reacted to his instruction. I know he had to alter his teaching style somewhat, but I don't think it was because of my "special needs" status. I think it was because he was beginning to see something that he thought he would never see again. Something he had seen only once in his life as a young child—a true prodigy.

Later, I would learn his history and come to a true understanding of the complexities of the man, but in those moments, I was elevated beyond any tier that I had previously existed on. I was forever changed, and the difference was more than tangible. From those days forward, I was utterly transformed into something other than the kid who was more than somewhat off.

I can't explain it. Looking back, it was probably a lot less seamless than I am making it out to be. I was reborn, or reauthorized, or retrieved from a reality that was now fantasy, and set on a quest that would encompass all of my days ahead.

It didn't take long before I started spending the bulk of each day at the course. Somewhere in there, maybe after lesson number five, Jim told Taylor he could keep an eye on me during the summer months when school was out. Sick of spending considerable treasure on day care personnel, it took Taylor less than a nanosecond to agree.

He'd drop me off early and pick me up sometime in the late afternoon.

I was desperate to be useful, so Jim and the guys who worked in the shop let me run the ball washing machine, pick up empty buckets from the range, and snag their lunches from the snack bar or restaurant.

My compensation for those deeds was that I got to hit as many balls on the range as I wanted.

A couple of years later, I became the full-time range boy and took over the responsibility for everything except mowing the grass of the practice area.

I set the markers in the morning, even on the winter weekdays before I headed to school. I had my own cart replete with a heavy-duty ball scooper. When I picked the balls by the fence, I sported this jury-rigged dog bed set-up: two mattresses draped over my shoulders like a sandwich board, held by a couple of strong straps. My noggin was protected by a full-grille lacrosse helmet.

Anyone who has ever done that job has likely experienced the same oddity. Whether I was out there on foot or in the cart, it seemed that every range participant took on the challenge of trying to target me with their shots. As soon as my presence amongst the landscape of balls and yard markers was established, the incoming started from everyone—little old ladies, juniors, the guys still in their suit pants after stopping on their way home from the office, the high school team; it did not matter.

I was just a twelve-year-old kid, nearly bolted to the Earth by thirty pounds of gear, or encased in the cage of my cart trying to do my job. These people felt that it was absolutely okay to try to ping a ball off my body or my equipment. I got bonked more than a few times, and I still have a knot on the upper part of the radius bone of my left arm that I incurred one hazy, August afternoon.

In the beginning I called these snipers out, racing to their location to scream at them to cease. Most would hang their heads in obviously feigned shame. Their stock response was that they were not gifted enough at the game to know where the ball was going. That could have been true in some of the cases, but I was not blind. As soon as I resumed my duties, it started up again.

I worked that range until I turned pro at eighteen.

Every so often, Jim would saunter over during one of my practice sessions and adjust this or that, but mostly he wanted me to try to figure out everything on my own.

I don't think I played a full round on the course for the entire first year that I played the game, but often during those late afternoons, Jim would drive up in his cart, and tell me to grab my bag.

We would start on the first hole, a shortish par five. The setting sun repelled any view of the fairway or the green, which was a good 500 yards to the west.

I'd play that hole, the sixth—a short par three—and the par five ninth. Those last swings taking place during the gloaming of the southern California sky.

Usually, I'd play a minimum of three balls, and Jim would discuss the cause and effect of my choices for each swing. Those par fives were beasts to me at that age, but the knowledge that he imparted is as relevant now as it was then.

What I remember most were all the little details of how the course changed during those final moments of daily waning light.

There was a glazing of moisture that appeared on the tips of the grass, and the *Poa annua* would have completed its daily flowering amidst the suddenly visible footprints on the greens.

The first hole played into the sun, the sixth had it to my left, and the tee shot on nine was completely backlit before the dogleg turned it to my right. It was truly a full circle, and it ended those days with a sense of completion.

After, I would lock my sticks up in the ball-washer closet. Sporting a blissful smile on my face, I'd make my way to the nearly empty parking lot, and the headlights that beckoned me to the passenger seat of Taylor's car.

If there were words exchanged on the ride home, I do not remember their context or content. For me, it was to bed and the hope that the morning would put me back there as soon as Taylor could convey me.

10

"The decision is . . . Not now," Deidre said before I even got out the word "Hello."

It hit me hard. I instinctually blamed the phone, ripped it away from my ear and stared at it. This was some old behavior where I once blamed inanimate objects for not cooperating with my lack of knowledge or clumsiness. Deidre was still speaking. I clapped it back to my ear in time to catch:

". . . tell you right away. I don't like delaying any news, bad or good," she said.

Her voice sounded so cold and distant through a speaker occluded with the dried sweat of a thousand inmates before me.

"Are you there? Did you hear me?" she asked.

"Yeah."

"It sounds bad now."

"It does."

"But there is some good stuff too."

"I really thought they were listening to my story."

"Oh, they were, Mr. Dawson; we all were. Given your lack of flair in the retelling, I was actually amazed at how closely they were listening."

"I'm sorry, my lack of flair?"

"Yeah, you know, you have a way about you. You speak in a similar tone all the time. No one has told you that before?"

"Hmmm . . . I guess so."

"It's not altogether without a certain charm. It's interesting. It's like you kind of left space for their imaginations to create the pictures for them because you didn't try to stress anything for effect. I learned something there that I might be able to apply in my life. You do it naturally, but most of us don't have the balls to just let it all be, you know? You have to remember that the story is the important thing. And I think those who are self-conscious feel they have to provide colors, and a soundtrack. I know that I do at times."

I couldn't tell if there were a hint of self-denigration there. Listening to her in this instance, as opposed to seeing her face on a video feed, I heard someone who seemed kind of fragile.

There was a sudden clap of thunder in my brain at that moment, and I tried to recreate her image. The sweater. The pearls. I remembered the get-up, but other than the fascination with her un-pigmented iris, I could not conjure her hair color or any other physical feature.

"Are you there?" she asked.

"Yes ma'am," I said.

"Call me Deidre, okay?"

"Sure."

What did she look like? That wasn't like me to not know. That was weird.

"So, here's the good news, Charles. They want to process you through the MRP."

"The what?"

"Sorry. The Missouri Reentry Process. All inmates have to meet thresholds prior to release. There is a mandatory class you have to pass called *Avenues to Change*, which is a cognitive thinking course."

"You're kidding me," I said with half a laugh.

"You can't blow that off. They are serious about all their boxes being checked. They have a very definite need to make sure they put someone back into society who will not continue to be a criminal," she said.

"And how's that working out for them?"

"They clock in at around a 55 percent recidivism rate. That's the third highest in the country."

"Well, they could lower that figure if they let me go. I will not be reoffending."

"I'm sure that's true, but you still have to jump through all of the hoops."

"Do you have any idea how much cognitive behavioral therapy I've had in my life?" I asked.

"No. I was given very little about your history before your incarceration. That whole thing about the golf bet was completely new information for me."

"By the way, did you bring up my "specialness" at any point after I was gone?" I asked.

"I tried to bring up quite a few things. I brought up that, the lack of victim's statements, your model prisoner status, and your college degree, but they weren't going to move forward on your case because that's just the way they do things. Denial is the first response, always and ever. I have yet to have a client pass through to parole after only one hearing unless they were related to someone in the legislature or, you know, otherwise connected somehow."

"I don't want to sound arrogant, but I could probably teach that class that I have to pass," I said.

"Just get it done, Charles. This is good news, like I said. They could make you wait until you are approved to have to go through the process, which would tack months onto you being in there. Truly, you are the first client of mine to ever be offered this."

"Okay."

There was a finality approaching, though I felt a desire to continue our conversation. The persistent buzzing of the line reminded me that the call was possibly being archived, though even I knew that was a violation of the lawyer-client agreement. I became a little entranced by the noise and I endeavored to hear her breathing over the sound of the white noise.

"I do have a question, Charles."

"Call me Chuck."

"Okay, Chuck."

"Or Chunk. People who know me call me Chunk."

"Why?"

That was stupid of me. I'm not sure why I even thought to

mention it. I suppose I felt something akin to familiarity, but there was no reasoning to that at all. I didn't respond.

"Never mind. You said you had a question?"

"Last night, I was reading through some of the transcripts of your trial. Your counsel never explored the possibility that Ed Custis suffered his heart attack before you threw your golf ball at his car? I mean the guy was kind of a rager, right? He was a bird murderer. Couldn't he just have had his chest explode on its own without anyone's help?"

"Someone might have said something I think, but my attorney was an idiot. I wasn't represented by the likes of you," I said.

"No doubt. That would have been the substance of my defense—that you should carry zero blame in what was obviously an inevitable outcome. I would have brought up the pre-existing conditions found during his post-mortem, subpoenaed his doctor's files, the whole shebang. I would have put Ed's pulmonary system on trial, not you," she declared.

"The whole thing was kind of a charade. And then you had me as the accused, and that wasn't a positive. There wasn't a juror who didn't look at me and see anything but guilt. My implacability, so necessary in my profession that I label it a gift, did not sit well with my judgers. The deliberations took less than twenty minutes."

"Wow."

"Doesn't make sense to rehash it."

"No, you're right. You're getting out soon."

"We'll see."

"You are, Chuck, I swear," she said with what sounded like full conviction.

I certainly hoped she was right. I needed an infusion of something positive.

"All right. We'll be in touch soon. Is there anything else you need?" she asked.

I had a request, but I wasn't sure if it was appropriate. I asked anyway. It is my nature.

"Do you ever get down here to St. Joseph's?"

"I've been a time or two."

"Well, if you ever do, there is a golf course across the street from the W.M.D.C.C. I noticed it when they took me to the conference room for my hearing. If you get a chance, could you stop in there and get me a scorecard, maybe?" I asked.

"A scorecard? How would I do that?"

"Just walk into the clubhouse or the pro shop and ask for one. There will be no resistance. They will likely just be sitting there in a stack on one of the counters."

"Okay. That's it?"

"If you should be in the neighborhood."

"It sounds a little weird, but I'll take care of that when I get the opportunity."

"Thanks. And thanks for looking out for me, Deidre."

"You're welcome, Chuck."

There was a click on the line, and a recorded voice announced that our time was up. I hung up the phone, and told the guard I was ready to be escorted back to my cell.

Shorty died two days after my parole was denied. Sally and I never got to see him after he was removed from our housing unit.

The contrast between the way the two of us dealt with it was extreme.

I'd had this whole thing worked out for some time. I had known the day was coming, and that he was never going to suddenly pull a Lazarus and wake up one day free of the scourge that was rampaging inside his body. Death for him would be a release from the physical pain he had been forced to endure for longer than most mortals are capable.

All of those feelings and impressions were based in logic and pragmatism, and included a celebration of the time we had together.

They were also consistent with my diagnosis, and that freaked me out little. Was this who I was? Was my shell so dense that emotion was not possible?

I thought back to another person who had passed: Jim. I had been there at the moment of his death, and I recall that my reactions were similar. Of course, at the time, I think I just felt that I was carrying out his wishes, as he would not tolerate anything that smacked of sentimentality.

As for Sally's response to Shorty, she started crying the moment she heard. For weeks, her eyes were misty, and she verged on breaking down at the smallest things. She'd only known him for less than six months, and yet her grief was tremendously profound.

"I have a sadness inside me, darling, and when it gets triggered, I have a really hard time shutting it down," she said at some point.

I searched for the sadness in me, and I kind of came up empty. I wasn't sure if that labeled me sociopathic or not.

"In the past, I did things that weren't all together healthy when I was overtaken by grief and longing," she said.

The unraveling of Sally made me nervous. I felt a need to make sure that she didn't do anything stupid during this time of agitation, because those forces that were pissed off that she even existed were once again angling to make sure her punishment was more prejudicial than what she was currently experiencing.

I made sure to stay close to her during that summer. I believe she was coming to terms with the fact that she was going to be housed by the state for most of the rest of her life and that manifested in her as pure, unadulterated despair.

There were a couple of moments where I could sense a confrontation on the horizon with the guards who worked our cellblock. I did my best to deflect her, distract her, or even distort her perceptions.

In those instances, there was no gratitude offered for my intervention, but later, when the tide of emotion had ebbed, she would thank me for looking out for her.

All of that id being constantly in play was fascinating to me, because it was a trait that I believed had been permanently extinguished from my personality through most of my early therapeutic training.

I was never allowed to color outside of the lines that were

constantly being established by my parents, therapists, and health professionals, so to see someone so raw created questions that I wanted her to answer.

My discussion goals were dual-ended. I knew that she was amenable to opening up and discussing her sensitivity, and my hope was that if she did that on a regular basis, she wouldn't feel a need to act out. It was kind of a letting enough air out of a filling balloon so it wouldn't burst sort of thing.

Secondly, I was searching for a way to possibly remove the pesky tarp that seemed to be covering my feelings from being exposed to the world. It was a bit of a slippery slope for me, as I had convinced myself to that point that part of my success as a golfer was that my emotions very rarely came into play. But, that wasn't entirely true.

These were things that I had never, ever examined before, and the genesis for opening those portals came from getting Sally to open up about her feelings.

Things changed when she calmed down and began to turn the tables on me.

It happened out of the blue one afternoon when she asked with a look of astonished concern, "Have you ever been in love, Chunk?"

11

There was this game I used to play when I had unfettered access to the facilities at Sweetwater Valley Municipal Golf Course.

I played full rounds of the course on that driving range using my own targets as landing areas and green surfaces. Then after I'd charted the holes in my head, I would head over to the practice chipping/putting area and hole out. I could recreate most of the green contours by placing my ball on various parts of the practice green.

Within the confines of that specific game, I broke "par" for the first time when I was eleven. I didn't do that on the actual course until I was nearly thirteen.

Every day, I would try to break my standing record, but at some point, if I didn't hit the perfect shot, and I knew it wouldn't be possible to improve on a previous effort, I got a little pissed off.

Actually, I got a lot pissed off, and there were broken shafts and yards of gouged earth to prove it. I blamed everything—all disruptions; the wind; a bad range ball, it did not matter.

It got bad enough that a few patrons complained, perhaps out of concern for my well-being.

Jim knew what to do, though. He took me aside and told me that any outburst from that point forward would result in a suspension of my privileges. One week for a first offense, two weeks for a second, and banishment for the third. He said that golf is a game played by gentlemen and that I was to act accordingly. That my behavior was an insult to everything the game stood for, and he would not be a party to it.

Like magic, I acquiesced. This is one of the reasons why I see the game as my salvation. I'd been asked to make bargains in the past, and my acceptance could have only been described as iffy. Jim knew what I needed and that led to many conversations about the mental aspect of playing the game. Jim's tutelage became so ingrained, that the whole world could collapse in front of me and I would not react publicly.

In truth, that took a lot more time to develop than just the reaction to a single admonishment. But eventually, I was able to fully implant that uncanny implacability that I've mastered.

Because of who Jim was and what he represented, I took his expectations of me seriously. This thing of being an upstanding citizen in regards to the game became really important. I developed a very strong ethic when it came to etiquette and what he described as the responsibilities of this so-called gentleman.

A golf group, regardless of number, has a set level of duties to make the experience flow in a fashion that compresses time and space, and also focuses the group on the momentum required to tee it up on the first and hole it out on the eighteenth.

Each player is conscripted to be accountable for the things that need to be done throughout the round. It's paramount that everyone take responsibility for their part.

There are things like the order of play and the imperative to leave the golf course in the condition that you found it.

Jim taught me and the other young players all of this during our rounds as the junior program crew, and it really made an indelible impression on me through the years how few began their lives in the game without being instructed on the etiquette or the rules, or either.

When I started playing in competitions, somewhere just before my twelfth birthday, I was amazed at how little my opponents knew about any of this stuff.

I became totally caught up with herding my group of utter no-nothings into handling their chores, but few cared to listen to me or hold up their ends. My scores in those early tournament rounds were pretty bad. Likely because I placed nearly all of my attention on getting the round to move in the fashion that I saw fit.

These other kids, including the random parent who was masquerading as a marshal and scorekeeper, had zero interest in banding together for this common cause. Their only concern was their own game.

There were numerous rules violations that were overlooked because the participants hadn't the foggiest idea they'd committed an infraction.

I would attempt to educate, and there was more than one instance where I took the scorekeepers aside and told them that they had recorded the wrong score on a particular player because a rule had been broken.

I was vilified. Post-round, I ate my provided lunch—some type of soggy sandwich, a small bag of chips, and can of soda—alone. There was no recourse for me, though. I was not going to cave from my beliefs for the sake of being accepted. It was all too sacred to toss away the principles of the game.

After the fourth or fifth tournament, which was contested on a local course not far from SVMGC, Jim picked me up.

He clearly sensed something. Perhaps it was my body language as I trudged across the parking lot to his idling Buick.

"How'd it go?" he asked after I'd slammed the trunk closed and climbed into the passenger seat.

I shrugged. He didn't say anything until we were already on the road back to our course. We drove in silence past the mini-malls and horse corrals.

Finally, I unloaded. I launched into this lengthy monologue about my frustrations with the other players in my group—how slow they played, how I had witnessed them not adhering to the rules, how their etiquette was non-existent, and every other slight I could vomit up.

Jim didn't stop me. When I had finished, nearly red-faced with furor, he asked in his relaxed Texas drawl, "What'd ya shoot?"

"Fifty-two."

My age group and skill level were limited to nine hole events in those early competitions.

Jim nodded and looked into the rear-view mirror.

"How many putts?"

I didn't know. I dug the scorecard out of my back pocket.

"Nineteen."

"You must've missed a lot of fairways and greens," he stated.

"I guess. I didn't really pay that much attention."

"Look at the scorecard and let's replay the round. I know you can do that. Did you hit the fairway on the first hole?"

My mind went back to the moment to moment occurrences of the round, and the emotion of the struggle to deal with all of the outside elements during play just faded away.

We went shot for shot from the first through the ninth.

Most serious golfers can replay every single shot of a round with incredible detail. Most don't have any desire to hear about it, but Jim did. He knew my game and what I likely faced at every juncture, and at his insistence, I was now out there making the decisions on my own. He would weigh each instance, each strike of the ball, on the scale of whether I had followed his advice from the past or had begun to forge an identity with my game that was separate from his experiential orientation.

There were reins on me still at that age, but Jim had begun to loosen them in the hopes that maybe I could teach him a thing or two on subjects that he considered to be his weaknesses.

He was a guy who needed to play things safely at that point in his life and I know he was afraid to instill too much of that in me.

You see, Jim's life had been a rough and tumble affair. At the time we'd met, he was just keeping his head above water.

He had stopped drinking about a year before he was hired at SVMGC—a vice that had gotten him released from his prior seven jobs. Sobering up took a while, and there was a whole cache of repressed emotions that surfaced during that time. Jim dealt with all of them alone in his two-bedroom condo that was just up the hill from the course on Sweetwater Road.

It took the rest of his lifetime to relay the stories to me. He almost always did it in the guise of some lesson he was trying to teach me, though I'd like to think that in the end there was some cleansing, forgiveness, and eventual acceptance from him that things are just what they are. A life, you know.

It always came to me out of order, and it consisted of little prelude, just a recap of the highlights. Once I had framed it chronologically, I was in awe.

The young Jim had worked at Shady Oaks Country Club in Fort Worth, all the way up to his high school graduation. He'd picked up the game not long after becoming the range boy. As an employee, he wasn't allowed to practice on the grounds, but there was a municipal facility connected to the military base down the street from his house.

What he'd been lucky to experience was the opportunity to spend his days watching Mr. Hogan practice, and when the Hawk was in town, Jim often skipped school to be on the range when Hogan was there.

Hogan would hit about eight or nine shots in a row, take a seat to rest his fragile bones, and smoke cigarette after cigarette. It was during those breaks that Jim could digest what he had witnessed and think about how he could incorporate some of what Hogan was working on at the time.

When Hogan left the range, Jim hurried to tidy up his area—dumping ashtrays, throwing out the waste from his lunch, whatever he could do to keep the man's sanctuary in perfect shape for the next session.

He'd then rush over to the range at Tarrant Field to practice. He would hit balls until the darkness prevailed, off ground that rarely sported more than a couple of blades of crunchy, brown grass.

After high school graduation, he was invited to apprentice at Creekside Country Club in Fort Worth. He worked the cart shack, the club storage area, the range, and stocked the golf shop, all to give him an overview of a life ahead. He loved every second of it.

It wasn't long before he was relocated permanently into the pro shop, and subsequently amassed a small group of loyal students. Word spread quickly that the kid knew some secrets that no one else at the course did. When members' scores started dipping down, his stable of clients increased dramatically.

There was one issue that loomed, though: the head professional at Creekside. Possibly out of jealously, certainly out of the need to keep the sails on his own ship trim, that man demanded that Jim make a decision about whether he wanted to do this for a living.

His requirement was that Jim make a commitment to being his apprentice and learn everything there was to know about the business of golf. When he felt that Jim had learned all that he could teach him, he would make a recommendation to the local PGA chapter that he be considered for Class A status.

This was how they did it in the old days. There might have been a session with the chapter president that likely involved a beer and a shot of whiskey at their home club to seal the deal.

Now, there are classes and seminars, serious fees, a PAT (Player's Ability Test), and hoop after hoop just to be labeled as an associate.

Through his years of schooling, no one would have called Jim a promising student. But with subject matters that focused on things like retail sales of golf equipment, turf management, club alteration, and merchandising, he excelled. Long before Joseph Campbell coined the phrase about "following one's bliss," Jim had lived it.

Jim was never the greatest player, a common situation with great teachers, but in his early days he could get around the course at right around par, which was more than sufficient to prove his ability.

He rarely competed in any formal events, but got in a round each week with some of the other burgeoning associates of nearby clubs, where they would play Nassaus for cokes and silver dollars.

On an early spring day, a twenty-year-old Jim stood on the clubhouse balcony overlooking the eighteenth green at Creekside. He was fixated on the frost that laid atop the unmown grass. A rising sun was melting the crystalline ice. The vapor that formed produced a dense cloud that hugged the space just above the surface. He told me it was that moment when he knew there was a god, because that level of beauty could not have been achieved through randomness.

When I was in my middle teens, we were driving up north so I could play in the California Amateur. He told that story again, but with a second example of a creator's existence.

The divine beauty this time was Mildred Ella (Babe) Greene. a daughter of a prominent member of Creekside, who he'd been flirting with for the bulk of that particular summer.

The new story covered the ceremony of her societal debut.

Jim had volunteered to help with that yearly event, as he needed the extra money to pay for his PGA study materials.

Like all of the young ladies who rated that sort of recognition in Fort Worth, Babe was escorted by a young man in full uniform from the ROTC program at SMU.

In turn, as they reached the edge of the runway, all the white gowned women, small bouquets in their left hands, were expected to perform the "Texas Dip," an extreme curtsy where the person spreads their arms wide, lowers themselves to the floor by collapsing on their ankles, and then bends forward in a deep bow, before returning to a standing position.

It is not an easy move for anyone to pull off. There was the pressure of doing it in front of a couple hundred people, and many of the young ladies were likely new to wearing heels for an extended period of time.

When it was Babe's turn, she eased her arm off the bicep of the chiseled recruit. She made sure she caught sight of Jim who was removing glassware from the table directly in front of the runway. He thought she might have even hissed to get his attention, but Jim said he was fully aware of who was about to perform the next "Texas Dip." He had been counting down from the first debutante, so that he could be in position right at the front of the apron for Babe's arrival.

Like a fragile young fledgling spreading its wings for the first time, Babe opened herself up to the assembled. Her eyes were fixed on Jim as she slowly descended to the ground, the hem of her $1,000 dress forming a perfectly circular pool of taffeta and chiffon on the makeshift stage.

She took him into her gaze as she then bowed further, her forehead hovering just inches above the Masonite.

Okay, he thought at the time, that part was done.

To complete the "Texas Dip," one needs to then return to the perfectly erect posture that begat it. Jim knew that was the hard part—a good third of the field had already stumbled on the rise to that point—and he swore he tried to will Babe to her feet.

But, alas, Babe was a bit of a rebel. All of this presentation stuff was a bore to her. She had dealt with some pageants in her youth, cotillion, of course, since she was twelve, and now this was set in her mind to be the last time she would have to be put in this situation by her car dealer father, and her high-haired, Daughter of the American Revolution mother.

She could not resist taking the opportunity to do something spectacular.

She rolled her ankles to put herself back into a squat, but as she ascended, she tipped forward off the edge of the stage and fell toward Jim. The ROTC Captain reached for her, but because of the length of her gown, she was able to camouflage a tiny little spring of a leap that put space between her and the chivalrous trooper.

The crowd gasped as she plummeted toward Jim and the brimming bus tub that he held waist-high in front of him. He would always remember the private smile that emerged on her face just as he dropped the tub, became the cushion she fell upon, and secured her in his arms.

There was a scream or two, and Corny Greene and her brother, Tucker, rushed over to make sure she was okay. Babe continued the scene of the damsel as she extricated herself from Jim, and then bowed once more in a less-fanatical curtsy in gratitude for saving her.

"That was it, Chuck. The wasp had stung me and I knew right then and there that my life was going to change," he said with a nod.

I distinctly remember him blushing at that exact moment. It was the very first time he had related a story from his personal journey, and though I often asked for more, it seemed like ages before he exposed himself like that again.

12

Sally had asked the question, and I was aware I was taking a long time to give her an answer.

"Seriously, Chunk, have you ever been in love?" she asked again.

"Not sure," I finally said.

"Are you a virgin?"

"No."

"So, this 'not sure' thing. Is that because you've never been put in that situation, or is it that you're unsure of where your emotions are because of your issues?"

Sally always cut right to the bone. More often than not, I would be a little shocked at her bluntness, but that did not dissuade her when she was in the process of getting the answers she wanted via one of her interrogations.

"I guess that's it. I've never been someone to seek that out. I have spent most of my life being preoccupied," I said.

"By golf?"

"Yeah. All of my relationships have been connected to that in some way. My mentor was the most important person in my life, and we were inseparable. I practiced constantly and competed every chance I could. There was not a lot of room there for anything else."

"But you were attracted to other people?"

"Sure."

"Women?"

"Yeah."

"But you're what, shy?"

"Well, yeah, there was that," I said.

"So, a developing young lad like yourself. You didn't have certain urges?"

"Of course, I did."

I wasn't quite sure what she was trying to get at. We'd been having a lot of dialogues since Shorty passed. We both missed him; perhaps these chats provided us a way to fill a void created by his absence.

"Look, I knew plenty of guys who aggressively pursued that in their lives, and the cautionary tales are legendary," I said.

She laughed, I knew, at the truth inherent in that statement.

"We're talking about consequences, aren't we?" she asked.

"Ha, I guess so. I'm a little terrified to split focus, you know?"

"So are you superstitious?"

"Not really. A couple of quirks when it comes to clothing—I don't wear green."

"Why?"

"I shot eighty-two at a local qualifier for the U.S. Open

when I was sixteen, wearing a forest green shirt. I got a letter from the USGA that basically told me if I should attempt to qualify again at some point and fail as miserably, I would not be allowed to ever try again."

"I'll assume you did not fail the next time."

"I didn't. I made it out of the local qualifier the next year, and finished fifth at the sectional. I ended up being the sixth alternate at the Open that year—the youngest with a potential to be in the field—but I didn't make it in the end."

"I'm sorry," she said.

"I should not have bogeyed seventeen during the sectional, my thirty-fifth hole of the day. I cold-hooked my second shot into a nasty plot of succulents and had to take an unplayable. If I had made par, I would have been at Shinnecock. Can't bitch when it's on you."

She smiled with a clear sense of irony. I suppose we could both take that as the truth. We were sitting at the table in our common room, only because we had put ourselves there.

"You remember that? That was like more than a decade ago?"

"I remember almost every important shot I've ever hit."

"How do you do that?" she asked.

"I think it's because I care about it."

"Fuck, how did we get back to golf? I was asking you if you've ever gotten laid."

"You asked me about superstitions," I said.

And yeah, I had gotten "laid" as she put it. I'd had some indoctrination by the women who hung around the restaurants frequented by touring pros in Canada.

It was the goal for some to become the wife of a professional golfer—a fantasy of glamor filled with private jets and five-star accommodations that was never, ever going to be met in most cases.

But there they were, every night, in every town the tour visited. It seemed that the smaller the city, the greater the number of attendees at the local steakhouse or fish place.

My first encounter was with a very sweet blonde named Carla, who was gentle, and understood my circumstances. It was not my idea, but she was persistent. Turned out she had a boyfriend and that was a bit of a problem in the end. Saskatoon was a town with ears and Carla liked to talk a lot. I skipped that event in the subsequent years that I played up there.

"Okay, wait a minute. There was a point to all of this and it wasn't about, you know . . . I'm not really interested in your sex life. I'm trying to get you to examine something within yourself."

"What?"

"I don't know. There's something about you that's hard to define. When I look at you, I fear that something has been drilled or beaten into you that has affected your spirit. You're a bit of a zombie sometimes."

"Huh. Really? Could it be the Asperger's? Many believe that's what actually defines me."

"I don't think it's that. It's something else. Perhaps it's genetic, but as I have proven, that can be altered."

I pondered all of this for a moment. There was something there in what she was saying. I mean, there is little doubt that the carrot and stick nature of all of the therapies I endured did lead to a certain level of cautiousness, but was it debilitating to my performance in some way? I always felt it gave me access to greater focus than most.

I continued to let her statement hang in the air between us.

"Okay. Let me ask you a question?" I began.

"Absolutely."

"Did you ever think through the possibility that you might be penalized for a crime that you committed, or did you enter into it with the belief that you would never get caught?"

She clapped her hands and laughed.

"Ah, I think you know what I'm getting at. Good on you, kid. Of course, I knew that there might be consequences for my actions, but that knowledge did nothing to prevent me from trying to accomplish my goal. You have to understand that the reason I went so long not getting apprehended on that last run was because I meticulously planned every moment that was about to come. I removed a lot of the cowboy, or I guess cowgirl, attitude that had driven me to act before."

"I guess you didn't cover everything, huh?"

"Honey, as much as you think you can control it, all good plans immediately go to shit as soon as you pass the note that says, 'Please put all of the cash in your drawer and the two next to you in this tote bag, or someone could get hurt.'"

"Well, you set a record."

"Yeah, I guess. A lot of that was luck, but there was probably something in my preparation that spared me an early capture. My timing was good. I chose the right locations, that kind of stuff."

So, what was she trying to tell me? That I played things too close to the vest? I'd hit drivers off the deck from 300 yards out to greens with water on three sides.

"Look around you, Chunk. You are surrounded by people who did not think or care about the consequences of their actions in the moment. For me, and them, it sucks that that is our nature. For you, because you lean toward thinking you might know the result, perhaps it's hampering your progress."

"I certainly didn't project the outcome when I lobbed that golf ball at Ed Custis's Mark VIII."

"Yeah, how out of character was that?" she asked with a laugh.

"I've got to ask you. Why are we talking about all this?"

"Well, you're getting out soon, and Shorty and I thought that there were some things that you needed to think about before heading back to your freedom."

"Shorty?"

"Oh, yeah. He did nothing but talk about you when you weren't around. He was really concerned that there were forces in your life that kind of conspired to keep you down. He made me promise that I'd bring it up because he died before he could."

I must have reacted physically to this revelation because Sally got a little defensive.

"This is not criticism, Chunk. Shorty was an athlete and he was trying to help you by coming at it from his experience. I'm a dangerous, transsexual, convicted felon, and I'm trying to do the same. You think about it."

I did, but in the end, I realized that both of them knew very little about the game of golf.

One could call it a sport, and there is a certain amount of athleticism required, but in its most naked form, it is a skill.

A practitioner is given some tools and asked to progress upon a preconceived diagram as efficiently as possible. It is never about being the fastest, or the strongest, or any of the disciplines that reward effort. Risk is managed to the best of one's ability.

I had a pretty amazing amateur career before I turned pro, and I won a fair amount on the mini-tours and nabbed the top spot on more than a few tournaments on all of the developmental tours I had played on, but I had not sniffed a win on the big circuit in any of the events that I had qualified for. I had actually missed every cut, and at my age, given my resume, that should not have been the case. That must have been what Shorty was talking about.

I knew that I'd continued to improve, however, and that could not be denied. One's progress cannot be measured by comparing it to another's.

While these thoughts were circling around my mind, I was subsequently enrolled in the *Avenues to Change* program.

I was right. I could have taught that course without notes. Maybe not the part dealing with substance abuse—a reason many had been thrown in jail in the first place—but all of the elements that dealt with correct behavior and assimilation into society's norms were presented at a remedial level to me.

This program was another benchmark the state wanted

you to attain before they turned you loose on the streets. It was another thing they could point to when issues like prison reform came up in political discussions.

From experience, it is not a program that can be completed within six years, let alone the six weeks that is the length of the course in the Missouri prison system.

The program was basically what we in the know call CBT: Cognitive Behavioral Therapy. In this form, the instructors work off the simple formula that there is a cycle in the way that we behave in the world, and by reinforcing what constitutes good behavior, a person will be an asset to society.

The instructor, an overmatched psychology student in the midst of getting his master's degree from Missouri Western State University, was up against it with the coterie of participants who had been selected for that particular term.

We had a passel of drug addicts, a few guys who served terms for violent crimes (a group that I was included in) and one accountant who was just finishing a six-year term for fudging the numbers of a rich guy who never served a day for massive tax evasion.

The teacher's name was Ned.

My gratitude for having been housed in the special unit abounded.

If I'd been offered the odds that more than half the men in that room would commit further acts of depravity, I would have loaded up on the over.

When I looked into the eyes of the accountant, David Bergman—a template for every stereotype of a nerdy CPA—I could see what all those years among the real hardened criminals could do to one's psyche.

In comparison, the emotional toll associated with being incarcerated had been somewhat benign for me, though the days, weeks, and years certainly did a number on my soul.

Yeah, I didn't participate in the day-to-day machinations of the general population; the terror that guys like David Bergman must have had to transcend never was part of my experience, but I was sure to be scarred anyway.

I was the only one who had spent his entire term at the W.M.D.C.C. Everyone else had been shipped in from one or another of the facilities for just this class.

Alas, poor Ned did not have a grasp of his surroundings when he launched into his opening spiel. Being new to each other, every one of the men felt they had to establish a hierarchy—the same procedure that had occurred on their initial introduction to the system.

It appeared that Ned might end up being a stand-in for the fire hydrant that these men needed to lift their legs on.

Accountant Bergman and I did our best to try to disappear. One of the cons, a shaved head Aryan brother, blue ink tattoos coiled around his neck like an ascot, began sniffing the air and screwing up his face as if to indicate that there was an offensive odor in the room.

"Is everything all right, Mr. Pierson?" Ned asked.

"I smell a Jew," he said.

Ned's eyes grew a little bigger, and in my peripheral vision I saw David shift to the edge of his seat.

"That's funny. I smell white pussy," said a guy whose Afro do added six inches to his already prodigious height.

He, and the person sitting to his right exchanged some kind of personal handclasp.

The Aryan started to stand, and you could feel the whole room brace for what was to come. I'd immediately begun to scope out a possible escape route when David rose up onto his left butt cheek and ripped the loudest fart I had ever heard.

"Maybe y'all should smell this?" he asked.

That was followed by a moment of stunned silence.

"I finish this course and I'm released. No one in this room is going to stop that from happening," David said.

It was said with astonishing conviction.

"That's the same for all of us, right? We're heading toward some kind of parole procedure by taking this course. You may not be getting out right away, but the wheels are in motion. You can screw it up for yourself, but you will not screw it up for me. I've got a wife, and parents, and kids who miss their dad," David said.

Ned was eyeing the door, wondering if he should alert the guard stationed outside that things were falling apart in the room.

I couldn't take it anymore. For the first time since I'd lofted that golf ball toward a moving vehicle, my brain went on tilt. I stood up and did something that might be considered out of character.

"Thoughts create emotions. Emotions create behaviors. Behaviors reinforce thoughts," I said as forcefully as I could, which probably wasn't too impactful because the assembled turned to me like I had just left behind my own sort of stench.

"What's your name, inmate?" Ned asked.

"Charles Dawson."

"May I ask how you knew that phrase?"

"Because I lived it for the first eleven years of my life."

"You've done cognitive behavioral therapy before?"

I nodded in assent.

"You want a lesson on what works and what doesn't?" I asked.

"Yeah, that would be awesome," Ned said.

I walked up to him and asked if I could have one of the worksheets that he had piled on the chair next to him. He handed me one. I quickly scanned the first few tasks.

"Oh boy." I muttered.

"What?" Ned asked.

"Journaling?"

"I've found it helps to focus where one's feelings are. That can often be the onset of identifying thought processes. Adjustments of those can then lead to behavioral changes," Ned said.

I looked out to the class.

"He's right. But we've got six weeks, not ten years. Let me ask this question. How many of you have a driver's license?"

Only David raised his hand.

"I had one, but it probably expired like ten years ago," the Aryan said.

"Let's start there," I said to Ned. "Have everyone write down the reasons that they might need a driver's license when they get out, and then let's see if you can get some applications in here that will allow them to apply for one."

Ned didn't think it was such a bad idea.

"Okay. I can do that. So tonight, everyone write down five reasons why having a driver's license would be a good thing. We can read them all tomorrow," Ned said.

I took my seat. Ned took a good, long breath, then took the temperature of the room again.

"Thank you, Charles."

"You're welcome."

"But you said 'they.' Don't you need a driver's license?"

"Not in Missouri. I live in California."

"Oh. Well, that makes sense."

There were some looks my way. I really wanted to shrug off any thoughts that I was going to be the teacher's pet.

"You won't ever see me in this state again."

I must have said that with some assurance because Ned turned away from me, and looked, it seemed, for someone else he could connect with. He ended up speaking to some spot on the back wall.

"So, let's go around the room and get to know each other," Ned said.

Everyone loosened up a little, even David. Ned worked through some of the things we were expected to accomplish to pass the course. When the session ended, he stopped me at the door.

"I saw what you did there, Charles. You asked them to do a de facto journal looking for something positive."

"My most successful therapists were stringently specific. I froze when things were too vague. My guess is you are dealing with a whole slew of eleven-year-olds here."

"Well, thanks again." Ned said.

"You're welcome."

13

I was just short of my twelfth birthday when my world changed for good. During the year before, Jim had been unsubtly dropping hints to Taylor that he could keep an eye on me for the times the course was open—dawn to dusk.

Our school year routine would have Jim pick me up at daybreak and get me to the course, where I would help set up the range and practice for a bit before catching the school bus that stopped just up the hill.

School was from eight to nearly three. That same bus would drop me off on the return trip. I would help the maintenance crew break down the day, and putt and chip until Jim would turn off the lights in the shop.

It worked out for everyone. Taylor was thrilled that he no longer had to pop for post-school childcare, plus on many of the weekends, I would just stay at Jim's, so Taylor could scurry after a couple of potential Mrs. Dawsons.

When middle school came about, I moved into Jim's

two-bedroom condo permanently, as Taylor had found her—an Australian heiress.

After getting sober for the final time, Jim had thought a great deal about the concept of atonement. Unknown to any of us in the moment, his plan involved installing me as a surrogate who would be the recipient of his repentance.

In the end, my presence in Jim's life was symbiotic beyond whatever definition you use for that word. I got a fully engaged parent who had my best interests at heart, and he got a living, breathing reason to stay sober and alive.

It was the perfect union.

Babe and Jim's relationship grew into something of weight within a couple of months of the debutante ball. The folks in town could find them at most of the social gathering spots, be it the Lariat or Bowie Boulevard drive-ins, Nick's or Kincaid's burger joints, or any of the houses where the parents were away for the weekend.

They might have been physically present, but they did not interact much with the hoi polloi, and seemed to everyone to travel in a world of two.

She was still not yet seventeen and of the legal age of consent in Texas, so they concealed their liaison from the older folks.

When it came out that they were dating, the list of dissenters was long and included Jim's boss, her parents and extended family, the clergy from her church, and most of her peers who'd attended the most expensive, single-sex, parochial school in all of north Texas.

The pair stood tall, though, and weathered the gale of snubs and scorn. These headwinds drew them ever closer, and sometime in the spring of her senior year, she announced that she was expecting.

The two made plans to wed the week after graduation. Anyone who wished to attend could, but no one showed up for her side at the courthouse ceremony, but her brother, Tucker.

Jim's family had the opposite reaction and attended en masse, but they were not of the class of the Greene clan, and the party that followed was a picnic at Harmon Field Park between the softball diamonds and the banks of the Trinity River.

It took the arrival of their first grandson to bring Cornelius and Bettina Greene to heel. All was forgiven, and Babe's parents set them up in a modest ranch style home not far from their mansion with a singular condition: Jim would have to give up his job at the golf course and come to work for the old man at one of his three Ford, Lincoln, Mercury dealerships that dotted the Dallas-Fort Worth metroplex.

Jim did not have to wrestle too much with making the move. He had become increasingly disillusioned with the prospects of having a career in golf after having had to serve under the head pro at Creekside.

There is a long history of where the position of golf pro at a private club sits within the hierarchy of prestige. For many, it is at a level that might register just above the janitorial professions. An apprentice like Jim, no matter how helpful he had been in elevating the games of the membership, was not to be considered as anything other than an employee.

Jim had no patience for most of it. He did his job with the best of his ability, and let the whispers of those interested in innuendo dissipate into the humidity.

When young Benjamin made his way into the world, a lot changed. Jim had some stellar parenting himself, so priorities shifted hard once the youngster appeared. He took Corny's offer to work in the family business. A new hero's journey was defined; to provide for, and protect, his wife and progeny.

He told me that he was aware that a lot of this was about Corny and Bettina needing to control things for their grandchild, but his golf career had become an either/or after having to deal with his boss and the membership.

In a bit of a twist, Corny nominated Jim for membership, and given where Corny stood within the community, Jim was easily accepted. He even regained his amateur status and captured three consecutive club championships at Creekside before the decibel level of complaints that he was once a pro became too great.

It was about that time when he was first diagnosed with rheumatoid arthritis. The only real treatment then was pain mitigation.

Booze helped. There was plenty to be had in the Greene corporate culture; lunches with his father-in-law went three or four vodkas deep and Babe would always meet him at the door with a highball. Jim could handle it in those days.

Young Ben crawled, walked, and started nursery school. Jim was there for every event, every meeting, and every milestone.

Babe initially thrived on her return to the bosom of her

family. She had returned with her head held high and retained a tremendous amount of leverage for adding a twig to a branch of the family tree.

There were nurses and maids at her beck and call. If she wanted to swim, she only had to drive the short mile to the Greene colonial estate.

But Babe was just an asteroid traveling in an elliptical loop around a provincial planet. Her path had brought her back into the gravitational pull of her parents, but it was only temporary. She began to act out about the time that Ben entered elementary school.

The country was in a cultural revolt and there were temptations that beckoned from far beyond the outskirts of Tarrant County. A rejection of the life as a mother, wife of a car dealer, and country club member appeared to be part of her latest mandate. She had defied the gentry by marrying a lowly golf pro, and now that person had become the exact thing she had rebelled against.

Jim never saw it coming. Perhaps his focus was on other things like work and his son, though later he blamed the alcohol for bringing a fuzziness to his existence that could have exacerbated his myopia.

He came home one afternoon to find two suitcases missing along with the family's Country Squire wagon, his wife, and their son.

There was no note.

Jim canvassed everyone who knew her, and the responses

were consistently similar: "We had no idea." "She never said a word to me." "It makes no sense." "I just feel terrible."

Corny and Bettina hired a private dick, whose investigation got as far as Flagstaff, Arizona, and a hazy description of Babe from a gas jockey.

The car was sold in Bishop, California. Jim got a call from the new owner to ask if he had an original copy of the owner's manual.

A month after that, Babe called from a pay phone outside Carmel to tell him that she and Ben were fine, and if he wanted to come and get their son, she would arrange an exchange with someone she knew at a neutral site.

He took a Pacific Southwest Airlines flight to San Francisco two hours after the phone call. He and Ben were reunited at a Sambo's diner outside of Mountain View.

Ben seemed no worse for wear. The two of them had been apart for just over a month, and Jim swore that there were no lingering issues that had resulted from the separation.

He never remarried.

Babe didn't resurface for well over 500 full moons. There were rumors that she had moved to Spain, or Bali, or Malta.

As for the youngster Ben, he did all right. He was not really interested in athletics, especially something as mundane as golf. He wrestled a little in high school and was accepted on an academic scholarship to Texas A&M, where he immediately joined the Corps of Cadets.

Jim thought his own father might have been responsible

for that; his stories of Tarrant Field during the war years always seemed to excite the lad.

His choices could have also been in homage to Babe's genetics, as Benjamin wanted nothing of the life that might have been handed down to him via the Corny Greene Ford, Lincoln, and Mercury multi-megastore empire.

Upon graduation, he was accepted into the Marine Corps and entered Officer's Basic School at Quantico, Virginia. Twenty-six weeks later, Jim was there for his graduation.

The end came swiftly. Benjamin, like most true Marines, always chose infantry when queried about where they would like to be posted. Having graduated near the top of his class, he was granted his wish.

He joined the 24th Marine Amphibious Unit as a raw Second Lieutenant at their home at Camp Lejeune, North Carolina. Two weeks later, they were on a ship to relieve the 22nd MAU, who had been performing peacekeeping duties in Lebanon during a brutal civil war.

Benjamin wrote to his father about their daily contact with hostile forces and the constant barrage of mortars and rockets that landed in the vicinity of their barracks at the Beirut airport.

He was never really in mortal danger, he wrote, and after a couple of months, he and his fellow Marines just took it all in stride. His unit had been there before and knew most of the ins-and-outs of the geography and the players in the conflict. He was studying Arabic and considering applying for a position in intelligence when his next rotation request came about.

On an October morning, just a couple of months into

their deployment, the Marine barracks were deliberately driven into by a nineteen-ton Mercedes truck that was carrying 2,000 pounds of explosives.

Benjamin's billet was right in the front of the building at nearly the exact point of contact. The only part of Benjamin to make it back to Jim were his melted dog tags.

Jim tumbled pretty hard at that point. His physical condition had deteriorated in the years since his arthritis diagnosis, but other than some frozen joints and the acceptance of a more deliberative gait, he only had to compensate for the pain.

There hadn't been a trace of existential or psychic anguish in all the time it had just been he and Benjamin. If a reservoir of emotion had been filling during that period, he was not aware of it.

He'd been proud of the job he'd done in raising his son, and any tethers to old ideas like ambition and following one's own path had been severed in service of the aforementioned hero's journey.

He made it through the memorials, the national mourning, and the continual attempts from the Fort Worth and Creekside Country Club communities to reach out with their thoughts and prayers.

He even got a condolence note from Mr. Hogan, who had been informed by a member at Shady Oaks that he used to work there.

At some point, the dam broke. Jim sat down and drank the emptying lake in the form of some fairly decent rye whiskey.

Eventually, a group of family, friends, and co-workers

gathered him up and had him committed to a hospital to dry out.

That was followed by a stint at a rehabilitation facility in the California desert.

On his third day in Rancho Mirage, during a group session, he met Dave "Halfy" Sears, a former PGA champion, who was trying to get straightened out. Booze was only a symptom for Halfy. He had more than one screw loose.

He'd gotten his nickname sometime the decade before, and it was not meant to venerate him. Halfy was short for "half in the bag," an archaic term that designated its recipient as being drunk.

Halfy always had a bottle in his golf bag, and later, Jim found out, a gun, as well. Halfy told him that he'd begun to fantasize about a scenario where he shanked a ball, reached into his golf bag, and blew his brains out on the national TV broadcast. During that time, well into a binge, Halfy confessed this to a fellow golfer, who called social services. He was subsequently placed on lockdown at a mental hospital. Seventy-two hours later he was ferried to the desert to take the cure.

There were about sixty golf courses within about ten miles of the facility Jim and Halfy were living at, most of them private. At some point, Halfy and Jim were permitted to borrow one of the center's golf carts and take a recess period to hit balls with rental clubs at the municipal track down the block.

They had talked fundamentals for a couple of weeks, and Halfy had taken so many shadow swings on Jim's instruction that he couldn't take it anymore. He had to test Jim's theories so he could dream once again that a life existed beyond the grueling period of detoxification.

It was like a magic trick for Halfy. From the first shots he struck, he knew that everything Jim had told him about his swing was exactly right.

Jim took a few swings himself, but his hands had already begun to become the inert claw-like figures that he would live with the rest of his life. It just hurt a little too much for it to be any fun for him.

A fire had been kindled in Jim again, though. And when he returned to Fort Worth and his life selling cars, clean and sober for the time being, he knew another transformation was in the offing. A return to his first avocation was imminent.

Dave "Halfy" Sears was back out on tour and playing fairly well. He'd been touting Jim's genius to his fellow pro journeymen, and all it took was a phone call from "Halfy" to get Jim out of Fort Worth and onto the range of the next tour event.

He spent a month out there, sleeping in cheap motels, and eating diner food. His new students were showing improvements, but the pay was meager, and the nights were brutal and lonely.

When it became pretty obvious that "Halfy" had gotten back on the sauce, Jim started to rethink everything.

He returned to Fort Worth, sold his house to one of the Greene cousins, and headed to Arkansas to work as an assistant pro at a private club near Hot Springs.

There were new rules in place for gaining the Class A status that used to be granted by a handshake and a toast. There were academic courses, fees, and something called a PAT: a Player's Ability Test.

Luckily, Jim had a little money in his pocket from the sale of the house, so the fees that needed to be paid were not a burden. It would take a long time to go through the different levels, nearly four and a half years, but he was committed to seeing it through this time.

The playing test was going to be tough. He could hold a golf club, but the torque that was required to swing it hurt like a son-of-a bitch.

He couldn't really practice much for the thirty-six-hole test, except on and around the green, where the toll on his joints was less taxing.

The folks at the PGA make it pretty easy. The courses that are chosen are not that difficult and are often municipal facilities. Yet, fewer than 20 percent end up being able to pass the test.

Jim had a plan that involved a combination of prescription analgesics and some injected anti-inflammatory medication. An orthopedist at his club administered the cortisone and wrote him a prescription for the hyper-strong Ibuprofen.

He burned a nice little hole in his stomach from ingesting all of the medication required for the effort, but shot 78–80 and qualified on the number. He had to make a fifty-five-foot twisting putt on eighteen to get it done.

He eventually became a Class A Professional, and he never played a full round of golf again.

He continued to struggle with the alcohol, though, which led to a cycle of hire, fire, rehab, and repeat.

His hiring at Sweetwater Valley Municipal was his last chance.

14

It took me some time to become competitive in tournaments, but once I started to perform up to my capabilities, I won pretty much everything that was contested in my local area.

As Jim had told me time and again, transcending all of the petty distractions so I could focus more on my own experience would turn out to be the key.

I still had an ocean of thoughts in my mind during a round, but I had gotten to a place where the vast majority of them were dealing with the task at hand, and not the shiny objects of annoyance that had previously vexed me.

Anyone could see that I was physically gifted with hand/eye coordination. Like a great guitarist or painter, there was effortless precision in my movement.

I lacked the intellectual component of how to play at first by virtue of my condition. I was the explicit example of the see it, hit it, chase it, see it and hit it again school.

As I progressed, I began to acquire the tools to understand the relationship between skill and the decisions that needed to be addressed with each shot. The introduction of that information was so exciting, so different on an empirical level from anything I had learned in school or therapy.

There were times when I got overwhelmed with too much information to process. That often led to a type of paralysis akin to rigor mortis, but with Jim's guidance and experience, the frequency of those incidences dissipated rather quickly.

I talk about my ability with a lack of humility because I can state with absolute authority that all of those guys who play on the big tours in the U.S., Europe, or Asia are similarly blessed with many, if not all, of the tools that I possess.

Maybe not the Asperger's, but certainly the physical attributes and the ability to execute under duress.

The difference between a great golfer and one who can successfully make a living on tour is a gulf as wide as the Atlantic Ocean.

I rapidly progressed through the junior circuit in San Diego County. As a twelve-year-old, I was winning the one-day nine-hole events for my age group by five or six shots.

It didn't help my popularity any. If I'd been ostracized for being a stickler before, I was now being downright reviled for kicking everyone's ass.

The parents hated me as much as their kids did. At some point, a cabal of the concerned was formed and the committee responsible for putting on the tournaments agreed to "advance" me to the next age group: the thirteen and fourteen-year-olds.

I thought it was great because those events got to play the back nine, too. I finished second by a shot my first time out at a really nice private track in the northern part of the county.

I then won the next seven events in a row.

I took my age group at the Junior World as a thirteen-year old, and made the match play of the Junior Am later that summer. It wasn't long before there was a coterie of multi-colored polo shirt wearing followers making up the bulk of the gallery when I competed.

They were the assistants for the major college golf programs, and they were ubiquitous until my run-in with the USGA and the golf world at the Junior Am that one year.

There was one head coach who showed up at SVMGC one fall afternoon out of the blue, though. He'd done his research and learned that I played out of there, and worked the range and the shop.

Jim brought him out to the practice tee where I was testing a new shaft I'd put into my driver. Much to my chagrin, I had obviously gotten my calculations wrong.

Like Hogan had done, I was trying to perfect a power fade, and I felt that the previous shaft wasn't stiff enough to get the ball moving left to right without a ton of swing manipulation.

But the shaft I chose was just too dang rigid, and I was hitting slices that seemed to start at the far left of the driving range before flaring into the netting on the right.

Jim snickered a bit after each incidence. He'd warned me that I would go too far. He was open to most of my harebrained theories because he felt self-exploration and self-education were the most important tools for long-term success.

He wanted me to be a scientist about the game, which is kind of hilarious given my origins.

The coach, who helmed one of the most prestigious university golf programs in the country, stood silently by as I continued to struggle.

"Hey Chunk, this is Coach Cameron Zantz."

I just kind of nodded at them and kept teeing them up, churning that butter all over the place.

"Chunk, stop what you're doing and say hello to the man. He's driven a long way to talk to you."

I sighed and said, "Please, not now. I'm really trying to figure this out."

"Goddammit, Chunk . . ."

"It's okay," Cameron Zantz said. "I'm fine, really."

"Charles . . ."

His tone of voice and the evocation of my formal first name stopped me in my tracks. I had crossed a line, and I immediately apologized for being rude.

"It's cool, Mr. Dawson, really," Coach Zantz said again.

He had this unbelievably wide grin stretched across his face. His teeth could not have been whiter.

"I'm testing a new shaft. This one might be a little too stiff," I said to the coach.

"Ya think?" Jim asked.

"Let me ask you something, Charles. You don't mind if I call you that, do you?"

"No, I answer to nearly everything."

"If I asked you to hit a hook right now, do you think you could do it?" the coach asked.

"I don't know. I haven't gotten the head to square up once."

"Yeah, but you're trying to hit cuts, are you not? I'm asking you to hit a big ole hook."

"Maybe, I could."

"I mean, if you needed to hit a hook because your life depended on it, could you do that? If it was a matter of life and death, or meant all the money in the world, or the affections of a beautiful girl, do you think you could hit a draw with the club you're holding right now?"

"I'll try."

"You need to do more than try. This is everything; you understand me?"

"Yeah," I said feeling the emergence of a chip burgeoning on my shoulder.

I caught a glimpse of Jim out of the corner of my eye. He seemed intrigued by the challenge.

"Let's sweeten it. You hit a draw, and we'll have burritos from Salcedo's for dinner," Jim said.

I teed up the cleanest, newest ball from the pile that was scattered in front of me. I stood back behind the ball and looked down the line of flight, visualizing an arc that started somewhere to my right and curved hard to the left.

I went full old school by strengthening my left hand grip (twisting my wrist to the right) and weakening my right hand so it was almost under the club. I moved the ball back in my stance a bit and closed myself off to promote the most in-to-out swing path I could generate. I took an imaginary swipe where I took the club back on an inside path and then laid it off even more. I must have looked an idiot, but this swing was manufactured to do just one thing and that was to hook the crap out of that range ball.

Coach Zantz joined us for the burritos. I wouldn't call what I hit an actual hook, but I produced an arc that slightly turned to the left, which was deemed a success. Within seconds of us sitting down, he offered me a full ride scholarship to his elite private university up in Los Angeles. I was not yet fifteen years old.

"I really hadn't thought about going to school again after I finish high school. I feel like I've been going to some form of school since I could walk. And I'm not so sure I'd be able to get in based on my grades," I said.

"I'm not concerned," Coach Zantz said. "We have remedies for all that. There will be resources made available to you, like tutors and special help."

"Oh boy, really?" I asked with extreme indifference.

"Yeah, our athletes get the best assistance."

"I want to be polite and not make you or anyone else mad, but do you have any idea what I've gone through for all of my life?"

I looked over to Jim and bade him to step in as my advocate, but he really wanted me to explain myself without any outside reinforcement.

In retrospect, I've realized that from the moment he became

my mentor and guardian, he also innately understood how to execute the most efficacious course of lessons for me to develop beyond the limitations placed on me by the awesome power of my diagnosis.

"You see, Coach, I've always struggled with nearly everything—people, school—and someone has always been there to help with it. They've told me what to do, how to act, what to know, and I am sick of listening to all of them. When I finish school, I won't ever have to deal with stuff like that again, and I can't wait for that day to come. I just want to do the one thing I have ever truly loved—play golf."

Jim smiled. I knew that I had explained myself sufficiently, and hadn't even mentioned anything about my specific pathology. Coach Zantz sat back in his chair and shook his head.

"I get it," he said.

"You do?" I asked.

"Oh yeah. The bummer for me is I know you're right."

"How so?" Jim asked.

"I knew all about your stats, and I was made aware by countless alumni that you were a promising player. To be honest, I just wasn't interested, until someone told me about that thing at the Junior Am."

"That's when the other coaches ran for cover," Jim said with a laugh.

"It's the only reason I drove down here. I've spent fifteen years trying to choose players based on character. I haven't sniffed a National Championship. Those guys are good players and solid human beings, but the game just isn't the basis of their survival.

That's the competitor I'm looking for, and something tells me that you carry that with you somehow."

I felt bad for the coach. He looked really unhappy in the moment. I was almost wooed to the point of considering his offer.

"Look, Charles, I'm just being selfish. You are going to do something great in this game. I am dead certain of that. I rescind the offer, okay. It is off the table."

We talked about other things, the Masters and his short professional experience. Then, he stood up, handed both Jim and me his card, dropped a hundred-dollar bill on the table, and said, "If either of you need anything, give me call. It's been a pleasure. Great burrito. Now, don't break my heart, Charles. Bring it."

He walked out into the dying light of the day and we never saw him again. Three years later, his team won their first of four consecutive National Championships.

I had reached my limit in the amateur game while still in high school. I won the California Amateur just before my seventeenth birthday. I wasn't the youngest ever, but I *was* the youngest in thirty-five years.

I played high school golf as a freshman and sophomore, partly because I really wanted to be able to wear a varsity letterman's jacket on the few days of California winter where that kind of coverage was appropriate. I was too dense to understand that the little golf bag on the letter was something that the jocks snickered about when I passed by.

Our "team" was made up of me, a Korean kid named Josh,

who occasionally broke eighty, and four guys from the football team who just wanted to hang out and giggle. Our coach was the special team's coach for the football team.

We never won any of our matches as a team, but I won the county high school golf championship as an individual both years. They were one-day, eighteen-hole events, and as a sophomore I shot 62 and won by nine shots.

The team was disbanded after the football players graduated, and since you needed six players to compete, high school golf was over for Josh and me.

It was Lee Trevino who said that until you can regularly beat every single person within a fifty-mile radius, you shouldn't even think about trying to make a living playing tournament golf.

It's always surprised me that very few have ever taken that advice. The lower levels of the pro experience are littered with guys who will never, ever be able to make a go of it. Don't get me wrong; I'm not saying they shouldn't be out there trying. Players like me would never be able to survive if legions of the deluded didn't plunk down their entry fees for mini-tour events.

Those two hundred bucks is the gamble that we would take to make eight hundred to a thousand more, and that's if you won. You'd end up losing money if you finished fifth in a field of fifty. It's a bit of an ugly pyramid scheme, where the many feed the few.

I turned pro at seventeen, and mini-tour events were the only game in town for me. All of the other tours were off-limits until I was of legal age. I had become an employee at SVMGC about the time I turned fifteen—minimum wage pay for about four hours of work each day—and at some point my bank account held fourteen hundred bucks.

For my debut, I plunked two hundred of it down to enter a one-day event that was being played at a track at the county's eastern edge.

I'd shot a 68 from the men's tees in a junior event there a couple of years before, and won the event by three shots. Though playing from the tips stretched the course out about 400 yards more, I still thought I could break par and collect something from the purse.

I shot 71 and was handed a handwritten check for a hundred and ten bucks for finishing in a tie for sixth. My original stake was already ninety in the hole. I'd been told by a playing partner to take it straight to the bank if I wanted it to make sure the check would clear.

That was one of the first real eye-openers for me in the game: pros don't mess around. On most days, you shoot somewhere around even—a score that often wins at the amateur level—and you will get rolled over like a tidal wave. Some of these guys are trying to make enough to pay their rent, their car payment, or for even just a plate of tacos, and a golf course or opponent is not going to keep them from getting the job done.

There was not a lot of camaraderie amongst the ranks of those who played our little upstart circuit—the SoCal TOUR sponsored by Prince Harold's Realty.

The whole tour survived for only seven months before someone (Prince Harold, I think) went belly-up or ran off with the profits. Either way, it was over until the next guy who wanted to try to exploit a group of desperate souls hung up their shingle to announce the emergence of a new mini-tour.

Turns out whenever one of these things sprung to life, it was like a piranha attack on the carcass of a calf who'd fallen into the river. Marginal guys who didn't have status on any of the major tours, those who were in their forties and trying to hang on for a shot at the senior circuit, or those who had struggled with addictions or bad relationships all descended on the locales where the twice weekly events were being held.

There were more than a few local dreamers, unrealistic club pros, and groups of regional players who needed a place to compete between trying to get bartending gigs to fill out the fields.

These tours pop up in the snowbird environments every fall and winter in Florida, Arizona, and California. And all the pirates sail to them to take their shot at acquiring a mere ounce or two of gold.

A seventeen-year-old like me had absolutely no business with this group. I got murdered at the outset, but like many things for me, I started to figure it out. By the end of the Prince Harold thing, I had quintupled my stake to the point that I could afford to go through the qualifying process for one of the bigger tours as soon as my birthday passed.

Prince Harold still owes me my winnings from the last two events.

15

The package came on a Tuesday—a plain Manila envelope with a Missouri Department of Corrections seal and a couple of check marks signifying that the contents had been examined.

Inside was the mental health care remedy I had asked Deidre to try her best to provide. She had come through in spades because what spilled out of the mouth of the enclosure was not only the scorecard for the golf course across the street, but a players' guide and brief history of the club.

She also included copies of whatever golf publications she could find at a local newsstand. Sally strangely grabbed those in the hopes of expanding her woeful knowledge of the game.

It turned out that the track across the street was called Kiama Golf Club; it had been established in the 1920s by a once popular fraternal organization called the Shriner's, a sect of the Freemasons.

I was curious about the name Kiama and enlisted the help

from one of my *Avenues to Change* classmates. He said Kiama, though altered into some form of bastardized American English in a futile attempt to conceal its Arabic origins, was actually the word, qiyamah.

He said that qiyamah means resurrection. In the Koran, it has something to do with the resurrection of all peoples on the Day of Judgment, regardless of their core beliefs. He argued, quite vociferously, that most of that idea is bullshit, and that if you were an actual infidel, you would perish in a ball of flame or at the tip of a spear, no matter what, because that was how God willed it.

I saw some kismet in the resurrection theme, though, even if my agnosticism personified me as nothing but a blasphemer. I spent many a night staring at the ceiling of my cell visualizing every hole of the course.

Kiama played slightly under 6,200 yards from the tips, but still carried a decent slope of 130 for a par 71. The player's guide gave a little diagram of the holes, their hazards, and suggestions of the best way to play them.

When the doors had been locked and the lights extinguished, I attempted to play the entire course in my head. Shepherds might count sheep, golfers play imaginary holes until their eyes close for the night. I can't say I ever made it to the back nine.

My dreams were those of the anxious—recurring nightmares of trying to get to a golf course for a tee time or falling behind my group and never catching up to them again.

As the weeks passed, a lightness began to prevail.

Even if my parole never came through, I was still deep into the back-end of the halfway mark of my sentence.

Towards the end of the third week of the *Avenues to Change* program, Ned was running out of mundane tasks to assign to the class. We'd done all of the busy paperwork we could get from the Missouri DMV, and did a series of exercises filling out applications for everything from state assistance, to jobs, to admittance to a local junior college.

The tensions that existed amongst the factions never really abated and Ned always looked like he was one raised voice away from bolting the room.

Strangely, it was David Bergman's presence that always kept the lid on the pressure cooker. If things started to go off the rails, he would interject himself into the fray and demand that all efforts to be disruptive needed to cease immediately.

I did what I could to keep Ned on track, and as the fourth week began, he had me running the show. We were moving into the anger management portion of the curriculum, and I decided that Ned should split the groups into two teams with David and me as captains.

The exercise was kind of a disaster; it all ended up devolving into a bit of the antithesis to anger management.

When Ned excused us, I hung around a bit to debrief with David. We'd never had an actual conversation to that point, but there was something about his demeanor that intrigued me and I wanted to spend some of the remaining time we would have together to see what all of that was about.

"Hey, Dave, can I ask you a question about your time here?" I began.

"Only if you never call me Dave again. I'm not the dude who rotates your tires. My name is David."

"Oh, I'm sorry," I said.

"I'm just fucking with you. What do you want to know?" David asked.

I asked him about all kinds of things. How he survived in the general population, what he was going to do when he got out, and if he thought he was going to have to go through a transitional period.

His answers were thoughtful and filled with hope, but also a fair amount of anxiety about the unknown.

"What did you do before you ended up here, Charles?" he asked.

"Professional golfer."

"Cool. Well, that's a merit-based pursuit. No one can hold you back from that. You succeed or fail on your own efforts, right?"

"Yeah," I said, but I still wasn't so sure that it'd be that easy to just step back into it all.

"I'm looking into stuff like that now. Things I can do from home, like investments, brokerage, things where I'm no longer an employee. I worked for a lot of dipshits, Charles. Not anymore. My money's been working for me while I've been in here, but it's going to be working a lot harder when I can get my hands back on it."

"That makes sense," I said.

The guard appeared in the threshold and beckoned David to come out. They would be heading over to the other side of the facility. I didn't need an escort since I was already on my side of the building, a short pitch over a bunker away from my special wing.

Later that day, Sally and I discussed this reintegration into society and the things I had to consider in regards to the reclamation of my freedom.

For her, that first return had been daunting. But then, there were many things in her world that were elevated to epic status because of her heightened state of emotions. If her well ran deep, as she often said, I was like the bucket that floated on top of the water.

I'd been in a sort of jail for the entire first third of my life. I felt the transition to normalcy wasn't going to be that difficult.

"This David seems like a good guy. But there is pain in his future," Sally said after I had described our conversation.

"He seems to have an understanding of the hardships," I said.

"He has no clue, honey. He needs to reconnect to relationships that have gone sideways for such a long time. Everyone has figured out a way to get along without him, and now they will have to make some serious adjustments. It takes a willingness, and I'm not sure most people want to disrupt their lives like that."

"Well, I'm not going to have that problem," I said.

"Why?"

"Now don't cry, please, but when I get out there will be no

one there to meet me, and not a soul in this world that I will be going home to. No one is going to have to make any adjustments for me. I feel a little relief about that, honestly."

Sally didn't heed my request. Her face screwed up into the classic visage of sorrow. She shook her head, rose from the table, and almost got her face turned away from me before the first whimper escaped. She was full-out sobbing by the time she got to her cell door.

I continued to worry about what would become of Sally once I was released. Since she'd been housed at the W.M.D.C.C., it seemed that every so often, some district attorney in some county where one of her bank heists had taken place petitioned the judge who presided over her case to have her remanded to the general population at one of the maximum security facilities in the Missouri prison system.

For Sally's part, her formidable legal team was still trying to get her housed with the female population. This was as much a political statement as anything else—an acknowledgement of transgender rights that the state was trying to resist using the shield of their omnipotent god and his savior son.

As the time of her incarceration passed, Sally became content with just where she was, thank you. But my departure was about to change all of that, and as much as she wanted me to go, she couldn't help but ponder her own circumstance without a friend in the vicinity.

Most of the other guys on our block were there for reasons having to do with mental incapacity or serious medical issues. With Shorty dying, there was one less person to converse with.

When I was gone, there would be none. I kept reminding her that they would not be leaving my cell empty, and perhaps the new inmate might be different from the others.

"Oh come on, you've got to stop it, Chunk. You said that after Shorty passed, and they replaced him with a guy who can't walk and is hooked up to a machine to help him breathe," she said.

I was trying to help, but as the time ticked away, she became more and more depressed. I honestly feared that she had become suicidal at some point, but when I told her that she was frightening me, she showed me that anger that I have since cataloged as lore.

"Why would you think that?" she screamed.

"You just seem so bummed out all the time, and that kind of scares me. It always has. People don't think I react to those things, but it makes me uncomfortable. The woman who acted as my mother spent most of our years together in that state, and when she left, I felt relieved that I didn't have to feel that way anymore."

"God, were you ever diagnosed with narcissism, too? This all seems to be about you, you know?"

"Not me. I just feel bad for you."

"Listen to me, I'm not depressed; I'm emotional! There is a difference. Do you think if I were ever clinically depressed, I would be alive? I was born into the wrong body, I lived a life of crime in the hopes that I could change that, and now I'm going to spend the bulk of my life being housed by the state! Do you hear me talking about not wanting to be alive?" she seethed.

"No," I whispered.

"Do you think for even a second that I would ever give the people who wish I didn't exist the pleasure of knowing I killed myself?"

Cappy walked out of his safe room with a rubber sap in his hand. He slowly tapped it against his thigh as he tried to figure out what all the yelling was about. His de facto response:

"Goddamn it, Dio, stop this crazy shit right now!"

Sally jumped up from the table.

"Or what, Cappy. You really think you've got the balls to beat my ass? Let's go, asshole. Let's do this in front of all of these witnesses. Bring it, motherfucker!"

I immediately jumped in front of Sally. I could feel that she was welcoming whatever was about to ensue, and I was equally sure that this would be the thing that would haunt her forever.

If this thing were to go any further, she'd be out of the W.M.D.C.C. regardless of her legal Seal Team. In that chaotic moment, heart pounding out of my chest, I suddenly exploded.

"If you want a piece of her, Cappy, you better take me out first," I screamed.

I was suddenly possessed with a particular fervor that drew from some of the tantrums of my youth. Once that showed up, I plugged into that energy and unleashed a torrent of expletives until I could feel Sally's aggression begin to abate.

My behavior was so out of character that Cappy was stunned into paralysis. I even advanced toward him without even thinking of the recriminations. It was at that point that two things happened simultaneously: 1) Cappy snapped out of his reverie and readied his weapon, and 2) Sally grabbed me, and with surprising strength, pulled me as far away from Cappy as she could.

"What the fuck, Chunk?"

I was still pretty high with the adrenaline rush, and I must have started to smile, because she spun me around so that Cappy couldn't see my face.

"Okay, honey, come back to Earth now," she said with a voice that reminded me of Jim.

I started to cry for one of the few times in my life. The spell had broken. Yeah, I had come out of it, but I was left with an emptiness like nothing I had every felt before.

There it was—the emotions of the last five or so years being expelled in that moment: Jim's death, my subsequent feelings of insecurity and loneliness, my altercation with Ed Custis, and my experience with crime and punishment that had led to these years of enervating incarceration.

Sally led me back to my cell past the gawking faces of the other inmates on our block. I sobbed for the rest of night.

There was video footage of the incident, but Cappy had it suppressed by the operator. The last thing he wanted was any examination of the monitoring system that often found fault with the staff over the convicts.

He never mentioned it, and when I emerged from my cell the next morning, Cappy acted like it never happened. Sally stayed pretty chilly for the next couple of weeks or so.

Unless something strange happened, I figured that I had about a year left at that point. Ned, the *Avenues to Change* instructor, had petitioned someone in the Warden's office to allow me to help him run the class for at least the next session. I did that, and the one that followed.

I did not know a couple of things that were out there in the wind, and those were that Deidre was maneuvering behind the scenes to at least get me a second parole hearing on the grounds that my initial presentation had been cut short.

At some point, she began collecting references to bolster her case, and Ned generously offered to give me the highest marks if asked.

Cappy, of all people, also signed off on an affidavit that I had been a model prisoner, and that I'd given no one trouble throughout the service of my sentence.

My lack of awareness of these actions aside, my thoughts still began to wander to the realities of life outside of the walls of the W.M.D.C.C. There was going to be a lot that needed to be done. I had no idea where to start.

"So, when you got out the first time, what was that like?" I asked Sally one night after dinner.

"What do you mean?"

"I mean there were things you had to do, right? You had to go to where you used to live and get your stuff. You had to find your car and see if it would start, that sort of thing?"

"Sweetie, I was a serial bank robber; I slept most nights in a motel and I always rented a car, usually from some independent outfit that didn't ask a ton of questions. I was not part of any grid for many, many years."

I knew I had to go home. I knew I had to find a way to resurrect my career. And I knew that I had to take all that I had learned—not just what had happened in prison, but everything—and apply it to my desires and goals.

"C'mon, Chunk, don't you teach other convicts how to return to their lives? Why is this a thing?"

"I don't know."

Because I had paid a price for my actions, was I now a man who had no fear of consequence? Was I finally the guy who Coach Zantz wanted so desperately to recruit?

Again, all of this existential thought was becoming debilitating. It made my head hurt. In the past, when worry, anxiety, or the torment of puzzlement preoccupied me to the point of discomfort, I could always quell those thoughts and feelings by hitting a pyramid of balls on the driving range.

In my current state of restrictiveness, that was not an option. So, I tried to block it all out by just focusing on something else. Wherever I was, the dining area, my cell and cellblock, or Ned's class, if an undertow of perplexity began to pull me down, I would switch my brain to playing the different holes at Kiama Golf Club.

Sally caught me mid-reverie one day and asked me why I seemed to be constantly in a quasi-fugue state.

I explained my coping mechanism; she thought that it was a healthier way to deflect aggravation than what most mortals use.

"So I've been thumbing through those golf magazines that your lawyer sent you," she said.

"Yeah, I saw you gobble them up. What did you learn?"

"There are some serious fashion issues, I'll tell you that. What did you wear when you played?"

"I just tried to match the colors of the hat and the pants, you know, and let the shirt be what it was. I never wore a belt until I played a national event as a pro. It was in Canada, and it was a tour where a high finish on their order of merit bumped you to the next level of competition. Some semi-washed up player in his forties, possibly just to screw with my head, hammered me for the whole first nine about how stupid I looked because I wasn't wearing a belt. When we made the turn, I ducked into the pro shop and bought one. I spent four times what I should've, just so he could tell me how right he was the entire back nine."

Sally smiled. We were certainly opposites when it came to stuff like that, as I had no self-awareness of how I looked. If I took a peek into a mirror in the clubhouse before a round, a rarity, and something was awry, I'm not sure I would have clocked it. I had to be told by someone that my fly was open or I had missed the bottom button on my golf shirt.

My expressions of vanity were strictly related to my game performance. I honestly never thought about whether I was attractive, how my hair should look, that kind of thing. I left those things up to other people, like barbers or clothing reps. I shaved every day because Jim had done that.

"You are a trip, Chunk," Sally said. "I've had a girlfriend or two who would've fallen for you in a second. I knew this pretty little thing in Branson who couldn't decide if she wanted to get off the fence with me, but she would have dropped down to the ground if you'd shown up."

"Whoa, whoa, whoa, you just said like five things there that, like, what?"

"That I've been to Branson? Yeah, they had some good deals back in the day, and a felon could really disappear there if things got a little too hot down in the valley."

"No, no, no, Sally. C'mon, you just said something about a girlfriend."

"What about it? For your information, darling, I have never had a boyfriend."

"Okay, wait, how come I don't know this?"

"Because you don't ask about stuff like that. You get a tad uncomfortable every time I ask you about women. I've seen the look on your face when the subject comes up," she said with a dramatic roll of her eyes.

Why hadn't I known this?

16

My first foray at the qualifying process was a bust. Arrogance was the likely culprit, but like everything else for me in this life, it was another reminder that all endeavors require a learning curve.

Eighteen by the time the United States Developmental Tour qualifying tournament was set to kick off, I was allowed to put down my twenty-seven hundred bucks to play in the required pre-qualifying tourney.

It's a fifty-four-hole affair and was a newly added step when I first competed.

Back in Jim's day, the qualifying tournament was three stages in length. Anyone who wanted to press their luck could plunk down the fee and tee it up in one of the first stage events.

If you finished in some upper percentage, you got to play in stage two, where a more experienced field—with an influx of exempted players—awaited.

If you made it through that, you were invited to play six

rounds with another group of exempt players and your fellow qualifiers for a shot at being one of the twenty-five who got some status on the big tour.

There are dozens of reasons why things have changed. Guys who made the big tour for the first time were very rarely successful. Rich dilettantes often littered the first stage, and that created problems in regards to sizes of fields, hence the introduction of the pre-qualifying event.

There were other reasons, but suffice it to say, they changed things so that all of the qualifying would lead to the second-tier United States Development Tour; if you wanted to make it to the big show, you had to prove yourself on that level first.

I shot three rounds in the sixties in the pre-qualifier to make it to the first stage with ease, where I had to complete my entry fee by delivering another twenty-eight hundred dollars to the powers that be. It was the last bit of cash I had in the world.

There was this indelible moment that became part of lore. I had the lead in that pre-qualifier through the first two rounds, and when I warmed-up before the final round, I took a spot in the middle of the range and just starting hitting these lasers out to the two hundred flag with a five iron. If every one of those shots were given a metric by some type of optical device, the deviation to the right or the left would have been measured in microns.

A crowd of parents and friends of the other competitors began to gather behind me. I could hear their oohs and ahs each time the ball made contact with the dead center of the clubface. I had never hit the ball so straight in my entire life. Maybe with the Walmart walloper, but that was fifteen feet into a garage door.

"Hey!" came the wail of a raspy voice from over at the putting green.

All eyes turned to find Jim, a little hitch in his giddy-up, hoofing it double-time after parking the car.

"What the hell do you think you're doing?" he asked when he had about reached the distance where the spectators had gathered.

I turned to him with a sheepish grin; I knew what he was going to say.

"C'mon, Chunk, you gotta stop hitting that straight shit right now! It's either coming from the left or coming from the right, but I will not stand here and let you take that straight bullshit out onto the course!"

The entire crowd gasped. They were clearly stunned by the brazen attempt of this yelling individual to try to put an end to the beauty they believed they were witnessing.

Like I said, I could have told you this was coming; I just was kind of enjoying the attention. Jim had learned from Hogan that when the heat of competition was applied, you could likely no longer rely on your standard shot.

I breezed through that round—it took a 62 by a guy who started five shots back of me to beat me by a shot—and never really thought about trying to hit a single shot straight. That was Jim also understanding the complexity of my mind. He knew my decision-making would be swifter and more confident if I eliminated one side of the golf course on every shot by moving the ball the way my eyes saw the hole.

My competition for that pre-qualifier were guys who, like me, had no status at all, and the contrast between them and the fellas that showed up for the first stage was staggering.

I played fairly well at that first stage, and got rolled over by a field the likes of which I had never competed against before.

This was something other than a national amateur competition, or even a mini-tour event. That field was flat-out desperate. The fervor they had for protecting their fifty-five hundred dollar investment was a quantum leap up from my days with the Prince Harold crowd. It took an entire realignment of my perspective to comprehend what I'd faced that first time out in the real professional golf world.

Being broke, I returned to the range at SVMGC and prepared for my next opportunity. Jim and I debriefed on what had happened, and came to the conclusion that there were two areas we needed to concentrate on—putting (naturally), and trying to spin the ball a heck of a lot more than I did.

Now when I say spin, I don't just mean backspin. I mean imparting forces upon the golf ball that curve it at all levels to the right and left, as well as either getting the ball to roll out or stop where I wanted it to land.

I had to wait eight more months to give it a go for one of the sub-USDT circuits. The one I chose was played in the summertime in Canada, and the top five from their Order of Merit (money list) moved up to the USDT for the following season.

I drew from my previous experience and qualified for the Canadian tour handily. Homesick, and living on a monk's budget, I played every event and garnered enough money to finish in the top forty on the money list.

This would have exempted me from having to pre-qualify for the USDT tour, but I was out of cash.

My placing did exempt me into Canada for the following year, which I made the most of by finishing in the sixth position on the money list. That exempted me into second stage of the USDT qualifying, where I crashed and burned, and ended up gearing up to play in Canada for a third straight year.

Are you sensing a pattern here? I was not yet twenty-one, and by all accounts I had achieved a good deal, but I had to take it a single step at a time.

And that's how I went around the board of life, a roll of the die that kept coming up number one.

By the time I was twenty-five, I had won a couple times on every tour, including the USDT, and was handed my PGA Tour card at a ceremony after the USDT finals. I had finished third on the money list on that tour that season, and that cemented my status as a member of the big show for the following season.

The first tournament was three weeks away when, on the day I was supposed to pack up the car and head north for that event, Jim collapsed in the driveway. His big heart had had enough, I suppose.

He didn't die. That just wasn't his way. He hung in there for four more months before the clock actually stopped.

It was a great time for us—a coda to the extraordinary symphony of his life. Everything from the peaks of his existence to the depth of his regrets were explored.

Out of the blue, Babe showed up. No one ever explained to me how she knew he was sick and approaching the end, but one day she walked into the hospital and asked to see him.

He was not pissed off, and I think her appearance—though initially confused as some kind of post-death hallucination—comforted him in the end.

She spent two hours alone with him, then emerged from the room with tearful eyes, which she dabbed dry with a logoed napkin from a Hawaiian airline. She shook my hand, smiled, and walked away.

For one of the only times in the years that I'd known him, he truly seemed at peace. The demons had disappeared, off to haunt other souls, as their presence had been exorcised by his late-in-life adherence to love, morality, and penitence.

After Babe departed, there were long moments where I sat at the edge of his bed and he just stared at me. There was no judgement. There would be momentary smiles as a thought or memory crossed his mind.

And then one afternoon, he raised his arm and presented me with his gnarled left hand. It took all of his effort, but he contracted those frozen joints to simulate a good-bye wave.

His labored breathing, ever increasing, began to soften, and he died inside of the next minute.

I sat there in stunned silence for at least an hour. A nurse on rotation entered the room, surveyed the situation, tapped me on the shoulder, and told me that they would need to remove him and prepare the room for the next person.

I nodded and walked out into the hallway. That was the last time I saw my father. I did not express any emotion. I drove back to SVMGC and hit balls until sunset. I told everyone who knew him the next day that he was gone.

In the end, I was left confused, untethered, and angry.

My confusion was rooted in the realization that for the first time in nearly fifteen years, I was without something or someone that I could call family. I'd been on my own playing all around North America for the last five years, but that was for my job. Each week there was a new motel in a new city, and not one of those places ever evoked the feelings of what I would call, "home."

For the first time, there were no filial reins on me and that was discomfiting. I had to develop routines to stay grounded during the next couple of weeks.

And selfishly, I was miffed that I had missed the first four months of the tour schedule. I hung around for just long enough to get my game in some sort of shape before heading east to catch up with the traveling carnival.

I ended up being tried and convicted in Missouri only three months after I illegally buried his urn by the sixteenth tee at SVMGC, a downhill par three that was the high spot of the course.

All those feelings aside, Jim would have understood my predicament—the folly of one's life and all, but he probably would not have communicated that to me. He would have wanted for me to figure it all out, and to gain whatever wisdom there was to be gleaned.

I have still not understood most truths, and I was pretty sure that I was bound to stay ignorant until they let me out of my interminable confinement.

17

The end to my time at the W.M.D.C.C. came so quickly that I didn't even realize it was happening.

I had just wrapped up the second of the *Avenues to Change* class sequences that I had helped Ned instruct. I was heading back to my unit when a voice barked at me from the other end of the hall.

"Dawson?"

I spun around to see a flunky administrator walking toward me with an overstuffed Manila envelope in his hands.

"You're Dawson, right?"

"Yeah."

"Congratulations, I guess," he said as he handed over the envelope.

I held the bulky item in my arms like a newborn as he turned on his heels and headed back toward the end of the hall. He moved briskly, obviously out of place and desirous of the safety that the security door supplied.

I entered my unit and was waved to the second door by Cappy, with a flaccid nod. There was no acknowledgement of the package in my hands. I could've been carrying a pipe bomb and he wouldn't have noticed.

When I got to my cell, I finally looked down at the addressee. There was my name as the recipient and a red stamp from the Missouri State Parole Board in the upper left corner.

I think I might have said, "Holy shit," at that point, and I know my heart began to race like few times before.

It was as advertised—the paperwork granting me parole from the Missouri state prison system. I checked for authenticity and leafed to the last page. Above the straight lines designated for their placement were the signatures of the president of the board and the dang governor of the state.

I had ten days to get my head together. The rush of anxiety was visceral. There were things to do before my departure; number one on the list was squaring away the situation with Sally's future.

We met at our usual communal space, the picnic table down on the main floor of our unit. I was not going to waste time talking about me, but Sally knew something was up.

"I want you to talk to the woman who has been representing me for the parole stuff. She seems to know this system pretty well. She can help you with where they keep you," I began.

"Why, did something happen?" Sally asked.

I just shrugged off the question. The gap between her two front teeth was revealed as she offered a rare smile. She was on to me, but I plowed ahead anyway.

"I think she can help," I repeated.

"I don't need any more lawyers, Chunk. I got more than I need right now. I got three who have argued in front of the U.S. Supreme Court, and my guess is they are all angling to try to do it again with my case. What I'm trying to get them to understand is that I don't want them to feel that they have to be the ones who have to lose so the case can move up the chain. That's what terrifies me, dear. If they throw me into the general male population while they bat the decision around the various courts, I won't survive for long."

"What if the other option is just to stay here for the length of your term? What if I can teach you the basics of what I've done to help the poor fellow who is teaching the cognitive behavior course here? Maybe you could fill in for me after they let me out."

"That sounds like fun," she said with a roll of her eyes.

"Perhaps they would just house you here because it's so close," I offered.

She laughed at that.

"You forget that my status is a hell of a lot different than yours. You don't need to be shackled just to leave our unit and enter the hall. I do."

She was right about that. There definitely was a different vibe about her than anyone else on our block, and it wasn't just because of the issues with her gender identification. Everyone in the Missouri system of justice saw her as a hardened criminal.

"And besides, it's not like they're ever going to shorten my stretch or put me on a glide path toward my release. My case is not about that. I'm not getting out before my time. My case is only about where I want to be housed," she added.

There was truth there. I moved to another item of interest and asked a question that had been in the back of my mind for a while, one that she had sloughed off on numerous occasions.

"So are you going to tell me about this girlfriend you mentioned before?"

She blushed, but it was clearly not out of embarrassment.

"What do you want to know?" she asked.

That was a genuine first. She had never offered anything in my previous inquiries about the subject. I almost croaked out my first question.

"Was it before you were . . ."

"Me?"

"Uh, you know, before . . ."

"No."

She mercifully cut me off before I could stumble out the next question.

"Have you ever heard me talk about male attractiveness?" she asked.

"Uh, no."

"And why is that, do you think?"

Oh, boy. Questions like those were well above my pay grade.

"Cause, uh, you have high standards and no one you've met can meet them?"

She started to laugh, and I mean really, really laugh. She fell from her seat and rolled on the floor. There was snot coming out of her nose and rivulets of tears streaming from her eyes. I saw Cappy get up from his chair. He leveled a vacant stare at her through his office window.

I tried to get her to stop, but she just couldn't. It was one of the most absurd things I'd ever seen.

At last, she became composed enough to return to the table, but it still took her a long time to be able to speak more than two words without busting up all over again.

"God, I needed that, Chunk. I haven't laughed like that for a decade, at least," she sputtered.

I just sat there as she threw all her effort behind trying to compose herself. She eventually took a couple of really deep breaths, and resumed her explanation.

"Look, it's probably best that I don't ask you anymore questions," she said with giggle.

"That sounds like a solid policy," I said.

"So here's the deal. No offense to you, but I hate everything about men. Everything. I hated being one, and I certainly hated dealing with them in any capacity. That eventually translated to an understanding that I could no longer live as one. But you see, as a former member of the male population, I had been attracted to women like many of you for a whole set of reasons. I was curious about their habits, and also interested in the sexual stuff from a hormonal standpoint. Years of therapy revealed a whole hell of a lot of issues like envy, longing, and the need to be inside the thing I wanted the most in the world."

That last statement caused me to blush, but it was out of embarrassment this time.

"Sorry, I keep forgetting that you're a virgin."

"I am not," I said.

"In fact, what you can call me is a transgender lesbian. That gives me two of the four of that initialization. You can cross off the B and the G with extreme prejudice, unless the G is under the category of the L."

I started to think about what this meant in terms of the nature of her incarceration. There were only two options that would be satisfactory then; the third—the one she had been threatened with—was unthinkable.

Yeah, she was a convicted bank robbing, super-felon, who had terrorized more than a score of lowly paid tellers at the various branches she had knocked off. Who should give a damn where the hell she ended up serving her debt to society?

Me, I guess.

"I think I'm understanding what you're saying," I said.

"I hope so. It's pretty clear. Just don't mention it to anyone, including your lady lawyer."

"Why?" I asked.

"The last thing I want is to have anyone form an opinion that I actually want something for reasons other than what I've stated. I want to be housed with females because that is who I am. I don't want anyone to think that there is an ulterior motive linked to my preferences."

"I won't say anything," I said.

"Thanks. I think that's the best path," she said.

She knew something was up with me. She made a motion with her hands like it was time to give it up.

"I got my parole papers," I said.

"I knew it! You are a sorry poker player, Chunk," she said as she clapped her hands in glee.

"Ten days from today, the fifth."

She jumped up from the table and started pacing nearby. I saw Cappy raise his head for a second, but for now, he didn't seem interested in trying to restrain her.

"Where's your paperwork?" she asked.

"In my room," I said.

"Well, get it. I'll help you fill it out. There is this whole section about salient factors that is intended to inform them about your release. We are going to have fun with that one."

'Why?"

"Cause it's a bunch of questions about whether you are going to be a recidivist, or drug user, or buy weapons upon your release. You might be the first con to ever answer those questions truthfully. Also, did you get any information about the level of supervision you are going to be required to have? That could really screw you. You've got to ask your lady lawyer to try to get you supervised in California. You don't want to have to stay in this state any longer than it takes to get to the bus station."

It was as if she were getting released. I got the envelope. There were mounds of forms and questionnaires. For a second, I thought that ten days might not be enough time to complete it all.

Seven days out, I got a message from Deidre that I should call her when I had the opportunity. I scheduled a time that fit with her schedule and informed Cappy.

He escorted me to the phone when the time came.

"So, they're letting you out?" he asked.

"Apparently."

"You going to go back to playing golf?"

"I've got nothing else, really."

He nodded, while biting the inside of his cheek.

Deidre was fairly excited on the other end of the call.

"I'm telling you, Chuck, this never happens," she said with a giddy lilt.

"I wouldn't know."

"Of course, why would you? So, here's the deal. A week from now, you will wake up to find some of your personal items have been staged with your attendants. These will likely be some clothing and whatever you had on you when they took you to begin your sentence."

"Oh god," I said, "I think I'd rather wear the denim and shirt on issue. That suit is an absolute jinx. I don't even know if I'd fit in it."

"Have you gotten bigger or smaller while you've been in there?" she asked.

"Most of what I'd built through training is likely gone, so smaller, I guess. I don't know. I haven't thought about strength stuff, just trying to maintain flexibility."

"Did you have any money when you turned in your stuff?"

"Maybe a hundred bucks."

"Have you drawn from your prison account for the work you did here?"

"Toothpaste, and stuff like that."

"So, there might be something there."

"Yeah, I guess. It isn't a fortune."

"The state will provide you with a bus ticket."

"To California?" I asked hopefully.

"No. But you might be able to get as far as Dallas, and from there you can get anywhere."

"All right, I guess that's something."

"And speaking of leaving the state, because of your profession, Missouri is going to allow you to finish your parole without having to remain in the state. They'll assign a proxy officer in California. You'll have to pay for that."

"For how long?" I asked.

"For sure a year, maybe longer. It's up to them. In my experience, they always let the time lag. The proxies and the state like the steady paycheck."

"How much?"

"There will be an interstate transfer fee and then around a hundred bucks a month to Missouri, and fifty or so a week to the proxy."

"Oh, that's not too bad."

"Are you going to have trouble coming up with that?"

"I should have four plus years of rental income from my condo in an escrow account. I'll be fine there."

"Well, all right. I'm very happy for you, Chuck. It's always a pleasure for me when things work out. I can't say that is normal in my life and work, but it is pretty cool when it actually happens. If you ever need me for anything, you've always got my number."

"Thanks, Deidre."

We both went silent. I don't know if she had more to say, or if there should have been some other type of response coming from my end, but I just wanted to hear her breathe for a little bit. I really wanted to have that as a memory. It probably went on for nearly a minute.

"Anything else?" she asked.

There was, but I chickened out. I waited to hear another breath.

"No, thanks again. Thanks again for all you have done."

"So long, Chuck."

"Bye."

And the line went dead for a moment before it buzzed, and a mechanical voice asked, "Have you completed your call? If so, please hang up and exit the area. There are likely others who are waiting on line."

I hung up the phone. That was that.

The day was at hand. I had not slept much the previous night. I might have actually gotten to the back nine at Kiama at some point, but then my thoughts went to so many other things.

Bleary-eyed, I got up, put on my uniform, and sat on the edge of the ratty mattress that was supported by a fifty-year-old concrete platform.

It was last call for that ten by eight-foot space. Like that moment with Deidre the week before, where I commanded myself to try to remember the tone and timing of her respiration, I attempted to memorize every bit of my surroundings.

There was a method in play here and it had to do with something that Shorty had told me on my very first day.

"You need to see it all, son," he said, "you need to take this whole thing into your soul because one day you are going to walk back out that there door, and the last thing you want to do is forget that you were ever in here."

I had thought it was a little pushy at the time. We'd just met. I was freaked out to begin with and this giant string bean with a chemo-suppressed hairline was ordering me to begin some type of philosophical journey.

"Pay attention," he commanded.

To what? The competing realities of four to five years of inertial stasis versus my lustful desires to get back to trying to get a little ball to travel four hundred and fifty yards into a four and a quarter inch diameter hole in the fewest amount of strikes possible?

Was this the wisdom I was supposed to attain?

Sitting in my cell on that last day, I finally got what Shorty was trying to tell me.

Pay attention.

This had surely been an issue for me. Every therapist, sitter, "parent," or teacher had demanded that I perform that task. At the time, I resisted their requests with all my might.

Even Jim had to break through that wall. He had to remind me that awareness was a vital part of everything that went into playing the game we loved. He often said that was the biggest takeaway from his moments spent observing Hogan; that extraordinary deference to detail that only existed if one noticed everything around them.

Sally broke my reverie.

"What are you doing?" she asked.

"Cataloging these surroundings."

"Why?"

"Something that Shorty said about paying attention. He

told me when we first met that you could get lost in here and not find your way back home."

"Words of a sage," Sally said soberly.

"Yeah," I concurred.

She handed me a scrap of paper from one of the golf magazines that Deidre had given to me. It was a tear-out insert that one could mail in to get more information about some product. There was scribbling all over it. I had to squint a little to find a long string of numbers.

"What's this?"

She stepped back onto the row to make sure there was no one who could possibly be eavesdropping.

"This is a very crude code. Add one number to each existing number. Zero becomes one, one becomes two, two becomes three, nine becomes zero, get it?"

"I guess."

"Then group the numbers together into six numeral segments starting at the beginning, and finishing at the end, okay?"

"What is this?"

"Just listen; create these six numeral segments."

"Now?"

"No, not now. Did I say do it now?"

"I'm just trying to keep up."

"Place a decimal after the first two numerals of each one, okay? Then place another after the next two numerals of each one. You should end up with six sequences of six numerals each, each with two decimals."

She checked outside again.

"Now take the first two sequences and put a minus sign between them. Then do the same to the other two. You should have a number that starts like three seven, or maybe three eight or nine. After the minus sign, that next group will start with a nine. That will be true for all three."

"Are you going to tell me why I'm supposed to do this?" I asked.

"Repeat what I just told you."

I did, to the best of my ability. I was probably listening more at the end than in the beginning, so I screwed up the first step of adding one number to the existing one.

"Start again," she said after I realized I'd screwed it up.

I repeated the whole deal a second time and got it right.

"One more time."

"Really?"

"Just do it, Chunk."

I did, got it right, and she nodded her approval.

"Are you going to tell me what this is?" I asked in exasperation.

"Shush now, dear, and listen very carefully. Each one of those numerical sequences, all three, are the longitudes and latitudes of specific locations here in Missouri. I would suggest that you don't try to visit them for a few months or so, but that is up to you and your needs."

"What are you talking about?"

One last look into the hall prefaced her explanation.

"You're likely strapped, and I will never get the opportunity unless something very, very strange happens. At each one of those locations, all public places, exactly three feet down is buried a bundle that contains ten thousand totally clean dollars."

I gasped.

"I want you to have it to further your life since mine is pretty much over. We can call it an inheritance. Not a lot in the scheme of things, but something."

"No," I stated flatly, "I mean thanks, but I don't want your money."

"Don't worry. I have way more than that. Go get it. It's a gift. I would feel so much better. Please."

"No, thank you, Sally, but I won't be digging up any money. And I'm not likely to ever set foot in this state again once my bus crosses the state line."

I handed her back the mail-in card. She took it and stared at it.

"But I did so much work," she said with a sigh.

"Someone else will come along. You might be able to give it to them at some point. Maybe after you get that transfer to Chillicothe or Crossroads."

"Missouri ain't inviting me to any of their women's facilities, Chunk."

"You have no way of knowing that."

She smiled. We both knew how slim the chances were. As that gapped tooth smile faded, she tore the insert in two.

"Shit, I pretty much figured you'd say no. Rules of golf, right?"

"Yeah, pretty much. Don't worry, Sally, I'll figure it out somehow. I've gotten this far."

"If you want to write, you can," she said.

"As soon as I get home, I will. Then you'll have my address."

Cappy appeared at the threshold completely out of breath from the one flight climb.

"You ready, Dawson?"

"Yes, sir."

"Well, let's get you processed out then."

I nodded, rose up from that platform for the last time and headed for the door. Sally grabbed me as I walked past and enveloped me in a hug. She was strong. My lungs nearly collapsed. Cappy let it happen.

"Hit 'em far and straight, Chunk," she said as we unclasped.

"Haven't you heard," I said, "it's either coming from the right or left, but never, ever straight."

She laughed. I'd told her the story of Jim and me at tour school that first time.

"What the fuck are you talking about?" Cappy asked.

"Nothing. Inside joke, sir," I said.

In contrast to my earlier adherence to Shorty's emotional retention regimen, I did not turn around once I vectored to the exit. I did not want to see Sally's response. Either emotive or placid, it made no difference. Both would hit me on a level that I was only beginning to experience. I did not want to venture there when freedom was my paramount motivation.

We passed through the groups of doors that led into the special unit and entered the hall where a right turn would have taken me back to the classroom where I'd spent the last five months helping Ned teach my fellow convicts.

We took the left, the same direction I had taken on the day of my parole hearing. The day I had met Deidre on the monitor.

We passed into another set of doors on the right, similar to the two sets that led into our special unit.

I handed over my paperwork. My identity was verified three times via a visual description, obvious questions like birthdate and social security number, and finally by a biometric thumbprint scanner. I marveled at the new technology. That seemed to annoy the clerk who was responsible for checking me out.

"Sign this," he commanded.

I did without really knowing what I was putting my signature to.

Cappy entered from the hallway and handed me a zippered bag with some of the things that I had turned in at the commencement of my sentence.

There was a handful of change, my wallet that had a little over ninety bucks in it, as well as two expired credit cards.

There was a set of keys to all the various locks that had once existed in my life. Crushed inside a mylar bag was the suit I'd worn on my last day in court. Actually, it was the suit I'd worn every day in court, as golf drag was not considered to be appropriate attire by my legal eagles.

"You can change over there," the clerk said pointing to an anteroom.

"Where do I turn in my stuff?"

I was referring to the prison garb, underwear, shoes, and

towel. The last three I was still holding in a bundle wrapped with my denim jacket.

"Not to me."

He turned away from the window and rolled back to his desk. Another guard came over to him and handed him another package. He frowned and quickly looked up to me just as I was about to turn away.

"Hey, Dawson!"

"Yes, sir?" I replied.

"This just came for you!"

I heard his message through the vents of the tiny speaker hole.

"Ah shit, I'll get it," Cappy said.

He returned with the package, a flattish box like something you might find in a department store.

"I'll need to watch you open it," Cappy said.

I was pretty sure it had already been opened. I used my thumb to slit the tape that had been hastily slapped back on to hold the top to the bottom.

Inside was a card addressed to *Charles.*

I hope they fit. Congratulations. Enjoy your life, read an inscription on the card. It was signed, *Deidre.*

All I could think about was the unpigmented iris in that one eye. My heart skipped a little bit, something that felt strange, but a little wonderful.

Nestled below where the card had been were a pair of shorts, a belt, and a shirt from one of the boutique golf apparel companies.

I wouldn't have need for that suit. I entered the anteroom, changed into my new duds, and turned in my requisitioned gear to the attendant.

"Here you go, two pairs of pants, two pairs of underwear (I was wearing one), two T-shirts, one jacket, two pairs of socks (I was wearing one pair), one sheet, one pillowcase, one blanket, one pillow, one towel, one washcloth, and one laundry bag."

The attendant could only offer a grunt.

"What about my shoes?" I asked.

"What about them?"

"Do I need to turn them in?"

He looked over the counter to survey my over worn sneakers.

"When did they issue those to you?"

"God, had to be a couple of years now."

"Nah, you can keep them," he said as he gathered my other things and threw them in a barrel. I wondered who was going to get to wear that stuff next. He made some check marks on a piece of paper, smacked it emphatically with a stamp, and handed it to me.

"Give this to the discharge guy."

"Okay, thanks."

He did not acknowledgement my politeness.

I headed back to Cappy and the clerk sporting Deidre's gift. The feel of the fabric on my skin was so foreign. I felt like I wasn't wearing anything at all. I'd had no idea that I had spent the last four plus years feeling so much discomfort at every waking hour.

Cappy almost smiled when he saw me emerge. I handed the

paper to the discharge guy. He had me sign more forms and give my thumbprint a couple more times on that scanner. Finally, he slipped me a thin envelope through a slot.

"You're done," was all he said as he turned away again.

I stood there with the mylar bag and the envelope, not knowing what to do next.

"Get out of here, Dawson," Cappy said.

I wanted to obey him, like always, but I wasn't sure what I was supposed to do.

"Uh," I stammered.

"Walk out the door, dipshit. Right there. Turn the handle and walk out the door."

He stood there waiting with the same sourpuss look that he always sported.

I did as he said, turned away without a closing salutation, turned the handle to the left, felt the cylinder actually give, and released the door.

The rush of cold morning air hit my face first and I immediately knew I would always remember that tingle, regardless of my adherence to Shorty's demand or not.

I was on a side street just to the west of the prison. There were a couple of cabs down at the corner, and I figured that one of them could either take me or point the way to the nearest bus station.

I opened the envelope that the clerk had given me; two slips of paper were tucked inside. One was a voucher for a bus trip that was worth one hundred and fifty dollars.

The other piece of paper was kind of unexpected. It was a

check with a net value of four hundred and seven dollars issued by the state of Missouri. My accumulated employee compensation from the state for all of the days that I was incarcerated, minus the withholding taxes.

Like I'd told Deidre, I had used some of what was in the account to buy a few essentials along the way, but I had no idea that I had amassed such a fortune.

Missouri inmates earn about thirty-five cents a day for being in the can, regardless of whether you end up doing any actual work, apparently. I did some kitchen stuff when I first got there, but later my duties were confined to our cellblock and keeping it clean.

There was no extra compensation for helping Ned teach.

I started to walk over to the cabstand.

As I approached, I heard a familiar noise from off in the distance. It was the unmistakable sound of the old two cycle gas engines that powered the maintenance carts around SVMGC. They were the kind that would stutter to life and shutter to silence as the throttle was applied and withdrawn. It had been so long since I'd heard anything that resembled traffic, let alone life on the outside, but this specific timbre was etched in my memory.

One of those carts appeared at the end of the road. It made a beeline toward me. I stopped to watch it fly past. Behind the wheel was a younger man, maybe twenty-five or so, dressed in an outfit that was not dissimilar to the one I was wearing.

He released the gas pedal, the cart shut down, and came to a stop.

"Mr. Dawson?" he inquired.

"Uh, yeah?"

"Great. I'm Brady Wisch. I'm the assistant pro at Kiama and I'd like to invite you to come play a round with me this fine morning."

"Um, what?" I asked.

"My name is Brady. I'm one of the assistants to Kurt Longley, the head pro, across the street at Kiama Golf and Country Club?

"Uh, huh," I said in a fog.

"It's Monday, the course is closed to the membership and your lawyer thought it might be fun for you to get right back on the horse if you know what I mean," he said with a smile.

"I don't have any sticks. Wait a minute, Deidre set this up?"

"Miss Agugie . . . , Agugli . . ."

"Agugliero?"

"Yeah, that's it. She called my boss, Mr. Longley, and asked if it was a possibility. It's his day off, but I would love to play. Monday's my only day, you know. We keep the course open for the policemen and the firefighters, who get to play for free, but they're pretty terrible. To get to play with a touring pro would be a treat for me. And don't worry about the equipment. I've got you all set up. Are you up for it?"

It all seemed so odd. It was like a dream or something, or a stupid movie. I only thought about it for another second.

"Absolutely," I said.

"Hop on in."

I did, and we drove around the corner and up the street to the member's entrance of Kiama Golf and Country Club.

19

The round at Kiama was memorable, though not because of the play of either of us—Brady was a long way from being a competitive player.

No, what was great was the lively conversation, the feel of turf beneath my feet for the first time in over four years, and the aromas of fertilizer and fetid irrigation water that filled my senses with notes of home.

It was also a reset on some of the things I had missed over the last couple of years. Brady was a font of knowledge and he jabbered on about advances in technology and how the USGA and the Royal and Ancient had recently changed a few of the rules.

The range was closed, so we headed straight for the first tee. We both swung a couple of clubs to get warm. My hands found their home on the grips like a grandma holds her grand toddler's hand.

Brady had supplied me with a glove. The naturalness with which I slipped it on did not surprise me. Even with the hiatus, I'd had my left hand cloaked for more hours of the day than not in my life.

We waited for the green to clear of the threesome of paramedics, who were quickly putting out with the flagstick in the hole.

"That's a new rule," Brady said.

"What?"

"You can leave the stick in when you putt."

"Really?"

"Pace of play, pardsy. There's a whole bunch of changes. Did you know there is no penalty for a double hit?"

"What?"

"Yeah, you just play it from where it ends up. No penalty shot."

A double hit happens when you strike a ball twice during a single stroke. I'd been in a position to snag my first USDT victory when I double hit a flop shot out of grass bunker on the seventy-second hole of a tournament in Utah. That penalty had put me one shot out of a playoff for the title.

"Wow," I said.

I motioned to Brady to play away, and he hit a soft six iron down to the flat part of the fairway.

Seeing the hole in the flesh for the first time, I was amazed at how closely I had recreated it in my mind. It was a gentle starter, a downhill par four at 362 yards from the tees we were playing.

When I'd played the hole from the bed in my cell, I'd always imagined myself hitting driver into the front bunker, especially if the flag were positioned toward the back of the green.

I pulled out the big club, an oversized headed beast that reminded me of the plastic one of my youth.

I decided to hit a low cut and erase the half of the hole that had an out of bounds fence on the left.

That this was my first thought probably shows the level of arrogance that was both a blessing and curse in my sporting life. I hadn't stepped onto a golf course, let alone taken a full swing at a golf ball, in nearly five years.

I weakened my left hand a bit, took the club back a little on the outside and held the face open on contact.

I hit it squarely and the ball jumped off the club and flew straight over that fence onto the road that led to the maintenance area.

"Double cross," Brady opined.

"Yeah," I said with a laugh.

I reached to grab another ball.

"Forget it. You can play it from where it went out."

"No, I can't. I'm hitting three here. That was a one, and this is a four," I announced, holding up the ball for Brady to confirm the identifying number.

"Another new rule." he said, "They aren't going to do it for pro tournaments, but clubs are now allowed to institute a local rule that does away with stroke and distance. You take your relief down there where you went out. And, yeah, you lie three."

I didn't know what to say; that was sacrilege to me. Stroke

and distance was one of the most important applications of the rules of golf in my mind. Only cheaters played a lost ball or out of bounds as a two-stroke lateral penalty. But Brady had already jumped into the cart. He pulled up to the tee just as another group of first responders crested the hill to start their round.

"Let's go, pro," he said.

I climbed in and we were off.

Brady hit a sand wedge onto the lower level of the green, stuffed his club back in his bag, and drove us over to the area where I could take my relief. It was just short of being even with the bunker I had been trying to hit the ball into, but at an angle to the flag that squeezed the approach possibilities to hitting it to where Brady had played to, or way left of the flag on another tier.

"Well, I kind of screwed myself here," I said.

"Yeah, I was wondering why you were hitting driver. There is no real benefit to that unless you can get it in the front bunker."

"That's what I was trying to do. What's behind the hole?" I asked.

"Certain death. There's a big drop off into the trees."

I nodded, but decided to try to hit it on the upper tier anyway. Of course, I hit it a little too hard, with little spin coming from the rough, and the ball bounced off the back and into the oblivion that Brady had warned me to avoid.

I dropped behind the green, but the slope back down to the flag was so severe that the best I could do was barely keep it on the very front edge. I three-jacked it from there for a nice, big, fat, ten.

God, it was great to be out of jail and alive.

And that's kind of how the first nine went. I made a couple of pars and some other big numbers when I played the stupid shots that I had dreamed up in my cell during the multiple times my mind had ventured there.

The cool of the morning had eased, and in the end, it turned out that I was dressed perfectly. By the time we made the turn, I was hitting it pretty good.

I luckily dropped a thirty-five foot putt on eighteen for my lone birdie.

"The restaurant here is closed today," Brady said, "but we could grab a burger or something at the shack down the road."

"No offense, Brady, but I think I just want to head out and start my journey home, if that's all right."

"Sure, I have a car. Where do you want me to drop you?"

"A ride to the bus station in St. Joseph would be much appreciated," I said.

"Done," he replied.

"You wouldn't have an extra copy of the latest rule book?"

"Got one in my bag you can have," he said.

"That would be great."

Brady reached into the side pocket of his bag and pulled out the five and a half-inch by four-inch booklet that I expected to entertain me on my trip. He then drove into the cart shack and reemerged with a couple of Cokes.

"Let's hit it, pardsy. Did you have fun?"

"Yeah. I'm very grateful," I said.

"Well, you can thank that lady lawyer.."

I called Deidre from the decrepit pay phone in the lobby of the bus station, a single-story brick ruin on a dusty street a couple of blocks from the Missouri River.

Her voicemail picked up, and I hesitated before hanging up. In the moment, I swore to myself that I would call her back when we could actually speak. At least that's how I saw it at the time.

The bus crossed the Missouri state line a little over an hour into the trip. We were on U.S. I-35 heading for Texas by bisecting Oklahoma. I read the rule book for the first half-hour of the trip before I fell deeply asleep, lulled by the hum of the tires on the road, and the absolute blandness of the vistas that the Sooner State provided.

It was some sixteen hours to Dallas, and another little bit to make it to Fort Worth. I paid the extra sixteen bucks to have the trip end there.

I arrived at noon and could tell that my luck with the weather was about to run out. An icy rain was in the forecast, and the shorts and polo shirt were not going to be sufficient armor to shield me.

I ducked into a thrift shop just as the first drops began to fall, bought some old jeans, a soft flannel shirt, and some type of military parka. The whole outfit ran to just under twenty dollars.

I also bought a small duffel bag to house the clothing I had been gifted by Deidre. I donated my suit to charity. The old lady who ran the entire concession for her church rang me up.

I had formulated a plan to gather the funds to get me back to

California. My first dilemma was that I had to cash my Missouri prison separation check without a valid ID or a current bank account. The only option that made sense was to endorse the check to a third party and have them cash it for me.

As harebrained as it sounded, my plan involved getting to Fort Worth and looking up the biggest star I knew in golf—Gary Houston, the stud who blitzed me in the U.S. Junior Am way back when I was fourteen.

Through those junior years, we would run into each other at this tournament or the other, and later we teamed up as partners to try to qualify for the USGA Four Ball Championships.

Jim had become friendly with Gary's dad after we first faced off, and they had gotten the idea to have us give it a go. Gary was seventeen and had committed to enter Oklahoma State on a full ride. I was the current fourteen to sixteen-year-old Junior World champ.

The odds were astronomical of making the final field of a hundred twenty-eight sides of two, and we would have been the youngest pair to ever compete if we'd made it.

We finished in a three-way tie for fourth at the qualifier and had a brief playoff for an alternate position that we lost when one of our opponents holed out for eagle on the first playoff hole. It was fun, and we vowed to do it again, though we never did.

We didn't know it at the time, but neither Jim nor Gary's dad thought we had a chance in hell. They just wanted us to get a chance to play at Stone Beach, the host course for the qualifier, under USGA tournament conditions, and not have to pay the ridiculous cost of the green fee.

That ended up paying off for me when I won the California Amateur up there the following year.

Gary ended up becoming a two-time All-American at Okie State and was a vital part of the team that beat Coach Zantz's team in the NCAA finals his freshman year. Coach Z began his magical run only after Gary turned pro the summer before what would have been his junior year.

He'd dominated tour school and was promoted to the big show after winning three USDT events in his first five months.

At the time of my release from prison, he was the reigning Master's and PGA Champion. He also owned a restaurant with his non-golfing brother in Fort Worth.

We'd not seen each other in forever, but I was certain he would help me out by serving as my proxy in the cashing of the check.

There was this odd shame I felt about presenting myself as such a supreme fuck-up to this man who, though once a peer, was now an icon of worldwide renown. From what I knew about him, there would be no judgment as to my predicament. My memory was: I'd hit a few squirrelly shots during our one round as partners, and he was never less than upbeat and encouraging. I actually made the birdie on eighteen that got us into the alternate playoff, and he was just as excited for me as if he had made it himself.

His brother's restaurant was called "Downtown" and it was eponymous for its geographic location, which was smack dab in the center of a revitalized portion of Fort Worth.

I didn't think Gary would be there, but I was certainly

hoping his brother would be and I felt certain I could convince him that I was who I said I was.

I entered the business through the bar—an expansive room with a giant stone hearth that covered the entire wall. This was no roadhouse.

In the next room, presided over by a perky hostess, was a white tablecloth establishment, with warm yellow lights and a staff clad in crisp preppy outfits—pleasingly orderly and uniformly beautiful.

I was totally underdressed; I got that damp parka off my shoulders as quickly as if it had been lit on fire. I waited in the line at the hostess's podium as she finished with a couple in front of me.

"Good evening, sir. Do you have a reservation?" she asked, just as one of her underlings whispered in her ear about a table lingering too long after dessert. The hostess looked down at the monitor on her screen and produced a slight frown, before cheerily looking up at me again.

"No, I'm sorry, I don't have a reservation. I was wondering if Burt Houston was about?" I asked.

"And what is this regarding?"

"It's a personal matter. I'm an old friend of Gary's, and I'd just like to ask him a question if he's around."

"And your name is?"

"Charles Dawson, but Gary knows me as Chuck or maybe even Chunk," I said in exactly the way that I say things.

That is to say in a way that often makes people uncomfortable.

I could tell I was digging a bit of a trench every time I

opened my mouth. She called another woman over, and asked her, "Cass, can you take over for a moment?"

Cass did, and the hostess turned to me.

"Why don't you take a seat at the bar, Mr. Dawson? I'll find out if Mr. Houston has a moment."

I muttered a sheepish "Thanks," and took the stool over by where the bartender put up the drinks ordered by the dining room servers.

"Can I get you something, bud?" the bartender asked.

He waved to a server as he loaded an entire tray with goblets containing gelid banana daiquiris.

"No thank you. Maybe a glass of water?"

"Sure. Ice?"

"That would be great."

"Chuck?"

It was a voice trying to speak above the din of clinking glasses, adult contemporary alternative music, and the range of frequencies of human conversation. I looked around to find the source of the person trying to transcend it all. It was someone sitting at the bar.

Of all people, it was Babe.

"Oh my god, Babe?"

"Yes, sir. What are you doing here?"

"I could ask the same of you."

It had been nearly six years since I had seen her during Jim's last days. Though she would've been in her eighties by then, there was a teenager's twinkle in her eyes. It was the look that had so entranced Jim.

She had three fingers of bourbon in a rocks glass, and was sitting three people away between a guy in a suit and his much younger date. The date's purse was bigger than the dress she had on.

"Hey there, pal," Babe said to the guy in the suit, "could I get you to move down a seat? I'd like to sit next to my friend."

He obliged, as did his date, and Babe stood up and walked confidently over to take the stool to my left.

"All right, Chuck, it appears that we both have some type of epic story to tell. Should we get a table and have a little dinner?" she asked.

"I'm not really dressed for the dining room."

"Nonsense."

She turned and motioned over to whoever was currently manning the hostess station. The substitute hostess rushed over.

"Yes, Mrs. Wellington?"

I realized for the first time that either she had never remarried or decided to retain Jim's name to this day.

"Could you find us a table for two? Something quiet?"

"Yes, of course, ma'am."

She exited as the perky hostess strode up to us.

"I'm sorry, Mr. Dawson, but Mr. Houston is not available at this time," she said.

"That's all right. I was just taking a shot in the dark. Thanks for trying to find him."

"What do you mean he's not here? I saw Burt in the bar not half an hour ago," Babe piped up.

I was hoping that Babe wouldn't get into it. It was kind of a stupid idea to begin with and the poor hostess looked flustered that Babe had contradicted her.

"I think he must have run out for some reason, Mrs. Wellington," she said.

The other hostess arrived with a pair of large leather-clad menus and a wine list the size of an old phone book.

"Your table is ready, Mrs. Wellington."

"Thank you. Come along, Chuck."

Babe and I spent the next hour giving each other condensed versions of the six years that had passed since Jim's death.

For her part, she had returned to the Big Island for a spell, but when her brother died, she realized that she was the only member of the Greene family who had a wit of knowledge about the family business.

Tucker's kids had passed on taking over, so Babe returned to the colonial mansion, pulled the heavy drapes off the leaded glass windows, and moved back in lock, stock, and barrel.

The car business certainly wasn't what it had been during the last century, but she kept the company and its work force together amidst the chaos of changing tastes and financial vagaries.

In a way, I guess it was quintessential Babe. She was always going to go left if she was expected to turn right.

She'd lived in caves in Greece and huts in the rain forests of Ecuador, but those days were behind her, she claimed.

My story was a little shorter. I sketched out my act of

criminality and the years of my confinement. I also spoke a fair amount about Jim, and that combined with the bottle of wine she drank caused her eyes to mist over right about the time that Burt Houston obsequiously showed up at our table.

The subject of the cashing of the check never came up with Burt. I had pivoted and substituted some baloney about just passing through town and wanting him to tell his brother and his father that I wanted to say hello.

Burt bought it. He probably would never offer my salutations, but if he ever did, Gary would surely fill him in on what had happened to me. The gossip at the time had swirled through all of the levels of the golf world, and most of the players were aware.

Babe readily agreed to cash my check when I asked her. She took me back to the mansion that night and installed me in her childhood bedroom.

A menagerie of stuffed animals stared, button-eyed, as I slumbered. When I awoke the next day, I felt a significant sense of panic related to my sudden displacement.

It took a while for me to emerge into the sunlit kitchen for a delicious breakfast that had been prepared by Babe's live-in caretaker, a middle-aged Latina named Alma.

It was the first time I'd slept on an actual bed or had a personal shower in half a decade, and all I was trying to do was stay in the moment and let it all happen in the way it was going to happen anyway.

Babe arrived, heavy-lidded, and went to the coffee pot.

"How'd you sleep, Charles?" she asked.

"Good, thanks."

She nodded.

"Let me know when you want to start the day."

"I'm at your mercy," I said.

"Hardly. That is the biggest fallacy told in this world. We all have free will, and its exercise is the only healthy way to live this crazy life."

Alma laughed.

"You know, Babe, that's something only rich people can say," Alma said.

Babe smiled in agreement.

"Yeah, but it sounded good."

She reached into her robe, and pulled out a pack of cigarettes and a lighter. She stepped out the back door and went about the yard smoking and refilling the bird feeders.

20

Babe had the whole day planned. She contacted the woman who did her travel and tasked her with doing the research on how to get me home to Southern California.

She also had her personal banker waiting for our arrival, so he could pay the funds on my check from the state of Missouri.

Babe had offered to just give me the cash (and likely more) from the large stash she kept around the house. I just wanted what I'd earned.

She tried to point out the silliness of my argument. She had plenty of money and it would be no strain on her. We jousted for a bit until she ceded to my position.

"Oh my god, Chuck, what did Jim do to you?" she asked.

"Taught me how to live with rules, I suppose."

"Of course, he did. He used to say things like that when we first had Benjamin. That he was grateful for golf because it taught him things like the value of honesty. That it made it easier to live without hating yourself so much."

Alma, the granddaughter of Babe's primary childhood nanny, was hanging about for that part of our conversation. She looked up from the kitchen sink.

"What's with all the darkness, Babe?" she asked.

"Ah you know, dear. I could never measure up to his expectations. And he wasn't the only one. My parents, this town, my son—it's why I ran as far away as I did, as fast as I could."

"Huh. I guess I didn't know him back then, but I never really felt that he put any expectations on me, except the ones where I proclaimed a desire to try to achieve something. And then, he would do everything he could to get me there," I said.

Babe burst into tears. It was just like an episode that Sally would have had and I was as perplexed as ever.

Alma went over to her and put her arms around her shoulders.

"Did you take your pills today, Babe?" she asked.

"No," Babe said with a whimper.

"Well, why don't you get that done, so we can get our guest here, Mr. Chuck, on his way home."

Babe nodded and left the room, but not before mouthing the words, "I'm so sorry" to me on her exit.

Alma just shrugged, smiled, and went back to her doings at the sink.

While at the bank, Babe got a call from her travel agent about the exact spelling of my name to match my ID. I guess I'd forgotten that getting on a plane was akin to getting into a clean room for the space program and I suddenly felt that my plan of getting back to San Diego on something other than a bus was probably a non-starter.

Babe had a solution, of course. We walked to the Tarrant County Sheriff's substation up the street where she ordered them to create some identification for me. The task was completed in a half-hour. She tracked down the Sheriff himself and had him contact someone at the airport to tell them to look out for me.

My flight was at 6:00 p.m. DFW to San Diego International with a stop in Phoenix.

All that was done by nine-thirty. We had the rest of the day to kill, so Babe drove her vintage Mustang Boss 302 around the town to show me where she and Jim came of age.

We slipped by their first house, the country club where they met, their high school, and had an early burger at Kincaid's.

Babe ordered a chocolate malt to go before she fired up the Mustang again. We headed west on I-20 and took the turn off for US-281 south.

I quizzed her on our next stop, but she remained tight lipped on that subject. On just about everything else she was an absolute chatterbox.

We stayed on the road for a good hour as she prattled on about her designs for the future.

She had already willed the house to Alma. She sketched out her plans for the Corny Greene vehicle empire, as well as the parameters of her funeral celebration. Highlights included a local high school band and fireworks.

The declaration of her desires exhausted, she got around to asking me a question. Of course, it had nothing to do with me.

"You must have formed a bit of an impression of me, right Chuck? I mean, I assume that Jim warned you about consorting with women who exhibited traits like mine."

The fishing pole was out. The line was cast. And I was certainly reluctant to bite.

The way I saw it, she was still looking for absolution for her sins of rejecting both her spouse and child.

Everyone else in the equation was dead. I felt no compunction to fill in the blanks for her since she'd certainly survived, even with all of that sadness and self-flagellation. What was the point?

She liked to hide behind the tough, independent Texas exterior with her pronounced drawl and wizened demeanor, but there must have been a tremendous fragility that she was determined to cover. I got the impression that she devoted most of her energy to keeping it under wraps. I think the pattern was that every time it was exposed, she fled.

She sat there demanding an answer. I attempted to be gentle.

"Jim blamed himself for most of what happened in his life. I can honestly say he never used your name in vain, or gave me the sense that you were responsible for his fate and destiny," I said.

That didn't seem to mollify her, and she pressed on.

"He once told me that he hated my guts," she said.

"That really seems out of character for the guy I knew."

"He did. He said that he hated me because he couldn't fix me," she said.

"I think he might have hated himself for feeling that he failed. He used to agonize at night about not being able to help someone with their game."

She got teary-eyed again. She had this story she had spun that kept her from jumping off a cliff and I was screwing up the flow of her narrative. I steered the conversation over to me.

"I will say that he fixed me, though. And I don't just mean the stuff having to do with golf," I said.

"He seemed to feel that you saved his life when I saw him that last time," she said in the timbre of a soft sob.

"I think we both saw it as the other way around, so it made for a great relationship. I surely miss him," I said.

I saw a sign flash by—"Visit the home of Dr. Pepper!" Was this the eventual destination of this excursion of nostalgia?

"So, where are we?" I asked.

"It's a place I've never been to, but it is a place that Jim would have wanted to visit," she said.

We left the hilly landscape and entered a small town. The sign said, "Welcome to Dublin, Texas, Population 3,762." My synapses lit up.

I didn't need to tell anyone the contents of the subtitle: "The boyhood home of the champion golfer Ben Hogan."

"Are we?" I asked.

"Yes," she said.

She pulled into the modest parking lot of the Ben Hogan Museum. Wow. It was fantastic; I will forever be grateful to her for taking me there. We were the only patrons that day.

The docent was a middle-aged native Dubliner.

At one point, I heard Babe gasp and point to a photograph on a wall covered with them.

I walked over to find her eyes welling up again, because the picture was one of Mr. Hogan on the range at Shady Oaks sometime during the era after the car accident.

Babe pointed to a slightly out-of-focus figure just to the left of the Hawk. It was a young man holding a bucket of ice in his left hand and a pretty healthy slug of some darkish liquid in a short squat glass in his right.

"Ah, yes, that's at Shady Oaks up in Fort Worth," the lady said.

"That little boy would grow up to be my husband and this young man's guardian," Babe announced, pointing it out for the docent.

I leaned in closer and sure enough, it was Jim—cleared eyed and in obvious awe of the great man lashing at a golf ball before him.

"Well, that's pretty special," the lady said.

"I don't suppose you have a copy of that, do you?" Babe asked.

"I don't think so, ma'am."

"Perhaps the negative is in an archive somewhere?"

"I'm not the person to ask."

"Well, I'll tell you what," Babe said with a full dose of all the gravitas that coursed within her, "if you could find that out, and you could print up another copy or two, or maybe digitize the one you have right here, I would be willing to make a big enough donation to make it worth everyone's while."

The woman was not offended. She walked back to the register by the gift shop and snagged a post-it and a pen.

"Write down your information, and I'll have someone get back to you," she said.

I wandered away to the area where they had examples of all the clubs that Hogan played through all of the different eras of his golfing life.

My very first adult irons was a set of Hogan Apex II's that Jim had been presented by the Hogan Company rep when he was at SVMGC. To this day, I still consider them the most beautiful golf clubs I have ever seen.

They were exacting blades with red painted numbers on the sole and the coolest silhouette of Mr. Hogan on the back of the clubface.

I didn't find them amongst all the sticks that were arrayed in the display, but I think I remember that they came out at about the time that Mr. Hogan passed, so he might not have ever played them in competition.

It was at that moment that a rush of anxiety swept through me. I was some forty hours out of confinement, and I had yet to feel my feet firmly on the ground. I needed to be around something familiar, to feel the comforting yoke of home. I sought out Babe.

"I think we should get to the airport," I said.

Everything worked out as it was supposed to. The airport employee that the sheriff had contacted met me on the street side of security and escorted me around all of the metal detectors and radar machines by flashing his badge at everyone who wore a uniform.

My temporary ID didn't come into play at all. I handed my boarding pass to the boarding agent, took my seat in the back of the crowded plane, and waited for that wheel's up moment.

Four hours later, the metabolites of two ginger ales and a mini bag of pretzels coursing through my bloodstream, we touched down on the short runway of San Diego International Airport.

I splurged for a taxi from the airport to a motel in the neighborhood close to Jim's condo and SVMGC.

The Jacaranda Motor Inn probably never had a heyday. It was built sometime in the 1950s and was the definitive example of a motor court hotel. I paid cash for two nights in advance. That about tapped me out.

I bought a couple of tacos from a place up the street and watched some old Master's highlights on the cheap motel TV.

I slept, if you can call it that, fitfully. The vertical plastic blinds on the windows brought about memories of the bars I had looked at for such a long time.

I turned on the overhead fan and produced enough of a current to get them to swirl in motion. The clashing of the rigid slats was a raucous sort of white noise that drowned out the drunks outside returning to their rooms after the bars closed.

I rose early and put on my thrift store clothes. There would be warmer temperatures later in the day, but I needed something to ward off the dense fog that typified southern California mornings at that time of year.

I walked the mile down the hill to Jim's condo and saw that the tenants who lived there were keeping the place in decent shape.

I crossed the country road that separated the city of Chula Vista and the county land of San Diego. I stood on the shoulder by the traffic light in almost the same exact spot that I had bolted from Taylor's car more than twenty years before.

It was still early enough that no one had made it to eighteen yet. I took the same path into the culvert and walked up the cart path to the green and on to the clubhouse that was just across the recently resurfaced parking lot.

I walked into the golf shop.

"Oh my god, look who has risen from the dead," said the voice of the head pro. "The Chunk skunk!"

"Hey, Josh," I said.

Josh moved out from behind the counter and offered his hand. I think he wanted to pull me in for a hug, but he knew as much as anyone that wasn't my thing.

"Hey brah, you good? When did they let you out?"

"A couple of days ago. I got to town last night."

"Oh dude, what a nightmare, huh?"

"Yeah. But it's over," I said.

I think I mentioned Josh Lee. He was the only other high school teammate of mine who could actually play some golf. He was second generation Korean, but spoke like a surf bum from Imperial Beach.

Josh played a little golf at the local junior college and then signed on to be Jim's assistant as my career began to take off. He went through all the apprentice stuff while I was in Canada. Jim got him ready for his play ability test that he passed breezily. In fact, under Jim's tutelage, he became a pretty good player, worlds away from his high school results.

The board of directors hired him as Jim's replacement after his death. I offered them my testimony that I felt confident that Josh would mirror all that Jim had been if they gave him the job. Looking around the shop and from what I'd seen of the track, I knew I'd been right.

"So, where are you going to live?" Josh asked.

"A question without an answer at the moment."

"You could always return to Jim's condo, right? He gave it to you."

"Yeah, but I don't plan on staying put for too long. Besides, that will be my only source of guaranteed income when I head back out."

"Well, you must have saved some cash from renting the place, huh?"

"Yeah, I'm sure there will be charges for repairs and taxes and stuff, but there should be some in an escrow account I would think," I said without a wit of evidence.

"I'd let you stay with us, but it might be a little tight. Devon and me just had a little booger about three months ago," Josh said with a glint of wonder.

"Oh my god, congratulations, man."

"It's freaky, homes. I can hardly sleep, you know. Scared he ain't going to wake up and shit.

"Wow, I bet."

"This place is yours, though, man. You can go all Hogan on the range, and hit balls until your hands bleed. You can give lessons at my station on the practice tee. Hell, I'd bet that there are whole bunches of peeps who'd rather take a lesson from you than me."

"C'mon, Josh, you are such a better teacher than me."

"Thanks for saying that, but I ain't no Jim. You know, that's what we named the little one. Not James, but Jim."

"So cool."

I'll admit to a pang of something at that moment. I'd never conjured even the slightest notion that I would ever have a child, but the infinitesimally tiny part of my brain that might have harbored this thought also included the child to be male, affixed with the moniker of Jim.

"Do you think I could use the phone in the cart shack?"

"Of course, dude. You have full run of the place."

"Thanks."

"Glad they sprung ya, dude."

"Me too."

I walked out of the shop, waited for a squadron of carts to pass before crossing over to the cart shack.

Hernando and Javier Galan were hanging out in the back room, drinking their own-brewed, gourmet coffee, and fiddling with the battery connections of a dismantled golf cart.

They were both glad to see me. They sandwiched me in years, and had pretty much grown up around the course like I had—helping their dad who served as the head of maintenance for twenty years. He died when the boys were just out of high school and they took over for him.

They could fix anything, and no one cut golf holes with the precision of Javier.

I've seen way more imperfections at exclusive country clubs than I ever saw at SVMGC. And you never saw a green scarred by an oil leak from a mower, or a browned-out section of the fairway caused by a neglected, faulty sprinkler head.

While the local PGA section were publishing their suggested maintenance schedules for a coming year, the Galan brothers would be out following the insect populations, sighting bird flock migrations and monitoring the ornamental Asian pear trees that lined the driveway to the course.

After collating all of their personal data points, they set their yearly schedule for turf aeration, fertilizer application, winter over-seeding, and water allocation.

They were so far ahead of the curve of the changes in climate, that two local country clubs sent their greenskeepers over to SVMGC to try to find out why their course always looked so good.

They now had seven children between them and Javier had built a house on what was once his father's property, so both families could be together.

Jim and I often went to barbeques on their compound, and I can honestly say that I've had some of the best meals of my life with their family and friends.

We talked for a bit, but I had some pressing concerns that I needed to deal with before we could formally catch up. Nando poured me a cup of coffee, and they left me in privacy to make my phone calls.

I had two that couldn't really wait.

The first was to the management company I had tasked with handling all of the business around Jim's (now my) condominium.

They had been hastily conscripted to deal with all of the contingencies in the hours between the time the judge sentenced me and when I began serving my term.

I chose them on a lark because they were the first thing that popped up on the search engine when I entered the words, "property management San Diego."

For a reasonable monthly fee, it was their job to empty the apartment of most of the personal items, rent the space as a fully furnished unit, collect the rent, pay the property taxes, and be on call to fix anything that might break or become worn.

I never followed up beyond that initial contact except to check in at the one-year mark to hear that the space had been rented by a family on an initial lease with terms that were renewable on an annual basis.

I was also given the unit number at the storage facility where my personal effects were housed. That monthly fee would be added to my expenses.

The number was local, a Chula Vista prefix, but there was no answer and no voice mail. I told myself it was still pretty early and maybe no one had come into the office yet.

The second call was to Raymond Suarez, who had been

selected by the state of Missouri to serve as my proxy parole officer in California.

He answered the phone on the first ring.

"Suarez," he said in a cop voice.

"Ah yes, Mr. Suarez, my name is Charles Dawson and I am officially checking in as a newly-minted parolee from the Missouri Department of Corrections."

"Are you some kind of smart ass, Dawson?"

"No, sir."

"Then what's this newly-minted shit?"

"Uh, I'm sorry, I'm just trying to be cordial, I guess."

"Jesus, I'm just messing with ya, Dawson. You and I are going to have to find a rhythm. Why don't you meet me for breakfast?"

"Sure," I said.

"Where are you now?"

"In the cart shack at Sweetwater Valley Municipal Golf Course."

"Oh, yeah, you're the pro golfer?"

"Yes, sir."

"I'll be there in an hour. We can eat. And, Mr. Dawson, you know how to cure a wicked slice?"

"Perhaps."

"One hour in the restaurant, okay?"

"Yes, sir."

I hung up the phone.

I tried the number for the property management company again. Nothing.

Javier had an old Ping Anser 2 putter in a barrel by the door—he liked to be the first one to drain a putt on every new hole he cut. I picked it out of the bin and grabbed a couple of old Titleists that were clanging around inside the drawer of his desk.

I spent the next hour hitting lag putts from the greatest distance away from a hole as I could create. It was one fifty-footer after another. I think I might have scared the hole on one of them, but after forty-five minutes or so, I could start to feel my once pristine touch hazily reappearing from its nearly half-a-decade hibernation.

21

Raymond Suarez (nee Genaro Lopez Barilla) was in the ballpark of fifty years old, with close-cropped hair and a diamond stud in his left ear lobe. He had never seen his named spelled with the acute accent diacritical mark because it was not there when it was issued to him.

He'd had more life experience in his pinkie toe than 99 percent of the entire population had in their collective bodies.

A six-year stint with the Marines that included intelligence work with the First Recon outfit during the initial Gulf conflagration was followed by three years of college that netted him both a Bachelor's and a Master's.

He entered the FBI Academy at Quantico, where he trained in criminal counterintelligence.

He infiltrated the Culebras Locos Motorcycle Club that was based in Yuma and Nogales, Arizona, during the years that they had a working agreement with three different Mexican drug cartels, to provide security for contraband shipments after they crossed into El Norte.

I heard stories from him that would straighten your hair faster than sticking your finger in a light socket.

To maintain the deepest of covers, he committed unimaginable crimes to maintain his credibility with his fellow club members. The Culebras were a monstrous set, and they often killed the entire families of those who'd betrayed them.

Ray said that the job was easy because most of his fellow members were so dumb, damaged, and addicted, they could easily be manipulated. He rose high enough to be elected a First Vice-President of his chapter.

When the Feds rounded them up and pulled Ray out of his twelve-year long assignment, he had to take a long sabbatical to spiritually return to something resembling a human being.

Retired at forty-two, he lasted just two years in an Idaho ski town before he had a massive breakdown after being engulfed by a blazing wildfire of PTSD that had probably been licking at his heals since his days post-USMC.

His fifteenth therapist suggested that he try his hand at service to his fellow man as a way to pave a road to renewed health.

A new identity was concocted and he was reborn as a drug counselor and freelance parole officer with accreditation for cases for those coming to California from nearly all fifty states.

In my case, some flunky bureaucrat in Missouri had picked him out of a hat. When I met him that first time, he scared the living shit out of me.

Ray liked to work without a schedule, and he would do things like he had done to me when he set our first meeting not an hour after I checked in with him.

He would show up at his parolees' places of work, their residences, or just call out of the blue and demand that they meet him around the corner for a cup of coffee.

He was perusing the menu in the clubhouse restaurant when I walked in. There was a thick stack of paperwork that took up the place across from him in the booth.

"Are you too handicapped to fill that shit out?" he asked.

"No," I replied.

"That's the intake stuff. You can take it home, and do it when you can. Why they haven't gone to a digital solution by now is beyond me. But, you know, Missouri."

I put the paperwork on the seat next to me and slid in across from him.

"What's good here?"

"You can't go wrong with eggs," I said.

"That's bullshit, amigo. Eggs can be supremely fucked up in so many ways."

He waved the waitress over. Her name was Melinda. She had been hired during the years I'd been away.

"You want coffee," Ray asked me.

"No, sir."

"I'll have a cup," Ray said.

He flipped over the Buffalo mug, and she filled it nearly to the brim.

"What do you want for breakfast, Dawson?" Ray asked.

"I guess I'll have pancakes and sausage," I said.

"And you, sir?" Melinda asked.

"I'll have three eggs over medium, hash browns and an English muffin."

He didn't explain why he'd made that choice after his initial declaration. I sat in silence, averting my gaze and looking down at the paper placemat that depicted a wizard figure pointing and screaming, "COLOR ME!"

"You got plans, Dawson?"

"Yes, sir."

"Tell me."

"Got to get my game in shape and head back out to compete."

"So, that means leaving the state at some point?"

"Yes, sir."

"We'll see," he said with a shrug.

He took a sip of his coffee, then offered an expression that signaled he wasn't disappointed.

"Where are you living?" he asked.

"That's still a little up in the air. Right now, I'm at the motel up the street from the golf course."

"Do you have other options?"

"Not really. I own a condo not far from here, but it's rented now and I don't know when the current lease ends."

"What do you mean, you don't know?" Ray asked.

"I had a property management company take over the day-to-day when I went to prison. I haven't gotten a hold of them yet to figure out where everything stands."

"Has this management company been keeping your part of the rental income in an escrow account?"

"I expect so. I've never gotten a statement and have no clue what the balance is, but it's got to be something. I figure I can use that to get an apartment until I can get back out playing professionally."

Our food arrived and Ray began doctoring every item on the plate. Tabasco for the eggs, ketchup for the taters, and butter and strawberry jam on the over-toasted muffin. He then hit the whole thing with four or five stabs from the saltshaker.

I had nothing else to offer for a minute or two as he shoveled in half of the food. He laid his fork down and slurped some coffee.

"Okay, kid, enough about you. Can you fix my golf swing?" he asked.

"I can probably make it better," I said.

"You haven't seen it. What makes you so confident?"

"I know the swing pretty well, sir. I had an extraordinary teacher who got a hold of me when I was a pre-teen. He broke it all down to the most basic of parts before even allowing me to execute a full repetition. For my part, I had talent."

"What the fuck does that mean?"

"Good muscle memory, hand/eye coordination, some other stuff. That allowed me to go from pretty good to exceptional. Do you think you have talent?"

"Beats me."

"Do you have your sticks in the car?"

"Yeah."

"When we're done eating, go grab a six iron and I'll meet you at the far end of the practice tee."

"How much is this going to cost me?"

"First lesson free," I said.

"You want to trade? My services are roughly fifty bucks a week, plus the hundred a month that's payable to the state of Missouri. If you show results, I would waive my fee and pay what you owe the state."

"That sounds fair," I said.

"Look kid, I know all about your case. You are not like a single parolee that I have ever had under my supervision. I even saw your parole board appearance. Your lawyer sent it to me after the assignment was logged. I'll say this with all the decorum I can muster: 'You got fucked, kid.' I know she thinks so. She told me that in a pretty straight forward way."

"I just want to put that all in the past tense, Mr. Suarez; you know, next shot, next hole . . . That's the only way I know how to live."

Ray nodded.

"Okay. We'll see what I've got. As for you, you need to get some things rolling for me. You need to reapply for a driver's license, open a bank account, and get yourself a debit card. And find a place to live."

"I can do that."

"I know you can."

After the meal, Ray met me at the teaching station on the eastern terminus of the driving range. It was the same place I'd met Jim for the first time nearly twenty years before.

I know this sounds weird, but I felt his presence there, and from that day forward, I only hit balls at that station.

I had this belief that he was there, and I will admit to having a conversation or two from time to time with something or someone that answered my particular question in the moment.

Ray was downright horrible. One of the worst swings I'd ever seen in my life. He created a fair amount of club head speed, but he was so out of sync with anything that resembled an actual golf swing, that there was only one remedy for his situation.

He had one of those swings that went haywire from the outset, and his entire experience was confined to trying to correct each successive mistake. It was like he was trying to control a full body dry heave.

"So?" he asked.

I had no words.

"That bad?"

"How long have you been playing?"

"I guess about ten years or so."

"Worse than bad. I've never actually seen anyone approach the golf swing with such a lack of rhythm, of timing, of anything that resembles athleticism. It's a damn shame because I can see that you are working to get on plane at every part of the swing and will never, ever get there. Ever."

"Okay, I can take it. How do I get better, smart guy?"

"I don't know. Guys who swing that bad usually just give up the game. There's got to be other stuff you can do where you have some semblance of grace, am I right?" I asked.

"Not really. You don't want to see how I dance, Dawson."

"No, I do not."

I knew this trade thing was a great deal for me, and if I could consolidate my meetings with my parole officer to being held here at my home golf course without ever having to go meet somewhere else, well, that would be amazing. I was worried about any possible repercussions, though. Suppose I couldn't fix this mess.

"Okay," I began after a moment of meditation, "are you willing to start all over?"

"What do you mean?"

"I mean, once a week for as long as I'm in town, and we begin at the very beginning. I'm going to teach you to play from scratch, as if you never had a club in your hand at any point in your life. It's going to be really frustrating because we both know that isn't true. You are going to want to move beyond a particular drill or a lesson at every turn, but if you do, I'm done. You got me?"

"Huh," he said with an indifferent shrug.

I wanted to back pedal immediately. I don't know what had come over me in that moment, but I think it was because I was so viscerally offended by having to watch what he had the gall to refer to as a golf swing.

"It's kind of funny, you know?" he said.

"What?" I said with a bit of a stammer.

"The way you just admonished me. There was really like no emotion, no anger or determination. You just said what you felt you had to say with little or no inflection. Like your parole board tape, it's kind of confusing to the recipient."

"Yeah, it's been said before."

"Okay, it's a deal. Do we start now?"

"Give me that club. I can't bear to watch you hold it like that."

He did.

"I have a book for you. I have to find it, so you won't get it until next week. We'll go chapter by chapter. Please forget you ever played this game. Because the reality is, you never really did."

"I've tried to forget a lot of things in my life, Dawson. I have been entirely unsuccessful. But I will try, okay?"

"Okay."

22

I continued to get no answer from Bay Cities Property Management. My wallet was nearly bare and I was forced to vacate the Jacaranda Motor Inn after my third evening in residence.

I spent the next night sleeping in a chair in the cart shack, bundled in my Air Force parka with my feet up on Javier's desk.

Hernando found me, head lolling to the side and a dribble of drool suspended from the corner of my mouth.

"Hey ese, what is wrong with you, bro?"

I didn't have a clue what I was dreaming about, but it was something, and I thought that I was still asleep. I mumbled some gibberish, I think.

Hernando went outside to find his brother. He might have been laughing as he exited. I got my legs off the desk and creakily got to my feet. I could smell the coffee brewing in the corner, and I veered toward the bathroom as the brothers returned.

"Let me guess, it's 5:15 a.m.," I said.

"It is, bro. You want to join us this morning?" Hernando asked.

"Sure."

"You can pick the pins if you want," Javy said.

"Nah, you've got your monthly rotation, right? Just stick to that."

"No way, ese. We're glad you're back, Chunk. I'll even give you the first roll at it. See if you remember the break."

"Let me pee first."

"I'll get the coffee," Nando said.

He grabbed the Thermos and a couple of cups.

I used the restroom, splashed a little water on my face, and emerged to the smell of fuel. Outside, Javy was pouring the gas and oil concoction into their maintenance cart.

That cart was as custom as they come. They had rigs to hold buckets of sand and seed and all the equipment they used on a daily basis. I found a place in the bag well amidst the strapped rakes and a pristine foot-activated hole cutter.

The engine roared to life and we headed out into the darkness. Hernando came to a stop in the middle of the ninth fairway, let the engine croak to a stop, and cocked his head to the heavy air around him. I heard the sounds of scrub jays and dark-eyed juncos mingling with some of the traffic noise coming from the south. When I was still a kid, Javy had taught me how to distinguish between every bird who frequented our part of the world.

"I think they're on seven," he said, referring to the mowing crew.

"They're doing the front first?" Javy said in disbelief.

"Yeah, they said that they were going to switch for the week because of that irrigation valve that blew up on sixteen."

"Oh yeah, that's right. Well let's just start at one then," Javy said.

Hernando started the cart up. We half spun out on the thick layer of dew. As we crossed the bridge that forded the wash, I caught sight of the crossbeam that the three of us carved our names into when we were in our teens.

We traversed the freshly mowed first fairway. The loose, detached grass coated the rubber wheels like special St. Patrick's Day frosting on a glazed donut.

A lone coyote froze in its tracks by a conical cypress tree. We'd screwed up his hunt, and it scattered when the racket from the cart neared.

We parked on the concrete path, each took a tool, and trudged out and onto the green surface. I started to veer off to the right green side bunker as I had chosen the most mundane of their duties to tackle—raking the old sand traps.

"Hey Chunk, where are we going to stick this one?" Javy asked.

I peered over the lip of the deep bunker.

"What day is it?" I asked.

"You're kidding, right?" Hernando asked.

"Honestly, I have no idea. Is today a weekend day?"

"Today's Monday."

"Okay. So, there's a spot about five paces from the right edge and six or so paces from the back fringe where the drainage takes it to road, but it breaks toward the hills for some reason. Put it there. I always loved that pin."

"What does it being a Monday have to do with it?" Hernando asked.

"I know," said Javy.

"Tell your brother," I said before heading back down into the middle of the bunker.

"Tough pin. Three whacks are no good when the course is crowded on the weekends; is that it, Chunk?"

"Yep," I said from down below.

Javy cut the hole where I had indicated. Hernando took the cutting tool from him and filled the previous location as Javy painted the rim with white spray paint before inserting the cup.

"Okay, man, let's go. Let's see if you can make it."

I finished the rake job, took Javy's putter from him, and he dropped a couple of balls about ten feet from the hole. It was still dark, but my eyes had adjusted and the murky lights in the parking lot provided just enough illumination for me to see that far.

I wasn't the greatest of putters. As opposed to nearly every other facet of the game, I was constantly searching for something that felt comfortable; I've been known to try multiple things during a round when the feel was sour or downright off.

A good portion of my time in prison had been focused on the analysis of my putting stroke. I eventually came to the conclusion that I would try to sync up the theories that I practiced with my golf swing—the angles, planes, and arcs—and try to find consistency from relying on the physics of the situation, not the feel in the moment.

This process involved making a little swing with the same properties of movement along an arc. That meant an opening of the face during the takeaway, a return to square and the closing of the face after the strike.

I'd made that stroke during my putt lagging session before my breakfast with Ray and it seemed to create the type of spin I have been trying to achieve for as long as I've played the game.

Jim probably told me about this at some point, but I obviously had to try everything else before really understanding what he was talking about.

I've gone crosshanded, chicken wing, claw, straight back/straight through (which from a physics standpoint is a misnomer as you actually have to twist the face open to make it work), and many other forced manipulations.

I've varied pace and had some success ripping anything within four feet or so at the center of the hole with ferocious speed. That worked until it didn't, and after blowing some short putts six or eight feet by the cup, I stopped that nonsense.

I've experimented with every conceivable head, shaft, shaft length, weight, and grip configuration, all with the notion that they all felt right at some point.

The Anser 2 in my hands felt familiar—I played most of my teens with one that was almost exactly like Javy's. The brothers were whispering something to each other, but I blocked out the distraction.

The surface was smooth, as the mower had swept up a good deal of the accumulated moisture. I knew the break like the back of my hand. I made a practice stroke, picked a spot about three inches outside the left and fired away. I missed on the low side, the result of not enough strike.

Javy and Hernando started laughing, but I soldiered on. I raked the other ball over, picked the same spot, took my stance and drilled it into the center of the hole.

"Odelay!" Javy said.

"That's what's up," I said.

"The Chunk is back!" Hernando said.

I sidled over and picked up both of the balls. I looked to the east and saw the sun just beginning its struggle to scale Mount Miguel.

"What was so funny?" I asked.

"Oh, that was Javy. We were talking about your situation and he came up with a good idea," Hernando said.

"La bola de chiclé," Javy said with a smile.

They started to laugh again.

My Spanish sucked, but I was actually familiar with that specific term.

"That's in the junkyard by now, isn't it?"

"No, bro, we fixed it up. It's looking good."

"La Bola!" Javy yelled to the sky.

"Would that be cool with your families?" I asked.

"Come on, man, you're family. Our kids haven't seen you in years, and both Dora and Yvette would love having someone else around to do the dishes," Hernando said.

I was overwhelmed by gratitude. La bola de chiclé! That was perfect for me.

The morning shadows were still long when we returned to the cart shack. I tried the after-hours number for Bay Cities Property Management. A recorded voice said it had been disconnected.

I extracted the storage locker information from my frayed wallet and called the number on the piece of paper.

The man who answered the phone had a pronounced European accent, and we initially had a bit of trouble trying to establish a means of communication. In a cold voice, he told me that most of my things were gone. There had been an auction at least three years back, and much of the stuff had sold.

He said that the profits had failed to satisfy the outstanding bill.

He had the rest of the stuff in an abandoned space, and if I wanted it, I had to pay the balance of what I owed which was about $1,600.

I explained my situation, but he cited policy from some script on his desk before hanging up the phone.

I was devastated. There were things that were some of the only physical links back to Jim, like some of his clothing and other mementos, but there were also things that I needed, like my own clothing, at least four full sets of golf clubs, and assorted wedges and putters.

My biggest fear was that it was all gone—my personal stuff, Jim's history, and even the condo. I realized that I had been ripped off, and most likely from the outset of my transaction of transferring the management of the property to someone that I did not know.

I really didn't know where to turn, so in a moment of inspiration, I called the only guy who I knew might know about this type of monetary dilemma: the ex-con accountant David Bergman.

I got right into the reason I was calling, so we could dispense with evaluating how our lives of freedom were proceeding.

David was super knowledgeable, but also pessimistic about my fortunes. He told me that my first step must be to find out if the property taxes had been paid, because if they hadn't, the property could be sold in forfeiture for the amount of the tax lien.

Also, the current lessees were paying rent to someone. That information could be obtained by engaging a real estate lawyer, who could figure out where those monthly checks were going.

He said something about hearing about these sham companies who did this sort of thing—often to prisoners or military personnel on extended deployments—and that I should check with the county authorities to see if they'd received complaints about their practices in the past.

There were the warnings to be careful because real estate issues are often complex and the rights of individuals (owners) are neglected in favor of what David deemed to be nonsensical laws.

All of this was way more than I wanted to deal with. I just wanted to hit balls and plot my return to competition.

I wanted to believe that it wasn't true, but after being

unsuccessful in my attempt to reach Bay Cities Property Management for the fifteenth time, I knew that it was.

At least I had a place to live, access to food, and transportation to and from the golf course.

"*La bola de chiclé*" was now my full-time residence.

Let me explain: For as long as I've known the Galans, there was this compact Shasta travel trailer that was parked in the middle of their property. It was a relic from the mid–1950s, and though they claimed it could sleep four to six, it clocked in at about eighty-four-square-feet of cramped living space.

Galan family lore said it was the first American home to their father, Fernando, and mother, Blanca. Granted five rocky acres on the mesa by the owner of the farm Fernando managed, *La bola* served as their residence during the time the family house was being constructed.

Fernando refurbished the interior with some nifty tuck and roll upholstery work and hit the exterior with a healthy dose of flame-hued, orange spray paint. A color that did not exist in nature.

It took Fernando three years to build his dream home, a handsome cement casita with terra cotta roof tiles and a natural scrub landscape. The central courtyard sported the most magnificent centuries-old oak tree you will ever see in this or any other lifetime.

The Galan family grew to four children including Nando and Javy's older sisters. When Blanca passed, she had seventeen grandchildren and four great-grandbabies.

The trailer had two aluminum wings that were supposed to

give it stability on the road. By the time I'd moved in, it hadn't seen pavement for fifty years.

It was somewhat oval in shape with a rounded back end. As an older man, I would have equated the visual to something that resembled a deconstructed Nike or Icarus in the fetal position, but as a special-needs child, I only saw one thing: a giant orange gumball.

La bola de chiclé means gumball in Spanish. And that name stuck harder and faster than the epoxy I used to put a new head on a driver when I screamed it out on my first viewing.

The Galan brothers' wives had been given the heads up on my installment, and when we arrived at the end of the workday, they had cleaned and decorated the interior with some local wildflowers.

Both families got together for dinner, and we all gorged ourselves on some of my favorites: tamales, chile rellenos, and rice and beans.

For a brief moment, I swept aside my problems, then slept like the dead in my cozy, orange womb.

23

"So, I don't have your book yet, sir. We'll have to just get to work anyway," I said to Ray Suarez on the next Saturday after our first meeting.

"Why don't you have it, Dawson?" he asked.

I launched into the explanation of my personal effects and their disposition within the storage facility lockup.

"What are you telling me? They've stolen your stuff?" he asked.

"Well, you can understand that the fees weren't paid," I said.

"What is wrong with you?"

"Huh?"

"Come on," he said.

He shoved his six-iron back into his golf bag, hoisted it on his shoulder, and started walking away. He turned back when he'd gotten ten feet or so away from me.

"Goddammit, Dawson, let's go! Right now, son!"

We got into his truck and he tore out of the parking lot.

I gave him the address of the company where my unit was supposed to be and subsequently told him all of the things that David Bergman had related to me about what could happen with the property that I thought I once owned.

He started to get mad. I mean, it appeared to be quite a righteous fit; a volcanic rage simmered just under the surface of his reddening face as every facet of the story I was telling him was absorbed.

He began to mutter expletives, and by the time we pulled in front of the gate to "You-Stow-It", I sensed that he might become unglued.

"Hold on, sir. Shouldn't we contact some authority before going in there?" I asked with a voice of panicked dread.

"I will be the goddamn authority, Dawson."

"It's just that if you do something rash, I will be seen as an accomplice, and I do not want to violate my parole in any way."

"Fine. Stay in the truck. Give me the number of your original locker."

I handed him the slip of paper from my otherwise empty wallet.

He reached into the recessed console and pulled out a laminated ID that was attached to a chain. He put it around his neck. It had his picture on it, but I did not see what it identified him to be.

He returned in less than five minutes, wordlessly started up the truck and pulled up to the gate. Immediately, there was mechanical movement and chains and pulleys opened the blockade.

"What did you say?" I finally asked.

"Does it matter?"

"Well . . ."

"Look, Dawson, I only had like a hundred ways to go here. And in the end, there was no other option. We were going to get your stuff."

Ray drove all the way to the end of the third row of closet-like cubicles that were faced with metal roll top doors. Every single one of them had a crimson red lock on the hasp. There were also placards with paragraphs of regulations announcing danger and criminal penalties for illegal actions.

Ray got out of the truck and produced a key for one of the red locks.

"Now, don't try to get things organized or anything. I don't want to see a whole OCD episode unfold, or some goofy trip down the nostalgia highway. Just start loading whatever's in this locker into the bed of the truck," he said.

"I don't think I have OCD," I said, though that was kind of a lie.

He rolled the metal door up; there were all the things I had left in the world. From the looks of it, the six-foot bed of Ray's pickup wouldn't end up being more than half-full when all was said and done.

There were some clothes, a lot of the plaques and trophies I had garnered during my killer amateur career, and a grouping of golf clubs—sans golf bag—stacked against the wall.

I found a box of books, and on top of that was one of the things I was hoping I would never lose.

It was all loaded in just three or four trips, and Ray returned the lock and the key to the European guy on our exit. I scrunched down in the seat in case he could have fingered me later as part of the crew that had cleaned out one of his deadbeat vaults.

When Ray climbed back into the cab, he was still a little pissed off.

"Monday, 8:00 a.m. sharp, you and me are going to pay a little visit to the county tax collector. I'll pick you up," he said.

I nodded.

"This guy here was a piece of work, Dawson. A real piece of work."

"So, are you going to tell me what you said that made it okay for me to get my things?"

"Not much, kid. Half of the shit in these facilities is likely contraband of some sort. You start asking questions and they freak the fuck out."

"Did you say you were a cop?"

"Nah, I said that we needed to clear out your locker because there was evidence there that was of interest to the city DA."

"And is there?"

"We shall see, Dawson."

"He didn't ask for a warrant?"

"Lord, no. It's so much easier for him to just say, 'yes.' I think he knew it wasn't legit that your stuff was still there."

"What does your ID say?"

He looked down at the plasticized thingie dangling in front of him.

"Ha. That's my gym membership lanyard. He didn't have the guts to study it. That happens about 99 percent of the time."

I laughed.

"I'm a professional liar, Dawson. I'm really good at it."

"Congratulations."

He laughed at that.

"Now, can you make good on our barter? Can I get the lesson still?"

"Of course," I said.

After we arrived back at the course, I rummaged through the box of books and found the one that I wanted to give him. It was the dog-eared copy of the book that had changed my life—*Ben Hogan's Five Lessons*.

And then we spent the next hour getting his grip right. He was not allowed to make a swing.

He did not protest. Not even once.

Later, after he'd left, I looked over the rest of the things we'd liberated from their own five-year stint in the clink.

The dank elements of the environment had done a pretty good number on much of the clothing and linens. I was going to have to see what was salvageable, but one item—the item I'd really hoped would still be there—was intact.

It was the last of the flat caps that Jim wore daily throughout the entire time I'd known him.

This would not be something for some shrine; I planned to wear it for the rest of my days or as long as it would stay together. It fit pretty damn well.

In the following days, it became apparent that Bay Cities

Property Management was a criminal enterprise and I was not its only victim.

No one had paid the property taxes during the time I was incarcerated and the tax lien had risen to a figure of $18,457 when Ray and I checked with the San Diego County Assessor's office on that Monday.

Luckily, the county government had been underfunded from a personnel standpoint for a pretty long time, and they had yet to get around to selling the condo to satisfy my tax debt, though there was a date scheduled to do just that a couple of months in the future.

Ray predicted that the property would end up being used as evidence in a future criminal proceeding and that they wouldn't be disposing of anything until that was wrapped up.

David Bergman suggested I try to begin remittance on the debt as soon as possible. Just the effort alone might show them my intentions were in good faith.

I had one monumental problem. I was flat-ass broke. Yeah, I was alive because of the generosity of those around me, but even two nickels weren't jockeying for space in my pants pocket at the same time.

Again, Ray came up with an idea. He got the wife of a buddy of his in the county clerk's office to notarize a letter to the current lessees to change where they were to pay their monthly rent.

He put his lanyard around his neck, knocked on the door to the condo and delivered the notice to the occupants.

Two weeks later, the first check, for $1,450, arrived at the pro shop at SVMGC.

I actually got to open a bank account for the first time in five years.

I agreed to have a thousand dollars a month impounded to the San Diego County Tax Collector in the hopes that they would see that I was at least trying to rectify my delinquency.

Ray's prediction aside, there was still no guarantee that they wouldn't put it up for sale.

I also applied for a new driver's license. The effort was facilitated because my birth certificate was in a folder of important papers (that included the deed to the condominium) at the bottom of the box that contained the stray books.

Over a space of time, I brought everything back to the Gumball for sorting. Much of the clothing ended up in the trash. Nando's wife, Dora, resurrected the items that survived.

She mended the sweaters and washed the lot. My slightly larger wardrobe soon took up most of the meager closet space in the Gumball.

Finally, as things became more squared away, I felt I could get back to the only thing I ever wanted to do.

The one set of clubs that had not drawn a single bid at auction just happened to be the first adult set of clubs that I'd ever possessed.

They were a full set of Hogan Apex II irons from the mid-1970s—those stern, unforgiving blades that were as handsome as a chiseled-chin matinee idol, the same exact clubs I'd described during my visit to the museum with Babe.

I remember that the first night they were mine, I parked

them next to my bed and stared at the relief of Hogan's face on the backside of the toe until I fell asleep.

That next morning, I confirmed that any truly great golf club—one you rely on—has a definable sweet spot in the center of the face.

During their initial tenure in my bag, I wore dime-size abrasions into the chrome, and like a master marksman, the dispersion pattern was as tight as a seal on an old, unopened pickle jar.

When I examined them, they were still in great shape, though the heads had probably been forged nearly fifty years before.

They were scuffed in parts and the ruby-red paint that used to sit in a well of the sole denoting their number was pretty much gone from every single club.

The grips were degraded, so I got Josh to front me some from his inventory in the shop. I changed them out myself.

Finally, with everything cleaned up and the grip adhesive set, I picked a bucket's worth of balls out of the washer that had a little less life on them than the others and headed out to the tee to strike the first full shots I'd hit since that round at Kiama on the day of my release.

I'm a six-iron guy when it comes to working on something because I think that's just the right amount of loft to create about the same amount of side-to-side spin as backspin.

The face of that six-iron was more decayed than the rest of the clubs, but when I first made contact with its center, it was like being born again. There was a distinctive click that only those old forged irons seemed to make. That was feedback in its purest sense.

"It's either coming from the left or coming from the right, but, for god sakes, stop with that straight shit right now!"

It was Josh, half-laughing, playing the part of Jim in the famous story everyone who'd ever met me had heard at some point.

Hernando and Javy were not far behind him. They too had big goofy smiles plastered on their faces.

The swing felt really good. It was that kind of thing where there was little or no thought going into it. I knew that was soon to change; in fact, it wouldn't be long before I would get really uncomfortable that I was having no thoughts. I just took the club back and let it go.

"All right, Joshie, you're right, enough with this straight stuff," I said.

I set up for a nice little cut into the mild breeze coming from the coast.

I weakened my grip ever so slightly, opened my stance a tad, and took the club back a touch outside of my regular plane. At the top of the backswing, I kept the face just a bit closed, maybe four degrees or so, before starting my downswing by rotating my lower body open a quarter of a second before I normally would. I felt a slight resistance to the natural movement of my arms and hands in trying to keep the clubface a little more open at impact. That earlier lower rotation took the club on a path that was the smallest bit out-to-in and I struck the ball with just the right amount of side spin to get it to move about three or four yards to the right from the line I was trying to start it on.

It was superior execution.

"Butter," Josh proclaimed as soon as the ball started to turn to the right.

His exhortation followed a really loud "PING" that could be heard all over the range. While my tiny gallery was admiring the circumscribed flight of the golf ball, the rest of those folks practicing around me jerked their attention to find the source of that awful noise.

I was looking down at the shaft of my club, which no longer had a club head attached to it.

The separation had been clean and bloodless, and somewhere out there among the debris that looked like thousands of hailstones was my forged steel club head.

"Shit," I think I might have said.

"Oh, brah, what a bummer," Josh said.

Nando and Javy were trying to keep from laughing.

"You know what this means, ese?" Javy asked.

"What?" I asked.

Hernando seemed puzzled at first by his brother's question, but like most things that happened in the brains of close siblings, he caught on and started laughing louder.

"What's so funny?" Josh asked them.

"Suit up, Chunk," Javy yelled.

And then I got it. He was telling me I had to get in my old mattress and helmet outfit and go out and search for the part of my club that had gone AWOL.

"You know I'm going to do it," I said.

"Nah, Chunk, we'll just shut down the range for a couple of minutes," Josh said.

The driving range was full, with a couple of people waiting to snag a spot as soon as someone else's pail of balls ran dry.

"No. I will not be responsible for pissing off fifty people because this pro needs a moment. Where's that gear?"

Hernando pointed to the cart shack.

"It might actually fit you now," he said.

I finally looked at the part of the shaft that was severed. There was some rust on its edges. Years of being relegated to a barrel somewhere, and then half a decade in a dank locker had taken its toll. I would need to re-shaft the whole set, which was a drag because I had just re-gripped every single member.

I did suit up and haul myself out into the area of the range where I thought the head might be. Most everyone stopped to watch and not a single person tried to launch a ball in my direction.

I found it about halfway to the 100–yard marker and was surprised that it had traveled that far.

Nonetheless, I was as gleeful as I'd been in a long, long time.

24

The United States Development Tour was going to visit our region in two months and I set my sights on that event for my professional return.

I had Josh download an application for the qualifier and filled it out. In the category of status, there was only one box I could check: Other Professional.

At one time, I could have included more categories all the way up to PGA Tour member. Five years before, I had been ranked the 269th best player in the world. My name no longer appeared on the list. I checked.

I held out some hope that my felonious past would not disqualify me from getting an opportunity to ply my trade. Way back when, there was a guy on the Prince Harold tour whom I was occasionally paired with. He was a recovering drug addict who'd spent three years in medium security for burglary—he blew up the safe from the pro shop where he worked. He dominated our tour and another in Arizona before regaining his status on the big tour. He played at the highest level for five years, but died of an overdose on the eve of the final round of a tournament in Florida.

If he could go back to work, why couldn't I?

Josh held a kid's clinic on Saturdays and he let me take that over. It was anywhere from eight to ten hellions for an hour and a half, but at fifty bucks a month from their parents, it was a cool four to five hundred that would cover my entry fee.

I practiced like I never had before. Jim would have finally gotten off my back if he were still around. I hoped if his presence were still in the ether somewhere, he noticed and approved.

I was pushing thirty, though only by a smidgeon and there was sure to be plenty of solid years ahead of me, but now I had to work. I put in a tremendous amount of time on my short game.

I'd always been pretty solid around the greens. My stats during the USDT season that resulted in me getting my tour card were stellar—top five in scrambling, for example, but I still struggled to be a consistent putter.

Always seeking the secret, I had amassed about twenty putters through the years, but only two were left when we raided the storage unit. The one I'd used in my last and best competitive season was gone. It was a very stable, mallet type, with a head as big as a bear's paw.

I came to terms with the loss. The technique that I was sure was the answer—the one I had conjured many a night before my eyes closed on my musty mattress in my cell—would not have lent itself to a big, heavy-headed putter. If it survived, I might have been tempted to switch back the very moment I started to feel uncomfortable with my new technique.

I was left with a knock off of a Wilson 8802 (my very first putter that Taylor had bought at a yard sale for five bucks) and a thirty-four inch Acushnet Bullseye.

The Wilson copy was pretty beat up, and had probably been in service at a miniature golf course before Taylor purchased it.

The Bullseye was a precision instrument. It had a milled, flanged blade of brushed brass, with a slightly offset head.

I was never fond of the grip, though, and the first thing I did was swap it out for the same one that was on Javy's Anser, a Ping PP58, a pistol grip that had a flat front.

My last season, I preferred holding the putter cross-handed, but that was not going to work with my new stroke.

As I continued my experimentation, my confidence grew. I developed a better sense of the line and a consistency in regards to aim emerged.

My only issue was that I had a lot less feel for distance. Since I was now manipulating the face, it felt like something unnatural was creeping into my stroke. The bigger the swing, the more manipulation, and that started to really get into my head when I was faced with anything over thirty feet. Because of the feel I had from ten feet and in, I stuck with it, though.

I began to play rounds very early in the morning and late in the afternoon, especially on the days when the wind was coming in from the west. I wanted to experience the full breadth of all possible conditions.

On the Tuesday before the qualifier, I mailed my application and a check for the entry fee to the tournament organizer. I checked Josh's computer on the following Saturday. I scrolled down to find that I had an 8:33 a.m. tee time off number one at a course I knew pretty well: Beaumont Oaks Golf Club.

Hernando lent me the old Altima that had been gathering dust out by the Gumball, and I gassed it up and headed out at four in the morning on the day of the qualifier. After, 1,835 days away, I was reclaiming my path from the interminable detour.

Three hours later, I arrived in Riverside County and took the Beaumont city exit. There was a battalion of hopefuls scattered about the parking lot who, like me, had a fast food franchise breakfast sandwich and a cup of coffee as fortification for the day.

When that first beam of light appeared in the east, there was a simultaneous sound of trunks being unlatched mixed with the scrunching of bags that had once contained the pre-game meal.

I had no caddy, so I used an old carry bag that was hanging around the cart shack—a castoff of an old rental set.

Because I was still nervous about whether there would be an issue with me playing in their event, I trudged up to the tournament leaderboard to see if the calligrapher had artistically engraved my name on to the pre-printed sheet of white with his special black pen.

There it was, Charles Dawson, written in a script that conjured the epitome of penmanship.

Feeling emboldened, I continued onto the tournament desk and notified them that I had arrived for my scheduled tee time.

Turns out, there were so many competitors trying to grab a spot for the week's event, that they were contesting the qualifier over two courses and that each course would produce four entrants for the tourney.

I warmed up with the same protocol that I always had—a few wedges to get loose before swapping out for my six-iron where I would see what adjustments I needed to hit a ball dead straight. Then, I never hit another straight ball again.

I finished by taking about ten swipes with the driver, using the same process as I had with the six.

I hit a few bunker shots, did a bit of chipping, and then moved over to the putting green that was just a flop shot away from the first and tenth tees. The stroke felt great on greens that were that fast.

I used the bathroom, a ritual, before heading for the first tee to meet my playing partners, get a pin sheet, and look out at the landing area of the first hole.

We were in foursomes, which is always a drag for me. I believe that extra player accounts for an overly long round and in that kind of one-day format, there is just so much wasted time waiting for everyone trying so stridently to get it right.

I was paired with two good friends from different colleges in Texas: Tyler and Travis. They had known each other since their days in junior golf, and both had conditional status on the USDT. They weren't exempt yet, so they were forced to try to qualify for each tournament in the hopes that if they could get in and win a little money, their priority number would change. That would preclude them from having to show up for those Monday events for the rest of the year.

The fourth in our group was an anomaly in the world of professional golf. His name was Julius, a young Black man with a remarkable story.

I am constantly amazed when someone rises as a player from humble origins. The opportunities are so stacked against those who do not have access to the game because of cost and circumstance.

Players like Hogan and Lee Trevino were the exception. The rule is that the majority of golf pros do not come from the caddy ranks or spend their youth surrounded by urban blight. They grow up with parents who exposed them to the game, provided them with the best equipment and expert instruction.

Julius grew up in Compton, California. His classmates played basketball and football in youth programs. There were gangs and other stuff that lurked in the open of impoverished neighborhoods.

His grandparents raised him because his father had been killed in Iraq, and his mother had passed from cancer when he was ten.

His grandfather was a starter at an inner-city golf course named for Charlie Sifford, the first African-American to play (and win) on the PGA Tour.

Julius hung around the golf course after school much like I had, and eventually got some attention from the club pro who steered him toward a local junior college program. Julius won the National Junior College Golf Tournament in both of the years he was eligible before turning professional as a nineteen-year-old.

He'd heard all of the stories about exclusion from his grandpa and the other mavens who hung out at the Sifford course. You could tell that stepping outside that familiarity gave him the feeling of being on the outside looking in. We had that in common.

The first hole at Beaumont couldn't be more benign, a short par four with plenty of landing area off the tee and a relatively flat green.

The course was a Pete Dye design from the early 1990s. Like many of his courses that I've played from that era, it followed a format of letting you ease into the round.

I muttered my obligatory, "Play well," to my partners, teed it up and hit a big draw up the right side that I started out in the desert before it curved over the cart path and into the fairway.

"Nice," Julius said.

He ripped one down the middle, on a rope, with a bit of roll out.

He had an interesting action to his swing, a lot of width in the takeaway that he compressed by laying the club off quite a bit at the top. It reminded me of the swing that Johnny Miller had at the height of his dominance. It produced shots that were a little lower than some, and really bored through the air. Pure rockets.

I nodded at him when he returned to his bag, and we waited for the Texans to play.

It was pretty obvious that they had studied with the same teacher. They had uncannily similar swings, and they both launched their drivers with tremendous height with what I would call an infant draw. It was an esthetically pleasing ball flight, but ultimately hollow.

That teacher, I found out later, was a guy named Fran Friendly. He was renowned and expensive, and ran a golf ranch near Austin, Texas. He pretty much only taught that one type of shot which fooled his disciples into believing that was all they needed.

The pin was in the easiest position on the green, four paces from the right, five paces from the front edge. Julius hit a low dart to about six feet from the flag.

I followed with a little slinger of a gap wedge that I'd choked up on. Because my tee shot hugged the right side, I had no obstructions to try to fly over. I just whipped a low spinner into the bank to the right side of the green. It fed down to tap-in length.

"Beauty," Julius said.

"Thanks," I muttered.

The Texans wedged up to inside ten feet. Each of us holed our putts.

It was weird because no one with the exception of me took the pin out of the hole. I was going to have to get used to that new rule.

We played on. I birdied the second, while the others just missed and made par.

The third hole was a par three that dropped down eighty

feet from the tee to the green. Playing from the tips, the tee shot came out of a shoot next to a hill that usually blocked the wind.

I had the honor and I walked out to the edge of the tee to try to get a feel for how much the breeze was going to affect the ball once it got out there and hung in the exposed air. I ended up hitting a cut six and left myself a fairly straight uphill twenty-footer.

Travis and Tyler sauntered over and watched me put my club away. I half held it up for them to see because I knew it wasn't going to make that much difference. They were never going to hit the same type of shot. There were no cuts in their bag or in their future.

Julius hit a bullet that ended up pin high. The Texans hit seven-irons that went really high, took on a little too much wind, and ended up on the lower third of the green.

As we made our way down the winding cart path and into the valley, an official's cart pulled up behind the green.

Most of these qualifiers use part-time officials, usually guys from the local PGA section who are easily identifiable because they wear the same color bucket style hat.

They are thought to be pretty clueless about both the rules and where they place themselves on the course. These "bucket heads" often have to be waved out of your line, or told to turn their walkie-talkie off when they come into close proximity with you.

Sure enough, this bucket head's walkie-talkie went off as we approached.

"Where are you, Joe?" squawked a voice out of the black plastic.

We all heard Joe say, "Back of three green."

Then this: "Is he there?"

"Yeah," Joe said.

We arrived and marked our balls. I looked out onto the back of the fourth green, about 500 yards away and I could see two more carts, each being piloted by a bucket head, working their way on the cart path against the flow of play.

I pretty much knew what was up. The Texans had zero clue, but Julius got really nervous all of a sudden and he three-putted after hitting his first putt five feet past the hole.

We were followed to the fourth tee by the walkie-talkie guy and joined by the other two carts as we made it to the tee box.

"What the fuck?" Julius whispered to me.

"Just keep playing, man." I said.

"Is this about me?" he asked.

"God, no." I answered.

"I think this is about me," he said.

"No. This is about me. I'll tell you later. Don't lose your focus."

I didn't take my own advice. The fourth hole was another medium distance par four.

I set up for a fade. I double crossed it and smoked my drive into a waste area on the wrong side of the cart path.

"Wow. That was pure," I said with a full dose of sarcasm.

As we headed away from the tee, I gave Julius the short version of why we had a bucket head brigade in tow. He remained dubious; his sensitivity to feeling that he didn't belong was certainly exacerbated by the posse of officials clocking our play.

Travis and Tyler had not spoken a word to either of us, though they had been joking and high-fiving each other.

Tyler spoke to the group for the first time.

"We're not playing slow, are we?" he asked.

To refute that possibility, I pointed to the group up ahead who had just reached the green.

Tyler nodded, turned to his fellow Texan and shrugged his shoulders.

My ball was lying next to some stout weeds, and it took a mighty whack with lofted club to get it to move about forty yards toward where the hole should be played from.

From there, I flew it over the green, couldn't hold the ensuing flop shot, chipped close and tapped in the putt for a double bogey.

I glanced over to our observers and I saw the original one nod positively. My assertion was confirmed.

There was one more slightly easy hole before the course got tougher; a par five with a small creek running through it. The carry over the creek at its shortest point was only about 280 yards, but if you tugged it left at all, you were wet.

I did just that, and while the rest of my group were making birdies, I settled for par.

I tried to use my extraordinary powers of concentration to block the distractions from affecting me, but I failed miserably.

We were tailed for the rest of the round and I ended up

shooting one under par, which just happened to be two shots out of the playoff for the final spot.

As I predicted, the Texas twins' swings betrayed them on the backside. They both turned at two under, but that little draw eventually became a hook and both of them ended up shooting even. Travis did it by doubling the eighteenth after snap hooking his drive onto Beaumont Boulevard.

Julius was one of the three guys who made the playoff at three under. I hung around to watch him make the field with a heroic birdie on the second playoff hole.

Not a single bucket head ever confronted me, or offered an explanation for the surveillance. My guess is that—in their clueless fashion—they didn't know what to do.

Travis and Tyler finished their respective rounds in moods that soured with every dip in their performances. After, seething with synergistically triggered anger, they marched on over to one of the rules guys and asked him why they were the group that garnered all the scrutiny. I'm not sure if they got an answer.

For my first foray in competition in five years, I'd done all right. I'd played like a pro, but putting up all that money and coming away with nothing was unacceptable.

I set my sights on the next qualifier that would be in my region, determined to work a little harder on my stamina, my focus and my swing.

The odds would be tougher in that one. I reminded myself that all I needed to do was follow my normal path: get incrementally better with each outing.

25

I should have gotten to the point where I just stopped telling Ray anything that I thought might piss him off, but the events of earlier in the week were at the forefront of my thoughts.

At our weekly meeting (lesson), I told him about what had happened on the Monday before. As I related my experience, his face gradually took on the color of a red hazard stake.

Ray's game was coming along. Each week, he'd arrived with a smile and no questions, ready for the next step. He hadn't even swiped at a ball since we'd started.

That Saturday, I was trying to get him to understand the optimal angles that the clubface should exhibit through the takeaway before we moved to the top of the backswing, but he lost focus when I started giving him details of my round at Beaumont.

"Wait, wait, wait, stop!" he said. "If they knew you were ineligible, why did they allow you to even tee it up?"

"I don't know. I've gone through the player's handbook for

both the USDT and the big tour. It started out looking very murky, you know, that I might be okay. There are references to integrity, which I think has to do with gambling. There is also a thing about sanctions associated with social media transgressions. Both of those have a lot of discretion."

"So, what's the deal?"

"I can only assume that they feel, because they are a private thing, that they can make whatever rules they want at the time."

"That's bullshit. You can't just make stuff up. People would sue them," he said as he adjusted his now perfect grip.

"Well . . ."

"What?"

"There is one thing . . ."

I hesitated because there was something that I'd found that could be considered problematic.

"There was this clause in the handbook that lists some of the things that can keep you from competing. I had to read it over a couple of times and then I had to go to the book that the body that oversees all things in professional golf uses."

"What does it say?"

I'd carried the salient piece of paper around for a couple of days. Maybe I was trying to wish that the words might change from having been tucked away in my golf bag. I pulled out the copy of the page from the tour handbook and handed it to Ray.

"Yeah, I see what you mean," he said with no enthusiasm.

It had stated: *A player will cease to be a member: If in the judgment of the tour policy board commits a serious breach of . . . Code of Ethics . . .*

And so, I told him I'd referred to the big handbook, the one that all professionals had to abide.

It basically said that a felony conviction was grounds for immediate and permanent expulsion from the association for life. No appeal. No recourse.

"Well, they can't do that," Ray said.

"They can do anything they want."

"I want to see the precedent. I want to see that tested."

"I'm going to do that in about three weeks."

"You are?"

"I'm going to submit an application to enter the four-spot qualifier for the San Diego Open," I said.

"Four-spot?" he asked.

"Yeah, they have them most weeks on the tour, a Monday event where the low four competitors get into that week's tournament."

"How many entrants?"

"Three hundred? Usually two courses, so two guys from each."

"Jesus. Well, good luck."

"I'd be surprised if they accept my entry after what happened at Beaumont, but I'm hoping that it just slips through, you know?"

"And if it doesn't?"

"I guess I'll call a lawyer."

"Good."

I wasn't convinced about any of it. I just wanted to play, but I had been thinking that if my life's ambition was going to be permanently blocked, I wasn't going to just sit by and take it. I had nowhere else to go.

"You want a caddy?" Ray asked.

"What?"

"I'll caddy for you. I can also kick some bucket head ass if it comes to that."

"Have you ever looped before?"

"What's loop?" he asked as if I were speaking Portuguese.

"Sure. You can be my caddy."

"Awesome," he said.

I submitted my application for the qualifier in the same timing that I'd used to enter the USDT event. It was at the last second again in the hopes that it might get overlooked in the late crush of entries.

I got an email two days later pointing me to a site that listed the tee times. And there I was, set to go at 8:14 a.m. from the tenth tee at Mount Miguel Country Club, a track that I'd played a fair amount of golf at during my high school years.

It rained the whole weekend before and I was little nervous that we might get washed out, but by the time Monday rolled around, we were on, and actually playing the ball down.

Ray drove me to the course. It was funny to witness how nervous he appeared to be.

"You know the caddy credo, right?" I asked.

"What are you talking about?"

"The caddy credo. Something all caddies need to live by."

"No. Enlighten me."

"Show up. Keep up. Shut up."

"Ha. I've already completed number one, so there."

"I'll help you out. More likely, you're going to get schooled by one of the pro caddies. If they tell you to do something, just say you're sorry, and do it right the next time."

"All right."

"Some of those guys can get really prickly with a newbie."

He looked even more nervous for some reason.

"I'll set everyone straight about your experience. It will be fine."

At the course, Ray took the clubs out of the bed of the truck.

"Just so you know, one of the things that drives people crazy is if the clubs clank with every step. I brought an extra towel, and if you find that happening at some point, or worse, someone mentions it to you, weave it around the shafts to make it quiet."

"Goddamn," he said, "you all are some crazy control freaks."

"You don't know the half of it," I said with a laugh.

Again, there was my name, smack dab on the leader board, and again, no one said a word to me when I checked in at the tournament table.

We warmed up, hit a few putts, I went to the can, and we marched up the hill to the tenth tee.

We were playing in foursomes again. One of my playing partners, Bryce Fleming, was a guy whom I'd played a lot with in Canada. He had no idea what had happened to me, and I didn't feel obliged to fill him in.

"Hey, man," I said, as I shook his hand, "how's it going?"

"Oh, you know, just trying to have a place to play this week."

"What's your status?"

"Fully exempt for the USDT, but we don't play again for another couple of weeks," Bryce said.

"Is that in Mississippi?" one of the other players asked with a pretty thick accent."

"Yeah."

"I'm new to all of this. I'm Mark Tinby from Adelaide," he said with his hand out.

An Aussie. I always loved playing with them. As a rule, they're tough, funny, and generous.

"This is Bryce; I'm Chuck."

Our fourth arrived just before the starter bellowed: "This is the eight-fourteen starting time. From Sandy, Utah, Chris Gehringer. Play away, please."

Chris Gehringer was on one of the local college teams and was trying to qualify as an amateur. He had a teammate on his bag.

Chris seemed rattled at having cut his arrival to the tee so close. He quickly put his peg in the ground, shakily got his glove on, took a quick swing and ripped it down the middle.

"Nice," I said.

I was next. The hole was a fairly short par four with an undulating green that was guarded by water on the left and a collection of bunkers on the right. I hit a three-iron, so I would have the perfect gap wedge distance into the back, left pin position.

Bryce and Mark followed my lead.

As we walked to our tee shots, I filled everyone in on Ray. I told them that this was his first time, so please go easy on him.

I also mentioned something about his law enforcement past, and that he'd spent years working undercover.

To a man, both caddy and player, they looked impressed. I knew that no one would mess with him.

Bryce and Mark hit it pretty close. I had exactly a hundred and two yards to the hole. I told Ray that we needed to hit it just a little beyond because the rains were sure to have softened the greens.

I hit it with a little cut, maximizing the amount of spin, and the ball landed, jumped up, and sucked right back into the jar for a two.

"Yeow!" Ray screamed.

"Nice start," Bryce muttered.

The high hands came at me from all directions.

"Thank you," I said. "Exactly as I drew it up."

The college kid was still shaken and the excitement of an eagle on the opener only seemed to make him more flustered. After consulting with his buddy, he flew his pitch into the water.

Things got kind of weird. After the eagle on ten, I birdied eleven, twelve, thirteen, fourteen, lipped out for birdie on fifteen, birdied sixteen with a two putt, parred seventeen, and birdied eighteen when I dropped a thirty-five foot double breaker.

My total for my first nine was twenty-eight, the first time I'd ever broken thirty for nine holes in competition.

"Holy shit," Ray whispered to me as we made the turn.

"Insane," I whispered back. "Let's just keep it going."

"That seemed pretty easy," Bryce said.

"Just lucky," I said.

We had a bit of a wait on the first tee, as is often the case when they split things up between the nines.

A voice called to us from over by the leaderboard.

"Mr. Dawson?"

I turned to find Don Cassell, a VP with the tour, and the guy who owned the title of head rules official.

"Could you step over here, please?" he asked.

Don was dressed in the costume befitting his position: blue Oxford shirt, striped tie, khaki pants, and a somewhat crappy, pale blue windbreaker. There was a passel of access lanyards around his neck.

"What's all this?" Mark Tinby asked.

I shrugged, though I was pretty sure that it might be that moment of reckoning I'd feared.

"Stay with these guys," I said to Ray.

"You sure?"

"Yeah. It's better if I talk to him alone."

"What's going on, Chuck?" Bryce asked.

"I don't know."

I walked over to Don Cassell. He shooed away a couple of bucket heads that were loitering nearby.

"I'm going to make this real simple, Mr. Dawson. Whoever accepted your application to compete in this qualifier made a mistake. I would ask that you and your caddy please leave the property. We will refund you the entry fee and I will ask you to never try to apply for entry again in any event sanctioned by the tour, okay?"

"Can you give me a reason?" I asked

"I don't have to do that. We are a closed society here, son. You have made yourself ineligible by your previous actions. You are not up to our level of ethics. Check the handbook. It's all there."

I snorted, or maybe just nodded. I was numb. Implacable. There was no use in fighting this guy in that moment. I turned around and waved Ray over. He was huddled with my playing partners and their caddies; it was obvious that he had filled them in on my history.

Mark Tinby was absolutely livid. A righteous anger—the type, I suppose, that can only come from someone who was raised in a former penal colony—rose up inside him and he charged over to where we stood.

"What the fuck, man! How can you do this?" he screamed to Don Cassell.

"Take it easy," Don said calmly.

But Mark got right up in his face. Luckily, Ray arrived, and found a way to shield the two from having a physical altercation.

"Go back and finish your round, sir," Don said.

"This is bullshit. The guy is going to break the course record. Let him finish his round. Deal with it later, mate."

"Mr. Dawson, was never an entrant, sir. He knows that."

"You call yourself an example of justice, right? You're some kind of custodian of the game? Bullshit. You know nothing. I want to file a formal complaint. You have disrupted my round of golf. You have violated the rules, sir."

"And what rule would that be?"

"I think 1.2 would fit, don't you," Mark said.

That would be kind of hard to apply to someone who wasn't competing, but I did see his point. This was disruptive for more than just me.

"You are welcome to withdraw at this time, sir."

Mark stared daggers into Don Cassell. After an extended moment, he turned to me and held out his hand.

"That would have been a hell of round, mate. Best I've ever seen."

I shook his hand. I pulled his scorecard out of my back pocket, tore off the perforated border that was used for my own tally and handed his over.

"I'm sorry. I certainly didn't mean for you to get upset," I said.

"Fuck that. You did nothing."

Then he shook Ray's hand.

"Thanks for looking out for me," he said.

"No problem. Go get 'em, Mark," Ray said.

Mark headed back to the first tee. Bryce had already hit and he was up.

"Go if you're ready, Chris," we heard him say as he approached.

"Let's go home," I said to Ray.

I handed Don Cassell the strip of paper with the score from my first nine holes.

"I'll guess I'll see you in court," I said.

Don did not respond. He dropped the piece of paper in the trashcan nearby, and Ray and I headed for his truck. The clubs clanked with every step.

26

I spent the next four days holed up in the Gumball, eating instant ramen and drinking gallon jugs of spring water.

I'd been confounded before, obviously, but this seemed different. Darkness and despair enveloped me. A loop of negativity kept compounding in my mind. With each intensifying circuit, I could hear it scream that I was finished.

These feelings were foreign. My Asperger's hadn't broken me. Neither had Jim's death or my stretch in prison.

From that first time that I whacked those plastic balls into the garage door, I had plotted my course. Somehow, some way, I knew I was going to do this thing for the rest of my life.

I'd worked hard, gotten excellent instruction, taken my lumps and earned my stripes. I wanted to test all of that experience and knowledge against the best in the world.

Could I be content with just enjoying the game without the competition? The answer that continued to come back was a resounding, "No!"

I felt like someone who had lost a limb. I was going to have to carry on with a part of me missing and I was having a hard time convincing myself that I could reclaim anything resembling normalcy.

I'd been trained to put on a smile and go forward and I had gotten really good at performing that act when confronted with resistance. The vagaries of day to day frustrations could always be diluted by the big picture—the next lesson, the new discovery, and most notably, the next tournament.

I was utterly flummoxed.

I tried to counter these dispiriting feelings by attempting to foresee a different future. I had thought about becoming a caddy, sure there was a gaggle of players who could benefit from my analytical expertise.

Ultimately, I'd decided against it. I would not be able to keep my exasperation hidden when my player failed to execute something that I could easily accomplish.

I researched all of the other tours around the world: Europe, Asia, Australasia, Japan, Korea, China, South America, but most had, at the least, a loose affiliation with the big tour.

There was no one taking advantage of the lesser players by promoting an alternate circuit at the time. Prince Harold had died.

Finally, I called the only lawyer I'd ever trusted. When I first heard her voice, I got that same feeling I'd had every time I had ever spoken with her. A distinct flutter in my bloodstream and the emergence of goose bumps on my skin.

I had been nervous on the golf course, especially when I was younger, but this was an entirely different sensation.

"Hello, it's Chuck," I said when she picked up.

"Yes?" she asked, almost leaving out the required lilt for a question.

"It's Charles Dawson."

"Yeah, I know who you are."

There was a long silence before I added, "You helped me with my parole hearing?"

"Yeah, Chuck, yeah, I know who you are. I'm just a little pissed off is all."

"Bad day?"

"Goddamn, you are one dense dude."

"Excuse me?"

"Now you call me? It's been seven months," she said.

"Oh, yeah. I tried to call you from the pay phone at the bus station to thank you for the clothing and the round of golf, but . . ."

"But you didn't."

"You make me nervous," I said after another long pause.

"I do?"

"You knew that."

"No, no, Chuck, I did not."

"Well, you do."

The silence that came next was excruciating.

"And yeah, I'm dense; it's part of my DNA," I said.

She laughed a little at that and things seemed to shift. We

made small talk: She'd been swamped at work and a tornado had taken two apartment buildings a quarter of mile from where she lived.

I told her about the Gumball and a little about Ray before launching into my whole dilemma with the tour and my expulsion.

She listened without interruption as I told the whole the story.

"I can see some complications here," she said after I'd finished.

"Like what?"

"Okay. Here's what I think. One, you could sue. I'd have to research it and find out if there have been attempts by others in the past, but you are just one person against an entity that has tremendously deep pockets. They would bleed you dry before your case even found its way to a hearing."

"Well, it's not like I have a lot of blood left anyway. I'm tapped out. I'm alive because I have some amazing and gracious friends. I would have to have someone take on the case with no guarantee of anything," I said.

"Exactly, so you know what I'm saying. Now number two is something I think you should really think about. It solves many of the issues that are presented in number one. You would be represented pro bono and have a much larger army on your side. An actual movement backing you."

I knew where this was headed.

"No, I don't want to do that."

"Hang on, hear me out. I have friends who could make a

few calls, and you could have some real substantial legal representation backed up by thousands of people who would march in the streets for your cause."

"No, thanks."

"I'm talking about serious lawyers. Arguing cases in front of the Supreme Court serious."

"You got a number three?" I asked.

"Why, Chuck? Why wouldn't you consider it? I think it would not only be effective, but you could do a lot of good by showing the world that someone with your 'situation' can rise to the top of a very difficult profession."

"That's not how it works."

"That's not how what works?"

I was silent. I wasn't going to budge.

"Okay, first off, there is nothing typical about my 'situation.' When they call it a spectrum, it's just that, a wide range of diagnoses. If my so-called parents had done nothing to address their fears about me, it is quite possible that I would still be who I am today," I said.

"You honestly believe that?" she asked.

"I don't know. I don't know a life without thousands of hours of one type of therapy or another."

"I think you do."

"There was this famous comedian, and he was on some talk show, and they were talking about his youth. He said something like, 'If that diagnosis stuff had been around when I was a kid, I definitely would have been put on that scale with the autistic or Asperger's kids.' Well, the backlash to that statement was so fierce. Parents who viewed their children as afflicted posted videos to his social media, proclaiming the devastation it caused in their lives. I know he was just joking, but he spent a year apologizing for those comments."

"Okay, but that's someone who never actually suffered. You did."

"Did I? I've told you that I think that just might be my special sauce. That might be why I've gotten as far in golf as I have."

"Is stubbornness a symptom of your disorder?" she asked.

"Most definitely." I said.

"Okay, then I think I know the answer of whether you're afflicted or not," she said with a smile in her voice.

"So, let me circle back. Do you have a number three?" I asked.

"I do. I've got a real 'Hail Mary.'"

"Bring it."

"First off, have we ever discussed why you pleaded to a Class B felony and not a Class D?"

"There was a chance I could get out early if I went with the B."

"Who told you that?"

"My attorneys."

"Wow, those guys were some real winners. I'll have to check where they are now and steer potential clients away."

"Why is that a problem?" I asked.

"Class B is listed under violent felonies. Class D can encompass a whole bunch of stuff that could be considered non-violent."

"Oh."

"Here's my thought," she began. "We could try to get your conviction vacated. This is something that the governor of the state can do and often does for people that he knows, or that can provide him with an interesting story. If you are no longer a felon, well they can't keep you from pursuing your dreams."

"And the Class B is a problem?"

"Yeah, he, or should it end up being a she someday, only considers Class D or below in these instances."

"Oh. Oops."

"I might be able to ask around. There might be a procedure to alter the classification from B to D, and since you've already served your sentence and time has elapsed, they might just do that. I'm sure it's complicated, but it's possible. Still, that would be the easy part. Putting it in front of the governor is a lot trickier."

"Huh, wow, that actually gives me some hope," I said.

"You'll need a lot more than that."

"It's so nice to hear your voice," I stammered.

This was out of left field for me, and to this day I cannot believe that I said it. That flutter inside of me became the flapping of the wings of a turkey vulture, and it had just slipped out.

The ensuing silence went on for way longer than I could stand.

"Really? You know it is nearly impossible to tell with you. It seems like whenever we've spoken in the past, I always thought I was bugging you," she finally said.

"Hardly," I said.

"Yeah, well the feeling's mutual. I wasn't sure why you pissed me off so much, but you did, and I guess that means something."

That response confused me a little. It sounded sincere, but how was I to know?

"Should I call you next week?" I asked in a more business-like tone.

"I'll call you when I have something. What's next for you?"

"I don't know. I don't think I've ever been this desperate about anything."

"Really? Because of golf?"

"Yeah, really. If I can't compete again, I . . ."

"Huh. I guess I don't have a feel for something like that. It's just a game, right?"

"Ha. Spend some time with me and it will become readily apparent how much it means."

It wasn't an invitation, and I don't think she took it as such, but it did create another void in the conversation.

"Can I ask you a question?"

"Of course," I quickly replied.

"You once said that some people call you, Chunk. Why?"

"Not everyone does that. Only special people."

"Are you going to tell me?"

"Someday," I said.

"Yeah, we'll see, I guess," she said sardonically.

I felt that I was disappointing her again, and though I would have liked to talk a bit longer, I started to feel the nervousness rise in me like it had before. I decided to cut my losses and hang my hat on the hopes that she'd provided with her counsel.

"So, next week?" I asked, forgetting that I'd already tried to fix a time and been rebuffed.

"We just went over that. I'll call you when I know more."

"Oh, yeah, okay, that's good."

"Bye, Chuck."

"Bye."

I walked back to the Gumball, endeavoring to recreate the conversation in the most positive light. I crawled back into my orange cavern and tried to use our talk to replace the other conversations rattling around in my head.

27

On awakening the next day, I felt something break loose in my soul. I sat on my metal stoop in the morning mist, and as my mind and the sky cleared, I remembered that I had one more card to play.

I starting hitting balls again that afternoon. When the following Saturday rolled around and Ray showed up for his lesson, I filled him in about what Deidre had told me. I also announced my next move, which I saw as a last chance.

There is one tournament that Mr. Hogan competed in more than any other: The United States Open Championship. During a remarkable stretch of over twenty years, he won the tournament four times, and never finished worse than tenth.

Post-accident, he won it three times. In those days, the final round was staged over thirty-six holes, so the fact that he could haul his fragile, previously smashed bones around a hilly track in the heat of the summer is truly remarkable.

My experience with the event was sketchy at best. I had

gone down the road of trying to qualify since the age of fifteen. I'd advanced to sectional qualifying five times in the ten years I had attempted to make it into the tournament, but never teed it up on any of those Thursdays in mid-June when it was traditionally contested.

Every year, the USGA accepts somewhere between 8,500 to nearly 11,000 applications to play in their championship.

These are the criteria for eligibility: 1) Be a professional, or an amateur with a certifiable handicap index of 1.4. 2) Submit an application with an entry fee of two hundred dollars by the deadline, which is toward the end of every April.

Nearly all of the hopefuls compete in eighteen-hole events in May—there are sometimes as many as a hundred and twenty held around the country.

From there, a handful of players at the top of each local qualifier move on to thirty-six holes of sectional qualifying two weeks before the championship kicks off.

Those events produce the seventy-four entrants who will be added to the group of the already exempt to make up the final field of one hundred and fifty-six.

There is nothing in the eligibility rules about being excluded for having been a hardened criminal and jailbird.

I chose the local qualifying event that was going to be contested closest to me during the second week of May. Four players in the field of ninety-four would move on to one of the ten sectional qualifying sites.

I had a little over two months to get ready.

Every day, I hopped a ride with the Galan brothers. Those

March mornings were cold, but when I saw the headlights of Hernando's truck inching up the rutted, dirt road toward the mesa, I got excited for what the day might bring.

It might have just been a Band-Aid for that interim time, a winch to pull me out of my spirit ditch, but during those two months, I was buoyed by the existence of possibility.

My refund check for the San Diego Open four-spot qualifier arrived and I used a portion of that to submit my application to the USGA. I used the rest to stock up on balls. I also bought a used driver and utility club from the bargain bin at a golf equipment warehouse in National City.

Amongst my possessions in the storage locker was an array of shafts; I spent the next month tinkering with the new driver head and trying to make one of those fit my needs.

Josh got an invite to check out the facility of a major club manufacturer in North County, and he asked me if I wanted to go.

We traveled north to Carlsbad on a Monday afternoon, and I had my mind blown by all of the testing equipment they had there. I could have spent a good three days taking readings off the launch monitor alone.

It was fun, but I had a little bit of a crisis at one point. Here I was, indoors with dim LED lighting, looking at numbers as they flashed on the screen, trying to better only those factors, and adjusting my approach to achieve that.

I began to feel strange, like I couldn't really take a deep breath; my heart rate was climbing.

I know I've mentioned what I felt when I got nervous, and that thing I felt coursing through my veins when I talked to Deidre, but this was neither of those.

I had to get outside. I had to feel the wind and smell something that resembled the real—turf, exhaust, garbage, whatever. After two minutes, I was back to normal, but it freaked me out.

On the way home, Josh thought it had to do with being enclosed in the testing room, and I had to agree with him. I felt like I was locked up again.

We laughed about it then, but that night, back in the Gumball, I thought about what had happened to me in the months since I'd been released.

I've detailed it here, but that is just anecdotal information. I was starting to realize that there were scars that had yet to heal.

The next day, I called the W.M.D.C.C. and asked to speak to Sally. I was told that she was no longer at that facility.

My local U.S. Open qualifier was held at the private club in Chula Vista. I'd played two rounds there in all the years I'd played the game.

As the crow flew, it was only four miles from SVMGC, but it might as well have been on another continent.

Its exclusivity in the county was well known, but the steep initiation and exorbitant monthly fees did provide one thing of value: the layout was always in pristine condition.

At just a shade over 7,000 yards, it was relatively short in comparison to most modern-day courses, but it was narrow and had beautiful old trees that framed every hole.

The greens were a combination of bent grass and *Poa annua*, and they could be cut to a length that could rival the speeds at Augusta National.

Those greens were the course's greatest defense, and during the practice round, I had to keep reminding myself that they would be trimmed to the bone for the competition.

Ray asked if he could carry my bag again. There wasn't a question. We'd been eight under through nine holes of our last round and I could always use a continuation of that mojo.

I'd requested an early tee time (I always do) and we went off in the third group at 8:21 a.m.

Again, due to the size of the field, we were in foursomes. I was paired with one other professional and two amateurs, both high school kids from a more upscale part of the county.

The professional was a man named Paul Rink; I had heard of him before because he was constantly voted as one of the best teaching pros in the San Diego Section. He ran the municipal course across the bridge (or around the strand) on the inaccurately named Coronado Island.

He was a jolly sort and sported the body to express it. How he got the club around his gut was a real thing of beauty.

The two high school kids were a bit of a distraction. They had their families about, and as often happens when teens are playing amongst pros, they do things that are annoying by anyone's standards.

They are constantly in the way, often walk across your putting line, show more emotion than they should whether the result is good or bad, and have this uncanny tendency to retrieve their ball from the hole by stepping on the edge of the cup.

I know this because I was one of them at one point. I had Jim, and he'd laid it out for me on more than one occasion.

Paul Rink's jolliness got tested by the time we had holed out on the second. He confronted one of the teens as we headed to the third tee.

"Hey, kid, let's get something straight. You are not the center of this experience, you got me?" Paul said, seething.

One of the teens' dads overheard the admonishment and got a little testy.

"Excuse me, sir?" the dad asked.

"I'm not talking to you. Are you playing in this group?"

"That is my son, sir."

"Congratulations, he has the makings of a good player. Could you have at least taught him some goddamn etiquette?" Paul asked.

Ray and I were doing all we could to keep from laughing. There was a moment when I tried to conceal myself behind the giant trunk of one of those old trees because I was afraid that I was going to absolutely lose it.

Paul dropped it at that point, and stomped away. He reached into his bag and pulled out a fresh pack of cigarettes. He didn't really say another word to anyone for the rest of the round, and he killed that pack over the next sixteen holes.

The whole incident rattled the kids, who hit it sideways from that tee to the end. I don't think either of them broke eighty-five.

"They've got letters coming," I whispered to Ray after they had both doubled-bogeyed sixteen.

"What do you mean?"

"The USGA doesn't appreciate it when you overstate your ability. They send you a letter that says that you should not try to qualify for their championship again."

"Really? How do you know that?"

"Because I got one. The first time I tried to qualify, I shot an eighty-two. I had to get an affidavit signed by a pro. I also had to show them how I'd performed over the last year. I'd made the quarterfinals of the Junior Am, so it's not like I was trying to pull the wool over their eyes. I was the medalist in local qualifying that second year."

"Growing pains?"

"Yeah. That's my M.O."

We finished the round. I turned in my card, and a red 68 was inscribed on the board next to my name. It was early, but it was four shots better than anyone among the six groups that had finished.

The result of the round was never in doubt. I made five birdies, all in the first twelve holes. My lone bogey came on the sixth, the result of a three-putt when I hit my seven-iron behind the hole.

I made par from thirteen all the way to the house.

Paul Rink and the fathers of the teens got into it in the parking lot while my score was being posted. At some point, the security people at the course had to amble out to break it up.

Paul had shot 75 and he had no reason to hang around to see if he was going to sectional qualifying.

We did. Ray bought us lunch, and while we were pounding our burgers, there was a player who posted a 66. Another hour or so later, a second 68 went up on the board, and that was it. We'd made it.

There was a playoff for the final spot between three players. Ray and I were already in the car and headed back to SVMGC.

A couple of days later, I finally tracked down Sally Dio. I had been scrolling through the Missouri prison system's database, trying to find where she had been sent and I was having no luck.

There was a moment when the thought crossed my mind that something bad had happened, but finally I found her.

I had been searching using the name that was considered to be her legal one: Salvatore Dio. I'd gotten nothing back.

The next day, I mistakenly put in Sally, and there it was. She was currently being housed in the maximum-security wing of the Chillicothe Women's Prison, a fairly new facility that was in the northern part of the state.

Wow, I remember thinking at the time. How did that happen?

I left a message on their voicemail with her name, her inmate number, and my phone number.

She called the next day at six in the morning, my time. I was already out on the range, hitting half-lob wedges to a beach towel that was fifty yards from me. It was still dark.

"Hello?"

"Sweetie, how are you?" she said in a voice that seemed softer than I remembered it.

"I'm good."

"As am I."

"I found you at Chillicothe. How did that happen?"

"Where are you living?" she asked.

"I'm squatting in a trailer some friends have on their property. It's been a bit of cluster since I've returned. So many things are up in the air."

"Do you have an address? Someplace that I can send a letter?"

"Yeah. I get my mail at the golf course. Do you have a pen?"

"Hang on," she said.

She must have put her hand lightly over the receiver because in a muffled voice I heard her say:

"Doris, my dear, could I please have a pen and piece of paper?"

"Okay, lay it on me," she said on her return.

I gave her the address.

"I'll give you all the details there. It could only happen in Missouri. Well, probably another dozen or so states, but definitely in Missouri. How's the golf?"

I told her about some of the things that had happened, like the whole condo fraud thing, and getting pulled off the course at the four-spot qualifier. That same anger that she might have displayed on hearing those stories wasn't there for some reason.

"So, you said, when you got out that first time, you didn't

know what to do with yourself and that led you back into trouble. What was that feeling?" I asked.

"You are not a criminal, Chunk. You know that, right?"

"It's not that. I just . . . I guess I'm kind of lost is all."

"Okay, let's look at that. You came home to no place to live. Your father, or the man who functioned as such, has gone to heaven. And your future pursuits are being foiled by powers beyond your control. That's a shit ton of low blows you've taken, don't you think?"

"I was in a room last week, and it was poorly lit, and the air was fake, and I kind of had this flashback to having been locked up."

She laughed, knowingly.

"Ask any ex-con and they will tell you that it happens all the time. I would make friends with that, sweetie, cause you're likely to have that around you for the rest of your life."

That made sense. It reminded me of something that Jim once said about Babe; that, though they could never be together again, she had never left him. It was painful for a long time, but he made friends with it and eventually came to see it all in a positive light.

"It's a lot easier to accept than to deny," Sally said.

Jim had said that too.

She continued, "There was somebody, a yoga instructor or counselor who once said to me, 'The past is depression, the future is anxiety, the now is where your feet are.' Does that make sense? That's worked for me in the past."

There was a click on the line. Her time was ending.

"Look for my letter. So great to hear from you."

"You too. Be well," I said.

"It will all be in the letter."

There was a final click and then the recorded voice which redundantly announced that the call had ended.

28

The now is where your feet are.

La Clarita was a stunning piece of property nestled in the canyons just east of Point Conception, near the central California coast. It was blessed with hundreds of century-old oak trees and the course designer had smartly used their natural positioning to inform his routing.

Basically, it was what some would label a "target course." You were expected to play it by advancing from point to point, as hazards often blocked any direct attack.

The hidden genius of La Clarita was that it could actually be played like any regular course. There was plenty of lush grass to land on, though how you got there was often a gamble.

When played from the tips, it could be a serious test.

If you wanted to use your length, you had to take extraordinary routes over corners, or fit your tee shot into a tiny area between some trees and a dangerous situation. If you could pull it off, the rewards were plentiful.

If you didn't, there were a lot of double bogeys to be had.

The greens were good. They were incredibly expansive, often multi-tiered, and not super-fast.

All around it was an excellent test of golf and the perfect venue for a sectional qualifier.

The event was thirty-six holes contested over a single day.

Ray and I left San Diego County at around ten-thirty on the night before. It was a good six hours from SVMGC, and since the course sat in the area known as the wine country of the central coast, a crappy motel room was still a couple of hundred bucks a night.

I slept most of the way. Ray had his headphones on, listening to some podcast or other about the aspects of a bone-chilling crime.

I woke up as we turned off the 101 and headed west on the two-lane road that terminated at the ocean's edge.

"Oh wow, let's stop here," I said. "There's a place that does Danish pancakes with lemon butter."

"I'm into that," Ray said.

We pulled into the parking lot. Even at four-thirty in the morning, it was pretty full.

We drank coffee and fortified ourselves with carbohydrates and breakfast meat. I picked up the check; Ray protested, but I told him that he should accept my generosity now because I was going to stiff him on the caddy fee later.

He was absolutely certain that he would have no problem making it through both rounds. I was dubious.

"You know, Jim told me that back when Hogan had a streak

of three wins in the Open in five tries, he had to qualify for them by playing in a sectional," I said when we were back in the car.

"You're kidding."

"There were no exemptions until much later. Past champions had to qualify like everyone else, even if they were defending."

"This must have been before television."

"Yeah."

"That shit ain't going to fly now," he said.

He was right about that.

Eighteen more miles down the road, we pulled into the parking lot. I directed him over to the western edge, close to the range and the practice area. It was still dark, but the crickets and birds were letting everyone know that was soon to end.

I grabbed my putter and lob wedge, pocketed a couple of balls, and crossed a dry wash to get to one of the practice greens.

The crunch of river rock under my feet reminded me that I was exactly where I wanted to be on Earth. That led to a strange release of what I can only call emotion and I had to stop on the bank on the other side, my feet shin-deep in the dew-drenched grass, and appreciate the moment.

The feeling was transient and quickly replaced with a rush of reality. I had to play well that day. I just had to.

I began to visibly shake.

Ray arrived with the rest of my clubs.

"You okay, man?" he asked.

"I don't know. I don't think I've ever felt this way before."

"What's up?"

"I think this might be too important."

"Bullshit."

"No, I'm serious. I've never, ever felt like this before a round," I said in a bit of a panic.

Ray just stared at me with a stupid grin on his face.

I struggled slightly as I walked over to the practice green. I dropped the balls in some four-inch rough nearby and tried to hit super high flop shots that were meant to only travel ten yards. I was trying to land them on the two-foot wide strip of fringe and let them trickle onto the green.

My focus came back and it allowed me to recall that yes, I'd had this feeling before. I flashed on the moment that I'd first struck that plastic ball in my backyard. After contact, all I wanted to do was repeat it. I realized that back then, my hands had also been shaking.

The sun finally showed up and the first hint of the coming breeze began to ripple the distance flags that dotted the driving range like pennants at a stadium.

I walked up to the area by the clubhouse and checked in. I took a moment to look at the board.

The field only had sixty-eight competitors and sprinkled among the names were a good deal of guys who had serious resumes.

Every local pro from the region who'd had some success appeared to be on the board, including Chip Astoria, who had won multiple times on the tour.

Based on the field size, it appeared that only four players would advance. There would also be two alternates selected from those who finished fifth and sixth.

I grabbed a bucket of balls and hit only drivers to warm up. I wanted to practice a big draw, because nearly every hole where you could tee it up and let it fly could be played right to left.

I wanted to take advantage of the somewhat benign conditions. The wind had not quite gotten cranked up yet, and given those circumstances, I decided to let it go.

We made our way to the tee, exchanged greetings with our playing partners, pocketed the pin sheet and waited for them to call my name.

The first hole was a medium length par five. I hit a driver into the fifteen yards available between a pond and one of those magisterial oak trees, cut a five iron into the bunker in front of the three-tiered green, chunked it out to let it run up to the second level and dropped a three-footer for a birdie.

I then made par on the next thirteen holes.

Some were close to being birdies, some were hair-raising adventures where more than one miraculous shot got me out of the trouble I'd put myself into by gambling like a fool.

I birdied the par five fifteenth. I hit another big drive that I started over a large hazard and drew back into a sliver of fairway. I followed that with a four iron to the front fringe, lagged it up to tap-in distance, and knocked it in without removing the flag. I stood on the sixteenth tee at two under par.

Ray had started making a low whistle as each hole was finished. I knew he was tense and I wasn't making it easy on him with my club selection and routing. The more I felt he was wishing I would play it a little more conservatively, the more I wanted to show him that I had the guts to hit the impossible shot. I do not know why that was the dynamic of that round, but it was definitely a factor, and to that point, it had worked.

By the time we got to sixteen, the wind had become a tangible element.

I continued with the formula. I pulled a driver out of the bag with the intention of starting the ball on the right tree line and drawing it into the left side of the fairway.

I snap hooked it and ended up in the middle of an unkempt part of the course, left with 200 yards, straight into the wind, to one of the smaller greens where there were deadly drop-offs at the back and to the right.

It took Ray and me a bit of time to find the ball, and when we did, it was sitting on a little mound of sand that must have been the remnants of an old ant hill.

"What are you thinking?" Ray asked.

"Go for it."

"Really? Why now? You're two under. This course is a bitch. I've got to think that your score would be good enough to be at or near the top."

He was right. I'd looked it up. Historically, being one of the four who'd made it at La Clarita in sectionals varied by score, but two round scores of 142 always advanced. There were twenty holes to go. If I played them at even par, that would be my number.

"Lay up to the area in front. You can chip it up and make your par."

"Nah, I got this," I said.

I could go over a grove of trees with a cut, or I could hit a low hook around a tree that stood forty yards away on the edge of the fairway.

I went for the high cut, caught it a little fat because of the sand underneath the ball. It got up into the air too quickly and the wind knocked it down into a grouping of gnarly trees.

"Let's hope we've got a way to the hole," I said.

Ray was silent. I realize then that this was new for him—me chopping it around a bit.

"We'll be fine," I said.

We found it. It wasn't completely stymied, but I had no line to the hole. I scuttled it out, chipped to about six feet and dropped the putt for a bogey.

"That's not bad. Could have been a lot worse," I said as we took the long walk to seventeen.

"You're still in the red," Ray said.

"Yeah. Let's get it back."

If I'd thought the wind was nasty on the sixteenth tee, seventeen was at a whole other level.

It had always been a really cool hole, a dastardly par three, easily one of my favorites at La Clarita.

It was relatively short at around one hundred and seventy-five yards, but it was at the highest point of the golf course, with a tee that sat on a promontory favored by these huge, beautiful California condors. They liked to chill up there between swoops down into the valley to snatch up a wild hare or gopher that had momentarily turned their backs to the sun.

It was about an eighty-foot drop to the green, which was guarded by out of bounds on the left and a wash that protected the front. There was no bail-out to the right because it dropped down toward the eighteenth tee. Behind the green was a steep rise, and if you hit it up there, you were lucky if you made a bogey.

Anywhere on the green was not only good, but an imperative.

My two playing partners had also bogeyed sixteen, so the honor went back to me from the birdie I'd made on fifteen. They were both young amateurs and were around four or five over par at that point. They hadn't provided much useful information yet and I wasn't expecting that to change.

I finally decided to cut the ball into the wind that was coming out of the right.

I chose a seven iron. I'd hit it to the center of the green and let the breeze adjust the spin, so it would feather straight down to the putting surface.

Somewhere in the process of executing the shot, there was another strong gust and that led me, in mid-swing, to try to cut the ball even more. The result was a skulled slice that cleared the wash but ricocheted off the oak sentinel to the right of the green. The ball ended up on a knoll by the cart path near the tee box for the closing hole.

"Huh," I muttered in fake amazement.

It was a total gag swing. The kind of thing you did when your commitment was weak and without foundation.

Ray didn't look up. He became a condor. His intense eyes

stared at the ground as if he were looking for a microscopic field mouse.

I pitched it up over the tree and two-putted from thirty feet for my second straight bogey.

There was still no panic, but there was something rising inside of me that was akin to anger. I alit on what I'd done wrong and now I just needed to make it back to the clubhouse unscathed, so I could work it out on the range between rounds.

Eighteen was like a lot of holes at La Clarita, where there was a preferred route down one side or the other that could make the hole easier for you but punish you if you didn't pull it off.

The hole was a straight-ahead par four that played about four hundred and twenty yards, but was directly into what was now a wind that you could hear.

There was a landing area at 250 that was the supposed target, but there was also a narrow strip up the right side that was guarded by a deep bunker on the left and some nasty rough if you went a little further to the right.

Looking to just make par, I chose the conservative route, taking a three wood and hitting a low draw into the most generous part of the fairway.

I got a little ahead of it and pushed it out to the right, where it scurried into some of that nasty rough.

I chopped it out to an area before the wash and the platoon of gum tress that rose up about fifty yards short of the green. I then had to find a way around one of those trees that was blocking my direct access to the hole. My shot caught a wisp of one of the upper branches, and the ball ended up on the front fringe. I was left with a sixty-footer up two steep tiers of slope.

I lagged up to five feet and made that when the ball fell in over the edge after pushing the putt. Another bogey, and a lucky one at that.

Round one was in the books and my 73 put me in roughly tenth place. Had I finished at two under, I would have been in second.

"Let's get something to eat," Ray suggested.

"No, I've got some issues to try to work out."

I picked up my bag. One of the cart guys pointed me to a barrel of balls inside the shed, and I filled a small bucket.

Jim would have never let this happen. He would have seen how I'd warmed up and told me that just wasn't going to do.

I'd gotten loose by hitting draws with my driver. I mistakenly set my base swing with that shot shape. I was keying off a shape that eventually became uncomfortable and I failed to recalibrate on the fly.

The afternoon round was going to be a completely different story for everyone. There would be no more free-lancing, because the wind would be blowing twenty-five miles per hour.

I hit a couple of six irons to try to find my center, but I caught most of them on the toe. I started to panic for real. I didn't have the time to try to figure out why my path was so messed up. It could have been ten different things. I tried a few fixes. Nothing worked for more than a few iterations. For a time, I thought about just hitting cuts, but hitting slices into a gale is a fool's errand.

Ray brought me down a sandwich from the snack bar and reminded me that we had about twelve minutes to get to the tee for round two. I knew it was obvious to him that I was more than a little rattled.

"I don't know," I kept repeating after every lash.

"What don't you know?" Ray asked after the eighth or ninth time.

"I think I might have lost it."

"Lost what?"

"My swing. Nothing seems right."

"Has this ever happened before?"

"Yeah, for a hole or two. Never for a whole round."

"Well, you've got to trust that it will be there."

There was some wisdom there, I'm sure, but I wasn't really listening. I handed him the club, took the sandwich and ate it as we walked to the tee.

"Let me ask you a question, Chunk. I've had to answer this one probably a hundred times in my life."

"What?" I asked.

"If you had to go into battle with no ammunition . . . check that, no weapon of any kind, what would you do?"

I knew there was something metaphorical or at least allegorical in all that, but I didn't have the context or life experience to believe that I would be able to answer it the right way.

"Is running the other way an option?"

"Sure, now mind you, you are leaving your brothers-in-arms with fewer numbers, but yeah, you can retreat."

"Well, you know I'm not doing that."

"Yep," he said.

"Is this one of those use what you have access to kind of thing? Rocks, glass bottles, bare hands?"

"Yeah. Fight until you die. I came close on about twenty occasions, but I'm still here."

"Yes, you definitely are."

And then we heard: "This is the one thirty-six starting time. First up from Chula Vista, Charles Dawson."

29

Jim told me a story about Hogan, who'd made his only trip across the Atlantic to compete in the Open Championship at Carnoustie in 1953.

Hogan had set sail two weeks early to prepare and familiarize himself with the smaller British ball. He had to qualify, of course, but made it handily. He shot 73 in the opening round of the Championship, but played progressively better and closed with a 68. He won by four shots.

He'd had to alter his game to deal with the wind. He tried to hit the ball lower to limit the side-to-side spin because he felt it scrubbed off the distance he needed for the longer holes. The smaller ball helped, sure, but he found through his practice that the key was actually making sure that you caught the ball in the center of the clubface. The eventual results were straight, boring shots that worked their way around the links, one precise strike at a time.

Before I put my tee in the ground, I had made the decision

to do what Ray had talked about: use whatever I had left (rocks, bottles, bare hands) to carry me through what was sure to be an ordeal.

There were no thoughts of fading it or drawing it. No thoughts of hitting into areas where trouble lurked, or doing anything that might be construed as fancy.

All I thought about was getting the club to meet the ball squarely in the exact center of the clubface.

For the first time in my competitive life, I was trying to hit every ball dead straight.

To say it was a grind is an understatement. I plotted a course to the widest parts of every fairway and the most generous portions of every green.

I marked down par after par, never really scaring the hole for birdie.

I turned at even par, one over for the day, and judging by the numbers my playing partners were putting up, I believed that to be one of the better nines out there.

Ray ran up to the snack bar to get a banana or two for sustenance, and though I told him not to look at the leaderboard, I assumed he got a flavor of the carnage that was taking place in the bluster of the afternoon. We did not discuss it as we waited to take on the incoming nine.

I made my first birdie on ten by chipping in from just off the green.

I followed that with a bogey on eleven—one of the easier holes on the course—because for the first time in that round, I got a little greedy and tried to cut the corner with my tee shot.

My ball nearly plugged into the face of a bunker. I smashed it out, wedged on and two-putted for the five.

The next three holes took us down into a small glen; the wind was less intense during that stretch. I stayed with my game plan and parred all three.

The fifteenth was the par five I had birdied earlier in the day. I played conservatively and wrote down a par when it was done.

We walked to sixteen even par for the second round, still one over for the thirty-three holes we'd played.

When we arrived at the tee, the sun was directly in front of us, trying to stay afloat in the sky. With the departing light, the wind had also begun to disappear.

That consistent blast that had confronted us earlier on that tee was just a meek zephyr when I stood there for a second time.

"So, what did you see on the leaderboard when we made the turn?" I asked Ray.

"What? Nothing. I didn't look."

"Wow. I can't imagine that worked at all in your former life. You said you were a professional liar, but that stunk."

"What?"

"Ray, what did you see?"

"That Chip Astoria guy shot thirty-three on his outgoing nine," he said with some sheepishness.

"Jesus. That's some serious golf. So, we've got to figure that there are only three spots left."

"What are you thinking?" Ray asked.

"I'm thinking we have to adhere to the historical data. We have to get to one forty-two."

We both knew what that meant.

I was still a little shaky, but the time had come to deviate from the more conservative approach.

I'd accomplished my goal of striking the ball in the middle of the clubface, and except for a couple of swings, I was able to hit it straight and get it in the area I was aiming at. There was no nuance at all, however, and that is why the results were so standard.

I had to hope that I was back to some kind of solid base, as if I had warmed up as I normally would by hitting a couple of straight shots.

With the wind down, I decided to aim at another of those huge oak trees on the left side of the fairway and cut the ball back into the fairway.

It was really do or die. Basically, it had come down to me making five more swings. Then, I had to make three putts from what I was hoping to be shorter distances than anything I'd had during the round to that point.

I pulled off the first two swings, that cut driver and a buttered six iron that left me with an eight-foot uphill putt.

I drilled it with the pin out. I took most of the break out by just banging it straight into the center.

"That's one," I said to Ray as we made the hike to seventeen.

"Fuck, yeah," was all he mustered.

Seventeen couldn't have played any different than it had earlier. The condors were gone, hunting in the gloaming. The winds that could have produced full ahead speed on a schooner had diminished to the point where the flag on the green lay limp as if it were exhausted from the day's work.

I hit an eight with a baby draw and damn near holed it out. I putted last and made the two-footer with all the determination of someone who was never going to miss a putt again.

On our way to the closing hole, I didn't say a word. Ray's eyes were kind of bugging out of his head. We just had to do it one more time.

I really tried to jump on the drive on eighteen. I hit it a little high on the face and the ball got a little too far up in the air. That would have killed me earlier, but I only had a full pitching wedge left and I hit it to about seven feet.

The putt was tricky. The pin was in a place on the green where two of the tiers came together and that produced an optical illusion.

Every read told me that it would defy gravity and break uphill. I knew the ocean lay off in that direction, but the drainage looked like it went the opposite way.

Also, as the day was waning, the *Poa annua* had started to bud and the larger blades were bowing toward the setting sun. The contradictions grew. I called Ray over to sort through all of the different scenarios.

I listed my litany of thoughts and asked for his opinion.

"You're kidding, right?" he asked.

"No. How would you play it?"

He thought about it for a moment. He knelt down and tried to see what I saw.

"I don't understand how you think that it will break uphill. That makes no sense," he concluded.

I took my stance and went with my first thought. I stroked it with some good pace. There was no wobble or side spin.

Ray and Isaac Newton were right. Gravity is a factor. The putt never broke uphill. It stayed perfectly straight and skimmed past on the left edge.

"Damn," I muttered.

I tapped in for a 70. 143. *Maybe that was going to be good enough*, I thought at the time.

I shook everyone's hands. The others in our group were destined for the parking lot. Ray headed to the bathroom and I went and authenticated my scorecard.

"Wow, nice round," the bucket head said after he'd totaled the numbers.

"Thanks."

He handed it over to the scorekeeper. I walked over to the board.

Chip Astoria was in at 139, which was truly remarkable.

I found a 141 and another 143. My score went up and you could hear the disappointed murmurs from those who stood at 144.

It looked like a quarter of the field had yet to post, so I hunted through the morning round scores to see how many threats were still out there.

Ray arrived with some water and a granola bar.

"It's tight. I'm tied for third, but there are still at least five guys out there who could change that," I said.

I continued to scan through the field.

"Oh boy, you've got to be kidding," I whispered in amazement.

"What?" Ray asked.

I pointed to the board.

"That guy. Oh geez, it had to be, right?"

"What the hell are you talking about?"

"It's a long story. I'll tell you later."

The name that I was focusing on was Billy Mars. The same Billy Mars who took me out with an ace during my first U.S. Amateur. He was in the last group. He'd shot two under in the morning round.

There would be about thirty minutes before he finished, so I popped my six iron out of my bag, and went to the shed for another bucket before heading down to the range. It would only take one more sub-144 score to extend the day for me.

Ray showed up after forty-five minutes.

"It's a playoff," he said.

"Damn. For alternate, right?"

"Well, kind of. A 142 came in. And that Billy Mars guy just posted 143. It's four guys for the last spot. The next two will be the alternates."

"Didn't I say 142 would get you through?"

"Yes, you did." Ray said.

"We're starting on ten, right?"

"Yup. Ten, then seventeen, and eighteen, if required."

I nodded. I knew the shot I wanted to hit off ten, but I didn't practice it. I just kept trying to make my strike on the balls within the parameters of that dime-sized indentation in the center of the clubface of my trusty six iron.

At the tenth tee there were probably thirty or so folks, most of them from Billy Mars' home club, milling about. The tension among the participants was visceral. Sudden death.

Along with Billy and me, there were two other pros.

They both were from up north and I'd heard of only one of them. The other was a lefty.

There were three bucket heads in tow, each with a cart. The players shook hands. Billy Mars did not acknowledge that we had a history and I didn't bring it up.

The lefty led off. He drove his ball into the hazard on the left and was kind of out of the hole by the time we arrived at the green.

I hit a big cut with a driver into the center of the fairway.

Billy and the other pro landed in the rough, but both got their balls onto the putting surface with their second shots.

I feathered a nine iron to ten feet. As I marked my ball, the lefty waded into the bunker to play his fourth shot.

I was, at the very least, going to be an alternate, but I had no interest in finishing second or third in this grouping.

The lefty marked his ball and never took his putter out of the bag.

Billy spent a good deal of time grinding over his putt and missed on the low side from twenty-five feet. The other pro really scared the hole, but left it on the lip.

So that was it. If I made it, I was heading to the Open.

I didn't consult Ray. He was staring at the ground again.

I focused on getting the speed right. I kept it inside the hole and tried to hit it a foot past. I didn't account for the day's growth and all of the footprints, and the putt finished just short, wiggling off to the right.

We headed to seventeen and the lefty and his caddy headed down the eighteenth fairway, knowing that it would be days before the pain of being eliminated would become bearable.

We climbed the hill to the tee of the par three. Only one of the condors had returned and he or she was sitting on the top branch of a big oak on the promontory.

I had retained the honor. I tried to recreate the exact same shot I'd hit about an hour before, the eight with baby draw, and pulled it off. I didn't have a two-footer, but I was hole high with eight feet for birdie.

The pro from up north went next and punched a seven. It ended up crawling just onto the front, around twenty feet away.

Billy Mars didn't hesitate. He yanked a club from his bag with some attitude and cut what I thought was a seven iron in there to three feet.

"Beauty," I said.

"Thanks, man,"

"Fuck," Ray muttered.

As we headed down the hill, Billy turned around and looked back at us.

"Have we met?" He asked me.

"U.S. Am thirteen years ago. You beat me two and one in the round of sixty-four."

"The ace!" He said gleefully and clapped his hands.

"Yeah."

"Could've used one right here," he said.

"You came pretty close," I said.

We trooped down the hill just as two returning condors did a flyby above us. They joined their full-bellied buddy on adjacent branches back up at the top of the hill.

The other pro missed his putt and then finished out.

I was certain that Billy would make it. He'd dropped putt after putt all of those years ago in the Am and I assumed that if it were a strength of his game then, it likely had not diminished.

At forty-one, he was just as tough an hombre as he'd always been. Those stockbroker guys often played for considerable sums on the weekend, and I'd bet he'd supplemented his bank account quite handsomely through the years.

I took a brief tour around the hole. There were more footprints than before, but the green sat in a pool of shade and the grass had retained its sheen from the morning. It was slightly downhill and toward the wash a bit, so I played it a ball outside right, and kissed it just off the toe of my Bullseye.

It never wavered and plopped into the cup without ever slowing down.

The gallery responded with a brief spate of applause, as the other pro hung his head in dismay. He was now the second alternate.

Billy took very little time and calmly dropped his putt.

Ray grabbed my putter and stowed it.

"Same as before?" he asked.

I nodded and he handed me the driver.

Billy sidled up on my right.

"Just like old times, right Dawson?" Billy asked.

"You ever play in the Open?" I asked.

"Two of the last five. Have yet to make the cut, though. Missed by one three years ago at Stone Beach."

"I've never made it," I said.

"Well, we both have a good shot. First alternates have been drawing into the field these days. That's how I made the last one," Billy said.

I wasn't interested in being an alternate. I wasn't interested in anything other than beating Billy Mars at that point. That conversation was a blatant bit of gamesmanship and I knew that he was trying in a nuanced way to see if he could reduce the fire that was burning inside of me.

The gist was, "Hey man, being an alternate is okay. You don't need to go all out."

The sectional was not likely to be included in the upper tier of those being contested, and priority for alternates came from field strength. It would take a sequence of extraordinary circumstances for the alternate from La Clarita to get in.

I absolutely smoked a power fade, employing the same swing I'd used on ten, to the right side of the fairway.

Billy hit a draw around the bunker. His ball ended up thirty yards behind me. His second shot clipped the same exact branch that I'd hit earlier in round one and the ball dropped down on that long apron just off the front. He was left with a good forty yards to the hole.

I had 114 yards, the wall of trees in my face and only one

option. I had to get the ball up quickly and still have enough on it to get it all the way to the back half of the green.

"Well, I guess that was kind of stupid," I said to Ray.

"What?"

"I hit it too far. I don't think my gap wedge is going get up fast enough, and my L-wedge would never make it to the green, let alone the hole."

"Rocks, bottles, bare hands," Ray said.

I laughed. He hadn't done much more than encourage and commiserate all day if he did anything at all, but those were the exact words I needed to hear in that moment.

"Give me an eight iron," I said.

"What are you going do with that?"

I pointed to a ten-foot gap between two of the gum trees.

"I'm going to hit through there with a little late hook."

"No, you're not."

"Yeah, I am."

I didn't wait for him. I snatched the eight iron out myself, scrubbed the grip with the towel, put the ball in the back of my stance and turned the clubface down slightly.

I didn't see Ray close his eyes and I didn't hear the murmurs in the gallery as they clearly came to the realization that I was not going over the trees—I was going through them.

I made a three-quarter swing, caught it flush, and the ball rocketed toward the gap. It passed through with five feet on either side, curved slightly to the left and came to rest eleven feet from the hole on almost the exact same line that I'd missed from in the final hole of regulation.

There was an explosion of obvious wonderment from the assembled. The gallery that had gone ahead was ringing the green and they clapped as we approached, though it might have been an exhortation to Billy to hole his next shot.

Billy was obviously rattled, though. He hit his chip a little fat and left himself a good fifteen feet for par.

I expected him to make it and he didn't disappoint. Right in the center with pace. The crowd went wild.

I didn't overthink it this time. I stepped up, aimed slightly left and rolled it right into the hole.

Ray fell to the ground.

There were gasps of disappointment from the partisan gallery. Billy took off his visor, shook my hand and walked away without a word.

A bucket head met me as I came off the green to inform me that I was an official invitee to the U.S. Open.

30

Josh put one stainless steel pail on the counter in the shop and another at that starter's shack with a note asking all to contribute to a fund to get me to the tournament.

By the time I showed up on that Tuesday morning after the qualifier, the buckets were half-filled with ones and the occasional five.

I haven't mentioned where the Open was being played. It seems a little silly to have withheld that information, but then the location was so obviously a "thing" that it could only be perceived as a literary cliché.

The U.S. Open I had qualified for was being played at Belleterre Country Club, and yes, that is the same one that exists in a suburb southwest of St. Louis, Missouri.

It's a long course with a venerable history, but more precise players have had success there over the years.

The sales rep whom Josh and I had visited—the one where I had my little crisis—called and asked me to come up to Carlsbad and test his equipment. His entire line was available free to me if I were interested. I spent five hours up there and didn't experience any of the same issues. I left with a new driver, about ten dozen balls and a nice array of solid colored shirts with the company logo.

When I returned to SVMGC, Josh had this goofy look on his face.

"Here are your keys. Thanks for letting me borrow your car," I said as I handed them over.

"You are not going to believe this, brah."

"What?"

"I had Javy collect the buckets to see how much we took in today for your expenses."

"Uh, huh," I said.

"There was like two fifty in cash, which was pretty good. We dumped it out on the sweaters over there and at the bottom of the bucket there was a cashier's check for two thousand buckaroos."

"What?"

"You're all set, my brother."

"Wait a minute. Where did that come from?"

"No say, dude."

Josh said that with an animated shrug, which was kind of a tell. Something was up. He knew way more about the source than he was letting on.

"Come on, man, who do I thank for that?"

"I can't . . ."

"Was it you?"

"Dude, you know what this gig pays. It wasn't me."

"Josh."

He handed me an envelope with all of the donations.

"Just give up, Chunk. You ain't going to get it out of me. Go make your plane reservations."

I must have stared at him for a while.

"Pack it in. It ain't going to happen," he said with a smile.

Back at the Gumball, I looked at the cashier's check to try to get a clue. It was drawn on a local bank and there was no way of telling who'd initiated it.

I put in a call to a woman named Debbie. It's funny: in all my years of dealing with her, I don't think I ever got her last name.

At one time, she was the go-to person for those of us on the various tours who needed to schedule air travel—often on short notice. The big tour and their affiliates had a deal with one of the airlines that saved some seats on their flights for players and caddies at discounted rates and Debbie was the conduit to getting those deals.

"Oh, my word, Mr. Dawson, where have you been?" Debbie asked in her tight-lipped Oklahoma drawl.

"I took a bit of a detour, Deb. But I'm back. I need to get to St. Louis from San Diego this Sunday," I said.

"You are playing in the Open, aren't ya?"

"Yes, ma'am."

"I'll need to pay for my ticket at the airport, if that's okay. I don't have a credit card to guarantee it at the moment."

"I can make that happen, dear. I can guarantee it for you."

"Thanks."

"That's what I'm here for. Okay let's see, San Diego to St. Louis. I can fly you non-stop on Sunday, the eighth, at 9:00 a.m. How does that work?"

"Perfect," I said.

"And your return?"

"Make it the following Monday. I'll be making the cut."

"That's what I like to hear. We'll get you home in the early evening. Plane departs at four-thirty."

"Great."

I gave her all of the pertinent information and she sent me the confirmation number. Another phone call beeped in, but I did not pick up.

"Will you need a ticket for your caddy?" Debbie asked.

I hadn't really thought about it. Did Ray want to make the trip? We hadn't talked about it.

"Let me get back to you on that."

"Sure thing, Charles. Good luck and play well."

"Thank you, Debbie."

I hung up and reviewed the missed call. It was not a number I recognized and there was no voicemail.

Because I was going to be gone, we moved up the time for Ray's weekly lesson. He didn't know it at the time, but he would actually be launching golf balls with his new swing that day.

"I've already got my ticket and a motel room, Chunk. You ain't thinking I'm not going to want to see that first hand?" Ray asked the next day.

"Was that a triple negative?"

"You know what I mean," he said.

"Do you want to carry the bag?"

"Man, I don't know if I can take it. Honestly, that last round at La Clarita and the playoff took more years off my life than anything I did with the FBI."

"That's a lie."

"Yeah, it is. But still, that was fucking insane, dude."

I grabbed a small bucket and dipped it into the barrel that was close to the teaching tee.

"You ready?"

"Oh shit, today?"

"Yeah. Just wedges. Grab the club with the most loft."

He took his L-wedge out and made a few practice swings. What he'd accomplished in the last couple of months was pretty impressive. What he had once called a golf swing bore no resemblance to what I was watching him perform in that moment.

It was funny. In the end, this whole thing about teaching the swing to Ray in the same fashion that Jim had taught me could not have come at a better time. It centered me, reinforced all that I had learned from Jim and made me feel useful on my return. I should also thank Mr. Hogan for his contribution.

I dropped a ball on the ground and pointed to the seventy-five-yard flag.

"Don't worry about how far. Just get lined up right."

"I guess I'm hitting it straight," he said with a hint of irony.

"Yeah, if you don't shank it. It's kind of hard to work an L-wedge anyway."

You could see his mind clicking as he put together the sequencing program we had programmed into this brain. If

I had taught him correctly, the muscles would follow those commands.

He set up, checked his alignment and grip, centered his weight, took the club slowly back on plane, paused ever so briefly and dropped his hands down as he turned his hips and began rotating toward the ball.

There was the distinctive sound of a "click" as club head met ball. It was a sensation he had never experienced before.

"Oh my god," he said, "that was incredible."

"Do it again," I said.

He did.

"Again," I said.

Later in the day, Ray took me to the bank, so I could cash my check, and then drove me out to the airport, so I could pay for the ticket that Debbie had reserved.

He queried me on the source of the two grand. After giving it a full day of thought, I was pretty sure I knew where it came from. I had eliminated all of the other suspects. I told him I intended to keep the identity to myself, because the donor's wish had been to remain anonymous.

"You might have done well working undercover," he said, "though that monotone you speak in comes off like you're high most of the time."

I laughed at that.

As I got back in the truck, my phone rang again. It displayed the same unfamiliar number that had beeped in when I'd been talking to Debbie. I sent it to voicemail and this time, the caller left a message.

I waited until I was alone, on the practice tee to have a listen.

"Hey Mister Dawson, my name is Artie Fishman; I'm a reporter with the St. Louis Mail and Tribune. I'm writing an article on your journey to the Open here next week and I wonder if you have a moment when we could chat. Call me back when you get a chance. Thanks."

That was the very last thing I wanted in the world. Who'd told him about me?

I knew it must have been Deidre, which really bummed me out.

I could see her point. If she were trying to get my case in front of the governor, or someone on his staff, what better way than to put me out there as a matter of public interest?

But she had to have known how that would make me feel. After our last discussion, she had to know.

I worked on my wedges all afternoon, but I was fairly distressed. I felt this odd sense of betrayal and that feeling continued to seep into my brain. It left me sapped of energy and I lost focus repeatedly.

How could she do that?

I didn't sleep much that night. There were snippets of dreams, but nothing coherent. I awoke feeling a sense of flatness, which is something completely counter to what I should have been feeling. It was very confusing.

I hadn't had a lot of experience with things that lingered on my periphery. Everything in my world always seemed to be ahead of me. I did not look back. And because of that, I'd had little experience with a shadow. I had just never noticed it, because I never turned around to look.

I rode in with Nando and Javy and helped them set up for the day. We got the mowers to come over and had them dial down the blades to see if we could get the practice green to quicken up. We were never going to get it anywhere near Open speed, but we did add about five feet on the stimpmeter.

By the time the sun was up, I was working on my stroke and chipping from the fully returned seasonal Bermuda collars.

Josh walked out and handed me an envelope. It was addressed to me in the distinct scrawl of a number two pencil. It was the letter from Sally.

I read it quickly. She had gotten her wish and they had moved her out of the W.M.D.C.C. and into one of the women's facilities of the Missouri state prison system.

I was very happy for her. I would love to have a similar outcome to my predicament with the repressive powers that be, though the forces that were keeping me from exercising my desires were not swayed by the political winds.

Just as I started back to work, the phone rang—Artie Fishman again.

I knew I had to deal with all of it. The distraction of Deidre's betrayal had become too much in the moment.

"Hello," I said.

"Oh great, Mr. Dawson?"

"Uh, yeah, this is Charles Dawson."

"Thanks for picking up. Do you mind if I record our conversation?"

"Uh, yeah, actually, I do mind."

"Okay."

There was an awkward pause, but Artie was a pro.

"So, Mr. Dawson, I saw where you made the field for the Open, and I think your story is quite fascinating."

"How do you know my story?" I asked.

"You are the Charles Dawson who served time at the Western Missouri Diagnostic Correctional Center, right?"

"Yeah, that's me."

"Anyway, someone had mentioned something about you and your situation to me awhile back, and I must have forgotten about it. But Monday night I was scrolling through the entrants for the Open, and there was your name. Kind of jogged my memory. So, I did a little digging . . ."

"Who mentioned me?"

"I don't know. It was in passing and whoever it was thought you might make a good subject for an article at some point. Might have been my editor."

"Okay."

"I read through your case. I made a few calls."

"To who?"

"People who knew Ed Custis."

"Uh, huh . . ."

"I talked to one of the members of your original legal team."

"Oh yeah? What did they have to say?"

"Not much. I don't think they remembered the case."

I laughed.

"Not surprising. I *am* kind of surprised they still have their licenses," I said.

That brought about a snort from Artie.

"You sure I can't record you?"

"Why?"

"I'm writing a story about you, Mr. Dawson. I would love to get your comments on a couple of things."

"Here is my only comment: I would prefer that you don't write an article about me, Mr. Fishman."

"Too late," he said, "we haven't hosted an Open here since 1965. Stories like this don't come along very often. This is human interest at its most glorious."

"I can't imagine that the angle is that I prevailed in a four-man playoff for the last spot out of the La Clarita sectional qualifier?" I asked.

"Your career is prominent, sure, but it doesn't take up more than a couple of graphs. I mention that you had a pretty impressive amateur career, and there's a certain uniqueness in that you turned pro at eighteen."

"I was actually seventeen when I started playing on the mini-tour circuit."

"I'll fix that."

"But that's not what you're interested in?"

"Not really."

I didn't know what to say. I didn't want this. I just wanted to show up on Monday at the course and play a practice round. Do the same thing on Tuesday and Wednesday, and be called to the first or tenth tee on Thursday.

"Look," he said," this isn't going to run in the sports pages, Charles. I'm not a sports writer by trade. It's a front-page feature. The angle is your perseverance to overcome both your Asperger's and the stigma that comes with being a convicted felon."

"I wish you wouldn't run it, but I realize you have a job to do. I have no comment, Mr. Fishman. I just want to be able to play golf," I said.

"It's going to run on Sunday. If you change your mind and want to talk, you have my number. For what it's worth, I think this will be a positive thing for you, Mr. Dawson."

"Have a nice day, Mr. Fishman."

I hung up the phone before he could reciprocate. I went over to the putting green and went back to work.

There were a group of players over on the cart path side of the practice green giggling about the speed difference.

"These are fast," one of them said to me.

"Not really," I said.

31

The flight was uneventful. I was way in the back, hoping that my clubs would be in the special baggage area when I finally made it down to the terminal.

During the boarding process, I passed Chip Astoria sitting in his first-class seat on the aisle. He gave me a nod of his head, which was kind of cool. I didn't know him from a coat hanger, but he'd had to stick around to get his silver medal at the sectional and he must have recognized me from when the USGA official ceremoniously handed me a tournament packet.

Ray was already on his way, having taken a flight that connected through Dallas. We would meet at the rental car row.

I was the last one off the plane. Ray had already gotten the car and was waiting at the curb. I loaded my clubs and luggage into the trunk and slid into the passenger seat.

Ray handed me the Sunday edition of the *St. Louis Mail and Tribune*. Below the fold was the headline: "Charlie's Odyssey, the Perseverance of a Professional."

"Does anyone call you Charlie?" Ray asked.

"Never," I said.

"It's not a hatchet job. At the very least, the guy is rooting for you," Ray said.

He was right about that. Artie Fishman was someone who wanted to see me succeed. I know that makes a better story, and to take up column inches in the front of the paper, it probably better be uplifting. I still hated seeing my name, my story and an old USDT media guide picture of me in newsprint.

There were only about twenty glaring inaccuracies, but the general tone and trajectory was pretty truthful.

There were the tropes of my triumph over my condition, the passing of me from biological mother to adoptive absentee caretakers to a true loving parent in Jim.

There were career highlights, and somehow he was able to recreate the tragedy that had struck just as I was in the process of striving toward the highest level.

The facts surrounding Jim's sickness and death, and the whole episode of dealing with Shorty's death in prison, were quite detailed. It got me thinking about who he'd gone to as a source on that.

The circumstances surrounding the reason for my incarceration were murky; there were mentions about how my trial team had failed me.

Interviews of those who knew Ed Custis were also bizarre. According to those he claimed to have interviewed, not a soul ended up having a single nice thing to say about the man I was determined to have killed.

Artie seemed to imply that I was somehow blameless.

A reader was bound to get the impression that I'd been railroaded for what had essentially been a non-crime, which wasn't really accurate.

He tagged the article with a note that I was a more interesting figure than the defending champion, and that is why the U.S. Open is the greatest golf tournament of all-time.

"Whew," I said as I put the paper on the seat.

"You worried you can't live up to it?"

"It's not true."

"It's a little true," Ray said.

"Doesn't meet my threshold."

"No offense, Chunk, but you don't count. We're way beyond that."

My phone rang.

"Hello?"

"When were you going to tell me you were coming to town?" Deidre asked with an edge in her voice.

"Uh . . ."

"I should have to read about it in the paper?"

I didn't answer. Hearing her voice both thrilled me and pissed me off a little. I froze, more confused than I could ever remember having been. I could see Ray studying me with a single eye, the other on the unfamiliar road ahead.

"Were you ever going to tell me?" she asked directly.

"Yes, of course."

"When?"

"Well, to be honest, I'm kind of upset with you."

"About what?"

"About using that newspaper to get my story out there. I thought we talked about that."

"Excuse me?"

"The way I figure it, it had to come from you."

"Are you serious?"

"Maybe we should talk about this later," I said with a recurrence of that stammer that seemed to show up when we'd converse.

"No, no, Charles, we'll talk now. Do you really think that I would do that when you told me that you didn't want to go in that direction?"

I waited a long time to answer, which she must have taken as confirmation that I thought that exact thing.

The line went dead.

"Hello?" I asked into the plastic thing in my hand.

"Who was that?" Ray asked.

"A girl. Shit."

"I didn't know you had a girl."

"I don't. Shit. I'm an idiot."

"Yeah, most of us are in the end," Ray said.

"No. I don't know what I'm doing."

"The definition of the word, idiot, right?"

The phone rang. The ID proclaimed it was Deidre again.

"Hey, can I call you when I get settled?" I asked.

"No. I don't trust you now. Where are you staying?" she asked.

I looked over to Ray.

"Where are we staying?"

"Who's that?" she asked.

"My caddy. My caddy and parole officer."

She laughed at that one.

"Really?"

"Yeah."

"We're at the Sleepy Time Inn and Suites in Westport," Ray said.

"Did you hear that?"

"Yeah. Hardly the Four Seasons," she said.

"Kind of on a budget," I said.

"I'll meet you in the coffee shop across the street at six-thirty. Be there."

"Okay."

"If you are not there, I will hunt you down."

"Okay."

She hung up. This was all becoming more than a little too much for me.

"You never said you had a girl, Chunk," Ray said with a stupid grin.

"I don't think I do. And if I ever did, I don't now."

"Your impression only, I guess. Don't stay out too late. We get up early."

I rolled my eyes at him.

The coffee shop was indeed across from the motel on what was a busy road. I walked down the street to the light. The last thing I wanted was to get cited for jaywalking. Just being outdoors in Missouri was a little nerve wracking.

I'm the golfer. I am never late. I actually slipped into a booth at six-fifteen.

It was too far into the evening on my clock for coffee, so I asked for some water and stared at the seventeen-page menu.

"You showed," she said.

I was on page fifteen. Side orders.

"Of course," I said.

She stood there, and I slid out to gentlemanly stand before her. I held out my hand.

"Pleased to finally meet you for real," I said stiffly.

She stepped forward and pulled me into a short hug.

"I guess it's on me to lead," she said as we parted.

"Uh . . ."

"That's right, we've never been in the same room together," she mused.

"No."

We sat. She had her contacts on, and the person I had first viewed over the video feed was missing.

The person who I'd spent an inordinate amount of time conjuring had one gray eye, not two hazel ones. She observed me staring at her face.

"What's wrong?"

"Why are you wearing your contacts?"

She blushed.

"Why do you think?"

"I don't know."

She moved the menu aside and placed her hands on the table.

"Okay, before we do anything here, I want you to look me

in the eyes and tell me that you know that I was not the one who contacted that reporter who did the story on you."

I knew right away that I had been horribly wrong. It was as a self-evident as the sun.

She clearly didn't intuit that I'd retreated from the accusation, and that, as I've said, is a fault of my nature. All she saw was that I was still staring at her eyes.

"What?" she finally asked in exasperation.

"I know you didn't tell him," I finally said.

"Good."

But still, I remained transfixed.

"What are you looking at?"

My awkward awareness kicked in and the spell was broken.

"Nothing," I said, as I searched for the menu.

"Look, Chuck, let me lay it out for you. I have a bit of a crush on you. For the life of me, I don't know how it developed or even where it came from, but it is there. I am beyond the age of denying my feelings, because doing that always depresses me, so screw it. I wore my contacts because I'm insecure about the way I look sometimes and honestly, I forgot that when you first saw me on the screen, I was not wearing them."

She was so beautiful. Even with the camouflaged eye, she was stunning.

"It's fine. I've imagined you many times since that first time and I never visualized you with two eyes of the same color."

I tried to remain distracted, but my gaze kept returning to her eyes.

She reached into her purse and took out a small bag. She

extracted a contact lens case and small bottle of saline solution. She slipped the contact out of her eye, squirted a puddle of solution into the case and dropped the lens into the cup.

"Better?" she asked as she put everything away.

"Yeah."

There she was. This was the person who was responsible for altering my body chemistry since our first exposure to each other.

"Okay. Should we order?" I asked.

She laughed.

"Sure."

I signaled the waitress. We both had our heads down in the tome of a menu when she arrived.

"What can I get you two?" she asked.

"Could I have a house salad, please? Ranch dressing. And, I'd like a couple of eggs, sunny side up, with some hash browns and wheat toast?" Deidre said.

"We can do that."

When the waitress turned her attention to me, I wasn't ready. I was just staring at Deidre as she ordered. She was so confident and sure of what she wanted. It was like the way she handled her profession. To hear her say she felt some insecurity was a bit baffling.

"You know, I feel everything that you feel, except for one thing," I said to her.

She got a little self-conscious with the witness standing just to her right. She clocked the nametag pinned to the waitress's smock.

"Do you want to order first? I don't think Edie is interested in . . ."

"I don't have anywhere to be. What have you got to say to her, slick?" Edie asked, cutting her off.

"I was going to say that whatever you feel, I feel exponentially."

"I don't know what that means, but it sounds good, right?" Edie asked Deidre.

"Yeah. It's good," Deidre said.

"I'll have what she's having. Eggs over, though, and ranch dressing on the side, please."

"Coming up," Edie said, then departed.

What followed was the longest, most awkward moment of my life. And I've had awkward moments that would make a baby cringe.

"We're going to figure this out," Deidre said.

There was that confidence again. I had relied on it before, and it had worked out pretty well.

We kissed in the parking lot under the blinking incandescent bulbs that spelled out the restaurant's logo.

We both had things to do the next day, but we agreed to meet for dinner at the same time, in the same place.

I floated back to my room. Ray's light was out next door and I tried to catch some sleep. It didn't work.

There were hazy, repetitive dreams, all tinted with a hue of what any psychiatrist would label as rampant anxiety.

I had my usual tee time ones where I couldn't find the course. There was the one where I needed to catch up with a group that had already started and the one where I made it to the first tee, but my clubs, or balls, or shoes were somewhere else.

At five, I got up to pee. On my return to the bed, I veered to the cheap desk that abutted the TV. In the large vinyl-covered folder that held brochures for all of the tourist attractions in the region, was a single sheet of white paper. It had the establishment's logo as a letterhead. There was also a branded pen, thin and black. A twist revealed the ballpoint.

I don't know why, but I started writing down names. They came to me in droves and I had to scribble them down quickly because the next one was cascading into my brain as soon as each was recorded. It brought to mind one of those range ball machines, where you put in a token and the balls clatter into the bucket (hopefully) like a wicked hail storm.

I filled the front page and started working on the back. After fifteen minutes, I was done. I crawled back into bed and fell into a deep sleep.

Ray was pounding on my door an hour later.

"I thought maybe you spent the night somewhere else," he said when I presented my half-dressed, bleary-eyed self at the threshold.

"Yeah, right."

"I'll bring the car around."

We arrived at the player's parking lot and I presented my temporary credentials to the cop who was stationed at the entrance.

He pointed over to an area that was only half-full with vehicles.

"We're here," Ray said with an unsubtle tone of amazement.

I felt a bit of that. We had passed through a couple of checkpoints at that point, all adorned with red, white, and blue bunting that screamed USGA.

I sensed the ghosts of all who had played in the Open, and even in my sleep-deprived, Deidre-obsessed mind, I became hyper-focused.

We parked directly behind the neo-colonial clubhouse, unloaded our stuff and headed for the men's locker room.

In the past, caddies hadn't usually been given access to the player's locker room or clubhouse proper, but many of the more accomplished players had trashed that regulation over the last decade.

As we approached, a very stocky African-American, a bone-white coverall obscuring his clothing and a terry cloth towel with a logo on it draped over his left arm, reached out to open the door for us.

"Thank you," I said.

"Mr. Dawson?" he asked, politely inquiring.

"Yes?"

That article had obviously destroyed my anonymity.

"Sorry to bother you sir, but my name is Samuel Williams, though everyone around here calls me "Stubby."

And then it hit me. The resemblance was uncanny. It was like I was looking at a version of the man through a funhouse mirror.

"Wait a minute. You're related to Shorty," I exclaimed.

"Yes, sir. My father was his brother."

I turned to Ray.

"Oh my god, this is Shorty's nephew. I've told you about Shorty."

"I don't think so."

"He was my best friend when I was locked up. He passed away from cancer?"

"Oh yeah. The ball player."

Ray stuck out his hand to shake Stubby's.

"Ray Suarez."

"Pleased to meet you, sir."

I finally got around to shaking Samuel's hand myself.

"I'm Chuck."

"I don't want to bother you, sir, but before he died, my uncle wrote me a note."

He pulled a folded-up paper from his back pocket and handed it to me. I recognized Shorty's primer-perfect cursive writing immediately.

The sentiment was sweet. It was an introductory note for Stubby, replete with his bona fides.

"That's so nice. But I have Ray here on my bag," I explained to Stubby.

"I understand, sir," Stubby said.

"Whoa, wait a second there, Chunk. What does the note say?" Ray asked.

"It says that Samuel here has been a caddy at Belleterre for nearly twenty years, and should I ever make it to the Open when it's held there, he's my man."

"How did your uncle know this day would come?" Ray asked Samuel.

"This venue has been on the USGA schedule from before I got sent away," I said.

"My uncle said Mr. Dawson was a player and it was just a matter of time before the whole world knew about it. I followed the results from the local and the sectional qualifiers. Someday, you'll have to tell me the story of that playoff," Samuel said.

Ray set the bag down.

"He's yours," Ray said without any remorse.

"Ray . . ."

"Are you kidding, Chunk, I ain't no caddy. This man has twenty years walking this track. You gotta do this. You gotta honor your cellmate's request. You just gotta. It's not even a question."

"Are you sure, Mr. Suarez?" Samuel asked.

"As sure as rain is water," Ray said.

Stubby picked up the bag.

"Do you need anything out of here now, sir?"

"No."

"Then should I meet you on the practice green or the range then?"

"The range, Mr. Williams."

"Call me, Stubby, sir."

"Call me Chunk.

We walked into the locker room and made our way to the check-in table.

There were no bucket heads at this level. Everything was extremely official and the man who took my information was efficient and welcoming.

He picked up his walkie-talkie from the desk and announced my arrival into the airwaves.

Before long I had a whole group of men in white suits, official lanyards around their necks, standing before me.

"Mr. Dawson, we'd just like to welcome you to the championship. I'm Claude Harling, the tournament director," one said.

He introduced the others; the rules official and the media relations coordinator."

"This is Ray Suarez," I said.

Claude handed over an envelope.

"There are eight passes in there, Mr. Dawson. If you need more, we can certainly make an inquiry as to availability."

"Eight is plenty," I said.

"If there is anything we can do for you, let us know."

"Practice rounds are first come, first served. Just sign up at the first tee. And we'll have the official pairings tomorrow morning," the rules guy said.

"Okay."

"And I'd like to schedule a time for your media availability," the media coordinator said.

"Oh, I don't think that will be necessary," I said.

"On the contrary, Mr. Dawson, your presence has caused a bit of a stir. There have been multiple requests for access to you, and we thought it best to make you available during the media crush tomorrow. Unless, you are interested in meeting with them on a one-on-one basis."

"Absolutely not," I said.

"So, what would be best? Morning or afternoon?"

I looked over at Ray. I'm sure I looked like a plaintive child—eyes aching, hoping Daddy would get me out of some mess.

He just shrugged.

"I guess, the afternoon?"

The official looked at his clipboard.

"Three forty-five?"

"Okay."

"The media tent is over by the eastern end of the facility. If you could be there at three-thirty, that would be great."

"I'll make sure he's on time," Ray said.

I laughed.

"Yeah, he will."

They didn't see any humor in our exchange. And honestly, why would they?

The huddle split apart and we went looking for the driving range.

Stubby had stationed himself by the water cooler in the middle of the range. Behind him, a large grandstand had been erected to seat the curious. It was about a quarter-full and I assumed the spectators were made up of friends and families of the contestants, this being Monday morning.

None of the stars had arrived yet.

"What side do you like to hit from?" Stubby asked.

"Middle works."

He took the slip of cardboard that had my name on it and slid it into the holder that identified my position on the range.

A whoop went up from a section of the crowd. I figured it was Ray, but when I turned around, I could see that it was a grouping of kids in their tweens. There were two adults nearby, who waved at me from their perch.

Uh-oh.

"Everything okay, Charles?" Stubby asked.

"I don't know. Let's go to work."

I proceeded to slide into my routine. I hit a couple of straight warm-up shots and then started peeling balls to the right. I followed that up with a couple of more straight shots, before I started hitting a series of draws and hooks.

"You play it both ways, Charles?" Stubby asked.

"I do. Never a straight ball."

"I like it," he said.

"Let's sign up for a round," I said.

I walked to the area around the tee and signed in. I joined a group of two that was scheduled to tee off thirty minutes later. I met Stubby over at the practice green.

After just two putts on the putting green, I slipped into a bit of a panic. It was immediately apparent that I had the wrong tool in my hands. The Bullseye was not going to work on those greens.

In California, where the *Poa annua* creates a surface that prefers a putt to get millimeters airborne, the bent grass greens they had at Belleterre reacted negatively to that action. Putts jumped off-line almost immediately. My putter had way too much loft.

Thankfully, I had thrown the 8802 copy in the bag as an afterthought. It had no loft at all. I was going to have to find a feel for it, but at least the ball would stay on the ground.

"So, this the hole where the bodies are buried?" I asked as we stood on the first tee.

My question was literal. The area of the first fairway had actually been a graveyard at one time. The headstones had been moved when the course was constructed, but the boxes with the bones remained under the emerald Zoysia turf.

"So, what should I hit here? Where is the best position to come into the green?" I asked.

Stubby shrugged. I thought that was a bit odd.

"You've done your research on our course, right?" he asked.

"Of course," I said.

"So, you know it's going to play differently since the last time we hosted a major championship."

"I know that they let the chipping areas they'd cut grow back in and they reseeded the collars with bent."

Stubby nodded. After another moment, he went on to say, "So here's what I propose, Charles. I want you to take me through how you thought each hole should play. Talk your way around the place. Give me all the information—club choice, shot shape, conditions, approach to different pin positions, green reads, whatever. Try to execute the shots you envisioned when you first read about the course. Trust your eye. When we're done, we'll debrief. We need to build a relationship of trust faster than normal. No sense in starting with what I know. I need to see what you see, what you know and what you can do. Only then can I be of service."

No pro caddy that I've ever worked with had ever had that approach. It was pure genius.

32

Deidre looked at me from across the table just like the curious cat she proclaimed to resemble at times.

"I'm confused. Shorty was like what, seven feet, and Stubby is like squat with short limbs?"

"Ray said the same thing."

"Where's the spin?"

"You mean, because it's literal."

"Yeah. Where's the nickname come from?"

"They can be literal. Some guys just take your name and add a 'y.'"

"Chunk? Where's that from?"

"Ah, I see where you're going here."

"Are you going to tell me?"

"Not now."

She tilted her head to the right, a direct declaration that my response was unacceptable.

"I guess I will have to ask him," I said.

"Who?"

"Stubby."

"No. That would be rude."

"Ray really wants to know."

"Okay, you ask him. Since it will be coming from you, it shouldn't make him uncomfortable. I reckon your general awkwardness can be an asset at times. I will want to know the answer, of course."

Edie delivered the same exact thing we'd had the night before. Neither of us had any interest in reinvestigating the menu. Deidre had spent a full day in court and I'd had a time-equaling stint at the golf course. Edie asked if there would be anything else, but she clearly could tell by the intensity that passed between her patrons that her presence wasn't required.

"A strange thing happened when I was warming up," I said.

"What's that?"

"There was this group of kids. I first caught sight of them on the driving range. They had a couple of chaperones with them and when we went to play, they followed us. They stayed half a hole behind us most of the time. They cheered at most everything I did, even when the results were less than satisfactory. In his way, Ray infiltrated them and found out that they were a bunch of kids from the local chapter of some Asperger's foundation. They had read the article in the newspaper and decided to take a field trip to watch me play the practice round."

She smiled. She didn't drop an *I told you so on me*, which would have been well within her rights.

"Did they come up to you? Did you get to meet them?"

"No."

She sighed.

"They were gone by the time we finished. Stubby and I got some sandwiches and did our debriefing in the garage," I said.

"So, what did Samuel have to say from watching you?"

"He said I got things right about 60 percent of the time. That was a lot more than he thought I would get, so he was encouraged."

"And what about you? Do you feel encouraged?"

I'm sure I gave her a shrug at that point. A shot is a shot. The course is the course. The wind is the wind. Though I possess most of the remedies for any situation, you never know what can happen.

Jim had said it: *"That's golf."*

She reached her hand across the table. There was a crackling spark that arced between our fields of electricity and I stopped talking at that point.

"I thought a lot about you today. It was kind of distracting," she said.

"I thought a lot about you, and it wasn't," I said.

She cocked her head again at my response.

"Did that sound strange?" I asked.

"A little. But you know that."

"I guess what I meant to say is that it didn't deter me from my job. Every time it came up, I was fueled by it. My concentration got really narrow. Does that make sense?"

That made her smile. It was not a lie.

She spent the night. We fell asleep on the bed with our

clothes on after talking for an hour after dinner. There had also been more kissing.

And, initial snuggling, but it was obvious that both of us needed something restorative.

My body needed to find its clock.

Ray pounded on the door again in the morning. He was not surprised to see I had a visitor.

I gave Deidre a tournament pass and a parking voucher. I told her that we'd probably move toward the first tee around eight, but she could show up at any time.

Ray and I drove over to the course. Stubby met us at the locker room door.

"Range?"

"Yep," I said.

Ray and I passed through the clubhouse and I left him in the restaurant. I signed up at the first tee for a practice round, joining a couple of pros whom I'd never met, but had certainly heard of before.

One was George Herrmann, who was in his early forties, and still winning a tour event each year. The other was Dylan Rumpert, who was exempt by virtue of a top five finish in the British Open the year before.

Dylan was a guy who had yet to win a major, but had garnered more top ten results than just about anyone on tour over the last decade. He was the current holder of the "best player never to win a major championship" mantle.

Next to the sign-up sheet were the pairings for the first round. I would be going off the tenth tee on Thursday at

2:16 p.m. My playing partners were two other sectional qualifiers I didn't know.

I walked back over to the practice tee and you could feel that Tuesday was a whole different vibe from Monday. The stands were nearly full and the names of the players striping balls onto the old plot of farmland were those that held prestige and status.

I found Stubby at the far-right end, holding a place that had recently been vacated. When he slid my name placard into the slot, there were no cheers from any section of the crowd. That was a relief.

"Sorry, boss, this is all the real estate that was left."

"No worries, Stub. Just got to aim left."

I went through my regular routine, and after about twenty swings, I tossed my six-iron to Stubby.

"I'm going to putt. Gotta get more comfortable with this flat stick," I said.

He handed me the 8802 copy. I was less panicked, though I'd putted better with the Bullseye than I had with anything else through my entire career. I just kept telling myself it was the stroke that made the difference, not the equipment.

"You know, they'll be at least a foot or two faster on Thursday," Stubby said after I'd hit a couple of long lags.

"Yeah, I bet."

"The breaks will be a lot more subtle when they get them to Open length."

"I'm sure. That's my biggest worry right now. I'm not that familiar with this putter, and I really had my speed dialed in with the other one."

"We'll get it right."

I nodded.

"I noticed that you went for a lot of pins yesterday. We're going to have keep your target orientation to spots, not flags, okay?" Stubby said.

"I'm all yours today."

"Okay. I'm going to hold you to that. Today is my day, Chuck. You are going to try to hit it exactly where I say. See how that makes your body react. Look for the resistance. I'm going to show you how to play this course. You and I will debrief after, just like yesterday."

"All right," I said.

That was it for me and my mouth. For the next five hours, I didn't question him once. I just did whatever he said.

Dylan and George didn't bring me into their conversation at all, but they were intrigued with where Stubby was taking me on every shot.

Deidre sent Ray a text as I was walking off the fourth green. He waved to me before he took off to go find her.

The fifth at Belleterre was a monster. It was 480 yards of a par four with a slanted fairway that kicked the ball hard to the right. The rough down there was nasty; a decision would always have to be made as to whether you wanted to lay up in front of the creek that angled across the front of the green or risk bouncing it off the back into certain death.

"Can you hook one into the left rough?" Stubby asked when it was my turn to hit.

"Sure," I said.

I hit kind of a snapper up the left side of the fairway, and the ball tumbled into the hay about ten yards from the second cut.

This was about the third time that Stubby had asked me to hit to a place that was less than optimal. I'd already been instructed to miss the green on the right side of two and hit it into the back bunker on the third.

George Herrmann couldn't take it anymore.

"What the fuck are you doing, son?" he asked me.

Stubby's eyes sought mine. I knew he felt restrained from answering because he worked for me, not George. I gave him an agreeable nod meant to release him from any non-disclosure pact.

"My man is going to hit a nice draw here, sir, so he can keep the ball from bounding off the fairway to the right. He's going to start the ball somewhere toward the left third, and if by chance he overcooks it, he'll be in the left rough. That is a much better angle into the green if you don't make the fairway. You can lay up on the apron over there, or if the lie is decent, have a go at the middle of the putting surface. I want him to know what his options might be should it happen in competition."

George presented the face of a man who was seriously impressed.

He waved his caddy over and they walked with us to where my ball sat in the rough that was four inches deep now, but would easily grow to five by the time the weekend rolled around.

I slashed it out. It took a hard bounce on the front fringe and rolled all the way to the very back edge of the green.

"That lie was pretty bad. You'll want to play it to the area on the left. You'd have the whole green to work with, and an uphill chip," Stubby said.

As with all things, Stubbyesque, it made complete sense.

George grabbed a ball out of his pocket and dropped it right next to where mine had been. He hit the shot that Stubby had suggested and the ball stopped short of the surface in an area that was far superior than where my ball had ended up. He turned to his caddy.

"We're going to do the same thing here. Stay left on this hole. Write it down," George commanded.

As we marched toward the green, Stubby said sheepishly, "That was okay, right?"

"Of course. George Herrmann's not stupid. He sensed that we were working on a different level. He's still gotta pull off the shot. I've never been one to keep information from others. No one really plays the game exactly alike."

Stubby nodded. I think he felt the same way I did.

Deidre showed up with Ray, behind the ropes that encircled the sixth tee. I walked over and greeted her. She waited for a kiss hello and for probably the first time in my life, I was up to providing it.

"Wow, so much better," she said.

"Will you let the man get back to work?" Ray said in full deadpan mode.

We completed the round. Stubby and I again grabbed some sandwiches and went into the garage to do our debriefing session.

It was weird. We both felt way more comfortable sitting in the vacant carts having our powwow than we would have felt in the stuffiness of the clubhouse or on the back patio. It was like home to me.

When I emerged, I met Ray and Deidre at a lemonade stand, where the media rep found us.

"Are you ready, Mr. Dawson?" he asked.

"Not really," I said.

"You know, that's his answer to nearly everything," Deidre said.

Ray snorted some lemonade through his nose.

The rep had a cart nearby and we all loaded in for the trip over to the media tent.

There was an area over by the back of the dais where some of the broadcast networks were doing standups either with their correspondents or interviewing some of the players.

Ray was a little starstruck and Deidre used that opportunity to give him a hard time.

"Look, that's the 'Puma,'" Ray said throwing a glance over to where Peter Forrest was being interviewed by one of the anchors from the Golf Network.

"Are you going to squeal like a little girl?" Deidre asked.

"Madam, you have no idea where you are," he said.

"You got that right," she said.

"This is Valhalla."

"Really? Where's the one they call Thor?"

I was enjoying the repartee. I couldn't keep up their pace, but it was fun to watch.

"You're next," the rep said to me.

"Who's in there now?" I asked.

He tilted his clipboard up.

"Gary Houston."

"Ha, perfect," I said.

Gary exited into a gaggle of assistant producers for the various electronic media conglomerates. They were all vying for a moment on camera with him. I crossed behind him and patted him on the back when I passed by.

"Hey, Gar," I said.

He turned to me.

"Holy shit, Chunk! I heard you were here."

"How's it going?" I asked, lamely.

"I gotta do some of these TV things, but you want to play a practice round tomorrow?" he asked, walking away.

"Sure. I go in the afternoon on Thursday, so I'm playing tomorrow around two."

"That works for me. Meet you on the range at one-thirty?"

"Sure."

And he was gone, swept into a vortex of microphones and cameras.

I slipped into the tent and was shocked to find that most of the media folk had not exited when Gary had finished.

Cameras flashed and the chitchat died. Ray and Deidre took up some space in the very back.

I sat down in front of a wall emblazoned with multiple renderings of the Belleterre/USGA Championship logo. The figure was a mash-up of a silhouette of the Open trophy fronting the mascot for the course: A river corsair from the days when the Mississippi was ruled by rogues and thieves. Not much had changed, I guess.

The rep sat down next to me and centered the microphone in front of him.

"We'd like to welcome to the Open, Charles Dawson, a sectional qualifier from Chula Vista, California. I think some of you know Charles' story. If not, I refer you to Artie Fishman's excellent feature in last Sunday's *Mail and Tribune*. So, without further ado, Charles Dawson."

No one clapped except for Ray and Deidre at the back, who abruptly stopped when they realized they were the only ones.

The rep pushed the microphone over to me. I cupped my right hand over it for privacy's sake.

"Can I say something first before we get into any questions?" I asked him.

"Sure. Go ahead."

I adjusted the mic, cleared my throat and let out a sigh.

"Hi. Um, I just wanted to say a few things if you don't mind. I know that golf is an individual game and that we succeed or fail on our own merits or lack thereof. And there is a kind of arrogant thing that happens when we discuss our game, or our goals. It's that thing about us doing it all on our own. That we only make money if we make the cut, blah, blah, blah. I'm sure you've all noticed that. But I feel a need to say that there is much more to it than that."

I tilted over, reached into my pocket and withdrew the

piece of motel stationery that I had scribbled onto in the early hours of Monday morning when sleep had eluded me.

"I would not be here, or anywhere for that matter, without the help of a group of people that would fill this tent like ten times over."

I held up the piece of paper.

"On this are some of the names of those who have helped me along the way. Without them, I am convinced that I would just be a special needs kid with no hope that there is a future for me beyond a semi-institutionalized life or menial employment existence. These people define me. Two of them are standing right there, my friends Ray and Deidre."

I pointed to the back and every single person turned around. Both of them blushed and desperately tried to hide in plain sight.

"There are two names on here that I want to single, or I guess double, out because they have much of the gratitude that exists in my body and soul."

I laid the piece of paper on the table. I no longer needed it for reference.

"First, is my teacher, my mentor, Jim Wellington, who also functioned as my father for over twelve of the most formative years of my life. He passed away nearly six years ago and I miss him every day. Second, and I know this is going to make her mad if it goes beyond this room, but Jim's wife, Babe Greene. She is the person responsible for providing me with the wherewithal to even get to this tournament. She tried to do it anonymously, but I am breaking her confidence to say that I am overwhelmed with gratitude for her for making this possible. Okay, that's it. Thanks for giving me a moment."

I sought out the rep. When I looked over to him, he was pointing to the people in the room.

"Yeah, Charles?" a voice called out.

I scanned for the source, but couldn't locate it.

"Over here," the voice said.

"Sorry."

"Rick Goshen from *Golf Day*. What do you think of the course?"

"Well, I think it's fantastic. I'm a big fan of all of Robert Trent Jones' designs, but the subtlety here is really amazing. By the way, someone who's not on this piece of paper was someone I just met yesterday: Samuel Williams. He's been a caddy here for two decades and he's been my Sherpa. Pretty lucky to have him on my bag this week."

There was another moment as everyone jotted or typed something of a seemingly editorial nature to my response.

"Hey, Charlie, Artie Fishman, *Mail and Tribune*."

"Hey, Artie," I said with a smile.

"I'm the guy who wrote the article."

"Oh, I know who you are. We talked on the phone. I have question for you. Which person did you interview that said they called me Charlie?"

"I don't remember."

"Not to be picky, but that's a thing you got wrong. Not a single person has ever referred to me as Charlie."

"I'll print a retraction."

"Thank you."

There was some soft laughter in the room.

"So, Charles, I heard that you had a gallery for your practice round from the Asperger's Foundation. Do you feel that you could be a role model for those afflicted with conditions such as autism or Asperger's, like yourself?"

Damn. He snared me. I was trapped. I sought out Deidre in the back. She was nodding and waving her finger in a circle. I took that as some universal signal to answer the question.

"Look, Mr. Fishman, that's an interesting question, but not something that I feel comfortable answering. I mean, does someone just stand up and declare that now they are a role model? Is that how it works? I think it's important that people understand that someone that falls on the spectrum like I have can alter aspects of their original diagnosis, but everyone's different. You get that, right? It's not black and white. That being said, I welcome anyone who wants to follow me around and watch me play."

Through the flaring of the blinding lights of the cameras, I could see some heads nodding in agreement. I hoped he wouldn't ask a follow-up. Thankfully, someone spoke up from right down in front.

"Pat Harbison, with *Golf Down Under*."

Ah, there was that cool Australian accent again.

"Yes?"

"What is your relationship with the tour, Mr. Dawson? I

ask because I heard the most amazing story on the driving range today from Mark Tinby."

"Oh, great. Mark made it? Cool," I butted in.

"He said he played in the same group as you in a Monday qualifier for the San Diego Open and tour officials pulled you off the course after nine holes. He said you shot a twenty-eight on your first nine."

"Yeah, I had it rolling. One of the funny things about that day was I had Ray back there on my bag. He'd never carried before and he thought that's how I always played."

The laughter was a little louder that time.

"Have you been banned from competing in tour events?" Pat asked.

"That's what I've been told," I said.

"Because, as my colleague detailed in his article, you were convicted of a felony?"

"Yeah, from what I understand, I have failed to live up to the ethics expected of competitors. I've been told I am in violation of a by-law in the association handbook that subsequently disqualifies me from competing in any events that are sanctioned by the tour. As you all know, that pretty much shuts me out from nearly every event on the planet."

"Are you planning on fighting their decision?" Pat asked.

"I'm planning on finding a remedy, yes. I've paid my debt to society. I believe I should be allowed to continue to make a living at my trade."

"And the USGA never said anything to you?"

I stole a glance at the media rep.

"The only requirement for entry in the U.S. Open Championship is you must be a professional or amateur with a handicap index of one-point-four or better. The entry fee is $200," I said.

The rep nodded and smiled, though he probably had no desire to deal with that issue.

"Have a great week," Pat said.

"Thanks."

I looked to the rep again, but this time I was hoping to convey that I'd had enough. He walked over, bent down, and spoke into the mic.

"All right, everyone, Peter Forrest is next," he said.

I hastily rose and exited before anyone else could ask a question. I pushed through the entourage that was accompanying the "Puma" into the tent and gathered in a deep breath in a quiet corner.

Ray and Deidre sauntered over.

"You sure talk funny," Ray said.

"Was it all right?"

"I thought you did great," Deidre said.

She planted one on my cheek.

"Are we done for the day?" Ray asked.

"Yeah, I am," I said.

"Where do we get Mexican food in this town?" Ray asked Deidre.

"You don't."

Just as we were heading out, Artie Fishman walked up.

"You didn't stick around for the "Puma?" I asked him.

"Not a sports guy. I remembered how I got onto your story. It was Sally Dio, the bank robber. She told me about you."

That made perfect sense.

There was slap on my upper arm. Deidre was not the perpetrator, and when I turned to her, she had a stern look on her face.

"Just wanted to clear that up. Play well, Mr. Dawson. I mean Charles," Artie said before he slipped away.

We took Ray over to the coffee shop. He got into a whole flirtation thing with Edie, and before we left, I gave her a tournament pass and told her what time I was teeing off on Thursday.

Deidre had parole hearings for most of the next day. I had more work to do with the putter in the morning before my practice round with Gary. We sat on the bumper of her Subaru and kissed as the rush hour traffic streamed by.

33

The parking lot was already full when we arrived at just after ten. There was this feeling in the air that was different from the two days before. It would continue to build until tomorrow, but even on the eve of the tournament, it was tactile. I likened it to something physical: electricity or a pressure drop accompanying an approaching storm.

The officer doing traffic control waved us over to a patch of dirt that had been cleared to accommodate the overflow. It was far enough away that we had to wait for a shuttle bus to make it to the clubhouse.

The tram ride added to the anticipation; I could really feel the excitement bubbling up inside of me. Its level of intensity brought about thoughts of those first days on the range with Jim, when I was learning the game as a ten-year-old.

Somewhere in there, I knew that all that crackling energy had another source. The thing with Deidre had caused a shift in my awareness, and not just to all things carnal. In the moment,

I thought I might have uttered an untruth when I told her at the diner that I wasn't distracted by her presence in my world at that time.

I chipped and hit bunker shots for an hour before pouring all of my focus into my putting. I met Gary Houston on the range at the prescribed hour. He had signed us up for a practice round at just after two o'clock.

His brother and father were both there, and they waved to me like an old friend. I played along.

Gary proposed a little wager for our round. It only seemed right that we should put something on it, which always amplified my focus and enjoyment. I couldn't afford to play for the stakes that made it thrilling for him, but we did play a match for twenty bucks for the front, twenty for the back, and forty for the overall. It was strictly a medal score bet.

I had maybe a hundred dollars in my wallet, so the incentive was there. That was my food money I was putting up.

Stubby and I followed our game plan from the day before and we turned the front in one under. Gary had recorded the same, so everything was pushed to the back nine.

"You want to double it?" Gary asked.

"I do, but I can't right now. I'm on a pretty strict budget."

"So, Chunk, why didn't I know about all this autism stuff you were dealing with when we knew each other as kids?" he asked.

I didn't correct him about my actual diagnosis. Instead, I almost started laughing and had to do a whole bunch of facial manipulation to mask my shock that he'd even made such a query.

Gary Houston was one of those people who never asked a question about another person. You interviewed him and maybe you hit on a topic of mutual interest, but mostly he just spoke about himself using your question as a departure point.

Even though we'd had this familiarity for over fifteen years, including teaming up as partners, he knew absolutely nothing about me.

Not that I was ever into volunteering anything anyway, so he shouldn't be held in too much contempt. And Gary was truly a nice guy.

"I don't know. I guess I didn't want it to be a thing. By the time we met, I'd gone through a lot of therapy, so it might have been hard to tell that I was afflicted by simple observation," I said.

"Huh," he said.

And that was it for that. Which surprised me. I was sure that now that his curiosity had been piqued, I was going to have to field a question about my time away downstate.

Instead, we spent the rest of the round discussing course nuance and clubs that we were likely to hit in different situations.

I birdied the last two holes to beat him by three shots.

"Your game looks good, Chunk," he said as whipped out a snakeskin wallet and withdrew a rigid hundred-dollar bill.

I presented the twenty in change.

"Thanks, but this track is going to look completely different tomorrow."

"Yeah, that's true. Those greens are fast already, but they'll be ridiculous tomorrow. Plus, there will be about 50,000 people wandering around. About 50 percent will be idiots."

"I don't have to worry about that. We'll have a gallery of ten. You're in the marquee group with Peter Forrest, right?"

"Guy's such an asshole," Gary whined.

"It's going to be fun."

"We'll see."

"Want to see if we can trade tee times?" I asked.

"Hah."

"Thanks for the round. You know, I stopped by you and your brother's place in Fort Worth awhile back. The food was really good."

"Yeah, I heard you dined with that wacky Babe Greene."

"I did. The food was great."

"Yeah, it ain't bad, if I do say so myself. Play well, tomorrow."

"You too," I said. "Thanks for the game."

I followed up the practice round with a session on the range and then putted until the moon muscled out the sun in the sky.

Deidre took Ray and me out to dinner at this really cool restaurant.

It was oddly quiet for a busy place. The walls were lined with books with subjects like how people can be nice to each other. The food was incredible, every dish built around a fresh herb. Ray declared that it might have been one of the top ten meals he'd ever eaten.

Deidre and I couldn't stop staring at each other, and when Ray wandered off to the restroom, we shared a kiss as deep as any in my lifetime. We were both charged up. There was no real need for restraint.

"You know where this goes next, right?" she asked.

"Yeah," I said flatly.

"Is that going to be all right?"

"I hope so," I said.

"Are you into it?" she asked with a hint of insecurity.

"Most definitely."

"God, it is so hard to tell sometimes."

"Do you want me to put it in writing?"

She smiled. She might have already known that was the best I could do in terms of answering. Of course, there might have been a certain amount of trepidation on my part because it had been a long, long time since those days in Canada. I was definitely a rank amateur.

It did not matter in the end. Nature takes its course. There were fumbles and stumbles, mostly from my side of the ledger, but it was still epic. It was unlike anything I'd ever felt or experienced with another human being.

Moments after, I cried for the second time in a year, and this time the source of the emotion was not sadness, but pure joy.

That outpouring of emotion, regardless of the provocation, was something I'd been told I could not experience, so again, it came as a shock when I just suddenly started bawling when we laid down next to each, pretzel legged, coated by a visible layer of sweat.

It didn't freak Deidre out. She just held me until the sobs became sniffles.

"So, why do they call you, Chunk?" she asked when I stopped quaking.

"Okay, you win."

"You said you'd tell me when I got to know you better. I know you pretty well now, don't I?"

"Better than nearly anyone in the world. You know things that no one knows," I said, truthfully.

"Okay, so what's the story?"

I turned to face her. We were close. It was that kind of close that only lovers can achieve. It was truly unique. A first for me. All the walls that I lived with were demolished.

"The word 'chunk' is a golf term," I said.

"What does it mean?"

"It's when you hit a little too far behind the ball. That is known as hitting it fat, or chunking it. The result is a weak shot that travels a short distance."

"So, it's a golf nickname? That seems a little banal given that you were being so mysterious about it."

"Everyone who calls me by that name assumes that is the origin, some golf related thing, but that's not true. I tell people who know me well that they can call me that, but I know it's because they know I'm a golfer and it's kind of a cool nickname."

"But . . ."

"It has nothing to do with golf at all."

I moved a lock of her hair that was covering her right eye. It was such a source of curiosity to me.

"Here's the real story. Back when I was in kindergarten and first grade, I was confined to what they called the special room, you know, that one that's close to the front of the school, a piece of red construction paper over the wire glass door window and stark black paint that says, "Special Ed." There wasn't much funding for those programs in public school and so, there was no separation between the different issues that each student had. We were a class of eleven, maybe twelve. We had the short bus and two teachers who knew very little about what they were doing. It was really a six-hour babysitting session for them. There were kids with Down's syndrome lumped in with those whose only issues were physical deformities. We were segregated from the main population at the school, so creating relationships beyond those who were in our room was rare."

Deidre got a little misty-eyed at that point, but I prattled on anyway.

"Anyway, I hung in the back with two kids, Kirby and Steve. Kirby had cerebral palsy, and among Steve's issues was that he was pretty much deaf and had speech problems. Kirby was one of the first guys to have an artificial voice set-up on a tablet attached to his wheelchair. No one understood him when he spoke, and since he was actually quite brilliant, he got frustrated to the point where he'd express himself with these thrashing outbursts that were really disruptive. One day he showed up with this translating tool with a mechanical voice. He was seriously spastic, and had very little muscle control except for his neck. It was weird that he could control only that part of his body, but I guess pathologies just can't be perfect. He wore a Velcro sweatband on his head and attached to it was a foot-long wand. He used that to hunt and peck at his tablet when he wanted to communicate. So, one day I did something to piss the teacher off; she blamed Steve, and he screamed out with his impediment meaning to say Chuck, 'It was Chunk!'" Well, Kirby started thrashing around laughing and programmed some kind of beat box thing on his tablet that screamed, 'Chunk, ka-Chunk, Chunk, Chunk, etc.,' and the nickname was born. Kirby went on to write these little ditties of rhythmic music that always had 'Chunk' in the lyrics, and every time I walked into the room, he would play one of them."

"Oh my god. That's so sweet."

"Yeah. Those friendships didn't last long. Kirby had moved away by the time I started second grade and Steve disappeared a couple of months into my third-grade year. My adoptive mom told me that his family had been transferred to another naval base, but I found out a couple of years later that he'd contracted pneumonia and died around Thanksgiving of that year."

A small rivulet of tears slipped from the eye I'd been staring at and moistened her pillow.

"I was moved into a mainstream class in fourth grade and things changed immeasurably. I liked the nickname, so I told kids to call me that. I think they thought it was stupid, but it stuck."

She came in for a kiss. The sex was better for her the second time around. She fell asleep in the crook of my arm after asking me what would be the most comfortable position for me given my need to perform as an athlete the next day. I laughed.

"I'm a golfer, not an athlete."

34

She left a note. Scrawled onto the back of her business card was what I thought might be a cautious sentiment: *Hope you slept in. I took one of your extra passes for a friend. See you later. D.*

I spent a good ten minutes trying to read more into it than just the text. Did she consciously not include the salutation, "love?" I noticed that was new for me and it led to some moments of confusion.

So much had changed over the last five plus years. Any common metric would classify it as "for the better," even with the bulk of that time being confined to a state facility.

The reality was that, during that span, my world had become expansive for the first time in my life. There were so many new additions, which was evidenced by the lack of empty space on my list of names that covered that once blank sheet of paper.

It had been a long struggle to get to that point. From my

initial diagnosis, to therapy, to golf, to Jim, to my professional life and eventually my time in prison.

My life had been so small for so long. Every step felt like a shuffle and not a stride, and yet, I believed, in that moment, it had all been worth it. Especially, if it had led me to the part of the journey that included Deidre.

My thoughts then shifted to the day at hand. That first round of the Open was going to be the first competitive tournament round I'd played since I missed the cut in my last tour event. That had happened just down the road, a fifth of my lifetime ago.

There was a notion that buzzed around my periphery that it could be one of my last, but I shoved that out of the way.

I brewed some crappy coffee with the in-room plastic device. The card that illustrated the numbered protocol of required steps reminded me of so many of the flash cards and therapy tools that my minders used to get me to progress toward functionality. I still screwed it up by adding the water at the outset instead of step three. I'm sure the coffee would have been just as bad had I not adlibbed. I took a shower, did some stretching and then found Ray, so we could get some breakfast across the street.

Ya feel that?" I asked him as we crossed at the light.

"What?"

I pointed toward the river.

"The wind has changed from yesterday. I'll bet it's blowing pretty good out there today."

The restaurant was empty. Edie had already told her

co-workers she'd be at the tournament that day, so a busboy got a battlefield promotion to server. He forgot Ray's coffee early on, but he did all right.

"How'd it go?" Ray asked in reference to last night's festivities.

"No comment."

"You nervous about today?"

"Yeah. But, you know, I love to compete, so it's a good kind of nerves, I guess. There's no dread, just excitement."

"No crazy 'it might be too important kind of thing like the sectional?'"

"No. I don't where that came from."

"I'm shaking in my boots," Ray said.

"Really?"

"Are you kidding me? This is the big one, baby. It's positively nerve-wracking for me to be so into it."

"I'll try not to kill you," I said with a smile.

"That would be good."

There was little talk on the ride to the course. Ray flashed my contestant's badge and delivered me to the clubhouse entrance before driving off to some space that was outside the orbit of just about everything. It was a long time before I saw him again.

Stubby and I hit the range and I went through my normal routine. My new driver had worked pretty well to that point. The shaft was probably a little stiffer than optimal, but I had dialed it in to allow me to cut the ball without fear of double-crossing it.

The practice green was indeed much faster than the one from the day before. The humidity was pretty high, so the moisture content was consistent, though you could tell that being exposed to the morning breezes was working to alter their texture.

The USGA was pretty spectacular when it came to changes in agronomical conditions. They'd lost golf courses before when they tried to get too cute, but it was before the cut and they had watered quite extensively over the last couple of days, even in the early morning hours before the first groups went off. There was no rain in the forecast, a blessing for the time being.

The wind was going to be a factor, though, and as we strolled to the tenth tee, we passed the big analog leaderboard by the clubhouse. There were only five scores in red, with the leader, Dylan Rumpert, at three under through fifteen.

I finally saw Ray as Stubby and I approached an open area that was about fifty yards from the tenth tee. The group in front of us was getting ready to hit, so I got the towel out of the bag, wiped the sweat off my face and chuffed it against the grip of my driver.

There was a fairly large gallery surrounding the tee. I don't remember seeing any marquee names going off around the same time, so I couldn't help wondering who was playing in front of us. Someone hit, and there was a round of polite applause.

"Hey, Dawson," said a voice from behind me.

I turned around to find Buzz, the caddy whom I'd spent time with in the yard at the W.M.D.C.C. that one day. He had a player's bag on his back, and though he'd gained a little weight, he had yet to grow a strand of hair on his head.

"Told you I'd be back," he said with a smirk.

"Who's your man?" I asked.

"I got a kid from the USDT this week, Sid Bash. He hits it a mile, but has no idea where it's going," he said in kind of a whisper.

"I'm playing with a Sid Bash."

"I know. I told him that if he gets out of line, you might have to waste him," Buzz said with a grin.

"Yeah, that's me," I said with as much sarcasm as I could muster.

The group in front cleared the tee, but only a smattering of the large gallery lit out to follow. I saw Deidre hanging by the ropes with a woman who was about her age.

I waved Stubby over to join me and we made our way to the official who guarded the entrance to the tee.

"Hey," I said to the official.

"So, you must be the famous guy, huh?"

"Not really."

"I think this crowd says something different."

It was then that I realized that the gallery was made up of some of the same people who had followed me on Monday, as well as, ten times that many from all around the city and the state.

They cheered as I came into view. It was a little disconcerting to say the least. I walked over to Deidre.

"Really?"

"Wait, you think I did this?" she asked.

"No. It's just . . ."

"You do. You have doubts, like with the article."

"No, I don't. It's just makes me uncomfortable."

"Are you seeking comfort in this environment?"

She had a point. I turned my attention to her companion.

"This is my friend, Molly," she said.

"Pleased to meet you," I said as I shook her hand.

"Okay then, go get 'em," Deidre said.

I leaned in and kissed her.

"My god, you've grown in the last few days, Chunk," she said, smiling slyly.

"We'll see."

A voice called out.

"Ladies and gentleman, this is the two-sixteen starting time. On the tee, from Chula Vista, California, Charles Dawson. Play away, please."

There was another outburst of applause. I tipped my cap and nodded, put the peg in the ground, lazily took a loosening swing, addressed the ball and smoked a power slice into the middle of the fairway.

"Beauty," Stubby whispered as I handed him my driver.

I was thinking about Ben Hogan and Jim as I walked down the tenth fairway. The Hawk had missed the Open the last time they'd come to Belleterre, and I was trying to remember why. Had he been ill?

There were two colorful tributaries that flowed along with Stubby and me as we crunched across the windblown turf. To the right and to the left were the various groups of kids who had come out to see me play.

Each cluster of twenty or so was clad in colorful T-shirts that had the logo of the organization or school that had had brought them to the tournament. Fire engine red would give way to a group in bright gold, to another group in sky blue, and so on. There was that spectrum thing again.

I had been a member of such a group on more than one occasion. The sight of them triggered memories of trips to the zoo, and to fairs or sporting events. I didn't know it at the time, but I came to understand that the T-shirts were part of the apparatus that the chaperones used to keep track of their charges.

It did appear that everyone had been instructed on how to act around the players and the other spectators. You could hear the warnings from kid to kid to remember to follow what they had been told.

There was a part of me that hoped there would be more mixing and the colors might blur—all that homogeneity dissipating into friendly chaos. I didn't think it would happen, but it would have been nice to see.

Because I am really good at it, all of those thoughts ebbed as I approached my ball. My focus narrowed and I looked to the treetops to see the angle that the wind was coming from.

The tenth was a fairly short par five, clocking in at 531 yards from the tees the USGA were using. The green was guarded by some tough bunkering and a creek that lazily wandered in front of it.

"Coming pretty hard from the left, don't you think?" I asked Stubby.

I checked the lie. The ball was sitting up in the Zoysia turf, showing me the manufacturer's logo and my special Sharpie mark of a blue circle beneath the number.

Two-eleven to the front," Stubby said.

I consulted the pin sheet. The green was twice as wide as it was deep and designed to accept something high with a lot of spin, not a long iron, or a five wood. The hole had been cut right in the middle, six paces from the front edge.

In anticipation of that particular hole and the par three sixth, and given the prevailing winds of the day, I had put my trusty hybrid utility club in my bag and shelved my four iron for the round.

The hybrid had twenty-two degrees of loft and there was a swing I often made where I hung back on it a bit and tried to launch it super high.

Stubby and I had come to terms with where we wanted our miss to be—definitely short, and in the worst case, let it bang off the face of the front bunker and eventually settle at the bottom with what I hoped would be a good lie.

My playing partners both laid up to about ninety yards, having missed the fairway on both sides.

I took that same lazy practice swing and set up for the shot. I was going to go for a high draw and curve it into the wind, with the hope that it would knock some of the forward out of the ball and get it to stop somewhere on the putting surface.

I took one last look at the target.

"Hit it good!" someone yelled.

There was an immediate chorus of screams that evoked "Shhhh," from almost the entire gallery. The excited young man who had made the mistake they'd all been told not to make started repeating the word, "sorry," over and over.

I backed off and took another lazy swing.

"I'm sorry," the young man said for the fifth time.

I sought him out and looked him in the eye.

"You want a good one?" I asked.

"Yes, sir," he said, brightly.

"Well, here goes. This is for you, bud," I said.

I stepped back into my stance, took the club back on plane, dropped it in a little inside on the downswing and turned my body to the left.

It was a direct center hit. The ball climbed to its apex quickly before starting on an arc to the left. As it ascended above the tree line, the brisk breeze that continued to blow from the direction of the river buffeted its movement.

The two forces fought each other with a vengeance—the wind trying to undo the counterclockwise spin and the rotating ball trying to maintain its speed and trajectory in the face of that competing force.

For a brief moment, it hung in the air like a tethered balloon, before giving into the forces that have always kept our feet to the ground.

The ball landed just over the bunker on a three-foot patch of fringe and plopped onto the bent grass green. I had a six-foot putt for eagle on the opening hole.

There was a good deal of recognition in the form of applause. I moved over to the ropes, gave the kid who yelled, a fist bump and said, "Thanks. Couldn't have done it without you."

With seemingly equal parts terror, awe, and awkwardness, he just stared at me as if I were a statue.

Stubby and I walked up behind the other two players.

"It's a goddamn circus out here," Buzz's guy, Sid Bash, said.

I didn't respond. Guys make excuses for their lots in the game all of time. A guy hits it in a divot, it plugs in the face of a bunker, etc. and they gnash their teeth and curse, and flap their wings to show everyone what a bad break they got.

That one comment said the guy was a blame-shifter. Bad play is never their fault. They always make the perfect swing, but it's the ball, or the club, or the elements like a hundred special needs kids in the gallery that made for a poor result. He wasn't worth engaging in conversation.

I putted last, and Stubby, who knew every bump, drainage point and elevation change on the course instructed me to keep it in the hole and to hit it firm.

Stubby's suggestion to hit it hard was meant to keep my mind clear. No need to have nuance on a six-foot uphill putt for eagle at the U.S. Open.

I ripped it right toward the middle of the hole and it fell over the ledge. It dove down with enough force that it actually popped back up for a moment before coming to rest at the bottom of the cup.

A celebration broke out among those gathered around the green.

I slapped hands with nearly all of those in attendance as I made my way through the gauntlet that spanned the distance to the eleventh tee.

I caught sight of Deidre, standing with Ray and her friend at the end of the line of colored T-shirts. She was shaking her head as if in wonder and smiling a smile that coated my heart with light.

Somewhere out there, Dylan Rumpert had made a double bogey.

On every digital scoreboard, throughout the entire course and the surrounding environs, a new name popped up at the very top.

It read: 1 C. Dawson -2 (1*).

Postscript

I did not win the U.S. Open that was held at Belleterre Country Club. I made the cut at even par, which was five shots clear of the line, shot a wonderful round of one over par on Saturday (in brutal conditions) and closed with the second best round of the entire field on Sunday with a three-under sixty-seven. That final round elevated me to a tie for eighteenth place at minus-two overall. I finished six strokes behind the champion, Peter "the Puma" Forrest, who won the tournament by two shots. It was his fourth U.S. Open victory.

Just turning in a scorecard for seventy-two holes ensured that I could skip local qualifying for the next Open.

I made $142,874 for my efforts, the most money I had made in any tournament, ever.

After, I hung around with Deidre for a couple of weeks. Finally, I headed back to Chula Vista to square my accounts. I enjoyed a somewhat embarrassing hero's welcome, but I did get an opportunity to personally thank the village that had taken care of me for nearly all of my days.

I called Babe, but she was busy. Alma, her caretaker and friend, said that she would convey my gratitude without ever admitting that she was the one who had called the pro shop.

We never spoke again and she passed a couple of months after the tournament.

I flew to Texas to attend the funeral. Babe's wishes were granted. A high school marching band played a song by The Drifters; the ceremony ended with a massive fireworks display. Alma took her ashes to Hawaii and tossed them off a cliff on the Big Island.

In deference to Jim, and the importance of our relationship together, there were provisions in her will for me, but there were multiple claims on her estate. It seemed that the resolution of it might take a decade or more.

Josh finally did admit that Babe had been the source of the money that got me to the Open. She had indeed called the shop, transferred money into Josh's checking account and had him draw the anonymous cashier's check at his bank.

He spilled it on the day that a four by five-foot wooden crate arrived via delivery service at SVMGC. The return address showed it was from Alma Reyes. The Greene family mansion's address was printed below her name.

In the crate was a framed photo of the pre-teen Jim with Ben Hogan on the range at Shady Oaks. It was the same one that Babe had offered the Hogan Museum docent a donation for a copy of. Professionals did an amazing job restoring and enhancing the image. We hung it on the wall behind the cash register next to Jim's awards and citations.

I put Dave Bergman in charge of everything financial in my world. He used some of my winnings to pay the back taxes on the condo, had the tenants sign a new lease and had future taxes and insurance premiums impounded into an escrow account that drew from the rental income.

Later, he created a thriving concern as a business manager for athletes. I'd been his first client.

I eventually moved out of the Gumball and got an apartment across the Mississippi River from Missouri in a sleepy bedroom community in Southern Illinois. There was a municipal golf course about a low, hard three wood away.

Ray ceded control of my parole to an officer who was in St. Louis and not particularly alert or organized. Deidre and I did a ton of painstaking documentation to list my movements to keep everything in order.

Two freeways, and roughly fifteen minutes, separated us. She and I saw each other nearly every day that I was in town.

I registered for tour school with the intention of going through the qualifying process to return to the USDT. My application was rejected.

I sued the tour with the help of an all-star team of litigators for reinstatement and they were able to get an injunction that would allow me to compete until my case was adjudicated.

In the meantime, the friend that Deidre had brought to the tournament was no random buddy. Molly was the lead legislative director for the incoming governor and she started the process of having the category of my conviction changed from Class B to Class D. She also readied a "Request to Vacate" document for when that day arrived.

Near the end of the summer, I Monday-qualified and went on to win the USDT event outside of Philadelphia. That exempted me into the second stage of tour qualifying school and gave me status on the USDT for the remainder of the season.

My pro bono lawyers, advocates for justice all, filed a further brief that allowed me to post my $4,500 entry fee and enter the qualifying process for the following season.

For the time being, I was back.

Ray broke eighty for the first time in his life. He took a picture of the scorecard and texted it to me. He also joined the Men's Club at SVMGC and finished second in the B flight of the President's Cup Tournament.

I did not forget Stubby. I had Dave issue Stubby a check for $15,000. I also made a $10,000 donation to the Asperger's and Autism Foundation of the greater St. Louis area.

For the Nerds
(I am proud to call myself one)

During the breadth of my incarceration, there were many changes to the Rules of Golf as administered by the Royal and Ancient Golf Club and the United States Golf Association.

On that bus that took me to Texas, perhaps during its run through Oklahoma, I read about this particular one.

The rule was 18-2b which read: *Ball Moving After Address—If a player's ball in play moves after he has addressed it (other than as a result of a stroke) the player is deemed to have moved the ball* ***and incurs a penalty of one stroke.***

This was the violation that Ed Custis had cited on the eighteenth hole of our match that fateful day.

As I learned, the rule had been amended to include a clause which demanded that the factors that caused the ball to move be known or virtually certain to be known.

Unless it can be determined that the player moved the ball by a metric that is greater than a 95 percent chance, it is deemed that the player had no influence on the movement and no penalty shall be incurred.

Tommy, the dermatologically challenged clubhouse boy, whose shrug Ed used for confirmation, could not have crested the threshold of 95 percent certainty. The hundreds of other witnesses would have to agree in unison that I had caused the ball's position to be altered. For the record, the ball never moved, so the entire scenario is rendered moot anyway.

What would have happened if we had played under the

new rule? I likely would have made par, albeit without chipping in, but would Ed still have blown his top? Would the ensuing episode have unfolded in exactly the same way? Would I have ended up having to endure nearly five years of being locked away from the world? Would I have met Deidre, or Ray, or Dave Bergman, or Stubby, or all of the others? I would guess not.

For me, I'm just striding forward. I continue to hit it, chase it, hit it again, and hopefully get it to settle in the bottom of the cup with the least amount of whacks.

And Finally:

Here is Sally's letter in full. The clue to who told Artie Fishman that I would be a good subject for a personal interest story is right there in the text. I missed it. Not a surprise.

Dearest Chunk,

I was so happy to hear your voice when we spoke. I would have written you sooner, but as you know, I did not have an address for you. Please tell me to stop if you get tired of hearing from me for the next forty years or so.

Here is the story of how I ended up at the women's prison at Chillicothe:

As you know, all of those righteous assholes who were out to get me incarcerated with the male population never gave up.

I guess I scare the shit out them.

Not long after your release, there was a lot pressure to get me moved into some place like Potosi or another place that houses maximum/high risk inmates.

One of my lawyers is a pretty brilliant guy. He let me know of the seriousness this time and I would have to fight with all I've got. I was just trying to be cool, you know? Not cause any waves, but those fuckers were not letting go. You just know that they have their own secrets, right?

So, I decided to throw in all the chips.

I don't know if you knew that before I ended up doing my current stretch, I was on a hormone regimen as transitional therapy. The court took away my Premarin that I'd been taking for over six months when I got popped.

I think you witnessed some of the effects of me being without my meds. A lot of that emotion—I was like a menopausal crone at that point.

So, on my lawyer's advice, I petitioned to have the state give me back my hormones.

The shit kind of hit the fan, but I had a long medical history to back me up and there was actually very little that they could do to stop it.

Turns out the Hippocratic oath is stronger than just about anything other than Jesus in Missouri, and if you can get enough doctors to testify on your behalf, you can pretty much tie their hands.

On top of all that, there was this incredible stroke of luck, if you can call it that. In Alabama, or Arkansas, or one of those places, a man—on trial for murder—was sentenced to death by a jury. They made that choice because he was gay and they believed that by sending him to prison for life, they would be providing him with the pleasure of being around a bunch of horny men. I swear to god this happened.

My lawyer seized on this whole gay thing. These stupid fuckers in this state think that I'm becoming a woman so I can be with men. I mean, we both know that I'm gay, right? I'm just a lesbian. Understanding the distinction would fry their brains, so my guy kind of led them to that story of the killer in Hicksville, Wherever, U.S.A. and asked them if they really wanted to let me roam among the cons at one of their prisons, especially if I were becoming a woman.

We thought that that was the clincher, but just to be sure, he got someone in the St. Louis paper to write an article detailing my reason for committing my crimes, my struggles with my identity and why the state was being so crazy about where they housed me.

Well, that did it. Suddenly, the state house here was filled with just about every kind of alternative lifestyle you can imagine.

These folks staked out assembly people and state senators. They hounded the governor and his staff.

Finally, someone got some number crunchers involved and they looked at the cost of having to fight all this in court. It was well into a least eight figures.

The demonstrations continued, and from what I have heard, they became quite flamboyant.

Someone cried "uncle" and suggested that they just drop the whole deal. They could claim some bullshit about granting my wish in the short term while they examined their policies blah, blah, blah.

So, that's what happened. I was transferred to Chillicothe, and have been part of the female maximum-security general population for about two months now.

I have a lovely girlfriend who is five years into a fifteen-year sentence. I've been reauthorized as pre-operative. It appears that the state will be on the hook for my transformation.

All's well that ends well. More to come, Chunk.

Love, S.

Gratitude

If I could recreate the roar around the sixteenth at TPC Scottsdale every February, I would ask that these folks bask in something even louder than that raucous affirmation.

My late mother, Ursula, deserves a rousing round of applause for being there for me since my arrival on Earth.

My wife, Saxon, who knows very little about the game, except for the day her parents demanded she give it a try at the military golf course at Parris Island, S.C., has always been a vocal advocate. Sadly, on the day of her first lesson, she pedaled her bike five miles on a hot, sticky afternoon only to collapse in front of the head pro at the Legends Course before he could put a club in her hands.

Max Flynn and Matt Craven have been my first readers for forever and have always devoured the most bloated versions of my work with enthusiasm.

Lane Witz, David Huffman, Dana Halstead, and my Hilltop High Golf teammate Rick Price were there to read and offer their valued comments on the version that exists here.

Daniel Pyne has gifted me with so many intangibles that have given me the opportunity to create without fear or anxiety. He retains the title of Mentor Supreme for all time.

This would not have been possible without my having met, befriended and eventually looped for pro golfer, NCAA National Golf Coach of the Year, master instructor, and all around amazing person, Chris Zambri. Much of the origination of this idea came from my experiences with him on the local mini-tour circuit, the Nike Tour and its subsequent other names, too many tour schools to count and the 1999 U.S. Open at Pinehurst #2.

Thanks also bestowed to PGA Class A professional Tim Terwilliger for his knowledge on the history of the Hawk.

For the first time, I got the opportunity to work with a world class editor, Benee Knauer, who shepherded me through revision after revision. Her enduring faith never waned.

Katie Pyne did the cool cover. Her inspiration spurred by the yardage books produced by "Gorjus" George Lucas.

And finally, Karen Richardson. She has always been my publication Sherpa and the person I've turned to when I've wanted to take one of my cockeyed dreams and transform it into reality.

Thank you all.

Erich Anderson is an actor by trade and author by choice. He was once a single digit handicap golfer and finished second one year at the Los Angeles City Golf Championships in the A Flight. He lives in Los Angeles with wife Saxon, and their dog, Becky.

Made in the USA
Las Vegas, NV
13 February 2024